Jules Verne

Dick Sands

the boy captain

Jules Verne

Dick Sands
the boy captain

ISBN/EAN: 9783337090562

Printed in Europe, USA, Canada, Australia, Japan

Cover: Foto ©Andreas Hilbeck / pixelio.de

More available books at **www.hansebooks.com**

DICK SANDS

THE BOY CAPTAIN

BY

JULES VERNE.

PART I.

AUTHOR'S ILLUSTRATED EDITION.

London:

SAMPSON LOW, MARSTON, SEARLE, & RIVINGTON,

CROWN BUILDINGS, 188, FLEET STREET.

1882.

CONTENTS.

LIST OF ILLUSTRATIONS.

DICK SANDS,

THE BOY CAPTAIN.

CHAPTER I.

THE "PILGRIM."

ON the 2nd of February, 1873, the "Pilgrim," a tight little craft of 400 tons burden, lay in lat. 43° 57′ S. and long. 165° 19′ W. She was a schooner, the property of James W. Weldon, a wealthy Californian ship-owner, who had fitted her out at San Francisco, expressly for the whale-fisheries in the southern seas.

James Weldon was accustomed every season to send his whalers both to the Arctic regions beyond Behring Straits, and to the Antarctic Ocean below Tasmania and Cape Horn ; and the "Pilgrim," although one of the smallest, was one of the best vessels of its class ; her sailing-powers were splendid, and her rigging was so adroitly adapted that with a very small crew she might venture without risk within sight of the impenetrable ice-fields of the southern hemi-sphere : under skilful guidance she could dauntlessly thread her way amongst the drifting icebergs that, lessened though they were by perpetual shocks and undermined by warm currents, made their way northwards as far as the parallel of

New Zealand or the Cape of Good Hope, to a latitude cor-
responding to which in the northern hemisphere they are
never seen, having already melted away in the depths of the
Atlantic and Pacific Oceans.

For several years the command of the " Pilgrim " had been
entrusted to Captain Hull, an experienced seaman, and one
of the most dexterous harpooners in Weldon's service. The
crew consisted of five sailors and an apprentice. This
number, of course, was quite insufficient for the process of
whale-fishing, which requires a large crew for manning
the whale-boats and for cutting up the whales after they are
captured ; but Weldon, following the example of other owners,
found it more economical to embark at San Francisco only
just enough men to work the ship to New Zealand, where,
from the promiscuous gathering of seamen of well-nigh every
nationality, and of needy emigrants, the captain had no
difficulty in engaging as many whalemen as he wanted for
the season. This method of hiring men who could be at
once discharged when their services were no longer required
had proved altogether to be the most profitable and convenient.

The " Pilgrim " had now just completed her annual voyage
to the Antarctic circle. It was not, however, with her proper
quota of oil-barrels full to the brim, nor yet with an ample
cargo of cut and uncut whalebone, that she was thus far on
her way back. The time, indeed, for a good haul was past ;
the repeated and vigorous attacks upon the cetaceans had
made them very scarce ; the whale known as " the Right
whale," the " Nord-kapper " of the northern fisheries, the
" Sulpher-boltone " of the southern, was hardly ever to be
seen ; and latterly the whalers had had no alternative but to
direct their efforts against the Finback or Jubarte, a gigantic
mammal, encounter with which is always attended with considerable danger.

So scanty this year had been the supply of whales that
Captain Hull had resolved next year to push his way into

far more southern latitudes ; even, if necessary, to advance
to the regions known as Clarie and Adélie Lands, of which
the discovery, though claimed by the American navigator
Wilkes, belongs by right to the illustrious Frenchman
Dumont d'Urville, the commander of the " Astrolabe " and
the " Zélée."

The season had been exceptionally unfortunate for the
" Pilgrim." At the beginning of January, almost in the
height of the southern summer, long before the ordinary time
for the whalers' return, Captain Hull had been obliged to
abandon his fishing-quarters. His hired crew, all men
of more than doubtful character, had given signs of such
insubordination as threatened to end in mutiny ; and he had
become aware that he must part company with them on the
earliest possible opportunity. Accordingly, without delay,
the bow of the " Pilgrim " was directed to the north-west,
towards New Zealand, which was sighted on the 15th of
January, and on reaching Waitemata, the port of Auckland
in the Hauraki Gulf on the east coast of North Island, the
whole of the gang was peremptorily discharged.

The ship's crew were more than dissatisfied. They were
angry. Never before had they returned with so meagre a
haul. They ought to have had at least two hundred barrels
more. The captain himself experienced all the mortification
of an ardent sportsman who for the first time in his life
brings home a half-empty bag ; and there was a general
spirit of animosity against the rascals whose rebellion had so
entirely marred the success of the expedition.

Captain Hull did everything in his power to repair the
disappointment ; he made every effort to engage a fresh
gang ; but it was too late ; every available seaman had long
since been carried off to the fisheries. Finding therefore
that all hope of making good the deficiency in his cargo
must be resigned, he was on the point of leaving Auckland
alone with his crew, when he was met by a request with
which he felt himself bound to comply.

It had chanced that James Weldon, on one of those journeys which were necessitated by the nature of his business, had brought with him his wife, his son Jack a child of five years of age, and a relation of the family who was generally known by the name of Cousin Benedict. Weldon had of course intended that his family should accompany him on his return home to San Francisco ; but little Jack was taken so seriously ill that his father, whose affairs demanded his immediate return, was obliged to leave him behind at Auckland with his wife and Cousin Benedict.

Three months had passed away, little Jack was convalescent, and Mrs. Weldon, weary of her long separation from her husband, was anxious to get home as soon as possible. Her readiest way of reaching San Francisco was to cross to Australia, and thence to take a passage in one of the vessels of the "Golden Age" Company, which run between Melbourne and the Isthmus of Panama : on arriving in Panama she would have to wait the departure of the next American steamer of the line which maintains a regular communication between the Isthmus and California. This route, however, involved many stoppages and changes, such as are always disagreeable and inconvenient for women and children, and Mrs. Weldon was hesitating whether she should encounter the journey, when she heard that her husband's vessel, the "Pilgrim," had arrived at Auckland. Hastening to Captain Hull, she begged him to take her with her little boy, Cousin Benedict, and Nan, an old negress who had been her attendant from her childhood, on board the "Pilgrim," and to convey them to San Francisco direct.

"Was it not over-hazardous," asked the captain, "to venture upon a voyage of between 5000 and 6000 miles in so small a sailing-vessel ?"

But Mrs. Weldon urged her request, and Captain Hull, confident in the sea-going qualities of his craft, and anticipating at this season nothing but fair weather on either side of the equator, gave his consent.

In order to provide as far as possible for the comfort of the lady during a voyage that must occupy from forty to fifty days, the captain placed his own cabin at her entire disposal.

Everything promised well for a prosperous voyage. The only hindrance that could be foreseen arose from the circumstance that the "Pilgrim" would have to put in at Valparaiso for the purpose of unlading ; but that business once accomplished, she would continue her way along the American coast with the assistance of the land breezes, which ordinarily make the proximity of those shores such agreeable quarters for sailing.

Mrs. Weldon herself had accompanied her husband in so many voyages, that she was quite inured to all the makeshifts of a seafaring life, and was conscious of no misgiving in embarking upon a vessel of such small tonnage. She was a brave, high-spirited woman of about thirty years of age, in the enjoyment of excellent health, and for her the sea had no terrors. Aware that Captain Hull was an experienced man, in whom her husband had the utmost confidence, and knowing that his ship was a substantial craft, registered as one of the best of the American whalers, so far from entertaining any mistrust as to her safety, she only rejoiced in the opportuneness of the chance which seemed to offer her a direct and unbroken route to her destination.

Cousin Benedict, as a matter of course, was to accompany her. He was about fifty ; but in spite of his mature age it would have been considered the height of imprudence to allow him to travel anywhere alone. Spare, lanky, with a bony frame, with an enormous cranium, and a profusion of hair, he was one of those amiable inoffensive *savants* who, having once taken to gold spectacles, appear to have arrived at a settled standard of age, and, however long they live afterwards, seem never to be older than they have ever been.

Claiming a sort of kindredship with all the world, he was universally known far beyond the pale of his own connexions,

by the name of " Cousin Benedict."   In the ordinary concerns
of life nothing would ever have rendered him capable of
shifting for himself; of his meals he would never think until
they were placed before him ; he had the appearance of
being utterly insensible to heat or cold ; he vegetated rather
than lived, and might not inaptly be compared to a tree
which, though healthy enough at its core, produces scant foliage and no fruit.   His long arms and legs were in the way of
himself and everybody else ; yet no one could possibly treat
him with unkindness.   As M. Prudhomme would say, "if
only he had been endowed with capability," he would have
rendered a service to any one in the world ; but helplessness
was his dominant characteristic ; helplessness was ingrained
into his very nature ; yet this very helplessness made him an
object of kind consideration rather than of contempt, and
Mrs. Weldon looked upon him as a kind of elder brother to
her little Jack.

It must not be supposed, however, that Cousin Benedict was
either idle or unoccupied.   On the contrary, his whole time
was devoted to one absorbing passion for natural history.
Not that he had any large claim to be regarded properly as
a natural historian ; he had made no excursions over the
whole four districts of zoology, botany, mineralogy, and geo-
logy, into which the realms of natural history are commonly
divided ; indeed, he had no pretensions at all to be either a
botanist, a mineralogist, or a geologist; his studies only
sufficed to make him a zoologist, and that in a very limited
sense.   No Cuvier was he ; he did not aspire to decompose
animal life by analysis, and to recompose it by synthesis ;
his enthusiasm had not made him at all deeply versed in
vertebrata, mollusca, or radiata ; in fact, the vertebrata—
animals, birds, reptiles, fishes—had had no place in his researches ; the mollusca—from the cephalopoda to the bryozia
—had had no attractions for him ; nor had he consumed the
midnight oil in investigating the radiata, the echinodermata,
acalephæ, polypi, entozoa, or infusoria.

Cousin Benedict.

No ; Cousin Benedict's interest began and ended with the articulata ; and it must be owned at once that his studies were very far from embracing all the range of the six classes into which " articulata " are subdivided ; viz., the insecta, the myriapoda, the arachnida, the crustacea, the cirrhopoda, and the anelides ; and he was utterly unable in scientific language to distinguish a worm from a leech, an earwig from a sea-acorn, a spider from a scorpion, a shrimp from a frog-hopper, or a galley-worm from a centipede.

To confess the plain truth, Cousin Benedict was an amateur entomologist, and nothing more.

Entomology, it may be asserted, is a wide science ; it embraces the whole division of the articulata ; but our friend was an entomologist only in the limited sense of the popular acceptation of the word ; that is to say, he was an observer and collector of insects, meaning by " insects " those articulata which have bodies consisting of a number of concentric movable rings, forming three distinct segments, each with a pair of legs, and which are scientifically designated as hexapods.

To this extent was Cousin Benedict an entomologist ; and when it is remembered that the class of insecta of which he had grown up to be the enthusiastic student comprises no less than ten[1] orders, and that of these ten the coleoptera and diptera alone include 30,000 and 60,000 species respectively, it must be confessed that he had an ample field for his most persevering exertions.

Every available hour did he spend in the pursuit of his favourite science : hexapods ruled his thoughts by day and

---

[1] These ten orders are (1) the orthoptera, *e. g.* grasshoppers and crickets ; (2) the neuroptera, *e. g.* dragon-flies ; (3) the hymenoptera, *e. g.* bees, wasps, and ants ; (4) the lepidoptera, *e. g.* butterflies and moths ; (5) the hemiptera, *e. g.* cicadas and fleas ; (6) the coleoptera, *e. g.* cockchafers and glow-worms ; (7) the diptera, *e. g.* gnats and flies ; (8) the rhipiptera, *e. g.* the stylops ; (9) the parasites, *e. g.* the acarus ; and (10) the thysanura, *e. g.* the lepisma and podura.

his dreams by night. The number of pins that he carried thick on the collar and sleeves of his coat, down the front of his waistcoat, and on the crown of his hat, defied computation; they were kept in readiness for the capture of specimens that might come in his way, and on his return from a ramble in the country he might be seen literally encased with a covering of insects, transfixed adroitly by scientific rule.

This ruling passion of his had been the inducement that had urged him to accompany Mr. and Mrs. Weldon to New Zealand. It had appeared to him that it was likely to be a promising district, and now having been successful in adding some rare specimens to his collection, he was anxious to get back again to San Francisco, and to assign them their proper places in his extensive cabinet.

Besides, it never occurred to Mrs. Weldon to start without him. To leave him to shift for himself would be sheer cruelty. As a matter of course whenever Mrs. Weldon went on board the " Pilgrim," Cousin Benedict would go too. Not that in any emergency assistance of any kind could be expected from him; on the contrary, in the case of difficulty he would be an additional burden; but there was every reason to expect a fair passage and no cause of misgiving of any kind, so the propriety of leaving the amiable entomologist behind was never suggested.

Anxious that she should be no impediment in the way of the due departure of the " Pilgrim " from Waitemata, Mrs. Weldon made her preparations with the utmost haste, discharged the servants which she had temporarily engaged at Auckland, and accompanied by little Jack and the old negress, and followed mechanically by Cousin Benedict, embarked on the 22nd of January on board the schooner.

The amateur, however, kept his eye very scrupulously upon his own special box. Amongst his collection of insects were some very remarkable examples of new staphylins, a species of carnivorous coleoptera with eyes placed above their head; it was a kind supposed to be peculiar to New

Caledonia. Another rarity which had been brought under his notice was a venomous spider, known among the Maoris as a "katipo;" its bite was asserted to be very often fatal. As a spider, however, belongs to the order of the arachnida, and is not properly an "insect," Benedict declined to take any interest in it. Enough for him that he had secured a novelty in his own section of research ; the " Staphylin Neo-Zelandus " was not only the gem of his collection, but its pecuniary value baffled ordinary estimate ; he insured his box at a fabulous sum, deeming it to be worth far more than all the cargo of oil and whalebone in the " Pilgrim's " hold.

Captain Hull advanced to meet Mrs. Weldon and her party as they stepped on deck.

"It must be understood, Mrs. Weldon," he said, courteously raising his hat, "that you take this passage entirely on your own responsibility."

" Certainly, Captain Hull," she answered ; " but why do you ask ? "

"Simply because I have received no orders from Mr. Weldon," replied the captain.

" But my wish exonerates you," said Mrs. Weldon.

"Besides," added Captain Hull, "I am unable to provide you with the accommodation and the comfort that you would have upon a passenger steamer."

" You know well enough, captain," remonstrated the lady, "that my husband would not hesitate for a moment to trust his wife and child on board the ' Pilgrim.' "

"Trust, madam ! No ! no more than I should myself. I repeat that the ' Pilgrim ' cannot afford you the comfort to which you are accustomed."

Mrs. Weldon smiled.

"Oh, I am not one of your grumbling travellers. I shall have no complaints to make either of small cramped cabins, or of rough and meagre food."

She took her son by the hand, and passing on, begged that they might start forthwith.

Orders accordingly were given ; sails were trimmed ; and after taking the shortest course across the gulf, the " Pilgrim" turned her head towards America.

Three days later strong easterly breezes compelled the schooner to sail on the port tack in order to get to windward. The consequence was that by the 2nd of February the captain found himself in such a latitude that he might almost be suspected of intending to round Cape Horn rather than of having a design to coast the western shores of the New Continent.

Still, the sea did not become rough. There was a slight delay, but, on the whole, navigation was perfectly easy.

CHAPTER II.

THE APPRENTICE.

THERE was no poop upon the "Pilgrim's" deck, so that Mrs.Weldon had no other alternative than to acquiesce in the captain's proposal that she should occupy his own modest cabin.

Accordingly, here she was installed with Jack and old Nan ; and here she took all her meals, in company with the captain and Cousin Benedict.

For Cousin Benedict tolerably comfortable sleeping-accommodation had been contrived close at hand, while Captain Hull himself retired to the crew's quarter, occupying the cabin which properly belonged to the chief mate, but as already indicated the services of a second officer were quite dispensed with.

All the crew were civil and attentive to the wife of their employer, a master to whom they were faithfully attached. They were all natives of the coast of California, brave and experienced seamen, and united by tastes and habits in a common bond of sympathy. Few as they were in number, their work was never shirked, not simply from the sense of duty, but because they were directly interested in the profits of their undertaking ; the success of their labours always told to their own advantage. The present expedition was the fourth that they had taken together ; and, as it turned out to be the first in which they had failed to meet with success, it may be imagined that they were full of resentment against the mutinous whalemen who had been the cause of so serious a diminution of their ordinary gains. ·

The only one on board who was not an American was a man who had been temporarily engaged as cook. His name was Negoro; he was a Portuguese by birth, but spoke English with perfect fluency. The previous cook had deserted the ship at Auckland, and when Negoro, who was out of employment, applied for the place, Captain Hull, only too glad to avoid detention, engaged him at once without inquiry into his antecedents. There was not the slightest fault to be found with the way in which the cook performed his duties, but there was something in his manner, or perhaps rather in the expression of his countenance, which excited the captain's misgivings, and made him regret that he had not taken more pains to investigate the character of one with whom he was now brought into such close contact.

Negoro looked about forty years of age. Although he had the appearance of being slightly built, he was muscular; he was of middle height, and seemed to have a robust constitution; his hair was dark, his complexion somewhat swarthy. His manner was taciturn, and although, from occasional remarks that he dropped, it was evident that he had received some education, he was very reserved on the subjects both of his family and of his past life. No one knew where he had come from, and he admitted no one to his confidence as to where he was going, except that he made no secret of his intention to land at Valparaiso. His freedom from seasickness demonstrated that this could hardly be his first voyage, but on the other hand his complete ignorance of seamen's phraseology made it certain that he had never been accustomed to his present occupation. He kept himself aloof as much as possible from the rest of the crew, during the day rarely leaving the great cast-iron stove, which was out of proportion to the measurement of the cramped little kitchen; and at night, as soon as the fire was extinguished, took the earliest opportunity of retiring to his berth and going to sleep.

It has been already stated that the crew of the " Pilgrim " consisted of five seamen and an apprentice. This apprentice was Dick Sands.

Dick was fifteen years old ; he was a foundling, his unknown parents having abandoned him at his birth, and he had been brought up in a public charitable institution. He had been called Dick, after the benevolent passer-by who had discovered him when he was but an infant a few hours old, and he had received the surname of Sands as a memorial of the spot where he had been exposed, Sandy Hook, a point at the mouth of the Hudson, where it forms an entrance to the harbour of New York.

As Dick was so young it was most likely he would yet grow a little taller, but it did not seem probable that he would ever exceed middle height, he looked too stoutly and strongly built to grow much. His complexion was dark, but his beaming blue eyes attested, with scarcely room for doubt, his Anglo-Saxon origin, and his countenance betokened energy and intelligence. The profession that he had adopted seemed to have equipped him betimes for fighting the battle of life.

Misquoted often as Virgil's are the words

" Audaces fortuna juvat ! "

but the true reading is

" Audentes fortuna juvat ! "

and, slight as the difference may seem, it is very significant. It is upon the confident rather than the rash, the daring rather than the bold, that Fortune sheds her smiles ; the bold man often acts without thinking, whilst the daring always thinks before he acts.

And Dick Sands was truly courageous ; he was one of the daring. At fifteen years old, an age at which few boys have laid aside the frivolities of childhood, he had acquired the stability of a man, and the most casual observer could scarcely fail to be attracted by his bright, yet thoughtful countenance. At an early period of his life he had realized all the difficulties of his position, and had made a resolution, from which nothing tempted him to flinch, that he would carve out for himself an honourable and independent career. Lithe and agile in his movements, he was an adept in every kind of athletic exercise; and so marvellous was his success in everything he undertook, that he might almost be supposed to be one of those gifted mortals who have two right hands and two left feet.

Until he was four years old the little orphan had found a home in one of those institutions in America where forsaken children are sure of an asylum, and he was subsequently sent to an industrial school supported by charitable aid, where he learnt reading, writing, and arithmetic. From the days of infancy he had never deviated from the expression of his wish to be a sailor, and accordingly, as soon as he was eight, he was placed as cabin-boy on board one of the ships that navigate the Southern Seas. The officers all took a peculiar interest in him, and he received, in consequence, a thoroughly good grounding in the duties and discipline of a seaman's life. There was no room to doubt that he must ultimately rise to eminence in his profession, for when a child from the very first has been trained in the knowledge that he must gain his bread by the sweat of his brow, it is comparatively rare that he lacks the will to do so.

Whilst he was still acting as cabin-boy on one of those trading-vessels, Dick attracted the notice of Captain Hull, who took a fancy to the lad and introduced him to his employer. Mr. Weldon at once took a lively interest in Dick's welfare, and had his education continued in San Francisco, taking care that he was instructed in the doctrines of the Roman Catholic Church, to which his own family belonged.

Throughout his studies Dick Sands' favourite subjects

were always those which had a reference to his future profession; he mastered the details of the geography of the world; he applied himself diligently to such branches of mathematics as were necessary for the science of navigation; whilst for recreation in his hours of leisure, he would greedily devour every book of adventure in travel that came in his way. Nor did he omit duly to combine the practical with the theoretical; and when he was bound apprentice on board the "Pilgrim," a vessel not only belonging to his benefactor, but under the command of his kind friend Captain Hull, he congratulated himself most heartily, and felt that the experience he should gain in the southern whale-fisheries could hardly fail to be of service to him in after-life. A first-rate sailor ought to be a first-rate fisherman too.

It was a matter of the greatest pleasure to Dick Sands when he heard to his surprise that Mrs. Weldon was about to become a passenger on board the "Pilgrim." His devotion to the family of his benefactor was large and genuine. For several years Mrs. Weldon had acted towards him little short of a mother's part, and for Jack, although he never forgot the difference in their position, he entertained wellnigh a brother's affection. His friends had the satisfaction of being assured that they had sown the seeds of kindness on a generous soil, for there was no room to doubt that the heart of the orphan boy was overflowing with sincere gratitude. Should the occasion arise, ought he not, he asked, to be ready to sacrifice everything in behalf of those to whom he was indebted not only for his start in life, but for the knowledge of all that was right and holy?

Confiding in the good principles of her protégé, Mrs. Weldon had no hesitation in entrusting her little son to his especial charge. During the frequent periods of leisure, when the wind was fair and the sails required no shifting, the apprentice was never weary of amusing Jack by making him familiar with the practice of a sailor's craft; he made him scramble up the shrouds, perch upon the yards, and slip down the back-stays; and the mother had no alarm; her assurance of Dick Sands' ability and watchfulness to protect her boy was so complete that she could only rejoice in an occupation for him that seemed more than anything to restore the colour he had lost in his recent illness.

Time passed on without incident; and had it not been for the constant prevalence of an adverse wind, neither passengers nor crew could have found the least cause of complaint. The pertinacity, however, with which the wind kept to the east could not do otherwise than make Captain Hull somewhat concerned; it absolutely prevented him from getting his ship into her proper course, and he could not altogether suppress his misgiving that the calms near the Tropic of Capricorn, and the equatorial current driving him on westwards, would entail a delay that might be serious.

It was principally on Mrs. Weldon's account that the captain began to feel uneasiness, and he made up his mind that if he could hail a vessel proceeding to America he should advise his passengers to embark on her; unfortunately, however, he felt that they were still in a latitude far too much to the south to make it likely that they should sight a steamer going to Panama; and at that date communication between Australia and the New World was much less frequent than it has since become.

Still, nothing occurred to interrupt the general monotony of the voyage until the 2nd of February, the date at which our narrative commences.

It was about nine o'clock in the morning of that day that Dick and little Jack had perched themselves together on the top-sail-yard. The weather was very clear, and they could see the horizon right round except the section behind them, hidden by the mainsail. Below them, the bowsprit seemed to lie along the water, with its stay-sail and the jibs attached like three unequal wings; from the lads' feet to the deck was the smooth surface of the fore-mast; and above their heads nothing but the top-gallant-sail and mast.

The schooner was running on the port tack as close to the wind as possible.

Dick Sands was pointing out to Jack how well the ship was ballasted, and was trying to explain how it was impossible for her to capsize, however much she heeled to starboard, when suddenly the little fellow cried out,—

" I can see something in the water ! "

" Where ? what ? " exclaimed Dick, clambering to his feet upon the yard.

'· There ! " said the child, directing attention to the portion of the sea-surface that was visible between the stay-sails.

Dick fixed his gaze intently for a moment, and then shouted out lustily,—

'· Look out on the starboard bow ! There is something afloat to leeward.   Look out !"

CHAPTER III.

A RESCUE.

AT the sound of Dick's voice all the crew, in a moment, were upon the alert. The men whose watch below it was rushed on deck, and Captain Hull hurried from his cabin to the bows. Mrs. Weldon, Nan, and even Cousin Benedict leaned over the taffrail to starboard, eager to get a glimpse of what had thus suddenly attracted the attention of the young apprentice. With his usual indifference, Negoro did not leave the galley, and was the only person on board who did not share the general excitement.

Speculations were soon rife as to what could be the nature of the floating object which could be discerned about three miles ahead. Suggestions of various character were freely made. One of the sailors declared that it looked to him only like an abandoned raft, but Mrs. Weldon observed quickly that if it were a raft, it might be carrying some unfortunate shipwrecked men who must be rescued if possible. Cousin Benedict asserted that it was nothing more nor less than a huge sea-monster; but the captain soon arrived at the conviction that it was the hull of a vessel that had heeled over on to its side, an opinion with which Dick thoroughly coincided, and went so far as to say that he believed he could make out the copper keel glittering in the sun.

"Let her go off, Bolton!" shouted Captain Hull to the helmsman; "we will at any rate lose no time in getting alongside."

"Ay, ay, sir," answered the helmsman, and the "Pilgrim" in an instant was steered according to orders.

In spite, however, of the convictions of the captain and Dick, Cousin Benedict would not be moved from his opinion that the object of their curiosity was some huge cetacean.

"It is certainly dead, then," remarked Mrs. Weldon; "it is perfectly motionless."

"Oh, that's because it is asleep," said Benedict, who, although he would have willingly given up all the whales in the ocean for one rare specimen of an insect, yet could not surrender his own belief.

"Easy, Bolton, easy!" shouted the captain, when they were getting nearer the floating mass; "don't let us be running foul of the thing; no good could come from knocking a hole in our side; keep out from it a good cable's length."

"Ay, ay, sir," replied the helmsman, in his usual cheery way; and by an easy turn of the helm the "Pilgrim's" course was slightly modified so as to avoid all fear of collision.

The excitement of the sailors by this time had become more intense. Ever since the distance had been less than a mile all doubt had vanished, and it was certain that what was attracting their attention was the hull of a capsized ship. They knew well enough the established rule that a third of all salvage is the right of the finders, and they were filled with the hope that the hull they were nearing might contain an undamaged cargo, and be "a good haul," to compensate them for their ill-success in the last season.

A quarter of an hour later and the "Pilgrim" was within half a mile of the deserted vessel, to windward. Waterlogged, with her gunwale awash, she had heeled over so completely that it would have been next to impossible to stand upon her deck. Of her masts nothing was to be seen; a few ends of cordage were all that remained of her shrouds, and the running rigging was hanging in shreds. Near her bows was an enormous hole.

" Something or other has run foul of her," said Dick.

" No doubt of that," replied the captain ; " the only wonder is that she did not sink immediately."

" Oh, how I hope the poor crew have been saved !" exclaimed Mrs. Weldon.

" Most probably," replied the captain, " they would all have taken to the boats. It is as likely as not that the ship which did the mischief would continue its course quite unconcerned."

" Surely, you cannot mean," cried Mrs. Weldon, " that any one could be capable of such inhumanity ? "

" Only too probable," answered Captain Hull; " unfortunately, such instances are very far from rare."

He scanned the drifting ship carefully and continued,—

" No ; I cannot see any sign of boats here ; I should guess that the crew have made an attempt to get to land ; at such a distance as this, however, from America or from the islands of the Pacific I should be afraid that it must be hopeless."

" Is it not possible," asked Mrs. Weldon, " that some poor creature may still survive on board, who can tell what has happened ? "

" Hardly likely, madam ; otherwise there would have been some sort of a signal in sight. But it is a matter about which we will make sure."

The captain waved his hand a little in the direction in which he wished to go, and said quietly,—

" Let her go off a bit, Bolton ! "

The " Pilgrim " by this time was not much more than three cables' lengths from the ship ; there was still no token of her being otherwise than utterly deserted, when Dick Sands suddenly exclaimed,—

" Hark ! if I am not much mistaken, that is a dog barking ! "

Every one listened attentively ; it was no fancy on Dick's part ; sure enough a stifled barking could be heard, as if some unfortunate dog had been imprisoned beneath the hatch-ways; but as the deck was not yet visible, it was impossible at present to determine the precise truth.

Mrs. Weldon pleaded,—

"If it is only a dog, captain, let it be saved !"

"Oh, yes, yes, mamma, the dog must be saved !" cried little Jack; "I will go and get a bit of sugar ready for it."

"A bit of sugar, my child, will not be much for a starved dog."

"Then it shall have my soup, and I will do without," said the boy, and he kept shouting, "Good dog ! good dog !" until he persuaded himself that he heard the animal responding to his call.

The vessels were now scarcely three hundred feet apart ; the barking was more and more distinct, and presently a great dog was seen clinging to the broken rigging. It barked more desperately than ever.

"Howick," said Captain Hull, calling to the boatswain, "heave to, and lower the small boat."

The sails were soon trimmed so as to bring the schooner to within half a cable's length of the disabled craft, the boat was lowered, and the captain and Dick, with a couple of sailors, went on board. The dog kept up a continual yelping ; it made the most vigorous efforts to retain its hold upon the rigging, but perpetually slipped backwards and fell off again upon the inclining deck. It was soon manifest, however, that all the noise the creature was making was not directed exclusively towards those who were coming to its rescue, and Mrs. Weldon could not divest herself of the im-pression that there must be some survivors still on board. All at once the animal changed its gestures. Instead of the crouching attitude and supplicating whine with which it seemed to be imploring the compassion of those who were nearing it, it suddenly appeared to become bursting with violence and furious with rage.

"What ails the brute ?" exclaimed Captain Hull.

But already the boat was on the farther side of the wrecked ship, and the captain was not in a position to see that Negoro the cook had just come on to the schooner's deck, or that it was obvious that it was against him that the dog had broken out in such obstreperous fury. Negoro had approached without being noticed by any one; he made his way to the bows, whence, without a word or look of surprise, he gazed a moment at the dog, knitted his brow, and, silent and unobserved as he had come, retired to his galley.

As the boat had rounded the stern of the drifting hull, it had been observed that the one word " Waldeck " was painted on the stern, but that there was no intimation of the port to which the ship belonged.   To Captain Hull's experienced eye, however, certain details of construction gave a decided confirmation to the probability suggested by her name that she was of American build.

Of what had once been a fine brig of 500 tons burden this hopeless wreck was now all that remained.   The large hole near the bows indicated the place where the disastrous shock had occurred, but as, in the heeling over, this aperture had been carried some five or six feet above the water, the vessel had escaped the immediate foundering which must otherwise have ensued; but still it wanted only the rising of a heavy swell to submerge the ship at any time in a few minutes.

It did not take many more strokes to bring the boat close to the lee bulwark, which was half out of the water, and Captain Hull obtained a view of the whole length of the deck.   It was clear from end to end.   Both masts had been snapped off within two feet of their sockets, and had been swept away, with shrouds, stays, and rigging.   Not a single spar was to be seen floating anywhere within sight of the wreck, a circumstance from which it was to be inferred that several days at least had elapsed since the catastrophe.

Meantime the dog, sliding down from the taffrail, got to the main hatchway, which was open.   Here it continued to bark, alternately directing its eyes on deck and below.

"Look at that dog!" said Dick; "I begin to think there must be somebody on board."

"If so," answered the captain, "he must have died of hunger; the water of course has flooded the store-room."

"No," said Dick; "that dog wouldn't look like that if there were nobody there alive."

Taking the boat as close as was prudent to the wreck, the captain and Dick called and whistled repeatedly to the dog, which after a while let itself slip into the sea, and began to swim slowly and with manifest weakness towards the boat. As soon as it was lifted in, the animal, instead of devouring the piece of bread that was offered him, made its way to a bucket containing a few drops of fresh water, and began eagerly to lap them up.

"The poor wretch is dying of thirst!" said Dick.

It soon appeared that the dog was very far from being engrossed with its own interests. The boat was being backed a few yards in order to allow the captain to ascertain the most convenient place to get alongside the "Waldeck," when the creature seized Dick by the jacket, and set up a howl that was almost human in its piteousness. It was evidently in a state of alarm that the boat was not going to return to the wreck. The dog's meaning could not be misunderstood. The boat was accordingly brought against the lee side of the vessel, and while the two sailors lashed her securely to the "Waldeck's" cat-head, Captain Hull and Dick, with the dog persistently accompanying them, clambered, after some difficulty, to the open hatchway between the stumps of the masts, and made their way into the hold. It was half full of water, but perfectly destitute of cargo, its sole contents being the ballast sand which had shifted to leeward, and now served to keep the vessel on her side.

One glance was sufficient to convince the captain that there was no salvage to be effected.

"There is nothing here; nobody here," he said.

"So I see," said the apprentice, who had made his way to the extreme fore-part of the hold.

"Then we have only to go up again," remarked the captain.

They ascended the ladder, but no sooner did they re-appear upon the deck than the dog, barking irrepressibly, began trying manifestly to drag them towards the stern.

Yielding to what might be called the importunities of the dog, they followed him to the poop, and there, by the dim glimmer admitted by the skylight, Captain Hull made out the forms of five bodies, motionless and apparently lifeless, stretched upon the floor.

One after another, Dick hastily examined them all, and emphatically declared it to be his opinion, that not one of them had actually ceased to breathe; whereupon the captain did not lose a minute in summoning the two sailors to his aid, and although it was far from an easy task, he succeeded in getting the five unconscious men, who were all negroes, conveyed safely to the boat.

The dog followed, apparently satisfied.

With all possible speed the boat made its way back again to the "Pilgrim," a tackle was lowered from the mainyard, and the unfortunate men were hoisted on board.

"Poor things!" said Mrs. Weldon, as she looked compassionately on the motionless forms.

"But they are not dead," cried Dick eagerly; "they are not dead; we shall save them all yet!"

"What's the matter with them?" asked Cousin Benedict, looking at them with utter bewilderment.

"We shall hear all about them soon, I dare say," said the captain, smiling; "but first we will give them a few drops of rum in some water."

Cousin Benedict smiled in return.

"Negoro!" shouted the captain.

At the sound of the name, the dog, who had hitherto been quite passive, growled fiercely, showed his teeth, and exhibited every sign of rage.

The cook did not answer.

" Negoro ! " again the captain shouted, and the dog became yet more angry.

At this second summons Negoro slowly left his kitchen, but no sooner had he shown his face upon the deck than the animal made a rush at him, and would unquestionably have seized him by the throat if the man had not knocked him back with a poker which he had brought with him in his hand.

The infuriated beast was secured by the sailors, and prevented from inflicting any serious injury.

" Do you know this dog ? " asked the captain.

" Know him ? Not I ! I have never set eyes on the brute in my life."

" Strange ! " muttered Dick to himself; "there is some mystery here. We shall see."

CHAPTER IV.

THE SURVIVORS OF THE " WALDECK."

IN spite of the watchfulness of the French and English
cruisers, there is no doubt that the slave-trade is still exten-
sively carried on in all parts of equatorial Africa, and that
year after year vessels loaded with slaves leave the coasts of
Angola and Mozambique to transport their living freight to
many quarters even of the civilized world.

Of this Captain Hull was well aware, and although he was
now in a latitude which was comparatively little traversed
by such slavers, he could not help almost involuntarily con-
jecturing that the negroes they had just found must be part
of a slave-cargo which was on its way to some colony of
the Pacific ; if this were so, he would at least have the
satisfaction of announcing to them that they had regained
their freedom from the moment that they came on board
the " Pilgrim."

Whilst these thoughts were passing through his mind,
Mrs. Weldon, assisted by Nan and the ever active Dick
Sands, was doing everything in her power to restore consciousness to the poor sufferers. The judicious administra-
tion of fresh water and a limited quantity of food soon had
the effect of making them revive ; and when they were
restored to their senses it was found that the eldest of them, a
man of about sixty years of age, who immediately regained
his powers of speech, was able to reply in good English to all
the questions that were put to him. In answer to Captain

Hull's inquiry whether they were not slaves, the old negro proudly stated that he and his companions were all free American citizens, belonging to the state of Pennsylvania.

"Then, let me assure you, my friend," said the captain, "you have by no means compromised your liberty in having been brought on board the American schooner ' Pilgrim.' "

Not merely, as it seemed, on account of his age and experience, but rather because of a certain superiority and greater energy of character, this old man was tacitly recognized as the spokesman of his party; he freely communicated all the information that Captain Hull required to hear, and by degrees he related all the details of his adventures.

He said that his name was Tom, and that when he was only six years of age he had been sold as a slave, and brought from his home in Africa to the United States; but by the act of emancipation he had long since recovered his freedom. His companions, who were all much younger than himself, their ages ranging from twenty-five to thirty, were all free-born, their parents having been emancipated before their birth, so that no white man had ever exercised upon them the rights of ownership. One of them was his own son; his name was Bat (an abbreviation of Bartholomew); and there were three others, named Austin, Actæon, and Hercules. All four of them were specimens of that stalwart race that commands so high a price in the African market, and in spite of the emaciation induced by their recent sufferings, their muscular, well-knit frames betokened a strong and healthy constitution. Their manner bore the impress of that solid education which is given in the North American schools, and their speech had lost all trace of the "nigger-tongue," a dialect without articles or inflexions, which since the anti-slavery war has almost died out in the United States.

Three years ago, old Tom stated, the five men had been engaged by an Englishman who had large property in South Australia, to work upon his estates near Melbourne.

Here they had realized a considerable profit, and upon the completion of their engagement they determined to return with their savings to America. Accordingly, on the 5th of January, after paying their passage in the ordinary way, they embarked at Melbourne on board the "Waldeck. Everything went on well for seventeen days, until, on the night of the 22nd, which was very dark, they were run into by a great steamer. They were all asleep in their berths, but, roused by the shock of the collision, which was extremely severe, they hurriedly made their way on to the deck. The scene was terrible ; both masts were gone, and the brig, although the water had not absolutely flooded her hold so as to make her sink, had completely heeled over on her side. Captain and crew had entirely disappeared, some probably having been dashed into the sea, others perhaps having saved themselves by clinging to the rigging of the ship which had fouled them, and which could be distinguished through the darkness rapidly receding in the distance. For a while they were paralyzed, but they soon awoke to the conviction that they were left alone upon a half-capsized and disabled hull, twelve hundred miles from the nearest land.

Mrs. Weldon was loud in her expression of indignation that any captain should have the barbarity to abandon an unfortunate vessel with which his own carelessness had brought him into collision. It would be bad enough, she said, for a driver on a public road, when it might be presumed that help would be forthcoming, to pass on unconcerned after causing an accident to another vehicle ; but how much more shameful to desert the injured on the open sea, where the victims of his incompetence could have no chance of obtaining succour ! Captain Hull could only repeat what he had said before, that incredibly atrocious as it might seem, such inhumanity was far from rare.

On resuming his story, Tom said that he and his companions soon found that they had no means left for getting away from the capsized brig ; both the boats had been crushed in the collision, so that they had no alternative except to await the appearance of a passing vessel, whilst the wreck was drifting hopelessly along under the action of the currents. This accounted for the fact of their being found so far south of their proper course.

For the next ten days the negroes had subsisted upon a few scraps of food that they found in the stern cabin ; but as the store-room was entirely under water, they were quite unable to obtain a drop of anything to drink, and the fresh-water tanks that had been lashed to the deck had been stove in at the time of the catastrophe. Tortured with thirst, the poor men had suffered agonies, and having on the previous night entirely lost consciousness, they must soon have died if the " Pilgrim's " timely arrival had not effected their rescue.

All the outlines of Tom's narrative were fully confirmed by the other negroes ; Captain Hull could see no reason to doubt it ; indeed, the facts seemed to speak for themselves.

One other survivor of the wreck, if he had been gifted with the power of speech, would doubtless have corroborated the testimony. This was the dog who seemed to have such an unaccountable dislike to Negoro.

Dingo, as the dog was named, belonged to the fine breed of mastiffs peculiar to New Holland. It was not, however, from Australia, but from the coast of West Africa, near the mouth of the Congo, that the animal had come. He had been picked up there, two years previously, by the captain of the " Waldeck," who had found him wandering about and more than half starved. The initials S. V. engraved upon his collar were the only tokens that the dog had a past history of his own. After he had been taken on board the " Waldeck," he remained quite unsociable, apparently ever pining for some lost master, whom he had failed to find in the desert land where he had been met with.

Larger than the dogs of the Pyrenees, Dingo was a magnificent example of his kind. Standing on his hind legs, with his head thrown back, he was as tall as a man.

His agility and strength would have made him a sure match for a panther, and he would not have flinched at facing a bear. His fine shaggy coat was a dark tawny colour, shading off somewhat lighter round the muzzle, and his long bushy tail was as strong as a lion's. If he were made angry, no doubt he might become a most formidable foe, so that it was no wonder that Negoro did not feel altogether gratified at his reception.

But Dingo, though unsociable, was not savage. Old Tom said that, on board the "Waldeck," he had noticed that the animal seemed to have a particular dislike to negroes; not that he actually attempted to do them any harm, only he uniformly avoided them, giving an impression that he must have been systematically ill-treated by the natives of that part of Africa in which he had been found. During the ten days that had elapsed since the collision, Dingo had kept resolutely aloof from Tom and his companions; they could not tell what he had been feeding on; they only knew that, like themselves, he had suffered an excruciating thirst.

Such had been the experience of the survivors of the "Waldeck." Their situation had been most critical. Even if they survived the pangs of want of food, the slightest gale or the most inconsiderable swell might at any moment have sunk the water-logged ship, and had it not been that calms and contrary winds had contributed to the opportune arrival of the "Pilgrim," an inevitable fate was before them; their corpses must lie at the bottom of the sea.

Captain Hull's act of humanity, however, would not be complete unless he succeeded in restoring the shipwrecked men to their homes. This he promised to do. After completing the unlading at Valparaiso, the "Pilgrim" would make direct for California, where, as Mrs. Weldon assured them, they would be most hospitably received by her husband, and provided with the necessary means for returning to Pennsylvania.

The five men, who, as the consequence of the shipwreck,

had lost all the savings of their last three years of toil, were profoundly grateful to their kind-hearted benefactors; nor, poor negroes as they were, did they utterly resign the hope that at some future time they might have it in their power to repay the debt which they owed their deliverers.

CHAPTER V.

DINGO'S SAGACITY.

MEANTIME the " Pilgrim " pursued her course, keeping as much as possible to the east, and before evening closed in the hull of the " Waldeck " was out of sight.

Captain Hull still continued to feel uneasy about the constant prevalence of calms ; not that for himself he cared much about the delay of a week or two in a voyage from New Zealand to Valparaiso, but he was disappointed at the prolonged inconvenience it caused to his lady passenger. Mrs. Weldon, however, submitted to the detention very philosophically, and did not utter a word of complaint.

The captain's next care was to improvise sleeping accommodation for Tom and his four associates. No room for them could possibly be found in the crew's quarters, so that their berths had to be arranged under the forecastle ; and as long as the weather continued fine, there was no reason why the negroes, accustomed as they were to a somewhat rough life, should not find themselves sufficiently comfortable.

After this incident of the discovery of the wreck, life on board the " Pilgrim " relapsed into its ordinary routine. With the wind invariably in the same direction, the sails required very little shifting ; but whenever it happened, as occasionally it would, that there was any tacking to be done, the good-natured negroes were ever ready to lend a helping hand ; and the rigging would creak again under the weight of Hercules, a great strapping fellow, six feet high, who seemed almost to require ropes of extra strength made for his special use.

Hercules became at once a great favourite with little Jack ; and when the giant lifted him like a doll in his stalwart arms, the child fairly shrieked with delight.

"Higher! higher! very high!" Jack would say sometimes.

"There you are, then, Master Jack," Hercules would reply as he raised him aloft.

"Am I heavy?" asked the child.

"As heavy as a feather."

"Then lift me higher still," cried Jack; "as high as ever you can reach."

And Hercules, with the child's two feet supported on his huge palm, would walk about the deck with him like an acrobat, Jack all the time endeavouring, with vain efforts, to make him "feel his weight."

Besides Dick Sands and Hercules, Jack admitted a third friend to his companionship. This was Dingo. The dog, unsociable as he had been on board the "Waldeck," seemed to have found society more congenial to his tastes, and being one of those animals that are fond of children, he allowed Jack to do with him almost anything he pleased. The child, however, never thought of hurting the dog in any way, and it was doubtful which of the two had the greater enjoyment of their mutual sport. Jack found a live dog infinitely more entertaining than his old toy upon its four wheels, and his great delight was to mount upon Dingo's back, when the animal would gallop off with him like a race-horse with his jockey. It must be owned that one result of this intimacy was a serious diminution of the supply of sugar in the store-room. Dingo was the delight of all the crew excepting Negoro, who cautiously avoided coming in contact with an animal who showed such unmistakable symptoms of hostility.

The new companions that Jack had thus found did not in the least make him forget his old friend Dick Sands, who devoted all his leisure time to him as assiduously as ever.

Mrs. Weldon regarded their intimacy with the greatest satisfaction, and one day made a remark to that effect in the
presence of Captain Hull.

"You are right, madam," said the captain cordially ; "Dick
is a capital fellow, and will be sure to be a first-rate sailor.
He has an instinct which is little short of a genius ; it supplies all deficiencies of theory. Considering how short an
experience and how little instruction he has had, it is quite
wonderful how much he knows about a ship."

"Certainly for his age," assented Mrs. Weldon, "he is
singularly advanced. I can safely say that I have never had
a fault to find with him. I believe that it is my husband's
intention, after this voyage, to let him have systematic
training in navigation, so that he may be able ultimately to
become a captain."

"I have no misgivings, madam," replied the captain ;
"there is every reason to expect that he will be an honour to
the service."

"Poor orphan !" said the lady ; "he has been trained in a
hard school."

"Its lessons have not been lost upon him," rejoined Captain Hull ; "they have taught him the prime lesson that he
has his own way to make in the world."

The eyes of the two speakers turned as it were unwittingly
in the direction where Dick Sands happened to be standing.
He was at the helm.

"Look at him now !" said the captain ; "see how constantly he keeps his eye upon the compass ; nothing distracts
him from his duty ; he is as much to be depended on as the
most experienced helmsman. It was a capital thing for him
that he began his training as a cabin-boy. Nothing like it.
Begin at the beginning. It is the best of training for the
merchant service."

"But surely," interposed Mrs. Weldon, "you would not
deny that in the navy there have been many good officers
who have never had the training of which you are speaking ?"

"True, madam ; but yet even some of the best of them have begun at the lowest step of the ladder. For instance, Lord Nelson."

Just at this instant Cousin Benedict emerged from the after-cabin, and completely absorbed, according to his wont, in his own pursuit, began to wander up and down the deck, peering into the interstices of the gratings, rummaging under the seats, and drawing his long fingers along the cracks in the deck where the tar had crumbled away.

"Well, Benedict, how are you getting on?" asked Mrs. Weldon.

"I? O, well enough, thank you," he replied dreamily ; "but I wish we were on shore."

"What were you looking for under that bench?" said Captain Hull.

"Insects, of course," answered Benedict ; "I am always looking for insects."

"But don't you know, Benedict," said Mrs. Weldon, "that Captain Hull is far too particular to allow any vermin on the deck of his vessel?"

Captain Hull smiled and said,—

"Mrs. Weldon is very complimentary ; but I am really inclined to hope that your investigations in the cabins of the 'Pilgrim' will not be attended with much success."

Cousin Benedict shrugged his shoulders in a manner that indicated that he was aware that the cabins could furnish nothing attractive in the way of insects.

"However," continued the captain, "I dare say down in the hold you could find some cockroaches ; but cockroaches, I presume, would be of little or no interest to you."

"No interest?" cried Benedict, at once warmed into enthusiasm ; "why, are they not the very orthoptera that roused the imprecations of Virgil and Horace? Are they not closely allied to the *Periplaneta orientalis* and the American Kakerlac, which inhabit—"

"I should rather say infest," interrupted the captain.

"Easy enough to see, sir," replied Benedict, stopping short with amazement, "that you are not an entomologist ! "

"I fear I must plead guilty to your accusation," said the captain good-humouredly.

" You must not expect every one to be such an enthusiast in your favourite study as yourself," Mrs. Weldon interposed ; "but are you not satisfied with the result of your explorations in New Zealand ? "

"Yes, yes," answered Benedict, with a sort of hesitating reluctance ; " I must not say I was dissatisfied ; I was really very delighted to secure that new staphylin which hitherto had never been seen elsewhere than in New California ; but still, you know, an entomologist is always craving for fresh additions to his collection.'

While he was speaking, Dingo, leaving little Jack, who was romping with him, came and jumped on Benedict, and began to fawn on him.

" Get away, you brute ! " he exclaimed, thrusting the dog aside.

" Poor Dingo ! good dog ! " cried Jack, running up and taking the animal's huge head between his tiny hands.

" Your interest in cockroaches, Mr. Benedict," observed the captain, " does not seem to extend to dogs."

" It isn't that I dislike dogs at all," answered Benedict ; "but this creature has disappointed me."

" How do you mean ? You could hardly want to catalogue him with the diptera or hymenoptera ? " asked Mrs. Weldon laughingly.

" Oh, not at all," replied Benedict, with the most unmoved gravity. " But I understood that he had been found on the West Coast of Africa, and I hoped that perhaps he might have brought over some African hemiptera in his coat ; but I have searched his coat well, over and over again, without finding a single specimen. The dog has disappointed me," he repeated mournfully.

"I can only hope," said the captain, "that if you had found anything, you were going to kill it instantly."

Benedict looked with mute astonishment into the captain's face. In a moment or two afterwards, he said,—

"I suppose, sir, you acknowledge that Sir John Franklin was an eminent member of your profession?"

"Certainly; why?"

"Because Sir John would never take away the life of the most insignificant insect; it is related of him that when he had once been incessantly tormented all day by a mosquito, at last he found it on the back of his hand and blew it off, saying, 'Fly away, little creature, the world is large enough for both you and me!'"

"That little anecdote of yours, Mr. Benedict," said the captain, smiling, "is a good deal older than Sir John Franklin. It is told, in nearly the same words, about Uncle Toby, in Sterne's 'Tristram Shandy'; only there it was not a mosquito, it was a common fly."

"And was Uncle Toby an entomologist?" asked Benedict; "did he ever really live?"

"No," said the captain, "he was only a character in a novel."

Cousin Benedict gave a look of utter contempt, and Captain Hull and Mrs. Weldon could not resist laughing.

Such is only one instance of the way in which Cousin Benedict invariably brought it about that all conversation with him ultimately turned upon his favourite pursuit, and all along, throughout the monotonous hours of smooth sailing, while the "Pilgrim" was making her little headway to the east, he showed his own devotion to his pet science, by seeking to enlist new disciples. First of all, he tried his powers of persuasion upon Dick Sands, but soon finding that the young apprentice had no taste for entomological mysteries, he gave him up and turned his attention to the negroes. Nor was he much more successful with them; one after another, Tom, Bat, Actæon, and Austin had all withdrawn themselves from his instructions, and the class at last was reduced to the single person of Hercules ; but in him the enthusiastic naturalist thought he had discovered a latent talent which could distinguish between a parasite and a thysanura.

Hercules accordingly submitted to pass a considerable portion of his leisure in the observation of every variety of coleoptera ; he was encouraged to study the extensive collection of stag-beetles, tiger-beetles and lady-birds ; and although at times the enthusiast trembled to see some of his most delicate and fragile specimens in the huge grasp of his pupil, he soon learned that the man's gentle docility was a sufficient guarantee against his clumsiness.

While the science of entomology was thus occupying its two votaries, Mrs. Weldon was giving her own best attention to the education of Master Jack. Reading and writing she undertook to teach herself, while she entrusted the instruction in arithmetic to the care of Dick Sands. Under the conviction that a child of five years will make a much more rapid progress if something like amusement be combined with his lessons, Mrs. Weldon would not teach her boy to spell by the use of an ordinary school primer, but used a set of cubes, on the sides of which the various letters were painted in red. After first making a word and showing it to Jack, she set him to put it together without her help, and it was astonishing how quickly the child advanced, and how many hours he would spend in this way, both in the cabin and on deck. There were more than fifty cubes, which, besides the alphabet, included all the figures ; so that they were of service for Dick Sands' lessons as well as for her own. She was more than satisfied with her device.

On the morning of the 9th an incident occurred which could not fail to be observed as somewhat remarkable. Jack was half lying, half sitting on the deck, amusing himself with his letters, and had just finished putting together a word with which he intended to puzzle old Tom, who, with his hand sheltering his eyes, was pretending not to see the difficulty which was being laboriously prepared to bewilder him ; all at once, Dingo, who had been gambolling round the child, made a sudden pause, lifted his right paw, and wagged his tail convulsively. Then darting down upon a capital S, he seized it in his mouth, and carried it some paces away.

"Oh, Dingo, Dingo ! you mustn't eat my letters !" shouted the child.

But the dog had already dropped the block of wood, and coming back again, picked up another, which he laid quietly by the side of the first. This time it was a capital V. Jack uttered an exclamation of astonishment which brought to his side not only his mother, but the captain and Dick, who were both on deck. In answer to their inquiry as to what had occurred, Jack cried out in the greatest excitement that Dingo knew how to read. At any rate he was sure that he knew his letters.

Dick Sands smiled and stooped to take back the letters. Dingo snarled and showed his teeth, but the apprentice was not frightened ; he carried his point, and replaced the two blocks among the rest. Dingo in an instant pounced upon them again, and having drawn them to his side, laid a paw upon each of them, as if to signify his intention of retaining them in his possession. Of the other letters of the alphabet he took no notice at all.

"It is very strange," said Mrs. Weldon ; "he has picked out S V again."

"S V !" repeated the captain thoughtfully ; "are not those the letters that form the initials on his collar ? "

And turning to the old negro, he continued,—

"Tom, didn't you say that this dog did not always belong to the captain of the 'Waldeck'?"

"To the best of my belief," replied Tom, "the captain had only had him about two years. I often heard him tell how he found him at the mouth of the Congo."

"Do you suppose that he never knew where the animal

came from, or to whom he had previously belonged?" asked Captain Hull.

"Never," answered Tom, shaking his head; "a lost dog is worse to identify than a lost child; you see, he can't make himself understood any way."

The captain made no answer, but stood musing; Mrs. Weldon interrupted him.

"These letters, captain, seem to be recalling something to your recollection."

"I can hardly go so far as to say that, Mrs. Weldon," he replied; "but I cannot help associating them with the fate of a brave explorer."

"Whom do you mean?" said the lady.

"In 1871, just two years ago," the captain continued, "a French traveller, under the auspices of the Geographical Society of Paris, set out for the purpose of crossing Africa from west to east. His starting-point was the mouth of the Congo, and his exit was designed to be as near as possible to Cape Deldago, at the mouth of the River Rovuma, of which he was to ascertain the true course. The name of this man was Samuel Vernon, and I confess it strikes me as somewhat a strange coincidence that the letters engraved on Dingo's collar should be Vernon's initials."

"Is nothing known about this traveller?" asked Mrs. Weldon.

"Nothing was ever heard of him after his first departure. It appears quite certain that he failed to reach the east coast, and it can only be conjectured either that he died upon his way, or that he was made prisoner by the natives; and if so, and this dog ever belonged to him, the animal might have made his way back to the sea-coast, where, just about the time that would be likely, the captain of the 'Waldeck' picked him up."

"But you have no reason to suppose, Captain Hull, that Vernon ever owned a dog of this description?"

"I own I never heard of it," said the captain ; "but still the impression fixes itself on my mind that the dog must have been his ; how he came to know one letter from another, it is not for me to pretend to say. Look at him now, madam ! he seems not only to be reading the letters for himself, but to be inviting us to come and read them with him."

Whilst Mrs. Weldon was watching the dog with much amusement, Dick Sands, who had listened to the previous conversation, took the opportunity of asking the captain whether the traveller Vernon had started on his expedition quite alone.

"That is really more than I can tell you, my boy," answered Captain Hull ; "but I should almost take it for granted that he would have a considerable retinue of natives.'

The captain spoke without being aware that Negoro had meanwhile quietly stolen on deck. At first his presence was quite unnoticed, and no one observed the peculiar glance with which he looked at the two letters over which Dingo still persisted in keeping guard. The dog, however, no sooner caught sight of the cook than he began to bristle with rage, whereupon Negoro, with a threatening gesture which seemed half involuntary, withdrew immediately to his accustomed quarters.

The incident did not escape the captain's observation.

"No doubt," he said, "there is some mystery here ;" and he was pondering the matter over in his mind when Dick Sands spoke.

"Don't you think it very singular, sir, that this dog should have such a knowledge of the alphabet?"

Jack here put in his word.

"My mamma has told me about a dog whose name was Munito, who could read as well as a schoolmaster, and could play dominoes."

Mrs. Weldon smiled.

"I am afraid, my child, that that dog was not quite so learned as you imagine. I don't suppose he knew one letter from another ; but his master, who was a clever American, having found out that the animal had a very keen sense of hearing, taught him some curious tricks."

"What sort of tricks?" asked Dick, who was almost as much interested as little Jack.

"When he had to perform in public," continued Mrs. Weldon, "a lot of letters like yours, Jack, were spread out upon a table, and Munito would put together any word that the company should propose, either aloud, or in a whisper, to his master. The creature would walk about until he stopped at the very letter which was wanted. The secret of it all was that the dog's owner gave him a signal when he was to stop by rattling a little toothpick in his pocket, making a slight noise that only the dog's ears were acute enough to perceive."

Dick was highly amused, and said,—

"But that was a dog who could do nothing wonderful without his master."

"Just so," answered Mrs. Weldon ; "and it surprises me very much to see Dingo picking out these letters without a master to direct him."

"The more one thinks of it, the more strange it is," said Captain Hull ; "but, after all, Dingo's sagacity is not greater than that of the dog which rang the convent bell in order to get at the dish that was reserved for passing beggars ; nor than that of the dog who had to turn a spit every other day, and never could be induced to work when it was not his proper day. Dingo evidently has no acquaintance with any other letters except the two S V ; and some circumstance which we can never guess has made him familiar with them."

" What a pity he cannot talk !" exclaimed the apprentice ; "we should know why it is that he always shows his teeth at Negoro."

"And tremendous teeth they are !" observed the captain, as Dingo at that moment opened his mouth, and made a display of his formidable fangs.

CHAPTER VI.

A WHALE IN SIGHT.

IT was only what might be expected that the dog's singular exhibition of sagacity should repeatedly form a subject of conversation between Mrs. Weldon, the captain, and Dick. The young apprentice in particular began to entertain a lurking feeling of distrust towards Negoro, although it must be owned that the man's conduct in general afforded no tangible grounds for suspicion.

Nor was it only among the cabin passengers that Dingo's remarkable feat was discussed ; amongst the crew in the bows the dog not only soon gained the reputation of being able to read, but was almost credited with being able to write too, as well as any sailor among them ; indeed the chief wonder was that he did not speak.

" Perhaps he can," suggested Bolton, the helmsman, " and likely enough some fine day we shall have him coming to ask about our bearings, and to inquire which way the wind is."

" Ah ! why not ? " assented another sailor ; " parrots talk, and magpies talk ; why shouldn't a dog ? For my part, I should guess it must be easier to speak with a mouth than with a beak."

" Of course it is," said Howick, the boatswain ; " only a quadruped has never yet been known to do it."

Perhaps, however, the worthy fellow would have been amazed to hear that a certain Danish *savant* once possessed a dog that could actually pronounce quite distinctly nearly twenty different words, demonstrating that the construction of the glottis, the aperture at the top of the windpipe, was adapted for the emission of regular sounds : of course the animal attached no meaning to the words it uttered any more than a parrot or a jay can comprehend their own chatterings.

Thus, unconsciously, Dingo had become the hero of the hour. On several separate occasions Captain Hull repeated the experiment of spreading out the blocks before him, but invariably with the same result; the dog never failed, without the slightest hesitation, to pick out the two letters, leaving all the rest of the alphabet quite unnoticed.

Cousin Benedict alone, somewhat ostentatiously, professed to take no interest in the circumstance.

"You cannot suppose," he said to Captain Hull, after various repetitions of the trick, " that dogs are to be reckoned the only animals endowed with intelligence. Rats, you know, will always leave a sinking ship, and beavers invariably raise their dams before the approach of a flood. Did not the horses of Nicomedes, Scanderburg and Oppian die of grief for the loss of their masters ? Have there not been instances of donkeys with wonderful memories ? Birds, too, have been trained to do the most remarkable things ; they have been taught to write word after word at their master's dictation ; there are cockatoos who can count the people in a room as accurately as a mathematician ; and haven't you heard of the old Cardinal's parrot that he would not part with for a hundred gold crowns because it could repeat the Apostles' creed from beginning to end without a blunder ? And insects," he continued, warming into enthusiasm, " how marvellously they vindicate the axiom—

' In minimis maximus Deus ! '

Are not the structures of ants the very models for the architects of a city ? Has the diving-bell of the aquatic argyroneta ever been surpassed by the invention of the most skilful student of mechanical art? And cannot fleas go through a drill and fire a gun as well as the most accomplished artilleryman? This Dingo is nothing out of the way. I suppose he belongs to some unclassed species of mastiff. Perhaps one day or other he may come to be identified as the 'canis alphabeticus' of New Zealand."

The worthy entomologist delivered this and various similar harangues ; but Dingo, nevertheless, retained his high place in the general estimation, and by the occupants of the forecastle was regarded as little short of a phenomenon. The feeling, otherwise universal, was not in any degree shared by Negoro, and it is not improbable that the man would have been tempted to some foul play with the dog if the open sympathies of the crew had not kept him in check. More than ever he studiously avoided coming in contact in any way with the animal, and Dick Sands in his own mind was quite convinced that since the incident of the letters, the cook's hatred of the dog had become still more intense.

After continual alternations with long and wearisome calms the north-east wind perceptibly moderated, and on the 10th, Captain Hull really began to hope that such a change would ensue as to allow the schooner to run straight before the wind. Nineteen days had elapsed since the " Pilgrim " had left Auckland, a period not so long but that with a favourable breeze it might be made up at last. Some days however were yet to elapse before the wind veered round to the anticipated quarter.

It has been already stated that this portion of the Pacific is almost always deserted. It is out of the line of the American and Australian steam-packets, and except a whaler had been brought into it by some such exceptional circumstances as the " Pilgrim," it was quite unusual to see one in this latitude.

But, however void of traffic was the surface of the sea, to none but an unintelligent mind could it appear monotonous or barren of interest. The poetry of the ocean breathes forth in its minute and almost imperceptible changes. A marine plant, a tuft of seaweed lightly furrowing the water, a drifting spar with its unknown history, may afford unlimited scope for the imagination ; every little drop passing, in its process of evaporation, backwards and forwards from sea to sky, might perchance reveal its own special secret ; and happy are those minds which are capable of a due appreciation of the mysteries of air and ocean.

Above the surface as well as below, the restless flood is ever teeming with animal life ; and the passengers on board the " Pilgrim " derived no little amusement from watching great flocks of birds migrating northwards to escape the rigour of the polar winter, and ever and again descending in rapid flight to secure some tiny fish. Occasionally Dick Sands would take a pistol, and now and then a rifle, and, thanks to Mr. Weldon's former instructions, would bring down various specimens of the feathered tribe.

Sometimes white petrels would congregate in considerable numbers near the schooner ; and sometimes petrels of another species, with brown borders on their wings, would come in sight ; now there would be flocks of damiers skimming the water ; and now groups of penguins, whose clumsy gait appears so ludicrous on shore ; but, as Captain Hull pointed out, when their stumpy wings were employed as fins, they were a match for the most rapid of fish, so that sailors have often mistaken them for bonitos.

High over head, huge albatrosses, their outspread wings measuring ten feet from tip to tip, would soar aloft, thence to swoop down towards the deep, into which they plunged their beaks in search of food. Such incidents and scenes as these were infinite in their variety, and it was accordingly only for minds that were obtuse to the charms of nature that the voyage could be monotonous.

On the day the wind shifted, Mrs. Weldon was walking up and down on the " Pilgrim's " quarter-deck, when her attention was attracted by what seemed to her a strange phenomenon.

All of a sudden, far as the eye could reach, the sea had assumed a reddish hue, as if it were tinged with blood.

Both Dick and Jack were standing close behind her, and she cried,—

"Look, Dick, look! the sea is all red. Is it a seaweed that is making the water so strange a colour?"

"No," answered Dick, "it is not a weed; it is what the sailors call whales' food; it is formed, I believe, of innumerable myriads of minute crustacea."

"Crustacea they may be," replied Mrs. Weldon, "but they must be so small that they are mere insects. Cousin Benedict no doubt will like to see them."

She called aloud,—

"Benedict! Benedict! come here! we have a sight here to interest you."

The amateur naturalist slowly emerged from his cabin followed by Captain Hull.

"Ah! yes, I see!" said the captain; "whales' food; just the opportunity for you, Mr. Benedict; a chance not to be thrown away for studying one of the most curious of the crustacea."

"Nonsense!" ejaculated Benedict contemptuously; "utter nonsense!"

"Why? what do you mean, Mr. Benedict?" retorted the captain; "surely you, as an entomologist, must know that I am right in my conviction that these crustacea belong to one of the six classes of the articulata."

The disdain of Cousin Benedict was expressed by a repeated sneer.

"Are you not aware, sir, that my researches as an entomologist are confined entirely to the hexapoda?"

Captain Hull, unable to repress a smile, only answered good-humouredly,—

"I see, sir, your tastes do not lie in the same direction as those of the whale."

And turning to Mrs. Weldon, he continued,—

"To whalemen, madam, this is a sight that speaks for itself. It is a token that we ought to lose no time in getting out our lines and looking to the state of our harpoons. There is game not far away."

Jack gave vent to his astonishment.

"Do you mean that great creatures like whales feed on such tiny things as these?"

"Yes, my boy," said the captain; "and I dare say they are as nice to them as semolina and ground rice are to you. When a whale gets into the middle of them he has nothing to do but to open his jaws, and, in a minute, hundreds thousands of these minute creatures are inside the fringe or whalebone around his palate, and he is sure of a good mouthful."

"So you see, Jack," said Dick, "the whale gets his shrimps without the trouble of shelling them."

"And when he has just closed his snappers is the very time to give him a good taste of the harpoon," added Captain Hull.

The words had hardly escaped the captain's lips when a shout from one of the sailors announced,—

"A whale on the weather bow!"

"There's the whale!" repeated the captain. All his professional instincts were aroused in an instant, and he hurried to the bows, followed in eager curiosity by all the stern passengers.

Even Cousin Benedict loitered up in the rear, constrained, in spite of himself, to take a share in the general interest.

There was no doubt about the matter. Four miles or so to windward an unusual commotion in the water betokened to experienced eyes the presence of a whale; but the distance was too great to permit a reasonable conjecture to be formed as to which species of those mammifers the creature belonged.

Three distinct species are familiarly known. First there

is the Right whale, which is ordinarily sought for in the northern fisheries. The average length of this cetacean is sixty feet, though it has been known to attain the length of eighty feet. It has no dorsal fin, and beneath its skin is a thick layer of blubber. One of these monsters alone will yield as much as a hundred barrels of oil.

Then there is the Hump-back, a typical representative of the species "balænoptera," a definition which may at first sight appear to possess an interest for an entomologist, but which really refers to two white dorsal fins, each half as wide as the body, resembling a pair of wings, and in their formation similar to those of the flying-fish. It must be owned, however, that a flying whale would decidedly be a *rara avis.*

Lastly, there is the Jubarte, commonly known as the Fin-back. It is provided with a dorsal fin, and in length not unfrequently is a match for the gigantic Right whale.

While it was impossible to decide to which of the three species the whale in the distance really belonged, the general impression inclined to the belief that it was a jubarte.

With longing eyes Captain Hull and his crew gazed at the object of general attraction. Just as irresistibly as it is said a clockmaker is drawn on to examine the mechanism of every clock which chance may throw in his way, so is a whaleman ever anxious to plunge his harpoon into any whale that he can get within his reach. The larger the game the more keen the excitement ; and no elephant-hunter's eagerness ever surpasses the zest of the whale-fisher when once started in pursuit of the prey.

To the crew the sight of the whale was the opening of an unexpected opportunity, and no wonder they were fired with the burning hope that even now they might do something to supply the deficiency of their meagre haul throughout the season.

Far away as the creature still was, the captain's practised eye soon enabled him to detect various indications that satisfied him as to its true species. Amongst other things that arrested his attention, he observed a column of water and vapour ejected from the nostrils. "It isn't a right whale," he said; "if so, its spout would be smaller and it would rise higher in the air. And I do not think it is a hump-back. I cannot hear the hump-back's roar. Dick, tell me, what do you think about it?"

With a critical eye Dick Sands looked long and steadil at the spout.

"It blows out water, sir," said the apprentice, "water, as well as vapour. I should think it is a finback. But it must be a rare large one."

"Seventy feet, at least!" rejoined the captain, flushing with his enthusiasm.

"What a big fellow!" said Jack, catching the excitement of his elders.

"Ah, Jack, my boy," chuckled the captain, "the whale little thinks who are watching him enjoy his breakfast!"

"Yes," said the boatswain; "a dozen such gentlemen as that would freight a craft twice the size of ours; but this one, if only we can get him, will go a good way towards filling our empty barrels."

"Rather rough work, you know," said Dick, "to attack a finback!"

"You are right, Dick," answered the captain; "the boat has yet to be built which is strong enough to resist the flap of a jubarte's tail."

"But the profit is worth the risk, captain, isn't it?"

"You are right again, Dick," replied Captain Hull, and as he spoke, he clambered on to the bowsprit in order that he might get a better view of the whale.

The crew were as eager as their captain. Mounted on the fore-shrouds, they scanned the movements of their coveted prey in the distance, freely descanting upon the profit to be made out of a good finback, and declaring that it would be a thousand pities if this chance of filling the casks below should be permitted to be lost.

Captain Hull was perplexed. He bit his nails and knitted his brow.

" Mamma ! " cried little Jack, " I should so much like to see a whale close,—quite close, you know."

" And so you shall, my boy," replied the captain, who was standing by, and had come to the resolve that if his men would back him, he would make an attempt to capture the prize.

He turned to his crew,—

" My men ! what do you think ? shall we make the venture ? Remember, we are all alone ; we have no whalemen to help us ; we must rely upon ourselves ; I have thrown a harpoon before now ; I can throw a harpoon again ; what do you say ? "

The crew responded with a ringing cheer,—

" Ay, ay, sir ! Ay, ay ! "

CHAPTER VII.

PREPARATIONS FOR AN ATTACK.

GREAT was the excitement that now prevailed, and the question of an attempt to capture the sea-monster became the ruling theme of conversation. Mrs. Weldon expressed considerable doubt as to the prudence of venturing upon so great a risk with such a limited number of hands, but when Captain Hull assured her that he had more than once successfully attacked a whale with a single boat, and that for his part he had no fear of failure, she made no further remonstrance, and appeared quite satisfied.

Having formed his resolve, the captain lost no time in setting about his preliminary arrangements. He could not really conceal from his own mind that the pursuit of a finback was always a matter of some peril, and he was anxious, accordingly, to make every possible provision which forethought could devise against all emergencies.

Besides her long-boat, which was kept between the two masts, the "Pilgrim" had three whale-boats, two of them slung to the starboard and port davits, and the third at the stern, outside the taffrail. During the fishing season, when the crew was reinforced by a hired complement of New Zealand whalemen, all three of these boats would be brought at once into requisition, but at present the whole crew of the "Pilgrim" was barely sufficient to man one of the three boats. Tom and his friends were ready to volunteer their assistance, but any offers of service from them were necessarily declined ; the manipulation of a whale-boat can only be entrusted to those who are experienced in the work, as a false turn of the tiller or a premature stroke of the oar may in a moment compromise the safety of the whole party. Thus compelled to take all his trained sailors with him on his venturous expedition, the captain had no alternative but to leave his apprentice in charge of the schooner during his absence. Dick's choice would have been very much in favour of taking a share in the whale-hunt, but he had the good sense to know that the developed strength of a man would be of far greater service in the boat, and accordingly without a murmur he resigned himself to remaining behind.

Of the five sailors who were to man the boat, there were four to take the oars, whilst Howick the boatswain was to manage the oar at the stern, which on these occasions generally replaces an ordinary rudder as being quicker in action in the event of any of the side oars being disabled. The post of harpooner was of course assigned to Captain Hull, to whose lot it would consequently fall first to hurl his weapon at the whale, then to manage the unwinding of the line to which the harpoon was attached, and finally to kill the creature by lance-wounds when it should emerge again from below the sea.

A method sometimes employed for commencing an attack is to place a sort of small cannon on the bows or deck of the boat, and to discharge from it either a harpoon or some explosive bullets, which make frightful lacerations in the body of the victim ; but the " Pilgrim " was not provided with apparatus of this description ; not only are all the contrivances of this kind very costly and difficult to manage, but the fishermen generally are averse to innovations, and prefer the old-fashioned harpoons. It was with these alone that Captain Hull was now about to encounter the finback that was lying some four miles distant from his ship.

The weather promised as favourably as could be for the

enterprise. The sea was calm, and the wind moreover was still moderating, so that there was no likelihood of the schooner drifting away during the captain's absence.

When the starboard whale-boat had been lowered, and the four sailors had entered it, Howick passed a couple of harpoons down to them, and some lances which had been carefully sharpened; to these were added five coils of stout and supple rope, each 600 feet long, for a whale when struck often dives so deeply that even these lengths of line knotted together are found to be insufficient. After these implements of attack had been properly stowed in the bows, the crew had only to await the pleasure of their captain.

The "Pilgrim," before the sailors left her, had been made to heave to, and the yards were braced so as to secure her remaining as stationary as possible. As the time drew near for the captain to quit her, he gave a searching look all round to satisfy himself that everything was in order; he saw that the sheets were properly tightened, and the sails trimmed as they should be, and then calling the young apprentice to his side, he said,—

"Now, Dick, I am going to leave you for a few hours: while I am away, I hope that it will not be necessary for you to make any movement whatever. However, you must be on the watch. It is not very likely, but it is possible that this finback may carry us out to some distance. If so, you will have to follow; and in that case, I am sure you may rely upon Tom and his friends for assistance."

One and all, the negroes assured the captain of their willingness to obey Dick's instructions, the sturdy Hercules rolling up his capacious shirt-sleeves as if to show that he was ready for immediate action. The captain went on,—

"The weather is beautifully fine, Dick, and I see no prospect of the wind freshening; but come what may, I have one direction to give you which I strictly enforce. You must not leave the ship. If I want you to follow us, I will hoist a flag on the boat-hook."

"You may trust me, sir," answered Dick; "and I will keep a good look-out."

"All right, my lad; keep a cool head and a good heart. You are second captain now, you know. I never heard of any one of your age being placed in such a post; be a credit to your position!"

Dick blushed, and the bright flush that rose to his cheeks spoke more than words.

"The lad may be trusted," murmured the captain to himself; "he is as modest as he is courageous. Yes; he may be trusted."

It cannot be denied that the captain was not wholly without compunction at the step he was taking; he was aware of the danger to which he was exposing himself, but he beguiled himself with the persuasion that it was only for a few hours; and his fisherman's instinct was very keen. It was not only for himself; the desire upon the part of the crew was almost irresistibly strong that every opportunity ought to be employed for making the cargo of the schooner equal to her owner's expectations. And so he finally prepared to start.

"I wish you all success!" said Mrs. Weldon.

"Many thanks!" he replied.

Little Jack put in his word,—

"And you will try and catch the whale without hurting him much?"

"All right, young gentleman," answered the captain; "he shall hardly feel the tip of our fingers!"

"Sometimes," said Cousin Benedict, as if he had been pondering the expedition in relation to his pet science, "sometimes there are strange insects clinging to the backs of these great mammifers; do you think you are likely to procure me any specimens?"

"You shall soon have the opportunity of investigating for yourself," was the captain's reply.

"And you, Tom; we shall be looking to you for help in

cutting up our prize, when we get it alongside," continued he.

" We shall be quite ready, sir," said the negro.

" One thing more, Dick," added the captain ; " you may as well be getting up the empty barrels out of the hold ; they will be all ready."

" It shall be done, sir," answered Dick promptly.

If everything went well it was the intention that the whale after it had been killed should be towed to the side of the schooner, where it would be firmly lashed.   Then the sailors with their feet in spiked shoes would get upon its back and proceed to cut the blubber, from head to tail, in long strips, which would first be divided into lumps about a foot and a half square, the lumps being subsequently chopped into smaller portions capable of being stored away in casks.   The ordinary rule would be for a ship, as soon as the flaying was complete, to make its way to land where the blubber could be at once boiled down, an operation by which it is reduced by about a third of its weight, and by which it yields all its oil, the only portion of it which is of any value.   Under pre-sent circumstances, however, Captain Hull would not think of melting down the blubber until his arrival at Valparaiso, and as he was sanguine that the wind would soon set in a favourable direction, he calculated that he should reach that port in less than three weeks, a period during which his cargo would not be deteriorated.

The latest movement with regard to the " Pilgrim " had been to bring her somewhat nearer the spot where the spouts of vapour indicated the presence of the coveted prize.   The creature continued to swim about in the reddened waters, opening and shutting its huge jaws like an automaton, and absorbing at every mouthful whole myriads of animalcula. No one entertained a fear that it would try to make an escape ; it was the unanimous verdict that it was " a fighting whale," and one that would resist all attacks to the very end.

As Captain Hull descended the rope-ladder and took his

The captain's voice came from the retreating boat.

E

place in the bows of the boat, Mrs. Weldon and all on board renewed their good wishes.

Dingo stood with his fore-paws upon the taffrail, and appeared as much as any to be bidding the adventurous party farewell.

When the boat pushed off, those who were left on board the "Pilgrim" made their way slowly to the bows, from which the most extensive view was to be gained.

The captain's voice came from the retreating boat,—

"A sharp look-out, Dick; a sharp look-out; one eye on us, one on the ship!"

"Ay, ay, sir," replied the apprentice.

By his gestures the captain showed that he was under some emotion; he called out again, but the boat had made such headway that it was too far off for any words to be heard.

Dingo broke out into a piteous howl.

The dog was still standing erect, his eye upon the boat in the distance. To the sailors, ever superstitious, the howling was not reassuring. Even Mrs. Weldon was startled.

"Why, Dingo, Dingo," she exclaimed, "this isn't the way to encourage your friends. Come here, sir; you must behave better than that!"

Sinking down on all fours the animal walked slowly up to Mrs. Weldon, and began to lick her hand.

"Ah!" muttered old Tom, shaking his head solemnly, "he doesn't wag his tail at all. A bad omen."

All at once the dog gave a savage growl.

As she turned her head, Mrs. Weldon caught sight of Negoro making his way to the forecastle, probably actuated by the general spirit of curiosity to follow the manœuvres of the whale-boat. He stopped and seized a handspike as soon as he saw the ferocious attitude of the dog.

The lady was quite unable to pacify the animal, which seemed about to fly upon the throat of the cook, but Dick Sands called out loudly,—

" Down, Dingo, down ! "

The dog obeyed ; but it seemed to be with extreme reluc-ance that he returned to Dick's side ; he continued to growl, as if still remembering his rage. Negoro had turned very pale, and having put down the handspike, made his way cautiously back to his own quarters.

" Hercules," said Dick, " I must get you to keep your eye upon that man."

" Yes, I will," he answered, significantly clenching his fists.

Dick took his station at the helm, whence he kept an ear-nest watch upon the whale-boat, which under the vigorous plying of the seamen's oars had become little more than a speck upon the water.

CHAPTER VIII.

A CATASTROPHE.

EXPERIENCED whaleman as he was, Captain Hull knew the difficulty of the task he had undertaken; he was alive to the importance of making his approach to the whale from leeward, so that there should be no sound to apprise the creature of the proximity of the boat. He had perfect confidence in his boatswain, and felt sure that he would take the proper course to insure a favourable result to the enterprise.

"We mustn't show ourselves too soon, Howick," he said.

"Certainly not," replied Howick; "I am going to skirt the edge of the discoloured water, and I shall take good care to get well to leeward."

"All right," the captain answered; and turning to the crew said, "Now, my lads, as quietly as you can."

Muffling the sound of their oars by placing straw in the rowlocks, and avoiding the least unnecessary noise, the men skilfully propelled the boat along the outline of the water tinged by the crustacea, so that while the starboard oars still dipped in the green and limpid sea, those to port were in the deep-dyed waves, and seemed as though they were dripping with blood.

"Wine on this side, water on that," said one of the sailors jocosely.

"But neither of them fit to drink," rejoined the captain sharply; "so just hold your tongue!"

Under Howick's guidance the boat now glided steadily on to the greasy surface of the reddened waters, where she appeared to float as on a pool of oil. The whale seemed utterly unconscious of the attack that was threatening it, and allowed the boat to come nearer without exhibiting any sign of alarm.

The wide circuit which the captain had thought it advisable to take had the effect of considerably increasing the distance between his boat and the "Pilgrim," whilst the strange rapidity with which objects at sea become diminished in apparent magnitude, as if viewed through the wrong end of a telescope, made the ship look farther away than she actually was.

Another half-hour elapsed, and at the end of it the captain found himself so exactly to leeward that the huge body of the whale was precisely intermediate between his boat and the "Pilgrim." A closer approach must now be made; every precaution must be used; but the time had come to get sufficiently near for the harpoon to be discharged.

"Slowly, my men," said the captain, in a low voice; "slowly and softly!"

Howick muttered something that implied that the whale had ceased blowing so hard, and that it was aware of their approach; the captain, upon this, enjoined the most perfect silence, but urged his crew onwards, until, in five or six minutes, they were within a cable's length of the finback. Erect at the stern the boatswain stood, and manœuvred to get the boat as close as possible to the whale's left flank, while he made it an object of special care to keep beyond the reach of its formidable tail, one stroke of which could involve them all in instantaneous disaster.

The manipulation of the boat thus left to the boatswain, the captain made ready for the arduous effort that was before him. At the extreme bow, harpoon in hand, with his legs somewhat astride so as to insure his equilibrium, he stood prepared to plunge his weapon into the mass that rose above the surface of the sea. By his side, coiled in a pail, and with one end firmly attached to the harpoon, was the first of the five lines which, if the whale should dive to a considerable depth, would have to be joined end to end, one after another.

"Are you ready, my lads?" said he, hardly above a whisper.

"Ay, ay, sir," replied Howick, speaking as gently as his master, and giving a firmer grip to the rudder-oar that he held in his hands.

"Then, alongside at once," was the captain's order, which was promptly obeyed, so that in a few minutes the boat was only about ten feet from the body of the whale. The animal did not move. Was it asleep? In that case there was hope that the very first stroke might be fatal. But it was hardly likely. Captain Hull felt only too sure that there was some different cause to be assigned for its remaining so still and stationary; and the rapid glances of the boat-swain showed that he entertained the same suspicion. But it was no time for speculation; the moment for action had arrived, and no attempt was made on either hand to exchange ideas upon the subject.

Captain Hull seized his weapon tightly by the shaft, and having poised it several times in the air, in order to make more sure of his aim, he gathered all his strength and hurled it against the side of the finback.

"Back water!" he shouted

The sailors pushed back with all their might, and the boat in an instant was beyond the range of the creature's tail.

And now the immoveableness of the animal was at once accounted for.

"See; there's a youngster!" exclaimed Howick.

And he was not mistaken. Startled by the blow of the harpoon the monster had heeled over on to its side, and the movement revealed a young whale which the mother had been disturbed in the act of suckling. It was a discovery which made Captain Hull aware that the capture of the whale would be attended with double difficulty; he knew that she would defend "her little one" (if such a term can be applied to a creature that was at least twenty feet long) with the most determined fury; yet having made what he considered a successful commencement of the attack, he would not be daunted, nor deterred from his endeavour to secure so fine a prize.

The whale did not, as sometimes happens, make a precipitate dash upon the boat, a proceeding which necessitates the instant cutting of the harpoon-line, and an immediate retreat, but it took the far more usual course of diving downwards almost perpendicularly. It was followed by its calf; very soon, however, after rising once again to the surface with a sudden bound, it began swimming along under water with great rapidity.

Before its first plunge Captain Hull and Howick had sufficient opportunity to observe that it was an unusually large balænoptera, measuring at least eighty feet from head to tail, its colour being of a yellowish-brown, dappled with numerous spots of a darker shade.

The pursuit, or what may be more aptly termed "the towing," of the whale had now fairly commenced. The sailors had shipped their oars, and the whale-boat darted like an arrow along the surface of the waves. In spite of the oscillation, which was very violent, Howick succeeded in maintaining equilibrium, and did not need the repeated injunctions with which the agitated captain urged his boatswain to be upon his guard.

But fast as the boat flew along, she could not keep pace with the whale, and so rapidly did the line run out that except proper care had been taken to keep the bucket in which it was coiled filled with water, the friction against the edge of the boat would inevitably have caused it to take fire. The whale gave no indication of moderating its speed, so that the first line was soon exhausted, and the second had to be attached to its end, only to be run out with like rapidity. In a few minutes more it was necessary to join on the third line ; it was evident that the whale had not been hit in a vital part, and so far from rising to the surface, the oblique direction of the rope indicated that the creature was seeking yet greater depths.

"Confound it !" exclaimed the captain; "it seems as if the brute is going to run out all our line."

"Yes ; and see what a distance the animal is dragging us away from the ' Pilgrim,' " answered Howick.

"Sooner or later, however," said Captain Hull, "the thing must come to the surface ; she is not a fish, you know."

"She is saving her breath for the sake of her speed," said one of the sailors with a grin.

But grin as he might, both he and his companions began to look serious when the fourth line had to be added to the third, and more serious still when the fifth was added to the fourth. The captain even began to mutter imprecations upon the refractory brute that was putting their patience to so severe a test.

The last line was nearly all uncoiled, and the general consternation was growing very great, when there was observed to be a slight slackening in the tension.

"Thank Heaven !" cried the captain; "the beast has tired herself out at last."

Casting his eye towards the "Pilgrim," he saw at a glance that she could not be less than five miles to leeward. It was a long distance, but when, according to his arrangement, he had hoisted the flag on the boat-hook which was to be the signal for the ship to approach, he had the satisfaction of seeing that Dick Sands and the negroes at once began bracing the yards to get as near as possible to the wind. The breeze, however, blew only in short, unsteady puffs, and it was only too evident that the "Pilgrim" would have considerable

difficulty in working her way to the whale-boat, even if she
succeeded at last.

Meantime, just as had been expected, the whale had
risen to the surface of the water, the harpoon still fixed
firmly in her side. She remained motionless, apparently
waiting for her calf, which she had far out-distanced in her
mad career. Captain Hull ordered his men to pull towards
her as rapidly as they could, and on getting close up, two of
the sailors, following the captain's example, shipped their
oars and took up the long lances with which the whale was
now to be attacked. Howick held himself in readiness to
sheer off quickly in the event of the finback making a turn
towards the boat.

"Now, my lads!" shouted the captain. "Look out!
take a good aim! no false shots! Are you ready, Howick?"

"Quite ready, captain," answered the boatswain, adding,
"but it perplexes me altogether to see the brute so quiet all
of a sudden."

"It looks suspicious," said the captain ; "but never mind;
go on! straight ahead!"

Captain Hull was becoming more excited every moment.

During the time the boat was approaching, the whale had
only turned round a little in the water without changing
its position. It was evidently still looking for its calf, which
was not to be seen by its side. All of a sudden it gave a
jerk with its tail which carried it some few yards away.

The men were all excited. Was the beast going to escape
again? Was the fatiguing pursuit all to come over a second
time? Must not the chase be abandoned? Would not the
prize have to be given up?

But no : the whale was not starting on another flight ; it
had merely turned so as to face the boat, and now rapidly
beating the water with its enormous fins, it commenced a
frantic dash forwards.

"Look out, Howick, she's coming!" shouted Captain
Hull.

The boat was well-nigh full of water, and in imminent danger of being capsized.

The skilful boatswain was all on the alert; the boat swerved, as if by instinct, so as to avoid the blow, and as the whale passed furiously by, she received three tremendous thrusts from the lances of the captain and the two men, who all endeavoured to strike at some vital part. There was a sudden pause. The whale spouted up two gigantic columns of blood and water, lashed its tail, and, with bounds and plunges that were terrible to behold, renewed its angry attack upon the boat.

None but the most determined of whalemen could fail to lose their head under such an assault. Calm and collected, however, the crew remained. Once again did Howick adroitly sheer aside, and once again did the three lances do their deadly work upon the huge carcase as it rolled impetuously past; but this time, so great was the wave that was caused by the infuriated animal, that the boat was well-nigh full of water, and in imminent danger of being capsized.

" Bale away, men ! " cried the captain.

Putting down their oars, the other sailors set to work baling with all their might. Captain Hull cut the harpoon-line, now no longer required, because the whale, maddened with pain and grief for the loss of its offspring, would certainly make no further attempt to escape, but would fight desperately to the very end.

The finback was obviously bent on a third onslaught upon the boat, which, being in spite of all the men's exertions still more than half full of water, no longer answered readily to the rudder-oar.

No one thought of flight. The swiftest boat could be overtaken in a very few bounds. There was no alternative but to face the encounter. It was not long in coming. Their previous good fortune failed them. The whale in passing caught the boat with such a violent blow from its dorsal fin, that the men lost their footing and the lances missed their mark.

"Where's Howick?" screamed the captain in alarm.

"Here I am, captain; all right!" replied the boatswain, who had scrambled to his feet only to find that the oar with which he had been steering was snapped in half.

"The rudder's smashed," he said.

"Take another, Howick; quick!" cried the captain.

But scarcely had he time to replace the broken oar, when a bubbling was heard a few yards away from the boat, and the young whale made its appearance on the surface of the sea. Catching sight of it instantly, the mother made a fresh dash in its direction; the maternal instincts were aroused, and the contest must become more deadly than ever.

Captain Hull looked towards the "Pilgrim," and waved his signal frantically above his head. It was, however, with no hope of succour; he was only too well aware that no human efforts could effectually hasten the arrival of the ship. Dick Sands indeed had at once obeyed the first summons; already the wind was filling the sails, but in default of steam-power her progress at best could not be otherwise than slow. Not only did Dick feel convinced that it would be a useless waste of time to lower a boat and come off with the negroes to the rescue, but he remembered the strict orders he had received on no account to quit the ship. Captain Hull, however, could perceive that the apprentice had had the aft-boat lowered, and was towing it along, so that it should be in readiness for a refuge as soon as they should get within reach.

But the whale, close at hand, demanded attention that could ill be spared for the yet distant ship. Covering her young one with her body, she was manifestly designing another charge full upon the boat.

"On your guard, Howick! sheer off!" bellowed the captain.

But the order was useless. The fresh oar that the boatswain had taken to replace the broken one was considerably shorter, and consequently it failed in lever-power. There was, in fact, no helm for the boat to answer. The sailors saw the failure, and, convinced that all was lost, uttered one long, despairing cry that might have been heard on board the " Pilgrim." Another moment, and from beneath there came a tremendous blow from the monster's tail that sent the boat flying in the air. In fragments it fell back again into a sea that was lashed into fury by the angry flapping of the finback's fins.

Was it not possible for the unfortunate men, bleeding and wounded as they were, still to save themselves by clinging to some floating spar? Captain Hull is indeed seen endeavouring to hoist the boatswain on to a drifting plank. But all in vain. There is no hope. The whale, writhing in the convulsions of death, returns yet once again to the attack; the waters around the struggling sailors seethe and foam. A brief turmoil follows as if there were the bursting of some vast waterspout.

In a quarter of an hour afterwards, Dick Sands, with the negroes, reaches the scene of the catastrophe. All is still and desolate. Every living object has vanished. Nothing is visible except a few fragments of the whale-boat floating on the blood-stained water.

CHAPTER IX.

DICK'S PROMOTION.

THE first feeling experienced by those on board the " Pilgrim," after witnessing the terrible disaster, was one of grief
and horror at the fearful death that had befallen the victims.
Captain Hull and his men had been swept away before their
very eyes, and they had been powerless to assist. Not one
was saved ; the schooner had reached the spot too late to
offer the least resistance to the attacks of the formidable
sea-monster.

When Dick and the negroes returned to the ship after
their hopeless search, with only the corroboration of their
sad foreboding that captain and crew had disappeared for
ever, Mrs. Weldon sank upon her knees ; little Jack knelt
beside her crying bitterly ; and Dick, old Nan, and all the
negroes stood reverently around her whilst with great devout-
ness the lady offered up the prayer of commendation for
the souls of the departing. All sympathized heartily with
her supplications, nor was there any diminution of their
fervour when she proceeded to implore that the survivors
might have strength and courage for their own hour of
need.

The situation was indeed very grave. Here was the
" Pilgrim " in the middle of the Pacific, hundreds of miles
away from the nearest land, without captain, without crew,
at the mercy of the wind and waves. It was a strange fatality that had brought the whale across their path ; it was a

fatality stranger still that had induced her captain, a man of no ordinary prudence, to risk even his life for the sake of making good a deficient cargo. It was an event almost unknown in the annals of whale-fishing that not a single man in the whale-boat should escape alive; nevertheless, it was all too true; and now, of all those left on board, Dick Sands, the apprentice-boy of fifteen years of age, was the sole individual who had the slightest knowledge of the management of a ship; the negroes, brave and willing as they were, were perfectly ignorant of seamen's duties; and, to crown all, here was a lady with her child on board, for whose safety the commander of the vessel would be held responsible.

Such were the facts which presented themselves to the mind of Dick as, with folded arms, he stood gazing gloomily at the spot where Captain Hull, his esteemed benefactor, had sunk to rise no more. The lad raised his eyes sadly; he scanned the horizon with the vain hope that he might perchance descry some passing vessel to which he could confide Mrs. Weldon and her son; for himself, his mind was made up; he had already resolved that nothing should induce him to quit the " Pilgrim " until he had exhausted every energy in trying to carry her into port.

The ocean was all deserted. Since the disappearance of the whale nothing had broken the monotonous surface either of sea or sky. The apprentice, short as his experience was, knew enough to be aware that he was far out of the common track alike of merchantmen or whalers; he would not buoy himself up with false expectations; he would look his situation full and fairly in the face; he would do his best, and trust hopefully in guidance from the Power above.

Thus absorbed in his meditations he did not observe that he was not alone. Negoro, who had gone below immediately after the catastrophe, had again come back upon deck. What this mysterious character had felt upon witnessing the awful calamity it would be impossible to say. Although with his eye he had keenly taken in every detail of the melancholy spectacle, every muscle of his face had remained unmoved; not a gesture, not a word betrayed the least emotion. Even if he had heard, he had taken no part, nor evinced the faintest interest in Mrs. Weldon's outpouring of prayer.

He had made his way to the stern, where Dick Sands was pondering over the responsibilities of his own position, and stood looking towards the apprentice without interrupting his reverie.

Catching sight of him, Dick roused himself in an instant, and said,—

"You want to speak to me?"

"I must speak either to the captain or the boatswain," answered the man.

"Negoro," said Dick sharply, "you know as well as I do, that they are both drowned."

"Then where am I to get my orders from?" asked the fellow insolently.

"From me," promptly rejoined the apprentice.

"From you! from a boy of fifteen?"

"Yes, from me," repeated Dick, in a firm and resolute voice, looking at the man until he recoiled under his gaze. "From *me*."

Mrs. Weldon had heard what passed.

"I wish every one on board to understand," she interposed, "that Dick Sands is captain now. Orders must be taken from him, and they must be obeyed."

Negoro frowned, bit his lip, sneered, and having muttered something that was unintelligible, made his way back to his galley.

Meantime, the schooner under the freshening breeze had been carried beyond the shoal of the crustaceans. Dick cast his eye first at the sails, then along the deck, and seemed to become more and more alive to the weight of the obligation that had fallen upon him ; but his heart did not fail him ; he was conscious that the hopes of the passengers centred in himself, and he was determined to let them see that he would do his best not to disappoint them.

Although he was satisfied of his capability, with the help of the negroes, to manipulate the sails, he was conscious of a defect of the scientific knowledge which was requisite for properly controlling the ship's course. He felt the want of a few more years' experience. If only he had had longer practice he would, he thought, have been as able as Captain Hull himself to use the sextant, to take the altitude of the stars, to calculate the true time with his chronometer; sun, moon, and planets should have been his guides ; from the firmament, as from a dial-plate, he would have gathered the teachings of his true position ; but all this was beyond him as yet ; his knowledge went no further than the use of the log and compass, and by these alone he must be content to make his reckonings. But he kept up his courage, and did not permit himself for one moment to despair of ultimate success.

Mrs. Weldon needed little penetration to recognize the thoughts which were passing in the mind of the resolute youth.

"I see you have come to your decision, Dick," she said. "The command of the ship is in your hands ; no fear but that you will do your duty ; and Tom, and the rest of them, no doubt, will render you every assistance in their power."

"Yes, Mrs. Weldon," rejoined Dick brightly ; "and before long I shall hope to make them good seamen. If only the weather lasts fair, everything will go on well enough ; and if the weather turns out bad, we must not despond ; we will get safe ashore."

He paused a moment and added reverently,—

"God helping us."

Mrs. Weldon proceeded to inquire whether he had any means of ascertaining the " Pilgrim's " present position. He replied that the ship's chart would at once settle that. Captain Hull had kept the reckoning accurately right up to the preceding day.

"And what do you propose to do next?" she asked. " Of course you understand that in our present circumstances we are not in the least bound to go·to Valparaiso if there is a nearer port which we could reach."

"Certainly not," replied Dick; "and therefore it is my intention to sail due east, as by following that course we are sure to come upon some part of the American coast."

"Do your best, Dick, to let us get ashore somewhere."

"Never fear, madam," he answered; "as we get nearer land we shall be almost sure to fall in with a cruiser which will put us into the right track. If the wind does but remain in the north-west, and allow us to carry plenty of sail, we shall get on famously."

He spoke with the cheery confidence of a good sailor who knows the good ship beneath his feet. He had moved off a few steps to go and take the helm, when Mrs. Weldon, calling him back, reminded him that he had not yet ascertained the true position of the schooner. Dick confessed that it ought to be done at once, and going to the captain's cabin brought out the chart upon which the ill-fated commander had marked the bearings the evening before. According to his dead-reckoning they were in lat. 43° 35′, S., and long. 164° 13′, W.; and as the schooner had made next to no progress during the last twenty-four eventful hours, the entry might fairly be accepted as representing approximately their present position.

To the lady's inexperienced eye, as she bent over the outspread chart, it seemed that the land, as represented by the brown patch which depicted the continent of South America extending like a barrier between two oceans from Cape Horn to Columbia, was, after all, not so very far distant; the wide space of the Pacific was not so broad but that it would be quickly traversed.

"Oh, we shall soon be on shore!" she said.

But Dick knew better. He had acquaintance enough with the scale upon which the chart was constructed to be aware that the "Pilgrim" herself would have been a speck like a microscopic infusoria on the vast surface of that sea, and that hundreds and hundreds of weary miles separated her from the coast.

No time was to be lost. Contrary winds had ceased to blow; a fresh north-westerly breeze had sprung up, and the *cirri*, or curl-clouds overhead indicated that for some time at least the direction of the wind would be unchanged. Dick appealed to the negroes, and tried to make them appreciate the difficulty of the task that had fallen to his lot. Tom answered, in behalf of himself and all the rest, that they were not only willing, but anxious, to do all they could to assist him, saying that if their knowledge was small, yet their arms were strong, and added that they should certainly be obedient to every order he gave.

"My friends," said Dick, addressing them in reply; "I shall make it a point of myself taking the helm as much as possible. But you know I must have my proper rest sometimes. No one can live without sleep. Now, Tom, I intend you to stand by me for the remainder of the day. I will try and make you understand how to steer by the aid of the compass. It is not difficult. You will soon learn. I shall have to leave you when I go to my hammock for an hour or two."

"Is there nothing," said little Jack, "that I can learn to do?"

"Oh yes, Jack; you shall keep the wind in order," answered Dick, smiling.

"That I will!" cried the child, clapping his hands, while the mother drew him to her side.

"And now, my men," was Dick's first order to his crew,

" we must brace the yards to sail before the wind. I will show you how."

" All right, Captain Sands ; we are at your service," said old Tom gravely.

CHAPTER X.

THE NEW CREW.

DICK SANDS, captain of the "Pilgrim," would not lose a moment in getting his ship under sail. His prime object was to land his passengers safely at Valparaiso or some other American port, and to accomplish his purpose it was in the first place necessary that he should ascertain the schooner's rate of speed and the direction that she was taking. This information was to be obtained readily enough by means of the log and compass, and the result of each day's observations would be entered regularly on the chart.

The log on board was a patent log, with a dial-plate and screw, by means of which the distance that is travelled can be measured accurately for any definite time; it was an instrument so simple that the negroes were very soon taught its use. The slight error in the reckoning caused by the action of the currents could only be rectified by astronomical observtaions, which, as already has been stated, were beyond Dick's attainments to make.

The idea more than once crossed Dick's mind whether he would not take the "Pilgrim" back again to New Zealand; the distance was considerably less than it was to America, and had the wind remained in the quarter whence it had been blowing so long, it is more than likely he would have determined to retrace his course. But as the wind had now veered to the north-west, and there was every probability that it was settled for a time, he came to the conclusion that he had better take advantage of it and persevere in making his way towards the east. Accordingly he lost no time in putting his ship before the wind.

On a schooner the fore-mast usually carries four square sails; viz. on the lower mast a fore-sail, on the top-mast a top-sail, on the top-gallant-mast a top-gallant-sail and a royal. The main-mast carries only a fore and aft main-sail and a top-sail. Between the masts upon the stays can be hoisted a triple tier of stay-sails; while the bowsprit with its jib-boom will carry the three jibs.

The jibs, the main-sail, the main-top-sail and the stay-sails are all managed with comparative ease, because they can be hoisted from the deck without the necessity of ascending the mast to let fly the ropes, by which they are fastened to the yards. With the sails on the fore-mast it is altogether a more difficult business. In order either to unfurl them, to take them in, or to reef them, it is necessary for a man to clamber up by the shrouds, either to the fore-top, or to the top-gallant cross-trees, and thence moving on to loose ropes extended below the yards, to hold on by one hand whilst he does his work with the other. The operation requires alike the head and arm of an experienced mariner; and, when a fresh breeze has been blowing, it is a casualty far from uncommon for a sailor, confused by the flapping of the canvas and the pitching of the vessel, to be blown overboard in the act.

For the unpractised negroes the danger would necessarily be very great. However, the wind at present was very moderate, and the ship ploughed her way over the waves without any violent oscillations.

At the time when Dick Sands, in obedience to the signal he received from Captain Hull, proceeded to make his way to the scene of the disaster, the "Pilgrim," as she lay to, was carrying only her jibs, main-sail, fore-sail, and fore-top-sail. In order, therefore, to put her as near as possible to the wind, it had been merely necessary to haul in the lee sheets and braces, a manœuvre in which the negroes had rendered all the assistance that was necessary. It was requisite now to do something more. To enable him to get straight before the wind Dick wanted to increase his sail, and was desirous of setting the fore-top-gallant and royal-sails with the main-top-sail and stay-sails.

He was himself standing at the wheel.

"Now, my men," he shouted to the negroes; "I want your help. Do exactly as I tell you. Let go, Tom!"

Tom looked puzzled.

"Let go! unfasten that rope, I mean. And, Bat, come along; do the same as Tom."

The men did what they were bidden.

"That's right!" continued Dick, and calling to Hercules, said,—

"Now, Hercules; a good strong pull!"

To give such a direction to Hercules was somewhat imprudent; the rigging creaked again under his giant strength.

"Gently, gently, my good fellow!" said Dick, laughing; "you will have the mast down."

"I declare I hardly touched the rope," answered Hercules.

"Well, next time, you must only pretend to touch it," said Dick; and, continuing his orders, shouted, "Now easy! let fly! make fast! now brace round the yards! all right! that's capital!"

The lee braces were loosened, the fore-sails turned slowly round, and, catching the breeze, gave a slight impetus to the ship. Dick's next orders were for the jib-sheets to be eased, and then he called the men to the stern.

"Now," said he; "we must look to the main-mast; but take care, Hercules, not to have it down."

"I will be as careful as possible, Mr. Dick," submissively replied Hercules, as though he were afraid to commit himself to any rash promise.

The manœuvre was simple enough. The main-sheet was gradually slackened, the great sail took the wind and added its powerful action to that of the fore-sails. The main-top-sail was next brought to bear; it was only stowed at the main-mast head, so that there was nothing to do except to pull the halyards, haul the tack and sheet, and unfurl it. But in pulling at the halyards the muscular energy of Hercules, which was supplemented by that of Actæon, not to forget little Jack, who had volunteered his assistance, proved to be overpowering, and the rope snapped in two. All three of them, of course, fell flat upon the deck; but fortunately neither of them was hurt, and Jack laughed heartily at his tumble as an excellent joke.

"Up with you!" cried Captain Dick; "there's no harm done; splice the rope, and haul away more gently next time."

It took but a few minutes to execute the order, and the "Pilgrim" was soon sailing away rapidly with her head to the east.

"Well done, my friends!" said Dick, who had not left his post at the helm; "you will be first-rate sailors before the end of the voyage."

"We shall do our best, I promise you, Captain Sands," replied Tom, making it a point to give the young commander his proper title.

Mrs. Weldon also congratulated the new crew upon the success of their first attempt.

"I believe it was Master Jack who broke that rope," said Hercules, with a sly twinkle in his eye; "he is very strong, I can tell you."

Jack looked as though he thoroughly appreciated the compliment, and evidenced his satisfaction by giving his huge friend a hearty shake of the hand.

All three of them fell flat upon the deck.

There were still several sails that were not yet set. Running well before the wind as the " Pilgrim " was, Dick nevertheless felt that the top-gallant, royal, and stay-sails, if brought into service, would materially assist her progress, and he determined not to dispense with their help. The stay-sails could be hoisted from below, but to bring the top-gallant and royal into play demanded more experience than any of his crew had had. Knowing that he could not entrust the task to them, and yet resolved not to be baulked of his wish to set them, he undertook the task himself. He first put Tom to the helm, showing him how to keep the schooner's head in the right direction, and having placed the other four at the royal and top-gallant halyards, proceeded to mount the foremast.

To clamber up the fore-mast and fore-top-mast shrouds on to the cross-trees was mere child's play to the active apprentice. In a few minutes he had unfurled the top-gallant-sail, mounted to the royal-yard, unfurled the royal, again reached the cross-trees, and having caught hold of one of the starboard back-stays, had descended to the deck; there he gave the necessary directions, and the two sails were made fast, and both yards braced.

Nor did this content him. The stay-sails were set between the masts, and thus the " Pilgrim " was running along, with all her canvas set and full. The only additional sails which Dick could possibly have employed would have been some studding-sails to windward, but as the setting of these was a matter of some difficulty, and they were not always readily taken in in case of a sudden squall, he contented himself without them.

Again he took his place at the helm. The breeze was manifestly freshening, and the " Pilgrim," almost imperceptibly heeling to starboard, glided rapidly along the surface of the water, leaving behind her a wake, smooth and clean, that bore plain witness to the skill with which she had been designed.

"This is good progress, Mrs. Weldon," he said; "may Heaven grant the wind and weather may continue thus favourable!"

The lady, in silence, shook the boy's hand; and then, worn-out with the excitement of the past hours, went to her cabin, where she lay down and fell into a troubled doze.

The new crew remained on watch. They were stationed on the forecastle, in readiness to make any alteration which the sails might require, but the wind was so steady and unshifting that no need arose for their services.

And Cousin Benedict? all this time, where was he? and what had he been doing?

He was sitting in his cabin; he had a magnifying-glass in his hand and was studying an articulata of the order orthoptera, an insect of the Blattidæ family; its characteristics are a roundish body, rather long wings, flat elytra, and a head hidden by the prothorax. He had been on deck at the time of the calamity; the ill-fated captain with the crew had been drowned before his very eyes; but he said nothing; not that he was unmoved; to think that he was not struck with horror would be to libel his kind and pitying nature. His sympathy was aroused, especially for his cousin; he pressed her hand warmly as if he would assure her of his truest commiseration; but he said nothing; he hurried off towards his cabin; and who shall deny that it was to devise some wonderfully energetic measures that he would take in consequence of this melancholy event?

Passing the kitchen, however, he caught sight of Negoro in the act of crushing a blatta, an American species of cockroach. He broke out into a storm of invective, and in tones of indignation demanded the surrender of the insect, which Negoro made with cool contempt. In a moment Captain Hull and his partners in death were all forgotten; the enthusiast had secured a prize with which he hastened to his own little compartment, where he was soon absorbed in proving to his own satisfaction, in opposition to the opinion of other entomologists, that the blattæ of the phoraspous species, which are remarkable for their colours, differ in their habits from blattæ of the ordinary sort.

For the remainder of the day perfect order reigned on board the " Pilgrim." Though they were unable to shake off the sickening feeling of horror roused by the frightful disaster, and felt that they had sustained a startling shock, all the passengers seemed mechanically to fall into their usual routine. Dick Sands, though avowedly at the wheel, seemed to be everywhere, with an eye for everything, and his amateur crew obeyed him readily, and with the promptness of a willing activity.

Negoro made no further overt attempt to question the young captain's authority, but remained shut up in his kitchen. Dick made no secret of his determination to place the cook in close confinement if he exhibited any future sign of insubordination. Hercules was ready to carry him off bodily to the hold, and old Nan was equally ready to take his place in the cooking department. Probably Negoro was aware of all this ; at any rate he did not seem disposed to give any further cause of offence at present.

As the day advanced the wind continued to freshen ; but no shifting of the sails seemed necessary. The " Pilgrim" was running well. There was no need to diminish her spread of canvas. Masts as solid and rigging as strong as hers could stand a far heavier breeze.

As a general rule, it is deemed prudent in case of a squall to shorten sail at night, and especially to take in top-gallant and royal sails ; but the weather prospects now were all so promising and satisfactory that Dick persuaded himself he was under no necessity to take this precaution ; he rather felt himself bound to take the strongest measures he could to expedite his reaching less unfrequented waters. He made up his mind, however, not to leave the deck at all that night.

The young captain made every effort to get an approximate reckoning of the schooner's progress. He hove the log every half-hour, and duly registered the result of each successive examination. There were two compasses on board; one in the binnacle close under the eye of the helmsman, the other an inverted compass attached to the rafters of the captain's cabin, so that without leaving his berth he could see whether the man in charge of the wheel was holding a proper course.

Every vessel that is duly furnished for a lengthened voyage has always not only two compasses but two chronometers, one to correct the other. The " Pilgrim " was not deficient in this respect, and Dick Sands made a strong point of admonishing his crew that they should take especial care of the compasses, which under their present circumstances were of such supreme importance.

A misfortune, however, was in store for them. On the night of the 12th, while Dick was on watch, the compass in the cabin became detached from its fastening and fell on the floor. The accident was not discovered until the following morning. Whether the metal ferule that had attached the instrument to the rafters had become rusty, or whether it had been worn away by additional friction, it seemed impossible to settle. All that could be said was that the compass was broken beyond repair. Dick was extremely grieved at the loss; but he did not consider that any one was to be blamed for the mishap, and could only resolve for the future to take extra care of the compass in the binnacle.

With the exception of this *contretemps*, everything appeared to go on satisfactorily on board. Mrs. Weldon, reassured by Dick's confidence, had regained much of her wonted calmness, and was besides ever supported by a sincere religious spirit. She and Dick had many a long conversation

together. The ingenuous lad was always ready to take the
kind and intelligent lady into his counsel, and day by day
would point out to her on the chart the registers he made as
the result of his dead reckoning; he would then try and
satisfy her that under the prevailing wind there could be no
doubt they must arrive at the coast of South America:
moreover, he said that, unless he was much mistaken, they
should sight the land at no great distance from Valparaiso.

Mrs. Weldon had, in truth, no reason to question the cor-
rectness of Dick's representations; she owned that provided
the wind remained in the same favourable quarter, there was
every prospect of their reaching land in safety; nevertheless
at times she could not resist the misgiving that would arise
when she contemplated what might be the result of a change
of wind or a breaking of the weather.

With the light-heartedness that belonged to his age, Jack
soon fell back into his accustomed pursuits, and was to be
seen merrily running over the deck or romping with Dingo.
At times, it is true, he missed the companionship of Dick;
but his mother made him comprehend that now that Dick
was captain, his time was too much occupied to allow him
any leisure for play, and the child quite understood that he
must not interrupt his old friend in his new duties.

The negroes performed their work with intelligence, and
seemed to make rapid progress in the art of seamanship.
Tom had been unanimously appointed boatswain, and took
one watch with Bat and Austin, the alternate watch being
discharged by Dick himself with Hercules and Actæon.
One of them steered, so that the other two were free to watch
at the bows. As a general rule Dick Sands managed to
remain at the wheel all night; five or six hours' sleep in the
daytime sufficed for him, and during the time when he was
lying down he entrusted the wheel to Tom or Bat, who under
his instructions had become very fair helmsmen. Although

in these unfrequented waters there was little chance of running foul of any other vessel, Dick invariably took the precaution of lighting his side-lamps—a green one to starboard and a red one to port. His exertions, however, were a great strain upon him, and sometimes during the night his fatigue would induce a heavy drowsiness, and he steered, as it were, by instinct more than by attention.

On the night of the 13th, he was so utterly worn out that he was obliged to ask Tom to relieve him at the helm whilst he went down for a few hours' rest. Actæon and Hercules remained on watch on the forecastle.

The night was very dark ; the sky was covered with heavy clouds that had formed in the chill evening air, and the sails on the top-masts were lost in the obscurity. At the stern, the lamps on either side of the binnacle cast a faint reflection on the metal mountings of the wheel, leaving the deck generally in complete darkness.

Towards three o'clock in the morning Tom was getting so heavy with sleepiness that he was almost unconscious. His eye, long fixed steadily on the compass, lost its power of vision, and he fell into a doze from which it would require more than a slight disturbance to arouse him.

Meantime a light shadow glided stealthily along the deck. Creeping gradually up to the binnacle, Negoro put down something heavy that he had brought in his hand. He stole a keen and rapid glance at the dial of the compass, and made his way back, unseen and unheard as he had come.

Almost immediately afterwards, Tom awakened from his slumber. His eye fell instinctively on the compass, and he saw in a moment that the ship was out of her proper course. By a turn of the helm he brought her head to what he supposed to be the east. But he was mistaken. During his brief interval of unconsciousness a piece of iron had been deposited beneath the magnetic needle, which by this means had been diverted thirty degrees to the right, and, instead of pointing due north, inclined far towards north-east.

Consequently it came to pass that the " Pilgrim," supposed by her young commander to be making good headway due east, was in reality, under the brisk north-west breeze, speeding along towards the south-east.

CHAPTER XI.

ROUGH WEATHER.

DURING the ensuing week nothing particular occurred on board. The breeze still freshened, and the " Pilgrim " made on the average 160 miles every twenty-four hours. The speed was as great as could be expected from a craft of her size.

Dick grew more and more sanguine in his anticipations that it could not be long before the schooner would cross the track of the mail-packets plying between the eastern and western hemispheres. He had made up his mind to hail the first passing vessel, and either to transfer his passengers, or what perhaps would be better still, to borrow a few sailors, and, it might be, an officer to work the " Pilgrim " to shore. He could not help, however, a growing sense of astonishment, when day after day passed, and yet there was no ship to be signalled. He kept the most vigorous look-out, but all to no purpose. Three voyages before had he made to the whale-fisheries, and his experience made him sure that he ought now to be sighting some English or American vessel on its way between the Equator and Cape Horn.

Very different, however, was the true position of the " Pilgrim " from what Dick supposed ; not only had the ship been carried far out of her direct course by currents the force of which there were no means of estimating, but from the moment when the compass had been tampered with by Negoro, the steering itself had put the vessel all astray.

Unconscious of both these elements of disturbance, Dick Sands was convinced that they were proceeding steadily eastwards, and was perpetually encouraging Mrs. Weldon and himself by the assurance that they must very soon arrive within view of the American coast ; again and again asserting that his sole concern was for his passengers, and that for his own safety he had no anxiety.

"But think, Dick," said the lady, "what a position you would have been in, if you had not had your passengers. You would have been alone with that terrible Negoro ; you would have been rather alarmed then."

" I should have taken good care to put it out of Negoro's power to do me any mischief, and then I should have worked the ship by myself," answered the lad stoutly.

His very pluck gave Mrs. Weldon renewed confidence. She was a woman with wonderful powers of endurance, and it was only when she thought of her little son that she had any feeling of despair ; yet even this she endeavoured to conceal, and Dick's undaunted courage helped her.

Although the youth of the apprentice did not allow him to pretend to any advanced scientific knowledge, he had the proverbial "weather-eye" of the sailor. He was not only very keen in noticing any change in the aspect of the sky, but he had learnt from Captain Hull, who was a clever meteorologist, to draw correct conclusions from the indications of the barometer; the captain, indeed, having taken the trouble to make him learn by heart the general rules which are laid down in Vorepierre's *Dictionnaire Illustré*.

There are seven of these rules :—

1. If after a long period of fine weather the barometer falls suddenly and continuously, although the mercury may be descending for two or three days before there is an apparent change in the atmosphere, there will ultimately be rain ; and the longer has been the time between the first depression and the commencement of the rain, the longer the rain may be expected to last.

2. *Vice versâ*, if after a long period of wet weather the barometer begins to rise slowly and steadily, fine weather will ensue; and the longer the time between the first rising of the mercury and the commencement of the fine weather, the longer the fine weather may be expected to last.

3. If immediately after the fall or rise of the mercury a change of weather ensues, the change will be of no long continuance.[1]

4. A gradual rise for two or three days during rain forecasts fine weather; but if there be a fall immediately on the arrival of the fine weather, it will not be for long. This rule holds also conversely.

5. In spring and autumn a sudden fall indicates rain; in the summer, if very hot, it foretells a storm. In the winter, after a period of steady frost, a fall prognosticates a change of wind with rain and hail; whilst a rise announces the approach of snow.

6. Rapid oscillations of the mercury either way are not to be interpreted as indicating either wet or dry weather of any duration; continuance of either fair or foul weather is forecast only by a prolonged and steady rise or fall beforehand.

7. At the end of autumn, after a period of wind and rain, a rise may be expected to be followed by north wind and frost.

Not merely had Dick got these rules by rote, but he had tested them by his own observations, and had become singularly trustworthy in his forecasts of the weather. He made a point of consulting the barometer several times every day, and although to all appearances the sky indicated that the fine weather was settled, it did not escape his observation

---

[1] This and several of the other rules are concisely concentrated in the couplet—

Long foretold, long last;
Short notice, soon past.

that on the 20th the mercury showed a tendency to fall. Dick knew that rain, if it came, would be accompanied by wind ; an opinion in which he was very soon confirmed by the breeze freshening, till the air was displaced at the rate of nearly sixty feet a second, or more than forty miles an hour ; and he recognized the necessity of at once shortening sail. He had already used the precaution to take in the royal, the main-top-sail, and the flying jib, but he now at once resolved likewise to take in the top-gallant, and to have a couple of reefs in the fore-top-sail.

To an inexperienced crew the last operation was far from easy ; but there was no symptom of shrinking from it. Followed by Bat and Austin, Dick mounted the rigging of the foremast, and with little trouble got to the top-gallant-yard. Had the weather been less unpromising he would have been inclined to leave the two yards as they were, but anticipating the ultimate necessity of being obliged to lower the mast, he unrigged them, and let them down to the deck ; he knew well enough that in the event of the gale rising as he expected, the lowering of the mast as well as the shortening of sail would contribute to diminish the strain and stress upon the vessel.

It was the work of two hours to get this preliminary operation over. There still remained the task of taking in the reefs in the top-sail.

The " Pilgrim " in one respect differed from most modern vessels. She did not carry a double fore-top-sail, which would very much have diminished the difficulty attending the reefing. It was consequently necessary to proceed as before ; to mount the rigging, by main force to haul in the flapping canvas, and to make the fastening secure. But critical and dangerous as the task was, it was successfully accomplished, and the three young men, having descended safely to the deck, had the satisfaction of seeing the schooner run easily before the wind, which had further increased till it was blowing a stiff gale.

For three days the gale continued brisk and hard, yet without any variation in its direction. But all along the barometer was falling; the mercury sank to 28° without symptom of recovery. The sky was becoming overcast; clouds, thick and lowering, obscured the sun, and it was difficult to make out where it rose or where it set. Dick did his best to keep up his courage, but he could not disguise from himself that there was cause for uneasiness. He took no more rest than was absolutely necessary, and what repose he allowed himself he always took on deck; he maintained a calm exterior, but he was really tortured with anxiety.

Although the violence of the wind seemed to lull awhile, Dick did not suffer himself to be betrayed into any false security; he knew only too well what to expect, and after a brief interval of comparative quiet, the gale returned and the waves began to run very high.

About four o'clock one afternoon, Negoro (a most unusual thing for him) emerged from his galley, and skulked to the bows. Dingo was fast asleep, and did not make his ordinary growl by way of greeting to his enemy. For half an hour Negoro stood motionless, apparently surveying the horizon. The heavy waves rolled past; they were higher than the condition of the wind warranted; their magnitude witnessed to a storm passing in the west, and there was every reason to suspect that the " Pilgrim " might be caught by its violence.

Negoro looked long at the water; he then raised his eyes and scanned the sky. Above and below he might have read threatening signs. The upper stratum of cloud was travelling far more rapidly than that beneath, an indication that ere long the masses of vapour would descend, and, coming in contact with the lower current, would change the gale into a tempest, which probably would increase to a hurricane.

It might be from ignorance, or it might be from indifference, but there was no indication of alarm on the face of Negoro; on the other hand there might be seen a sort of smile curling on his lip. After thus gazing above him and around him, he clambered on to the bowsprit, and made his way by degrees to the very end ; again he rested and looked about him as if to explore the horizon ; after a while he clambered back on deck, and soon stealthily retreated to his own quarters.

No doubt there was much cause for concern in the general aspect of the weather ; but there was one point on which they never failed to congratulate each other ;—that the direction of the wind had never changed, and consequently must be carrying them in the desired course. Unless a storm should overtake them, they could continue their present navigation without peril, and with every prospect of finding a port upon the shore where they might put in. Such were their mutual and acknowledged hopes ; but Dick secretly felt the misgiving lest, without a pilot, he might in his ignorance fail to find a harbour of refuge. Nevertheless, he would not suffer himself to meet trouble half-way, and kept up his spirits under the conviction that if difficulties came he should be strengthened to grapple with them or make his escape.

Time passed on, and the 9th of March arrived without material change in the condition of the atmosphere. The sky remained heavily burdened, and the wind, which occasionally had abated for a few hours, had always returned with at least its former violence. The occasional rising of the mercury never encouraged Dick to anticipate a permanent improvement in the weather, and he discerned only too plainly that brighter times at present were not to be looked for.

A startling alarm had more than once been caused by the sudden breaking of storms in which thunderbolts had seemed to fall within a few cables' lengths of the schooner. On these occasions the torrents of rain had been so heavy that the ship had appeared to be in the very midst of a whirlpool of vapour, and it was impossible to see a yard ahead.

The "Pilgrim" pitched and rolled frightfully. Fortunately

Mrs. Weldon could bear the motion without much personal inconvenience, and consequently was able to devote her attention to her little boy, who was a miserable sufferer. Cousin Benedict was as undisturbed as the cockroaches he was investigating; he hardly noticed the increasing madness of either wind or wave, but went on with his studies as calmly as if he were in his own comfortable museum at San Francisco. Moreover, it was fortunate that the negroes did not suffer to any great degree from sea-sickness, and consequently were able to assist their captain in his arduous task. Dick was far too experienced a sailor himself to be inconvenienced by the violent oscillations of the vessel.

The "Pilgrim" still made good headway, and Dick, although he was aware that ultimately it would probably be necessary again to shorten sail, was anxious to postpone making any alteration before he was absolutely obliged. Surely, he reasoned with himself, the land could not now be far away; he had calculated his speed; he had kept a diligent reckoning on the chart; surely, the shore must be almost in sight. He would not trust his crew to keep watch; he was aware how easily their inexperienced eyes would be misled, and how they might mistake a distant cloud-bank for the land they desired to see; he kept watch for himself; his own gaze was ever fixed upon the horizon; and in the eagerness of his expectation he would repeatedly mount to the cross-trees to get a wider range of vision.

But land was not to be seen.

Next day as Dick was standing at the bow, alternately eyeing the canvas which his ship carried and the aspect presented by the sky, Mrs. Weldon approached him without his noticing her. She caught some muttered expressions of bewilderment that fell from his lips, and asked him whether he could see anything.

He lowered the telescope which he had been holding in his hand, and answered,—

"No, Mrs. Weldon, I cannot see anything; and it is this

that perplexes me so sorely. I cannot understand why we have not already come in sight of land. It is nearly a month since we lost our poor captain. There has been no delay in our progress ; no stoppage in our rate of speed. I cannot make it out."

" How far were we from land when we lost the captain ?"

" I am sure I am not far out in saying that we were scarcely more than 4500 miles from the shores of America."

" And at what rate have we been sailing ?"

" Not much less than 180 knots a day."

" How long, then, do you reckon, Dick, we ought to be in arriving at the coast ?"

" Under six-and-twenty days," replied Dick.

He paused before he spoke again, then added,—

" But what mystifies me even more than our failing to sight the land is this : we have not come across a single vessel ; and yet vessels without number are always traversing these seas."

" But do you not think," inquired Mrs. Weldon, " that you have made some error in your reckoning? Is your speed really what you have supposed ? "

" Impossible, madam," replied Dick, with an air of dignity, " impossible that I should have fallen into error. The log has been consulted, without fail, every half-hour. I am about to have it lowered now, and I will undertake to show you that we are at this present moment making ten miles an hour, which would give considerably over 200 miles a day."

He then called out to Tom,—

" Tom, heave the log !"

The old man was quite accustomed to the duty. The log was fastened to the line and thrown overboard. It ran out regularly for about five-and-twenty fathoms, when all at once the line slackened in Tom's hand.

" It is broken !" cried Tom ; " the cord is broken !"

" Broken ?" exclaimed Dick : " good heavens ! we have lost the log !"

It was too true.   The log was gone.

Tom drew in the rope.   Dick took it up and examined it. It had not broken at its point of union with the log ; it had given way in the middle, at a place where the strands in some unaccountable way had worn strangely thin.

Dick's agony of mind, in spite of his effort to be calm, was intensely great.   A suspicion of foul play involuntarily occurred to him.   He knew that the rope had been of first-rate make ; he knew that it had been quite sound when used before ; but he could prove nothing ; he could only mourn over the loss which committed him to the sole remaining compass as his only guide.

That compass, too, although he knew it not, was misleading him entirely !

Mrs. Weldon sighed as she witnessed the grief which the loss manifestly caused poor Dick, but in purest sympathy she said nothing, and retired thoughtfully to her cabin.

It was no longer possible to reckon the rate of progress, but there was no doubt that the " Pilgrim " continued to maintain at least her previous speed.

Before another four-and-twenty hours had passed, the barometer had fallen still lower, and the wind was threatening to rise to a velocity of sixty miles.   Resolved to be on the safe side, Dick determined not only to strike the fore-top-gallant and the main-top-masts, but to take in all the lower sails. Indeed, he began to be aware that no time was to be lost. The operation would not be done in a moment, and the storm was approaching.   Dick made Tom take the helm ; he ascended the shrouds with Bat, Austin, and Actæon, making Hercules stay on deck to ease the halyards as required.

By dint of arduous exertion, and at no little risk of being thrown overboard by the rolling of the ship, they succeeded in striking the two masts ; the fore-top-sail was then reefed, and the fore-sail entirely stowed, so that the only canvas that the schooner carried was the reefed fore-top and one stay-sail.   These, however, made her run with a terrific speed.

Early on the morning of the 12th, Dick noted with alarm that the barometer had not ceased to fall, and now registered only 27.9°. The tempest had continued to increase, till it was unsafe for the ship to carry any canvas at all. The order was given for the top-sail to be taken in, but it was too late; a violent gust carried the sail completely away, and Austin, who had made his way to the top-sail-yard, was struck by the flying sheet ; and although he was not seriously hurt, he was obliged at once to return to deck.

Dick Sands became more uneasy than ever ; he was tortured by apprehensions of outlying reefs near the shore, to which he imagined he must now be close ; but he could discern no rocks to justify his fears, and returned to take his place at the helm.

The next moment Negoro appeared on deck ; he pointed mysteriously to the far-off horizon, as though he discerned some object, as a mountain, there ; and looking round with a malevolent smile, immediately left the deck, and went back to his galley.

CHAPTER XII

HOPE REVIVED.

THE wind had now increased to a hurricane; it had veered
to the south-west, and had attained a velocity little short of
ninety miles an hour. On land the most substantial of erections could with difficulty have withstood its violence, and a
vessel anchored in a roadstead must have been torn from its
moorings and cast ashore. The memorable storm that had
devastated the Island of Guadaloupe on the 25th of July,
1825, when heavy cannon were lifted from their carriages,
could scarcely have been more furious, and it was only
her mobility before the blast and the solidity of her structure that gave the "Pilgrim" a hope of surviving the
tempest.

A few minutes after the top-sail had been lost, the small
jib was carried away. Dick Sands contemplated the possibility of setting a storm-jib, made of extra strong canvas, as a means of bringing the ship a little more under his
control, but abandoned the idea as useless. It was, therefore, under bare poles that the "Pilgrim" was driven along;
but in spite of the lack of canvas, the hull, masts, and rigging
gave sufficient purchase to the wind, and the progress of the
schooner was prodigiously rapid; sometimes, indeed, she
seemed to be literally lifted from the water, and scudded on,
scarcely skimming its surface. The rolling was fearful.
Enormous waves followed in quick succession, and as they

travelled faster than the ship, there was the perpetual risk of one of them pooping her. Without sail, there were no means of escaping that peril by increase of speed ; the adroit management of the helm was the only chance of avoiding the hazardous shocks, and even this repeatedly failed.

To prevent his being washed overboard Dick lashed himself to his place at the wheel by a rope round his waist, and made Tom and Bat keep close at hand, ready to give him assistance, in case of emergency. Hercules and Actæon, clinging to the bitts, kept watch at the bow. Mrs. Weldon and her party, at Dick's special request, remained inside the after-cabin, although the lady, for her own part, would much rather have stayed on deck ; she had, however, yielded to the representation that she would thus be exposing herself to unnecessary danger.

The hatches were battened down, and it was to be hoped that they would withstand the heavy sea that was dashing over them; only let one of them give way to the pressure, and the vessel must inevitably fill and founder. It was a matter of congratulation that the stowage had been done very carefully, so that notwithstanding all the lurchings of the ship the cargo did not shift in the least.

The heroic young commander had still further curtailed his periods of rest, and it was only at the urgent entreaty of Mrs. Weldon, who feared that he would exhaust himself by his vigilance, that he was induced to lie down for a few hours' sleep on the night of the 13th.

After Tom and Bat had been left alone at the wheel, they were, somewhat to their surprise, joined by Negoro, who very rarely came aft. He seemed inclined to enter into conversation, but found little encouragement to talk on the part either of Tom or his son. All at once a violent roll of the ship threw him off his feet, and he would have gone overboard if he had not been saved by falling against the binnacle.

Old Tom was in a frantic state of alarm lest the compass should be broken. He uttered a cry of consternation so loud that it roused Dick from the light slumber into which he had fallen in the cabin, and he rushed to the deck. By the time he had reached the stern, Negoro had not only regained his feet, but had managed successfully to conceal the bit of iron which he had again extracted from beneath the binnacle where he had himself laid it. Now that the wind had shifted to the south-west, it suited his machinations that the magnetic needle should indicate its true direction.

"How now?" asked Dick eagerly; "what is the meaning of all this noise?"

Tom explained how the cook had fallen against the binnacle, and how he had been terrified lest the compass should be injured. Dick's heart sank at the thought of losing his sole remaining compass, and his anxiety betrayed itself in his countenance as he knelt down to examine its condition; but he breathed freely as he ascertained that the instrument had sustained no damage; by the dim light he saw the needle resting on its two concentric circles, and felt his fears at once relieved; of course, he was quite unconscious of the fact that the removal of the bit of iron had made the magnet change its direction.

The incident, however, excited his misgiving; although he felt that Negoro could not be held responsible for an accidental fall, the very presence of the man in such a place at such a time perplexed him.

"And what brings you here this hour of the night?" he asked.

"That's not your business," retorted Negoro insolently.

"It is my business," replied Dick resolutely; "and I mean to have an answer; what brought you here?"

Negoro answered sullenly that he knew of no rule to prevent his going where he liked and when he liked.

"No rule!" cried Dick; "then I make the rule now. From this time forward, I make the rule that you shall never come astern. Do you understand?"

Roused from his accustomed doggedness, the man seemed to make a threatening movement. Quick as lightning, Dick Sands drew a revolver from his pocket.

"Negoro, one act, one word of insubordination, and I blow out your brains!"

Negoro had no time to reply; before he could speak he was bowed down towards the deck by an irresistible weight. Hercules had grasped him by the shoulder.

"Shall I put him overboard, captain? he will make a meal for the fishes; they are not very particular what they eat," said the negro, with a grin of contempt.

"Not yet," quietly answered Dick.

The giant removed his hand, and Negoro stood upright again, and began to retreat to his own quarters, muttering, however, as he passed Hercules,—

"You cursed nigger! You shall pay for this!"

The discovery was now made that the wind apparently had taken a sudden shift of no less than forty-five degrees; but what occasioned Dick the greatest perplexity was that there was nothing in the condition of the sea to correspond with the alteration in the current of the air; instead of being directly astern, wind and waves were now beating on the port beam. Progress in this way must necessarily be full of danger, and Dick was obliged to bring his ship up at least four points before he got her straight before the tempest.

The young captain felt that he must be more than ever on the alert; he could not shake off the suspicion that Negoro had been concerned in the loss of the first compass, and had some further designs upon the second. Still he was utterly at a loss to imagine what possible motive the man could have for so criminal an act of malevolence, as there was no plausible reason to be assigned why he should not be as anxious as all the rest to reach the coast of America. The suspicion continued, however, to haunt him, and when he mentioned it to Mrs. Weldon he found that a similar feeling of distrust had agitated her, although she, like himself, was altogether unable to allege a likely motive why the cook should contemplate so strange an act of mischief. It was determined that a strict surveillance should be kept upon all the fellow's movements.

Negoro, however, manifested no inclination to disobey the captain's peremptory order; he kept strictly to his own part of the ship; but as Dingo was now regularly quartered in the stern, there was a tolerably sure guarantee that the cook would not be found wandering much in that direction.

A week passed, and still the tempest showed no signs of abating; the barometer continued to fall, and not once did a period of calmer weather afford an opportunity of carrying sail. The "Pilgrim" still made her way north-east. Her speed could not be less than two hundred miles in twenty-four hours. But no land appeared. Vast as was the range of the American continent, extending for 120 degrees between the Atlantic and the Pacific, it was nowhere to be discerned. Was he dreaming? was he mad? Dick would perpetually ask himself: had he been sailing in a wrong direction? had he failed to steer aright?

But no: he was convinced there was no error in his steering. Although he could not actually see it for the mist, he knew that day after day the sun rose before him, and that it set behind him. Yet he was constrained in bewilderment to ask, what had become of those shores of America upon which, when they came in sight, there was only too great a fear the ship should be dashed? what had become of them? where were they? whither had this incessant hurricane driven them? why did not the expected coast appear?

To all these bewildering inquiries Dick could find no answer except to imagine that his compass had misled him. Yet he was powerless to put his own misgivings to the test; he deplored more than ever the destruction of the duplicate instrument which would have checked his registers. He studied his chart; but all in vain; the position in which he found himself as the result of Negoro's treachery, seemed to baffle him the more, the more he tried to solve the mystery.

The days were passing on in this chronic state of anxiety, when one morning about eight o'clock, Hercules, who was on watch at the bows, suddenly shouted,—

"Land!"

Dick Sands had little reliance upon the negro's inexperienced eye, but hurried forward to the bow.

"Where's the land?" he cried; his voice being scarcely audible above the howling of the tempest.

"There! look there!" said Hercules, nodding his head and pointing over the port bow, to the north-east.

Dick could see nothing.

Mrs. Weldon had heard the shout. Unable to restrain her interest, she had left her cabin and was at Dick's side. He uttered an expression of surprise at seeing her, but could not hear anything she said, as her voice was unable to rise above the roaring of the elements; she stood, her whole being as it were concentrated in the power of vision, and scanned the horizon in the direction indicated by Hercules. But all to no purpose.

Suddenly, however, after a while, Dick raised his hand.

"Yes!" he said; "yes; sure enough, yonder is land."

He clung with excitement to the rigging; and Mrs. Weldon, supported by Hercules, strained her eyes yet more vehemently to get a glimpse of a shore which she had begun to despair of ever reaching.

Beyond a doubt an elevated peak was there. It must be about ten miles to leeward. A break in the clouds soon left it more distinct. Some promontory it must be upon the American coast. Without sails, of course, the " Pilgrim " had no chance of bearing down direct upon it ; but at least there was every reason to believe that she would soon reach some other portion of the shore ; perhaps before noon, certainly in a few hours, they must be close to land.

The pitching of the ship made it impossible for Mrs. Weldon to keep safe footing on the deck ; accordingly, at a sign from Dick, Hercules led her back again to her cabin.

Dick did not remain long at the bow, but went thoughtfully back to the wheel.

He had, indeed, a tremendous responsibility before him. Here was the land, the land for which they had longed so eagerly ; and now that their anticipations were on the point of being realized, what was there, with a hurricane driving them on towards it, to prevent that land being their destruction ? What measures could he take to prevent the schooner being dashed to pieces against it ?

At the very moment when the promontory was just abreast of them, Negoro appeared on deck ; he nodded to the peak familiarly, as he might have saluted a familiar friend, and retired as stealthily as he had come.

Two hours later, and the promontory lay abaft the port quarter. Dick Sands had never relaxed his watchfulness, but he had failed to discover any further indications of a coast-line. His perplexity could only increase ; the horizon was clear ; the Andes ought to be distinct ; they would be conspicuous twenty miles or more away. Dick took up his telescope again and again ; he scrutinized the eastern horizon with minutest care ; but there was nothing to be seen ; and as the afternoon waned away the last glimpse had been taken of the promontory that had awakened their expectation ; it had vanished utterly from their gaze ; no indication of shore could be seen from the " Pilgrim's " deck.

Dick Sands uttered a sigh of mingled amazement and relief. He went into Mrs. Weldon's cabin, where she was standing with her party.

" It was only an island ! " he said ; " only an island ! "

" How ? why ? what island ? what do you mean ? " cried Mrs. Weldon incredulously ; " what island can it be ? "

" The chart perhaps will tell us," replied Dick ; and hurrying off to his own cabin, he immediately returned with the chart in his hands.

After studying it attentively for a few minutes, he said,—

" There, Mrs. Weldon ; the land we have just passed, I should suppose must be that little speck in the midst of the Pacific. It must be Easter Island. At least, there seems to be no other land which possibly it could be."

" And do you say," inquired Mrs. Weldon, " that we have left it quite behind us ? "

" Yes, entirely ; almost to windward."

Mrs. Weldon commenced a searching scrutiny of the map that was outspread before her.

" How far is this," she said, after bending a considerable time over the chart ; " how far is this from the coast of America ? "

" Thirty-five degrees," answered Dick ; " somewhere about 2500 miles."

" Whatever do you mean ? " rejoined the lady, astonished ; " if the ' Pilgrim ' is still 2500 miles from shore, she has positively made no progress at all. Impossible ! "

In thoughtful perplexity, Dick passed his hand across his brow. He did not know what to say. After an interval of silence, he said,—

" I have no account to give for the strange delay. It is

inexplicable to myself, except upon that one hypothesis, which I cannot resist, that the readings of the compass somehow or other, have been wrong."

He relapsed into silence. Then, brightening up, he added,—

" But, thank God ! at least we have now the satisfaction of knowing where we really are ; we are no longer lost upon the wide Pacific ; if only this hurricane will cease, long as the distance seems, we are on our proper course to the shores of America."

The tone of confidence with which the youthful captain spoke had the effect of inspiring new hope into all who heard him ; their spirits rose, and to their sanguine mood it seemed as if they were approaching to the end of all their troubles, and had hardly more to do than to await the turning of a tide to bring them into a glad proximity to port.

Easter Island, of which the true name is Vai-Hoo, was discovered by David in 1686, and visited by Cook and Lapérouse. It lies in lat. 27° S., and long. 112 E. ; consequently, it was evident that during the raging of the hurricane the schooner had been driven northwards no less than fifteen degrees. Far away, however, as she was from shore, the wind could hardly fail within ten days to carry her within sight of land ; and then, if the storm had worn itself out, (as probably it would,) the " Pilgrim " would again set sail, and make her way into some port with safety. Anyhow, the discovery of his true position restored a spirit of confidence to Dick Sands, and he anticipated the time when he should no longer be drifting helplessly before the storm.

To say the truth, the " Pilgrim " had suffered very little from the prolonged fury of the weather. The damage she had sustained was limited to the loss of the topsail and the small jib, which could be easily replaced. The caulking of the seams remained thoroughly sound, and no drop of water had found its way into the hold. The pumps, too, were perfectly free. Dick Sands did not fear for the stability of his ship; his only anxiety was lest the weather should not moderate in time. Only let the wind subside, and the schooner once more would be under his control; but he never forgot that the ordering of the winds and waves was in the hands of the Great Disposer of all.

CHAPTER XIII.

LAND AT LAST.

IT was not long before Dick's sanguine expectations were partially realized, for on the very next day, which was the 27th, the barometer began to rise, not rapidly, but steadily, indicating that its elevation would probably continue. The sea remained exceedingly rough, but the violence of the wind, which had veered slightly towards the west, had perceptibly diminished. The tempest had passed its greatest fury, and was beginning to wear itself out.

Not a sail, however, could yet be hoisted; the smallest show of canvas would have been carried away in an instant; nevertheless Dick hoped that before another twenty-four hours were over, the "Pilgrim" might be able to carry a storm-jib.

In the course of the night the wind moderated still more, and the pitching of the ship had so far diminished that the passengers began to reappear on deck. Mrs. Weldon was the first to leave her enforced imprisonment. She was anxious to speak to Dick, whom she might have expected to find looking pale and wan after his almost superhuman exertions and loss of sleep. But she was mistaken; however much the lad might suffer from the strain in after-years, at present he exhibited no symptoms of failing energy.

"Well, Captain Dick, how are you?" she said, as she advanced towards him, holding out her hand.

Dick smiled.

"You call me captain, Mrs. Weldon," he answered, "but you do not seem disposed to submit implicitly to captain's orders. Did I not direct you to keep to your cabin?"

"You did," replied the lady; "but observing how much the storm had abated, I could not resist the temptation to disobey you."

"Yes, madam, the weather is far more promising; the barometer has not fallen since yesterday morning, and I really trust the worst is over now."

"Thank Heaven!" she replied, and after a few moments' silence, she added, "But now, Dick, you must really take some rest; you may perhaps not know how much you require it; but it is absolutely necessary."

"Rest!" the boy repeated; "rest! I want no rest. I have only done my duty, and it will be time enough for me to concern myself about my own rest, when I have seen my passengers in a place of safety."

"You have acquitted yourself like a man," said Mrs. Weldon; "and you may be assured that my husband, like myself, will never forget the services you have rendered me. I shall urge upon him the request which I am sure he will not refuse, that you shall have your studies completed, so that you may be made a captain for the firm."

Tears of gratitude rose to Dick's eyes. He deprecated the praise that was lavished upon him, but rejoiced in the prospect that seemed opening upon his future. Mrs. Weldon assured him that he was dear as a son to her, and pressed a gentle kiss upon his forehead. The lad felt that he was animated, if need be, to yet greater hardships in behalf of his benefactors, and resolved to prove himself even more worthy of their confidence.

By the 29th, the wind had so far moderated that Dick thought he might increase the "Pilgrim's" speed by hoisting the foresail and fore-topsail.

"Now, my men, I have some work for you to-day," he said to the negroes when he came on deck at daybreak.

"All right, captain," answered Hercules, "we are growing rusty for want of something to do."

"Why didn't you blow with your big mouth?" said little Jack; "you could have beaten the wind all to nothing."

Dick laughed, and said, "Not a bad idea, Jack; if ever we get becalmed, we must get Hercules to blow into the sails."

"I shall be most happy," retorted the giant, and he inflated his huge cheeks till he was the very impersonation of Boreas himself.

"But now to work!" cried Dick; "we have lost our topsail, and we must contrive to hoist another. Not an easy matter, I can tell you."

"I dare say we shall manage it," replied Actæon.

"We must do our best," said Tom.

"Can't I help?" inquired Jack.

"Of course you can," answered Dick; "run along to the wheel, and assist Bat."

Jack strutted off, proud enough of his commission.

Under Dick's directions, the negroes commenced their somewhat difficult task. The new topsail, rolled up, had first of all to be hoisted, and then to be made fast to the yard; but so adroitly did the crew carry out their orders, that in less than an hour the sail was properly set with a couple of reefs in it. The fore-staysail and second jib, which had been taken down before the tempest, were hoisted again, and before ten o'clock the "Pilgrim" was running along under the three sails which Dick considered were as much as it was prudent to carry. Even at her present speed, the schooner, he reckoned, would be within sight of the American shore in about ten days. It was an immense relief to him to find that she was no longer at the mercy of the waves, and when he saw the sails properly set he returned in good spirits to his post at the helm, not forgetting to thank the temporary helmsman for his services, nor omitting his acknowledgment to Master Jack, who received the compliment with becoming gravity.

Although the clouds continued to travel all the next day with great rapidity they were very much broken, and alternately the "Pilgrim" was bathed in sunlight and enveloped in vapours, which rolled on towards the east. As the weather cleared, the hatchways were opened in order to ventilate the ship, and the outer air was allowed again to penetrate not only the hold, but the cabin and crew's quarters. The wet sails were hung out to dry, the deck was washed down, for Dick Sands was anxious not to bring his ship into port without having "finished her toilet," and he found that his crew could very well spare a few hours daily to get her into proper trim.

Notwithstanding the loss of the log, Dick had sufficient experience to be able to make an approximate estimate of the schooner's progress, and after having pointed out to Mrs. Weldon what he imagined was the " Pilgrim's " true position, he told her that it was his firm impression that land would be sighted in little more than a week.

"And upon what part of South America do you reckon we are likely to find ourselves ?" she asked.

"That is more than I dare venture to promise," replied Dick ; "but I should think somewhere hereabouts."

He was pointing on the chart to the long shore-line of Chili and Peru. They both examined the outspread chart with still closer attention.

" Here, you see," resumed Dick, " here is the island we have just left ; we left it in the west ; the wind has not shifted ; we must expect to come in sight of land, pretty nearly due east of it. The coast has plenty of harbours. From any one of them you will be able easily to get to San Francisco. You know, I dare say, that the Pacific Navigation Company's steamers touch at all the principal ports. From any of them you will be sure to get a direct passage to California."

"But do you mean," asked Mrs. Weldon, "that you are not going yourself to take the schooner to San Francisco?"

"Not direct," replied the young captain; "I want to see you safe on shore and satisfactorily on your homeward way. When that is done, I shall hope to get competent officers to take the ship to Valparaiso, where she will discharge her cargo, as Captain Hull intended; and afterwards I shall work our way back to San Francisco."

"Ah, well; we will see all about that in due time," Mrs. Weldon said, smiling; and, after a short pause, added, "At one time, Dick, you seemed to have rather a dread of the shore."

"Quite true," answered Dick; "but now I am in hopes we may fall in with some passing vessel; we want to have a confirmation as to our true position. I cannot tell you how surprised I am that we have not come across a single vessel. But when we near the land we shall be able to get a pilot."

"But what will happen if we fail to get a pilot?" was Mrs. Weldon's inquiry. She was anxious to learn how far the lad was prepared to meet any emergency.

With unhesitating promptness Dick replied,—

"Why, then, unless the weather takes the control of the ship out of my hands, I must patiently follow the coast until I come to a harbour of refuge. But if the wind should freshen, I should have to adopt other measures."

"What then, Dick, what then?" persisted Mrs. Weldon.

The boy's brow knitted itself together in resolution, and he said deliberately,—

"I should run the ship aground."

Mrs. Weldon started..

"However," Dick continued, "there is no reason to apprehend this. The weather has mended and is likely to mend. And why should we fear about finding a pilot? Let us hope all will be well."

Mrs. Weldon at least had satisfied herself on one point.

She had ascertained that although Dick did not anticipate disaster, yet he was prepared in the case of emergency to resort to measures from which any but the most experienced seaman would shrink.

But although Dick's equanimity had been successful in allaying any misgivings on Mrs. Weldon's part, it must be owned that the condition of the atmosphere caused him very serious uneasiness.

The wind remained uncomfortably high, and the barometer gave very ominous indications that it would ere long freshen still more. Dick dreaded that the time was about to return in which once again he must reduce his vessel to a state of bare poles ; but so intense was his aversion to having his ship so wrested as it were from his own management, that he determined to carry the topsail till it was all but carried away by the force of the blast. Concerned, moreover, for the safety of his masts, the loss of which he acknowledged must be fatal, he had the standing rigging thoroughly set up.

More than once another contingency occurred to his mind, and gave him some anxiety. He could not overlook the possibility of the wind changing all round. What should he do in such a case ? He would of course endeavour by all means to get the schooner on by incessant tacking ; but was there not the certainty of a most hazardous delay ? and worse than this, was there not a likelihood of the " Pilgrim " being once again driven far out to sea ?

Happily these forebodings were not realized. The wind, after chopping about for several days, at one time blowing from the north, and at another from the south, finally settled down into a stiffish gale from the west, which did nothing worse than severely strain the masts.

In this weary but hopeful endurance time passed on. The 5th of April had arrived. It was more than two months since the " Pilgrim " had quitted New Zealand ; it was true that during the first three weeks of her voyage she had been impeded by protracted calms and contrary winds; but since that time her speed had been rapid, the very tempests had driven her forwards with unwonted velocity; she had never failed to have her bow towards the land, and yet land seemed as remote as ever; the coast-line was retreating as they approached it. What could be the solution of the mystery?

From the cross-trees one or other of the negroes was kept incessantly on the watch. Dick Sands himself, telescope in hand, would repeatedly ascend in the hope of beholding some lofty peak of the Andes emerging from the mists that hung over the horizon. But all in vain.

False alarms were given more than once. Sometimes Tom, sometimes Hercules, or one of the others would be sure that a distant speck they had descried was assuredly a mountain ridge; but the vapours were continually gathering in such fantastic forms that their unexperienced eyes were soon deceived, and they seldom had to wait long before their fond delusion was all dispelled.

At last, the expected longing was fulfilled. At eight o'clock one morning the mists seemed broken up with unusual rapidity, and the horizon was singularly clear. Dick had hardly gone aloft when his voice rung out,—

"Land! Land ahead!"

As if summoned by a spell, every one was on deck in an instant: Mrs. Weldon, sanguine of a speedy end to the general anxiety; little Jack, gratified at a new object of curiosity; Cousin Benedict, already scenting a new field for entomological investigation; old Nan; and the negroes, eager to set foot upon American soil; all, with the exception of Negoro, all were on deck; but the cook did not stir from his solitude, or betray any sympathy with the general excitement.

Whatever hesitation there might be at first soon passed away; one after another soon distinguished the shore they were approaching, and in half an hour there was no room for the most sceptical to doubt that Dick was right. There was land not far ahead.

A few miles to the east there was a long low-lying coast ; the chain of the Andes ought to be visible ; but it was obscured, of course, by the intervening clouds.

The " Pilgrim " bore down rapidly towards the land, and in a short time its configuration could be plainly made out. Towards the north-east the coast terminated in a headland of moderate height sheltering a kind of roadstead ; on the south-east it stretched out in a long and narrow tongue. The Andes were still wanting to the scene ; they must be somewhere in the background ; but at present, strange to say, there was only a succession of low cliffs with some trees standing out against the sky. No human habitation, no harbour, not even an indication of a river-mouth, could anywhere be seen.

The wind remained brisk, and the schooner was driving directly towards the land, with shortened sail as seemed desirable ; but Dick realized to himself the fact that he was utterly incapable of altering her course. With eager eyes he scrutinized his situation. Straight ahead was a reef over which the waves were curling, and around which the surf must be tremendous. It could hardly be more than a mile away. The wind seemed brisker than before.

After gazing awhile, Dick seemed to have come to a sudden resolution. He went quickly aft and took the helm. He had seen a little cove, and had made up his mind that he would try and make his way into it. He did not speak a word ; he knew the difficulty of the task he had undertaken ; he was aware from the white foam, that there was shallow water on either hand ; but he kept the secret of the peril to himself, and sought no counsel in coming to his fixed resolve.

Dingo had been trotting up and down the deck. All at once he bounded to the fore, and broke out into a piteous howl. It roused Dick from his anxious cogitations. Was it possible that the animal recognized the coast? It almost seemed as if it brought back some painful associations.

The howling of the dog had manifestly attracted Negoro's attention; the man emerged from his galley, and, regardless of the dog, stood close to the bulwark; but although he gazed at the surf, it did not seem to occasion him any alarm. Mrs. Weldon, who was watching him, fancied she saw a flush rise to his face, which involuntarily suggested the thought to her mind that Negoro had seen the place before.

Either she had no time or no wish to express what had struck her, for she did not mention it to Dick, who, at that moment, left the helm, and came and stood beside her.

Dick looked as if he were taking a lingering farewell of the cove past which they were being carried beyond his power to help.

In a few moments he turned round to Mrs. Weldon, and said quietly,—

"Mrs. Weldon, I am disappointed. I hoped to get the schooner into yonder cove; but there is no chance now; if nothing is done, in half an hour she will be upon that reef. I have but one alternative left. I must run her aground. It will be utter destruction to the ship, but there is no choice. Your safety is the first and paramount consideration."

"Do you mean that there is no other course to be taken, Dick?"

"None whatever," said Dick decidedly.

"It must be as you will," she said.

Forthwith ensued the agitating preparations for stranding. Mrs. Weldon, Jack, Cousin Benedict, and Nan were provided with life-belts, while Dick and the negroes made themselves ready for being dashed into the waves. Every precaution that the emergency admitted was duly taken. Mrs. Weldon was entrusted to the special charge of Hercules;

The sea was furious, and dashed vehemently upon the crags on either hand.

I

Dick made himself responsible for doing all he could for little Jack; Cousin Benedict, who was tolerably calm, was handed over to Bat and Austin; while Actæon promised to look after Nan. Negoro's nonchalance implied that he was quite capable of shifting for himself.

Dick had the forethought also to order about a dozen barrels of their cargo to be carried forward, so that when the "Pilgrim" struck, the oil escaping and floating on the waves would temporarily lull their fury, and make smoother water for the passage of the ship.

After satisfying himself that there was no other measure to be taken to ameliorate the peril, Dick Sands returned to the helm. The schooner was all but upon the reef, and only a few cables' length from the shore; her starboard bow indeed was already bathed in the seething foam, and any instant the keel might be expected to grate upon the under-lying rock. Presently a change of colour in the water was observed; it revealed a passage between the rocks. Dick gave the wheel a turn; he saw the chance of getting aground nearer to the shore than he had dared to hope, and he made the most of it. He steered the schooner right into the narrow channel; the sea was furious, and dashed vehemently upon the crags on either hand.

"Now, my lads!" he cried to his crew, "now's your time; out with your oil! let it run!"

Ready for the order, the negroes poured out the oil, and the raging waters were stilled as if by magic. A few moments more and perchance they would rage more vehemently than ever. But for the instant they were lulled.

The "Pilgrim," meanwhile, had glided onwards, and made dead for the adjacent shore. There was a sudden shock. Caught by an enormous wave the schooner had been hurled aground; her masts had fallen, fortunately without injury to any one on board. But the vessel had parted amidships, and was foundering; the water was rushing irresistibly into the hold.

The shore, however, was not half a cable's length away ; there was a low, dark ridge of rocks that was united to the beach ; it afforded ample means of rescue, and in less than ten minutes the " Pilgrim's " captain, crew, and passengers were all landed safely at the foot of the overhanging cliff.

CHAPTER XIV.

ASHORE.

THUS, after a voyage of seventy-four days, the "Pilgrim" had stranded. Mrs. Weldon and her fellow-voyagers joined in thanksgiving to the kind Providence that had brought them ashore, not upon one of the solitary islands of Polynesia, but upon a solid continent, from almost any part of which there would be no difficulty in getting home.

The ship was totally lost. She was lying in the surf a hopeless wreck, and few must be the hours that would elapse before she would be broken up in scattered fragments; it was impossible to save her. Notwithstanding that Dick Sands bewailed the loss of a valuable ship and her cargo to the owner, he had the satisfaction of knowing that he had been instrumental in saving what was far more precious, the lives of the owner's wife and son.

It was impossible to do more than hazard a conjecture as to the part of the South American coast on which the "Pilgrim" had been cast. Dick imagined that it must be somewhere on the coast of Peru; after sighting Easter Island, he knew that the united action of the equatorial current and the brisk wind must have had the effect of driving the schooner far northward, and he formed his conclusion accordingly. Be the true position, however, what it might, it was all-important that it should be accurately ascertained as soon as possible. If it were really in Peru, he would not be long in finding his way to one of the numerous ports and villages that lie along the coast.

But the shore here was quite a desert. A narrow strip of beach, strewn with boulders, was enclosed by a cliff of no great height, in which, at irregular intervals, deep funnels appeared as chasms in the rock. Here and there a gentle slope led to the top.

About a quarter of a mile to the north was the mouth of a little river which had not been visible from the sea. Its banks were overhung by a number of "rhizophora," a species of mangrove entirely distinct from that indigenous to India. It was soon ascertained that the summit of the cliff was clothed by a dense forest, extending far away in undulations of verdure to the mountains in the background. Had Cousin Benedict been a botanist, he could not have failed to find a new and interesting field for his researches; there were lofty baobabs (to which an extraordinary lon-gevity has often been erroneously ascribed), with bark resembling Egyptian syenite; there were white pines, tamarinds, pepper-plants of peculiar species, and numerous other plants unfamiliar to the eye of a native of the North; but, strange to say, there was not a single specimen of the extensive family of palms, of which more than a thousand varieties are scattered in profusion in so many quarters of the globe.

Above the shore hovered a large number of screeching birds, mostly of the swallow tribe, their black plumage shot with steelly blue, and shading off to a light brown at the top of the head. Now and then a few partridges of a greyish colour rose on wing, their necks entirely bare of feathers: the fearless manner in which the various birds all allowed themselves to be approached made Mrs. Weldon and Dick both wonder if the shores upon which they had been thrown were not so deserted that the sound of fire-arms was not known.

On the edge of the reefs some pelicans (of the species known as *pelicanus minor*) were busily filling their pouches with tiny fish, and some gulls coming in from the open sea

Surveying the shore with the air of a man who was trying to recall some past experience.

began to circle round the wreck : with these exceptions
not a living creature appeared in sight. Benedict, no doubt,
could have discovered many entomological novelties amongst
the foliage, but these could give no more information than
the birds as to the name of their habitat. Neither north,
nor south, nor towards the forest, was there trace of rising
smoke, or any footprint or other sign to indicate the presence
of a human being.

Dick's surprise was very great. He knew that the
proximity of a native would have made Dingo bark aloud ;
but the dog gave no warning ; he was running backwards
and forwards, his tail lowered and his nose close to the
ground ; now and again he uttered a deep growl.

"Look at Dingo!" said Mrs. Weldon ; "how strange he
is ! he seems to be trying to discover a lost scent."

After watching the dog for a time, she spoke again :—

"Look, too, at Negoro ! he and the dog seem to be on the
same purpose ! "

"As to Negoro," said Dick, "I cannot concern myself
with him now ; he must do as he pleases ; I have no further
control over him ; his service expires with the loss of the
ship."

Negoro was in fact walking to and fro, surveying the shore
with the air of a man who was trying to recall some past
experience to his recollection. His dogged taciturnity was
too well known for any one to think of questioning him ;
every.one was accustomed to let him go his own way, and
when Dick noticed that he had gone towards the little river,
and had disappeared behind the cliff, he thought no more
about him. Dingo likewise had quite forgotten his enemy,
and desisted from his growling.

The first necessity for the shipwrecked party was to find
a temporary shelter where they might take some refreshment. There was no lack of provisions ; independently of
the resources of the land, the ebbing tide had left upon the
rocks the great bulk of the "Pilgrim's" stores, and the

negroes had already collected several kegs of biscuit, and a number of cases of preserved meat, besides a variety of other supplies. All that they rescued they carefully piled up above high-water mark. As nothing appeared to be injured by the sea-water, the victualling of the party all seemed to be satisfactorily secure for the interval which must elapse (and they all believed it would not be long) before they reached one of the villages which they presumed were close at hand. Dick, moreover, took the precaution of sending Hercules to get a small supply of fresh water from the river hard by, and the good-natured fellow returned carrying a whole barrel-full on his shoulder.

Plenty of fuel was lying about, and whenever they wanted to light a fire they were sure of having an abundance of dead wood and the roots of the old mangroves. Old Tom, an inveterate smoker, always carried a tinder-box in his pocket; this had been too tightly fastened to be affected by the moisture, and could always produce a spark upon occasion.

Still they must have a shelter. Without some rest it was impossible to start upon a tour of exploration ; accordingly, all interests were directed towards ascertaining where the necessary repose could be obtained.

The honour of discovering where the desired retreat could be found fell to the lot of little Jack. Trotting about at the foot of the cliff, he came upon one of those grottoes which are constantly being found hollowed out in the rock by the vehement action of the waves in times of tempest.

" Here, look here ! " cried the child ; " here's a place ! "

" Well done, Jack ! " answered his mother ; " your lucky discovery is just what we wanted. If we were going to stay here any time we should have to do the same as the Swiss Family Robinson, and name the spot after you ! "

It was hardly more than twelve or fourteen feet square, and yet the grotto seemed to Jack to be a gigantic cavern. But narrow as its limits were, it was capacious enough to receive the entire party. It was a great satisfaction to Mrs. Weldon to observe that it was perfectly dry, and as the moon was just about her first quarter there was no likelihood of a tide rising to the foot of the cliff. At any rate, it was resolved that they might take up their quarters there for a few hours.

Shortly after one o'clock the whole party were seated upon a carpet of seaweed round a repast consisting of preserved meat, biscuit, and water flavoured with a few drops of rum, of which Bat had saved a quart bottle from the wreck. Even Negoro had returned and joined the group ; probably he had not cared to venture alone along the bank of the stream into the forest. He sat listening, as it seemed indifferently, to the various plans for the future that were being discussed, and did not open his mouth either by way of remonstrance or suggestion.

Dingo was not forgotten, and had his share of food duly given him outside the grotto, where he was keeping guard.

When the meal was ended, Mrs. Weldon, passing her arms round Jack, who was lounging half asleep with excitement and fatigue at her side, was the first to speak.

"My dear Dick," she said, "in the name of us all, let me thank you for the services you have rendered us in our tedious time of difficulty. As you have been our captain at sea, let me beg you to be our guide upon land. We shall have perfect confidence in your judgment, and await your instructions as to what our next proceedings shall be."

All eyes were turned upon Dick. Even Negoro appeared to be roused to curiosity, as if eager to know what he had to say.

Dick did not speak for some moments. He was manifestly pondering what step he should advise. After a while he said,—

"My own impression, Mrs. Weldon, is that we have been

cast ashore upon one of the least-frequented parts of the coast of Peru, and that we are near the borders of the Pampas. In that case I should conclude that we are at a considerable distance from any village. Now, I should recommend that we stay here all together for the coming night. To-morrow morning, two of us can start off on an exploring expedition. I entertain but little doubt that natives will be met with within ten or a dozen miles."

Mrs. Weldon looked doubtful. Plainly she thought unfavourably of the project of separating the party. She reflected for a considerable time, and then asked,—

"And who is to undertake the task of exploring?"

Prompt was Dick's answer :—

"Tom and I."

"And leave us here?" suggested the lady.

"Yes; to take care of you, there will be Hercules, Bat, Actæon, and Austin. Negoro, too, I presume, means to remain here," said Dick, glancing towards the cook.

"Perhaps," replied Negoro, sparing as ever of his words.

"We shall take Dingo," added Dick; "likely enough he may be useful."

At the sound of his name the dog had entered the grotto. A short bark seemed to testify his approval of Dick's proposal.

Mrs. Weldon was silent. She looked sad and thoughtful. It was hard to reconcile herself to the division of the party. She was aware that the separation would not be for long, but she could not suppress a certain feeling of nervousness. Was it not possible that some natives, attracted by the wreck, would assault them in hopes of plunder?

Every argument he could think of, Dick brought forward to reassure the lady. He told her that the Indians were perfectly harmless, and entirely different to the savage tribes of Africa and Polynesia; there was no reason to apprehend any mischief, even if they should chance to encounter them, which was itself extremely unlikely. No doubt the separation would have its inconveniences, but they would be insignificant compared with the difficulty of traversing the country *en masse*. Tom and he would have far greater freedom if they went alone, and could make their investigations much more thoroughly. Finally he promised that if within two days they failed to discover human habitation, they would return to the grotto forth-with.

"I confess, however," he added, "that I have little expectation of being able to ascertain our true position, until I have penetrated some distance into the country."

There was nothing in Dick's representations but what commanded Mrs. Weldon's assent as reasonable. It was simply her own nervousness, she acknowledged, that made her hesitate ; but it was only with extreme reluctance that she finally yielded to the proposition.

"And what, Mr. Benedict, is your opinion of my pro-posal?" said Dick, turning to the entomologist.

"I?" answered Cousin Benedict, looking somewhat bewil-dered, "Oh, I am agreeable to anything. I dare say I shall find some specimens. I think I will go and look at once."

"Take my advice, and don't go far away," replied Dick.

"All right; I shall take care of myself."

"And don't be bringing back a lot of mosquitoes," said old Tom mischievously.

With his box under his arm, the naturalist left the grotto.

Negoro followed almost immediately. He did not take the same direction as Benedict up the cliff, but for the second time bent his steps towards the river, and proceeded along its bank till he was out of sight.

It was not long before Jack's exertions told upon him, and he fell into a sound sleep. Mrs. Weldon having gently laid him on Nan's lap, wandered out and made her way to the water's edge. She was soon joined by Dick and the negroes, who wanted to see whether it was possible to get to the "Pilgrim," and secure any articles that might be serviceable for future use. The reef on which the schooner had stranded was now quite dry, and the carcase of the vessel which had been partially covered at high water was lying in the midst of *débris* of the most promiscuous character. The wide difference between high and low-water mark caused Dick Sands no little surprise. He knew that the tides on the shores of the Pacific were very inconsiderable; in his own mind, however, he came to the conclusion that the phenomenon was to be explained by the unusually high wind that had been blowing on the coast.

Not without emotion could Mrs. Weldon, or indeed any of them, behold the unfortunate ship upon which they had spent so many eventful days, lying dismasted on her side. But there was little time for sentiment. If they wished to visit the hull before it finally went to pieces, there must be no delay.

Hoisting themselves by some loose rigging that was hanging from the deck, Dick and several of the negroes contrived to make their way into the interior of the hull. Dick left his men to gather together all they could in the way of food and drink from the store-room, and himself went straight to the stern cabin, into which the water had not penetrated. Here he found four excellent Purday's Remington rifles and a hundred cartridges; with these he determined to arm his party, in case they should be attacked by Indians. He also chose six of the strongest of the cutlasses that are used for slicing up dead whales; and did not forget the little toy gun which was Jack's special property. Unexpectedly he found a pocket-compass, which he was only too glad to appropriate. What a boon it would have been had he discovered it earlier! The ship's charts in the fore-cabin were too much injured by water to be of any further service. Nearly everything was either lost or spoiled, but the misfortune was not felt very acutely because there was ample provision for a few days, and it seemed useless to burden themselves with more than was necessary. Dick hardly needed Mrs. Weldon's advice to secure all the money that might be on board, but after the most diligent search he failed to discover more than five hundred dollars. This was a subject of perplexity. Mrs. Weldon herself had had a considerably larger sum than this, and Captain Hull was known always to keep a good reserve in hand. There was but one way to solve the mystery. Some one had been beforehand to the wreck. It could not be any of the negroes, as not one of them had for a moment left the grotto. Suspicion naturally fell upon Negoro, who had been out alone upon the shore. Morose and cold-blooded as the man was, Dick hardly knew why he should suspect him of the crime of theft; nevertheless, he determined to cross-examine him, and, if need be, to have him searched, as soon as he came back.

The day wore onwards to its close. The sun was approaching the vernal equinox, and sank almost perpendicularly on to the horizon. Twilight was very short, and the rapidity with which darkness came on confirmed Dick in his belief that they had got ashore at some spot lying between the tropic of Capricorn and the equator.

They all assembled in the grotto again for the purpose of getting some sleep.

"Another rough night coming on!" said Tom, pointing to the heavy clouds that hung over the horizon.

"No doubt, Tom!" answered Dick; "and I think we may congratulate ourselves on being safe out of our poor ship."

As the night could not be otherwise than very dark, it was arranged that the negroes should take their turns in keeping guard at the entrance of the grotto. Dingo also would be upon the alert.

Benedict had not yet returned. Hercules shouted his name with the full strength of his capacious lungs, and shortly afterwards the entomologist was seen making his way down the face of the cliff at the imminent risk of breaking his neck. He was in a great rage. He had not found a single insect worth having ; scorpions, scolopendra, and other myriapoda were in the forest in abundance ; but not one of these of course could be allowed a place in his collection.

"Have I come six thousand miles for this?" he cried : "have I endured storm and shipwreck only to be cast where not a hexapod is to be seen? The country is detestable! I shall not stay in it another hour!"

Ever gentle to his eccentricities, Mrs. Weldon soothed him as she would a child ; she told him that he had better take some rest now, and most likely he would have better luck to-morrow.

Cousin Benedict had hardly been pacified when Tom remarked that Negoro too had not returned.

"Never mind!" said Bat; "his room is as good as his company."

"I cannot say that I altogether think so. The man is no favourite of mine, but I like him better under my own eye," said Mrs. Weldon.

"Perhaps he has his own reasons for keeping away," said Dick ; and taking Mrs. Weldon aside, he communicated to her his suspicions of the fellow's dishonesty.

He found that she coincided with him in her view of Negoro's conduct ; but she did not agree with him in his proposal to have him searched at once. If he returned, she should be convinced that he had deposited the money in some secret spot ; and as there would be no proof of his guilt, it would be better to leave him, at least for a time, uninterrogated.

Dick was convinced by her representations, and promised to act upon her advice.

Before they resigned themselves to sleep, they had repeatedly summoned Negoro back, but he either could not or would not hear. Mrs. Weldon and Dick scarcely knew

The entomologist was seen making his way down the face of the cliff at the imminent risk of breaking his neck.

what to think ; unless he had lost his way ; it was unaccountable why he should be wandering about alone on a dark night in a strange country.

Presently Dingo was heard barking furiously. He had left the opening of the grotto, and was evidently down at the water's edge. Imagining that Negoro must be coming, Dick sent three of the negroes in the direction of the river to meet him ; but when they reached the bank not a soul could be seen, and as Dingo was quiet again, they made their way back to the grotto.

Excepting the man left on watch, they now all lay down, hoping to get some repose. Mrs. Weldon, however, could not sleep. The land for which she had sighed so ardently had been reached, but it had failed to give either the security or the comfort which she had anticipated.

CHAPTER XV.

A STRANGER.

AT daybreak, next morning, Austin, who happened to be on guard, heard Dingo bark, and noticed that he started up and ran towards the river. Arousing the inmates of the grotto, he announced to them that some one was coming.

"It isn't Negoro," said Tom; "Dingo would bark louder than that if Negoro were to be seen."

"Who, then, can it be?" asked Mrs. Weldon, with an inquiring glance towards Dick.

"We must wait and see, madam," replied Dick quietly.

Bidding Bat, Austin, and Hercules follow his example, Dick Sands took up a cutlass and a rifle, into the breech of which he slipped a cartridge. Thus armed, the four young men made their way towards the river bank. Tom and Actæon were left with Mrs. Weldon at the entrance of the grotto.

The sun was just rising. Its rays, intercepted by the lofty range of mountains in the east, did not fall directly on the cliff; but the sea to its western horizon was sparkling in the sunbeams as the party marched along the shore. Dingo was motionless as a setter, but did not cease barking. It soon proved not to be his old enemy who was disturbing him. A man, who was not Negoro, appeared round the angle of the cliff, and advancing cautiously along the bank of the stream, seemed by his gestures to be endeavouring to pacify the dog, with which an encounter would certainly have been by no means desirable.

"That's not Negoro !" said Hercules.

"No loss for any of us," muttered Bat.

"You are right," replied Dick ; "perhaps he is a native ; let us hope he may be able to tell us our whereabouts, and save us the trouble of exploring."

With their rifles on their shoulders, they advanced steadily towards the new arrival. The stranger, on becoming aware of their approach, manifested great surprise ; he was apparently puzzled as to how they had reached the shore, for the "Pilgrim" had been entirely broken up during the night, and the spars that were floating about had probably been too few and too scattered to attract his attention. His first attitude seemed to betray something of fear ; and raising to his shoulder a gun that had been slung to his belt, he began to retrace his steps ; but conciliatory gestures on the part of Dick quickly reassured him, and after a moment's hesitation, he continued to advance.

He was a man of about forty years of age, strongly built, with a keen, bright eye, grizzly hair and beard, and a complexion tanned as with constant exposure to the forest air. He wore a broad-brimmed hat, a kind of leather jerkin, or tunic, and long boots reaching nearly to his knees. To his high heels was fastened a pair of wide-rowelled spurs, which clanked as he moved.

Dick Sands in an instant saw that he was not looking upon one of the roving Indians of the pampas, but upon one of those adventurers, often of very doubtful character, who are not unfrequently to be met with in the remotest quarters of the earth. Clearly this was neither an Indian nor a Spaniard. His erect, not to say rigid deportment, and the reddish hue with which his hair and beard were streaked, betokened him to be of Anglo-Saxon origin, a conjecture which was at once confirmed when upon Dick's wishing him "good morning," he replied in unmistakable English, with hardly a trace of foreign accent,—

"Good morning, my young friend."

He stepped forward, and having shaken hands with Dick, nodded to all his companions.

"Are you English?" he asked.

"No; we are Americans," replied Dick.

"North or South?" inquired the man.

"North," Dick answered.

The information seemed to afford the stranger no little satisfaction, and he again wrung Dick's hand with all the enthusiasm of a fellow-countryman.

"And may I ask what brings you here?" he continued.

Before, however, Dick had time to reply, the stranger had courteously raised his hat, and, looking round, Dick saw that his bow was intended for Mrs. Weldon, who had just reached the river-bank. She proceeded to tell him the particulars of how they had been shipwrecked, and how the vessel had gone to pieces on the reefs.

A look of pity crossed the man's face as he listened, and he cast his eye, as it might be involuntarily, upon the sea, in order to discern some vestige of the stranded ship.

"Ah! there is nothing to be seen of our poor schooner!" said Dick mournfully; "the last of her was broken up in the storm last night."

"And now," interposed Mrs. Weldon, "can you tell us where we are?"

"Where?" exclaimed the man, with every indication of surprise at her question; "why, on the coast of South America, of course!"

"But on what part? are we near Peru?" Dick inquired eagerly.

"No, my lad, no; you are more to the south; you are on the coast of Bolivia; close to the borders of Chili."

"A good distance, I suppose, from Lima?" asked Dick.

"From Lima? yes, a long way; Lima is far to the north."

"And what is the name of that promontory?" Dick said, pointing to the adjacent headland.

"That, I confess, is more than I am able to tell you," replied the stranger; "for although I have travelled a great deal in the interior of the country, I have never before visited this part of the coast."

Dick pondered in thoughtful silence over the information he had thus received. He had no reason to doubt its accuracy; according to his own reckoning he would have expected to come ashore somewhere between the latitudes of 27° and 30°; and by this stranger's showing he had made the latitude 25°; the discrepancy was not very great; it was not more than might be accounted for by the action of the currents, which he knew he had been unable to estimate; moreover, the deserted character of the whole shore inclined him to believe more easily that he was in Lower Bolivia.

Whilst this conversation was going on, Mrs. Weldon, whose suspicions had been excited by Negoro's disappearance, had been scrutinizing the stranger with the utmost attention; but she could detect nothing either in his manner or in his words to give her any cause to doubt his good faith.

"Pardon me," she said presently; "but you do not seem to me to be a native of Peru?"

"No; like yourself, I am an American, Mrs. ——;" he paused, as if waiting to be told her name.

The lady smiled, and gave her name; he thanked her, and continued,—

"My name is Harris. I was born in South Carolina; but it is now twenty years since I left my home for the pampas of Bolivia; imagine, therefore, how much pleasure it gives me to come across some countrymen of my own."

"Do you live in this part of the province, Mr. Harris?" Mrs. Weldon asked.

"No, indeed; far away; I live down to the south, close to the borders of Chili. At present I am taking a journey north-eastwards to Atacama."

"Atacama!" exclaimed Dick; "are we anywhere near the desert of Atacama?"

"Yes, my young friend," rejoined Harris, "you are just on the edge of it. It extends far beyond those mountains which you see on the horizon, and is one of the most curious and least explored parts of the continent."

"And are you travelling through it alone?" Mrs. Weldon inquired.

"Yes, quite alone; and it is not the first time I have performed the journey. One of my brothers owns a large farm, the hacienda of San Felice, about 200 miles from here, and I have occasion now and then to pay him business visits."

After a moment's hesitation, as if he were weighing a sudden thought, he continued,—

"I am on my way there now, and if you will accompany me I can promise you a hearty welcome, and my brother will be most happy to do his best to provide you with means of conveyance to San Francisco."

Mrs. Weldon had hardly begun to express her thanks for the proposal when he said abruptly,—

"Are these negroes your slaves?"

"Slaves! sir," replied Mrs. Weldon, drawing herself up proudly; "we have no slaves in the United States. The south has now long followed the example of the north. Slavery is abolished."

"I beg your pardon, madam. I had forgotten that the war of 1862 had solved that question. But seeing these fellows with you, I thought perhaps they might be in your service," he added, with a slight tone of irony.

"We are very proud to be of any service to Mrs. Weldon," Tom interposed with dignity, "but we are no man's property. It is true I was sold for a slave when I was six years old ; but I have long since had my freedom ; and so has my son. But here, and all his friends, were born of free parents."

"Ah ! well then, I have to congratulate you," replied Harris, in a manner that jarred very sensibly upon Mrs. Weldon's feelings ; but she said nothing.

Harris added,—

" I can assure you that you are as safe here in Bolivia as you would be in New England."

He had not finished speaking, when Jack, followed by Nan, came out of the grotto. The child was rubbing his eyes, having only just awakened from his night's sleep. Catching sight of his mother, he darted towards her.

"What a charming little boy !" exclaimed Harris.

" He is my little son," said Mrs. Weldon, kissing the child by way of morning greeting.

"Ah, madam, I am sure you must have suffered doubly on his account. Will the little man let me kiss him too ?"

But there was something in the stranger's appearance that did not take Jack's fancy, and he shrank back timidly to his mother's side.

"You must excuse him, sir ; he is very shy."

"Never mind," said Harris ; "we shall be better acquainted by-and-by. When we get to my brother's, he shall have a nice little pony to ride."

But not even this tempting offer seemed to have any effect in coaxing Jack into a more genial mood. He kept fast hold of his mother's hand, and she, somewhat vexed at his behaviour, and anxious that no offence should be given to a man who appeared so friendly in his intentions, hastened to turn the conversation to another topic.

Meantime Dick Sands had been considering Harris's proposal. Upon the whole, the plan of making their way to the hacienda of San Felice seemed to commend itself to his judgment; but he could not conceal from himself that a journey of 200 miles across plains and forests, without any means of transport, would be extremely fatiguing. On expressing his doubts on this point, he was met with the reply,—

"Oh, that can be managed well enough, young man; just round the corner of the cliff there I have a horse, which is quite at the disposal of the lady and her son; and by easy stages of ten miles or so a day, it will do the rest of us no harm to travel on foot. Besides," he added, "when I spoke of the journey being 200 miles, I was thinking of following, as I usually do, the course of the river; but by taking a short cut across the forest, we may reduce the distance by nearly eighty miles."

Mrs. Weldon was about to say how grateful she was, but Harris anticipated her.

"Not a word, madam, I beg you. You cannot thank me better than by accepting my offer. I confess I have never crossed this forest, but I am so much accustomed to the pampas that I have little fear of losing my way. The only difficulty is in the matter of provisions, as I have only supplied myself with enough to carry me on to San Felice."

"As to provisions," replied Mrs. Weldon, "we have enough and to spare; and we shall be more than willing to share everything with you."

"That is well," answered Harris; "then there can be no reason why we should not start at once."

He was turning away with the intention of fetching his horse, when Dick Sands detained him. True to his seaman's instincts, the young sailor felt that he should be much more at his ease on the sea-shore than traversing the heart of an unknown forest.

"Pardon me, Mr. Harris," he began, "but instead of taking so long a journey across the desert of Atacama, would it not be far better for us to follow the coast either northwards or southwards, until we reach the nearest sea-port?"

A frown passed over Harris's countenance.

"I know very little about the coast," he answered; "but I know enough to assure you that there is no town to the north within 300 or 400 miles."

"Then why should we not go south?" persisted Dick.

"You would then have to travel to Chili, which is almost as far; and, under your circumstances, I should not advise you to skirt the pampas of the Argentine Republic. For my own part, I could not accompany you."

"But do not the vessels which ply between Chili and Peru come within sight of this coast?" interposed Mrs. Weldon.

"No, madam; they keep out so far to sea that there would not be the faintest chance of your hailing one."

"You seem to have another question to ask Mr. Harris," Mrs. Weldon continued, addressing Dick, who still looked rather doubtful.

Dick replied that he was about to inquire at what port he would be likely to find a ship to convey their party to San Francisco.

"That I really cannot tell you, my young friend," rejoined Harris; "I can only repeat my promise that we will furnish you with the means of conveyance from San Felice to Atacama, where no doubt you will obtain all the information you require."

"I hope you will not think that Dick is insensible to your kindness, Mr. Harris," said Mrs. Weldon, apologetically.

"On the contrary," promptly observed Dick; "I fully appreciate it; I only wish we had been cast ashore upon a spot where we should have had no need to intrude upon his generosity."

"I assure you, madam, it gives me unbounded pleasure to

serve you in any way," said Harris ; "it is, as I have told you, not often that I come in contact with any of my own countrymen."

"Then we accept your offer as frankly as it is made," replied the lady ; adding, "but I cannot consent to deprive you of your horse. I am a very good walker."

"So am I," said Harris, with a bow, "and consequently I intend you and your little son to ride. I am used to long tramps through the pampas. Besides, it is not at all unlikely that we shall come across some of the workpeople belonging to the hacienda ; if so, they will be able to give us a mount."

Convinced that it would only be thwarting Mrs. Weldon's wishes to throw any further impediment in the way, Dick Sands suppressed his desire to raise fresh obstacles, and simply asked how soon they ought to start.

"This very day, at once," said Harris quickly.

"So soon?" asked Dick.

"Yes. The rainy season begins in April, and the sooner we are at San Felice the better. The way through the forest is the safest as well as the shortest, for we shall be less likely to meet any of the nomad Indians, who are notorious robbers."

Without making any direct reply, Dick proceeded to instruct the negroes to choose such of the provisions as were most easy of transport, and to make them up into packages, that every one might carry a due share. Hercules with his usual good-nature professed himself willing to carry the entire load ; a proposal, however, to which Dick would not listen for a moment.

"You are a fine fellow, Hercules," said Harris, scrutinizing the giant with the eye of a connoisseur ; "you would be worth something in the African market."

"Those who want me now must catch me first," retorted Hercules, with a grin.

The services of all hands were enlisted, and in a comparatively short time sufficient food was packed up to supply the party for about ten days' march.

"You must allow us to show you what hospitality is in our power," said Mrs. Weldon, addressing her new acquaintance ; "our breakfast will be ready in a quarter of an hour, and we shall be happy if you will join us."

"It will give me much pleasure," answered Harris, gaily ; "I will employ the interval in fetching my horse, who has breakfasted already."

"I will accompany you," said Dick.

"By all means, my young friend ; come with me, and I will show you the lower part of the river."

While they were gone, Hercules was sent in search of Cousin Benedict, who was wandering on the top of the cliff in quest of some wonderful insect, which, of course, was not to be found. Without asking his permission, Hercules uncere moniously brought him back to Mrs. Weldon, who explained how they were about to start upon a ten days' march into the interior of the country. The entomologist was quite satisfied with the arrangement, and declared himself ready for a march across the entire continent, as long as he was free to be adding to his collection on the way.

Thus assured of her cousin's acquiescence in her plans, Mrs. Weldon proceeded to prepare such a substantial meal as she hoped would invigorate them all for the approaching journey.

Harris and Dick Sands, meantime, had turned the corner of the cliff, and walked about 300 paces along the shore until they came to a tree to which a horse was tethered. The creature neighed as it recognized its master. It was a strong-built animal, of a kind that Dick had not seen before, although its long neck and crupper, short loins, flat shoulders and arched forehead indicated that it was of Arabian breed.

"Plenty of strength here," Harris said, as after unfastening the horse, he took it by the bridle and began to lead it along the shore.

Dick made no reply; he was casting a hasty glance at the forest which enclosed them on either hand; it was an unattractive sight, but he observed nothing to give him any particular ground for uneasiness.

Turning round, he said abruptly,—

"Did you meet a Portuguese last night, named Negoro?"

"Negoro? who is Negoro?" asked Harris, in a tone of surprise.

"He was our ship's cook; but he has disappeared."

"Drowned, probably," said Harris indifferently.

"No, he was not drowned; he was with us during the evening, but left afterwards; I thought perhaps you might have met him along the river-side, as you came that way."

"No," said Harris, "I saw no one; if your cook ventured alone into the forest, most likely he has lost his way; it is possible we may pick him up upon our road."

When they arrived at the grotto, they found breakfast duly prepared. Like the supper of the previous evening it consisted mainly of corned beef and biscuit. Harris did ample justice to the repast.

"There is no fear of our starving as we go," he observed to Mrs. Weldon; "but I can hardly say so much for the unfortunate Portuguese, your cook, of whom my young friend here has been speaking."

"Ah! has Dick been telling you about Negoro?" Mrs. Weldon said.

Dick explained that he had been inquiring whether Mr. Harris had happened to meet him in the direction he had come.

"I saw nothing of him," Harris repeated; "and as he has deserted you, you need not give yourselves any concern about him." And apparently glad to turn the subject, he said,

"Now, madam, I am at your service ; shall we start at once?"

It was agreed that there was no cause for delay. Each one took up the package that had been assigned him. Mrs. Weldon, with Hercules' help, mounted the horse, and Jack, with his miniature gun slung across his shoulder, was placed astride in front of her. Without a thought of acknowledging the kindness of the good-natured stranger in providing him so enjoyable a ride, the heedless little fellow declared himself quite capable of guiding the "gentleman's horse," and when to indulge him the bridle was put into his hand, he looked as proud as though he had been appointed leader of the whole caravan.

CHAPTER XVI.

THROUGH THE FOREST.

ALTHOUGH there was no obvious cause for apprehension, it cannot be denied that it was with a certain degree of foreboding that Dick Sands first entered that dense forest, through which for the next ten days they were all to wend their toilsome way.

Mrs. Weldon, on the contrary, was full of confidence and hope. A woman and a mother, she might have been expected to be conscious of anxiety at the peril to which she might be exposing herself and her child ; and doubtless she would have been sensible of alarm if her mind had not been fully satisfied upon two points ; first, that the portion of the pampas they were about to traverse was little infested either by natives or by dangerous beasts ; and secondly, that she was under the protection of a guide so trustworthy as she believed Harris to be.

The entrance to the forest was hardly more than three hundred paces up the river. An order of march had been arranged which was to be observed as closely as possible throughout the journey. At the head of the troop were Harris and Dick Sands, one armed with his long gun, the other with his Remington ; next came Bat and Austin, each carrying a gun and a cutlass, then Mrs. Weldon and Jack, on horseback, closely followed by Tom and old Nan, while Actæon with the fourth Remington, and Hercules with a huge hatchet in his waist-belt, brought up the rear. Dingo had no especial place in the procession, but wandered to and fro at his pleasure. Ever since he had been cast ashore Dick had noticed a remarkable change in the dog's behaviour ; the animal was in a constant state of agitation, always apparently on the search for some lost scent, and repeatedly giving vent to a low growl, which seemed to proceed from grief rather than from rage.

As for Cousin Benedict, his movements were permitted to be nearly as erratic as Dingo's ; nothing but a leading-string could possibly have kept him in the ranks. With his tin box under his arm, and his butterfly net in his hand, and his huge magnifying-glass suspended from his neck, he would be sometimes far ahead, sometimes a long way behind, and at the risk of being attacked by some venomous snake, would make frantic dashes into the tall grass whenever he espied some attractive orthoptera or other insect which he thought might be honoured by a place in his collection.

In one hour after starting Mrs. Weldon had called to him a dozen times without the slightest effect. At last she told him seriously that if he would not give up chasing the insects at a distance, she should be obliged to take possession of his tin box.

" Take away my box ! " he cried, with as much horror as if she had threatened to tear out his vitals.

" Yes, your box and your net too ! "

" My box and my net ! but surely not my spectacles ! " almost shrieked the excited entomologist.

" Yes, and your spectacles as well ! " added Mrs. Weldon mercilessly ; " I am glad you have reminded me of another means of reducing you to obedience ! "

The triple penalty of which he was thus warned had the effect of keeping him from wandering away for the best part of the next hour, but he was soon once more missing from the ranks; he was manifestly incorrigible; the deprivation of box, net, and spectacles would, it was acknowledged, be utterly without avail to prevent him from rambling. Accordingly it was thought better to let him have his own way, especially as Hercules volunteered to keep his eye upon him, and to endeavour to guard the worthy naturalist as carefully as he would himself protect some precious specimen of a lepidoptera. Further anxiety on his account was thus put to rest.

In spite of Harris's confident assertion that they were little likely to be molested by any of the nomad Indians, the whole company rejoiced in feeling that they were well armed, and they resolved to keep in a compact body. The way across the forest could scarcely be called a path; it was, in fact, little more than the track of animals, and progress along it was necessarily very slow; indeed it seemed impossible, at the rate they started, to accomplish more than five or six miles in the course of twelve hours.

The weather was beautifully fine; the sun ascended nearly to the zenith, and its rays, descending almost perpendicularly, caused a degree of heat which, as Harris pointed out, would have been unendurable upon the open plain, but was here pleasantly tempered by the shelter of the foliage.

Most of the trees were quite strange to them. To an experienced eye they were such as were remarkable more for their character than for their size. Here, on one side, was the bauhinia, or mountain ebony; there, on the other, the molompi or pterocarpus, its trunk exuding large quantities of resin, and of which the strong light wood makes excellent oars or paddles; further on were fustics, heavily charged with colouring matter, and guaiacums, twelve feet in diameter, surpassing the ordinary kind in magnitude, yet far inferior in quality.

Dick Sands kept perpetually asking Harris to tell him the names of all these trees and plants.

"Have you never been on the coast of South America before?" replied Harris, without giving the explicit information that was sought.

"Never," said Dick; "never before. Nor do I recollect ever having seen any one who has."

"But surely you have explored the coasts of Columbia or Patagonia," Harris continued.

Dick avowed that he had never had the chance.

"But has Mrs. Weldon never visited these parts? Our countrymen, I know, are great travellers."

"No," answered Mrs. Weldon; "my husband's business called him occasionally to New Zealand, but I have accompanied him nowhere else. With this part of Lower Bolivia we are totally unacquainted."

"Then, madam, I can only assure you that you will see a most remarkable country, in every way a very striking contrast to the regions of Peru, Brazil, and the Argentine republic. Its animal and vegetable products would fill a naturalist with unbounded wonder. May I not declare it a lucky chance that has brought you here?"

"Do not say chance, Mr. Harris, if you please."

"Well, then, madam; providence, if you prefer it," said Harris, with the air of a man incapable of recognizing the distinction.

After finding that there was no one amongst them who was acquainted in any way with the country through which they were travelling, Harris seemed to exhibit an evident pleasure in pointing out and describing by name the various wonders of the forest. Had Cousin Benedict's attainments included a knowledge of botany he would have found himself in a fine field for researches, and might perchance have discovered novelties to which his own name could be appended in the catalogues of science. But he was no botanist; in fact, as a rule, he held all blossoms in aversion, on the ground that they entrapped insects into their corollæ, and poisoned them sometimes with venomous juices. New and rare insects, however, seemed hereabouts to be wanting.

Occasionally the soil became marshy, and they all had to wend their way over a perfect network of tiny rivulets that were affluents of the river from which they had started. Sometimes these rivulets were so wide that they could not be passed without a long search for some spot where they could be forded ; their banks were all very damp, and in many places abounded with a kind of reed, which Harris called by its proper name of papyrus.

As soon as the marshy district had been passed, the forest resumed its original aspect, the footway becoming narrow as ever. Harris pointed out some very fine ebony-trees, larger than the common sort, and yielding a wood darker and more durable than what is ordinarily seen in the market. There were also more mango-trees than might have been expected at this distance from the sea ; a beautiful white ichen enveloped their trunks like a fur ; but in spite of their luxuriant foliage and delicious fruit, Harris said that there was not a native who would venture to propagate the species, as the superstition of the country is that "whoever plants a mango, dies !"

At noon a halt was made for the purpose of rest and refreshment. During the afternoon they arrived at some gently rising ground, not the first slopes of hills, but an insulated plateau which appeared to unite mountains and plains.

Notwithstanding that the trees were far less crowded and more inclined to grow in detached groups, the numbers of herbaceous plants with which the soil was covered rendered progress no less difficult than it was before. The general aspect of the scene was not unlike an East Indian jungle. Less luxuriant indeed than in the lower valley of the river, the vegetation was far more abundant than that of the temperate zones either of the Old or New continents. Indigo grew in great profusion, and, according to Harris's representation, was the most encroaching plant in the whole country ; no sooner, he said, was a field left untilled, than it was overrun by this parasite, which sprang up with the rank growth of thistles or nettles.

One tree which might have been expected to be common in this part of the continent seemed entirely wanting. This was the caoutchouc. Of the various trees from which India-rubber is procured, such as the Ficus prinoides, the Castilloa elastica, the Cecropia peltata, the Callophora utilis, the Cameraria latifolia, and especially the Siphonia elastica, all of which abound in the provinces of South America, not a single specimen was to be seen. Dick had promised to show Jack an India-rubber-tree, and the child, who had conjured up visions of squeaking dolls, balls, and other toys growing upon its branches, was loud and constant in his expressions of disappointment.

"Never mind, my little man," said Harris ; "have patience, and you shall see hundreds of India-rubber-trees when you get to the hacienda."

"And will they be nice and elastic?" asked Jack, whose ideas upon the subject were of the vaguest order.

"Oh, yes, they will stretch as long as you like," Harris answered, laughing. "But here is something to amuse you," he added, and as he spoke, he gathered a fruit that looked as tempting as a peach.

"You are quite sure that it is safe to give it him?" said Mrs. Weldon anxiously.

"To satisfy you, madam, I will eat one first myself."

The example he set was soon followed by all the rest. The fruit was a mango ; that which had been so opportunely discovered was of the sort that ripens in March or April; there is a later kind which ripens in September.

With his mouth full of juice, Jack pronounced that it was very nice, but did not seem to be altogether diverted from his sense of disappointment at not coming to an India-rubber-tree. Evidently the little man thought himself rather injured.

"And Dick promised me some humming-birds too!" he murmured.

"Plenty of humming-birds for you, when you get to the farm; lots of them where my brother lives," said Harris.

And to say the truth, there was nothing extravagant in the way the child's anticipations had been raised, for in Bolivia humming-birds are found in great abundance. The Indians, who weave their plumage into all kinds of artistic designs, have bestowed the most poetical epithets upon these gems of the feathered race. They call them "rays of the sun," and "tresses of the day-star;" at one time they will describe them as "king of flowers," at another as "blossoms of heaven kissing blossoms of earth," or as "the jewel that reflects the sunbeam." In fact their imagination seems to have shaped a suitable distinction for almost every one of the 150 known species of this dazzling little beauty.

But however numerous humming-birds might be expected to be in the Bolivian forest, they proved scarce enough at present, and Jack had to content himself with Harris's representations that they did not like solitude, but would be found plentifully at San Felice, where they would be heard all day long humming like a spinning-wheel. Already Jack said he longed to be there, a wish that was so unanimously echoed by all the rest, that they resolved that no stoppage should be allowed beyond what was absolutely indispensable.

After a time the forest began to alter its aspect. The trees were even less crowded, opening now and then into wide glades. The soil, cropping up above its carpet of verdure, exhibited veins of rose granite and syenite, like plates of lapis lazuli; on some of the higher ground, the fleshy tubers of the sarsaparilla plant, growing in a hopeless entanglement, made progress a matter of still greater difficulty than in the narrow tracks of the dense forest.

At sunset the travellers found that they had accomplished about eight miles from their starting-point. They could not prognosticate what hardships might be in store for them on future days, but it was certain that the experiences of the first day had been neither eventful nor very fatiguing. It was now unanimously agreed that they should make a halt for the night, and as little was to be apprehended from the attacks either of man or beast, it was considered unnecessary to form anything like a regular encampment. One man on guard, to be relieved every few hours, was presumed to be sufficient. Admirable shelter was offered by an enormous mango, the spreading foliage of which formed a kind of natural verandah, sweeping the ground so thoroughly that any one who chose could find sleeping-quarters in its very branches.

Simultaneously with the halting of the party there was heard a deafening tumult in the upper boughs. The mango was the roosting-place of a colony of grey parrots, a noisy, quarrelsome, and rapacious race, of whose true characteristics the specimens seen in confinement in Europe give no true conception. Their screeching and chattering were such a nuisance that Dick Sands wanted to fire a shot into the middle of them, but Harris seriously dissuaded him, urging that the report of fire-arms would only serve to reveal their own presence, whilst their greatest safety lay in perfect silence.

Supper was prepared. There was little need of cooking. The meal, as before, consisted of preserved meat and biscuit. Fresh water, which they flavoured with a few drops of rum, was obtained from an adjacent stream which trickled through the grass. By way of dessert they had an abundance of ripe mangoes, and the only drawback to their general enjoyment was the discordant outcry which the parrots kept up, as it were in protest against the invasion of what they held to be their own rightful domain.

It was nearly dark when supper was ended. The evening shade crept slowly upwards to the tops of the trees, which soon stood out in sharp relief against the lighter background of the sky, while the stars, one by one, began to peep. The wind dropped, and ceased to murmur through the foliage; to the general relief, the parrots desisted from their clatter; and as Nature hushed herself to rest, she seemed to be inviting all her children to follow her example.

"Had we not better light a good large fire?" asked Dick.

"By no means," said Harris; "the nights are not cold, and under this wide-spreading mango the ground is not likely to be damp. Besides, as I have told you before, our best security consists in our taking care to attract no attention whatever from without."

Mrs. Weldon interposed,—

"It may be true enough that we have nothing to dread from the Indians, but is it certain that there are no dangerous quadrupeds against which we are bound to be upon our guard?"

Harris answered,—

"I can positively assure you, madam, that there are no animals here but such as would be infinitely more afraid of you than you would be of them."

"Are there any woods without wild beasts?" asked Jack.

"All woods are not alike, my boy," replied Harris; "this wood is a great park. As the Indians say, 'Es como el Pariso;' it is like Paradise."

Jack persisted,—

"There must be snakes, and lions, and tigers."

"Ask your mamma, my boy," said Harris, "whether she ever heard of lions and tigers in America?"

Mrs. Weldon was endeavouring to put her little boy at his ease on this point, when Cousin Benedict interposed, saying that although there were no lions or tigers, there were plenty of jaguars and panthers in the New World.

"And won't they kill us?" demanded Jack eagerly, his apprehensions once more aroused.

"Kill you?" laughed Harris; "why, your friend Hercules here could strangle them, two at a time, one in each hand!"

"But, please, don't let the panthers come near me!" pleaded Jack, evidently alarmed.

"No, no, Master Jack, they shall not come near you. I will give them a good grip first," and the giant displayed his two rows of huge white teeth.

Dick Sands proposed that it should be the four younger negroes who should be assigned the task of keeping watch during the night, in attendance upon himself; but Actæon insisted so strongly upon the necessity of Dick's having his full share of rest, that the others were soon brought to the same conviction, and Dick was obliged to yield.

Jack valiantly announced his intention of taking one watch, but his sleepy eyelids made it only too plain that he did not know the extent of his own fatigue.

"I am sure there are wolves here," he said.

"Only such wolves as Dingo would swallow at a mouthful," said Harris.

"But I am sure there are wolves," he insisted, repeating the word "wolves" again and again, until he tumbled off to sleep against the side of old Nan. Mrs. Weldon gave her little son a silent kiss; it was her loving "good-night."

Cousin Benedict was missing. Some little time before, he had slipped away in search of "cocuyos," or fire-flies, which he had heard were common in South America. Those singular insects emit a bright bluish light from two spots on the side of the thorax, and their colours are so brilliant that they are used as ornaments for ladies' head-dresses. Hoping to secure some specimens for his box, Benedict would have wandered to an unlimited distance ; but Hercules, faithful to his undertaking, soon discovered him, and heedless of the naturalist's protestations and vociferations, promptly escorted him back to the general rendezvous.

Hercules himself was the first to keep watch, but with this exception, the whole party, in another hour, were wrapped in peaceful slumber.

CHAPTER XVII.

MISGIVINGS.

MOST travellers who have passed a night in a South American forest have been roused from their slumbers by a *matinée musicale* more fantastic than melodious, performed by monkeys, as their ordinary greeting of the dawn. The yelling, chattering, screeching, howling, all unite to form a chorus almost unearthly in its hideousness.

Amongst the various specimens of the numerous family of the quadrumana ought to be recognized the little mari-kina ; the sagouin, with its parti-coloured face ; the grey mora, the skin of which is used by the Indians for covering their gun-locks ; the sapajou, with its singular tuft over the forehead, and, most remarkable of all, the guariba (*Simia Beelzebul*) with its prehensile tail and diabolical counte-nance.

At the first streak of daylight the senior member, as choragus, will start the key-note in a sonorous barytone, the younger monkeys join in tenor and alto, and the concert begins. But this morning there was no concert at all. There was nothing of the wonted serenade to break the silence of the forest. The shrill notes resulting from the rapid vibration of the hyoid bones of the throat were not to be heard. Indians would have been disappointed and per-plexed ; they are very fond of the flesh of the guariba when smoked and dried, and they would certainly have missed the chant of the monkey "paternosters;" but Dick Sands and his companions were unfamiliar with any of these things, and accordingly the singular quietude was to them a matter of no surprise.

They all awoke much refreshed by their night's rest, which there had been nothing to disturb. Jack was by no means the latest in opening his eyes, and his first words were addressed to Hercules, asking him whether he had caught a wolf with his teeth. Hercules had to acknowledge that he had tasted nothing all night, and declared himself quite ready for breakfast. The whole party were unanimous in this respect, and after a brief morning prayer, breakfast was expeditiously served by old Nan. The meal was but a repetition of the last evening's supper, but with their appetites sharpened by the fresh forest air, and anxious to fortify themselves for a good day's march, they did not fail to do ample justice to their simple fare. Even Cousin Benedict, for once in his life at least, partook of his food as if it were not utterly a matter of indifference to him ; but he grumbled very much at the restraint to which he considered himself subjected ; he could not see the good of coming to such a country as this, if he were to be obliged to walk about with his hands in his pockets ; and he protested that if Hercules did not leave him alone and permit him to catch fire-flies, there would be a bone to pick between them. Hercules did not look very much alarmed at the threat. Mrs. Weldon, however, took him aside, and telling him that she did not wish to deprive the enthusiast entirely of his favourite occupation, instructed him to allow her cousin as much liberty as possible, provided he did not lose sight of him.

The morning meal was over, and it was only seven o'clock when the travellers were once more on their way towards the east, preserving the same marching-order as on the day before.

The path was still through luxuriant forest. The vegetable kingdom reigned supreme. As the plateau was immediately adjacent to tropical latitudes, the sun's rays during
the summer months descended perpendicularly upon the
virgin soil, and the vast amount of heat thus obtained combined with the abundant moisture retained in the sub-soil,
caused vegetation to assume a character which was truly
magnificent.

Dick Sands could not overcome a certain sense of mysti-
fication. Here they were, as Harris told them, in the region
of the pampas, a word which he knew in the Quichna dialect
signifies "a plain;" but he had always read that these
plains were characterized by a deficiency alike of water, of
trees, and rocks ; he had always understood that during the
rainy season, thistles spring up in great abundance and
grow until they form thickets that are well-nigh impenetrable ; he had imagined that the few dwarf trees and prickly
shrubs that exist during the summer only stamp the general scene with an aspect of yet more thorough bareness
and desolation. But how different was everything to all
this ! The forest never ceased to stretch away interminably
to the horizon. There were no tokens of the rough naked-
ness that he had expected. Dick seemed to be driven to
the conclusion that Harris was right in describing this
plateau of Atacama, which he had for his part most firmly
believed to be a vast desert between the Andes and the
Pacific, as a region that was quite exceptional in its natural
features.

It was not in Dick's character to keep his reflections to
himself. In the course of the morning he expressed his
extreme surprise at finding the pampas answer so little to
his preconceived ideas.

"Have I not understood correctly," he said, "that the
pampas is similar to the North American savannahs, only
less marshy?"

Harris replied that such was indeed a correct description of the pampas of Rio Colorado, and the llanos of Venezuela and the Orinoco.

"But," he continued, "I own I am as much astonished as yourself at the character of this region ; I have never crossed the plateau before, and I must confess it is altogether different to what you find beyond the Andes towards the Atlantic."

"You don't mean that we are going to cross the Andes ?" said Dick, in sudden alarm.

Harris smiled.

"No, no, indeed. With our limited means of transport such an undertaking would have been rash in the extreme. We had better have kept to the coast for ever rather than incur such a risk. Our destination, San Felice, is on this side of the range, and in order to reach it, we shall not have to leave the plateau, of which the greatest elevation is but little over 1500 feet."

"And you say," Dick persisted, "that you have really no fear of losing your way in a forest such as this, a forest into which you have never set foot before ?"

"No fear whatever," Harris answered ; "so accustomed am I to travelling of this kind, that I can steer my way by a thousand signs revealing themselves in the growth of the trees, and in the composition of the soil, which would never present themselves to your notice. I assure you that I anticipate no difficulties."

This conversation was not heard by any of the rest of the party. Harris seemed to speak as frankly as he did fearlessly, and Dick felt that there might be, after all, no just grounds for any of his own misgivings.

Five days passed by, and the 12th of April arrived without any special incident. Nine miles had been the average distance accomplished in a day ; regular periods of rest had been taken, and, except that Jack's spirits had somewhat flagged, the fatigue did not seem to have interfered with the general good health of the travellers.

First disappointed of his India-rubber-tree, and then of his humming-birds, Jack had inquired about the beautiful parrots which he had been led to expect he should see in this wonderful forest. Where were the bright green macaws? where were the gaudy aras with their bare white cheeks and pointed tails, which seem never to light upon the ground? and where, too, were all the brilliant parroquets, with their feathered faces, and indeed the whole variety of those forest chatterers of which the Indians affirm that they speak the language of nations long extinct?

It is true that there was no lack of the common grey parrots with crimson tails, but these were no novelty; Jack had seen plenty of them before, for owing to their reputation of being the most clever in mimicry of the Psittacidæ, they have been domesticated everywhere in both the Old and New worlds.

But Jack's dissatisfaction was nothing compared to Cousin Benedict's. In spite of being allowed to wander away from the rank, he had failed to discover a single insect which was worth the pursuit; not even a fire-fly danced at night; nature seemed to be mocking him, and his ill-humour increased accordingly.

In this way the journey was continued for four days longer, and on the 16th it was estimated that they must have travelled between eighty and ninety miles north-eastwards from the coast. Harris positively asserted that they could not be much more than twenty miles from San Felice, and that by pushing forwards they might expect in eight-and-forty hours to find themselves lodged in comfortable quarters.

But although they had thus succeeded in traversing this vast table-land, they had not seen one human inhabitant. Dick was more than ever perplexed, and it was a subject of bitter regret to him that they had not stranded upon some more frequented part of the shore, near some village or plantation where Mrs. Weldon might long since have found a suitable refuge.

Deserted, however, as the country apparently was by man, it had latterly shown itself much more abundantly tenanted by animals. Many a time a long, plaintive cry was heard, which Harris attributed to the tardigrades or sloths often found in wooded districts, and known by the name of "aïs;" and in the middle of the dinner-halt on this day, a loud hissing suddenly broke upon the air which made Mrs. Weldon start to her feet in alarm.

"A serpent!" cried Dick, catching up his loaded gun.

The negroes, following Dick's example, were in a moment on the alert.

"Don't fire!" cried Harris.

There was indeed nothing improbable in the supposition that a "sucuru," a species of boa, sometimes measuring forty feet in length, had just moved itself in the long grass at their side, but Harris affirmed that the "sucuru" never hisses, and declared that the noise had really come from animals of an entirely inoffensive character.

"What animals?" asked Dick, always eager for information, which it must be granted Harris seemed always equally anxious to give.

"Antelopes," replied Harris; "but, hush! not a sound, or you will frighten them away."

"Antelopes!" cried Dick; "I must see them; I must get close to them."

"More easily said than done," answered Harris, shaking his head; but Dick Sands not to be diverted from his purpose, and, gun in hand, crept into the grass. He had not advanced many yards before a herd of about a dozen gazelles, graceful in body, with short, pointed horns, dashed past him like a glowing cloud, and disappeared in the underwood without giving him time to take a shot.

"I told you beforehand what you would have to expect," said Harris, as Dick, with a considerable sense of disappointment, returned to the party.

Impossible, however, as it had been fairly to scrutinize the antelopes, such was hardly the case with another herd of animals, the identification of which led to a somewhat singular discussion between Harris and the rest.

About four o'clock in the afternoon of the same day, the travellers were halting for a few moments near an opening in the forest, when three or four large animals emerged from a thicket about a hundred paces ahead, and scampered off at full speed. In spite of what Harris had urged, Dick put his gun to his shoulder, and was on the very point of firing, . when Harris knocked the rifle quickly aside.

"They were giraffes!" shouted Dick.

The announcement awakened the curiosity of Jack, who quickly scrambled to his feet upon the saddle on which he was lounging.

" My dear Dick," said Mrs. Weldon, "there are no giraffes in America !"

" Certainly not," cried Harris; "they were not giraffes, they were ostriches which you saw ! "

" Ostriches with four legs ! that will never do ! what do you say, Mrs. Weldon ? "

Mrs. Weldon replied that she had certainly taken the animals for quadrupeds, and all the negroes were under the same impression.

Laughing heartily, Harris said it was far from an uncommon thing for an inexperienced eye to mistake a large ostrich for a small giraffe ; the shape of both was so similar, that it often quite escaped observation as to whether the long necks terminated in a beak or a muzzle ; besides, what nced of discussion could there be when the fact was established that giraffes are unknown in the New World? The reasoning was plausible enough, and Mrs. Weldon and the negroes were soon convinced. But Dick was far from satisfied.

"I did not know that there was an American ostrich!" he again objected.

"Oh, yes," replied Harris promptly, "there is a species called the nandu, which is very well known here; we shall probably see some more of them."

The statement was correct; the nandu is common in the plains of South America, and is distinguished from the African ostrich by having three toes, all furnished with claws. It is a fine bird, sometimes exceeding six feet in height; it has a short beak, and its wings are furnished with blue-grey plumes. Harris appeared well acquainted with the bird, and proceeded to give a very precise account of its habits. In concluding his remarks, he again pressed upon Dick his most urgent request that he should abstain from firing upon any animal whatever. It was of the utmost consequence.

Dick made no reply. He was silent and thoughtful. Grave doubts had arisen in his mind, and he could neither explain nor dispel them.

When the march was resumed on the following day, Harris asserted his conviction that another four-and-twenty hours would bring them to the hacienda.

"And there, madam," he said, addressing Mrs. Weldon, "we can offer you every essential comfort, though you may not find the luxuries of your own home in San Francisco."

Mrs. Weldon repeated her expression of gratitude for the proffered hospitality, owning that she should now be exceedingly glad to reach the farm, as she was anxious about her little son, who appeared to be threatened with the symptoms of incipient fever.

Harris could not deny that although the climate was usually very healthy, it nevertheless did occasionally produce a kind of intermittent fever during March and April.

"But nature has provided the proper remedy," said Dick; and perceiving that Harris did not comprehend his meaning, he continued, "Are we not in the region of the quinquinas, the bark of which is notoriously the medicine with which attacks of fever are usually treated? for my part, I am amazed that we have not seen numbers of them already."

"Ah! yes, yes; I know what you mean," answered Harris, after a moment's hesitation; "they are trees, however, not always easy to find; they rarely grow in groups, and in spite of their large leaves and fragrant red blossom, the Indians themselves often have a difficulty in recognizing them; the feature that distinguishes them most is their evergreen foliage."

At Mrs. Weldon's request, Harris promised to point out the tree if he should see one, but added that when she reached the hacienda, she would be able to obtain some sulphate of quinine, which was much more efficacious than the unprepared bark.[1]

The day passed without further incident. No rain had fallen at present, though the warm mist that rose from the soil betokened an approaching change of weather; the rainy season was certainly not far distant, but to travellers who indulged the expectation of being in a few hours in a place of shelter, this was not a matter of great concern.

Evening came, and a halt was made for the night beneath a grove of lofty trees. If Harris had not miscalculated, they could hardly be more than about six miles from their

---

[1] This bark, reduced to powder, was formerly known as "Pulvis Jesuiticus," because in the year 1649 the Jesuits in Rome imported a large quantity of it from their missionaries in South America.

destination ; so confirmed, however, was Dick Sands in his strange suspicions, that nothing could induce him to relax any of the usual precautions, and he particularly insisted upon the negroes, turn by turn, keeping up the accustomed watch.

Worn out by fatigue, the little party were glad to lie down, but they had scarcely dropped off to sleep when they were aroused by a sharp cry.

"Who's that ? who's there ? what's the matter ?" exclaimed Dick, the first to rise to his feet.

"It is I," answered Benedict's voice ; "I am bitten. Something has bitten me."

"A snake !" exclaimed Mrs. Weldon in alarm.

"No, no, cousin, better than that ! it was not a snake ; I believe it was an orthoptera ; I have it all right," he shouted triumphantly.

"Then kill it quickly, sir ; and let us go to sleep again in peace," said Harris.

"Kill it ! not for the world ! I must have a light, and look at it !"

Dick Sands indulged him, for reasons of his own, in getting a light. The entomologist carefully opened his hand and displayed an insect somewhat smaller than a bee, of a dull colour, streaked with yellow on the under portion of the body. He looked radiant with delight.

"A diptera !" he exclaimed, half beside himself with joy, "a most famous diptera !"

"Is it venomous ?" asked Mrs. Weldon.

"Not at all to men ; it only hurts elephants and buffaloes."

"But tell us its name ! what is it ?" cried Dick impetuously.

The naturalist began to speak in a slow, oracular tone.

"This insect is here a prodigy ; it is an insect totally unknown in this country,—in America."

"Tell us its name!" roared Dick.

"It is a tzetzy, sir, a true tzetzy."

Dick's heart sank like a stone. He was speechless. He did not, dared not, ask more. Only too well he knew where the tzetzy could alone be found. He did not close his eyes again that night.

CHAPTER XVIII

A TERRIBLE DISCOVERY.

THE morning of the 18th dawned, the day on which, according to Harris's prediction, the travellers were to be safely housed at San Felice. Mrs. Weldon was really much relieved at the prospect, for she was aware that her strength must prove inadequate to the strain of a more protracted journey. The condition of her little boy, who was alternately flushed with fever, and pale with exhaustion, had begun to cause her great anxiety, and unwilling to resign the care of the child even to Nan his faithful nurse, she insisted upon carrying him in her own arms. Twelve days and nights, passed in the open air, had done much to try her powers of endurance, and the charge of a sick child in addition would soon break down her strength entirely.

Dick Sands, Nan, and the negroes had all borne the march very fairly. Their stock of provisions, though of course considerably diminished, was still far from small. As for Harris, he had shown himself pre-eminently adapted for forest-life, and capable of bearing any amount of fatigue. Yet, strange to say, as he approached the end of the journey, his manner underwent a remarkable change; instead of conversing in his ordinary frank and easy way, he became silent and preoccupied, as if engrossed in his own thoughts. Perhaps he had an instinctive consciousness that "his young friend," as he was in the habit of addressing Dick, was entertaining hard suspicions about him.

The march was resumed. The trees once again ceased to be crowded in impenetrable masses, but stood in clusters at considerable distances apart. Now, Dick tried to argue with himself, they must be coming to the true pampas, or the man must be designedly misleading them ; and yet what motive could he have ?

Although during the earlier part of the day there occurred nothing that could be said absolutely to justify Dick's increasing uneasiness, two circumstances transpired which did not escape his observation, and which, he felt, might be significant. The first of these was a sudden change in Dingo's behaviour. The dog, throughout the march, had uniformly run along with his nose upon the ground, smelling the grass and shrubs, and occasionally uttering a sad low whine ; but to-day he seemed all agitation ; he scampered about with bristling coat, with his head erect, and ever and again burst into one of those furious fits of barking, with which he had formerly been accustomed to greet Negoro's appearance upon the deck of the " Pilgrim."

The idea that flitted across Dick's mind was shared by Tom.

" Look, Mr. Dick, look at Dingo ; he is at his old ways again," said he ; " it is just as if Negoro—"

" Hush !" said Dick to the old man, who continued in a lower voice,—

" It is just as if Negoro had followed us ; do you think it is likely ?"

" It might perhaps be to his advantage to follow us, if he doesn't know the country ; but if he does know the country why then—"

Dick did not finish his sentence, but whistled to Dingo. The dog reluctantly obeyed the call.

As soon as the dog was at his side, Dick patted him, repeating,—

" Good dog ! good Dingo ! where's Negoro ? "

The sound of Negoro's name had its usual effect; it seemed to irritate the animal exceedingly, and he barked furiously, and apparently wanted to dash into the thicket.

Harris had been an interested spectator of the scene, and now approached with a peculiar expression on his countenance, and inquired what they were saying to Dingo.

"Oh, nothing much," replied Tom; "we were only asking him for news of a lost acquaintance."

"Ah, I suppose you mean that Portuguese cook of yours."

"Yes," answered Tom; "we fancied from Dingo's behaviour that Negoro must be somewhere close at hand."

"Why don't you send and search the underwood? perhaps the poor wretch is in distress."

"No need of that, Mr. Harris; Negoro, I have no doubt, is quite capable of taking care of himself."

"Well, just as you please, my young friend," said Harris, with an air of indifference.

Dick turned away; he continued his endeavours to pacify Dingo, and the conversation dropped.

The other thing that had arrested Dick's attention was the behaviour of the horse. If they had been as near the hacienda as Harris described, would not the animal have pricked up its ears, sniffed the air, and with dilated nostril, exhibited some sign of satisfaction, as being upon familiar ground?

But nothing of the kind was to be observed; the horse plodded along as unconcernedly as if a stable were as far away as ever.

Even Mrs. Weldon was not so engrossed with her child, but what she was fain to express her wonder at the deserted aspect of the country. No trace of a farm-labourer was anywhere to be seen! She cast her eye at Harris, who was in his usual place in front, and observing how he was looking first to the left, and then to the right, with the air of a man who was uncertain of his path, she asked herself whether it was possible their guide might have lost his way. She dared not entertain the idea, and averted her eyes, that she might not be harassed by his movements.

After crossing an open plain about a mile in width, the travellers once again entered the forest, which resumed something of the same denseness that had characterized it farther to the west. In the course of the afternoon, they came to a spot which was marked very distinctly by the vestiges of some enormous animals, which must have passed quite recently. As Dick looked carefully about him, he observed that the branches were all torn off or broken to a considerable height, and that the foot-tracks in the trampled grass were much too large to be those either of jaguars or panthers. Even if it were possible that the prints on the ground had been made by aïs or other tardigrades, this would fail to account in the least for the trees being broken to such a height. Elephants alone were capable of working such destruction in the underwood, but elephants were unknown in America. Dick was puzzled, but controlled himself so that he would not apply to Harris for any enlightenment ; his intuition made him aware that a man who had once tried to make him believe that giraffes were ostriches, would not hesitate a second time to impose upon his credulity.

More than ever was Dick becoming convinced that Harris was a traitor, and he was secretly prompted to tax him with his treachery. Still he was obliged to own that he could not assign any motive for the man acting in such a manner with the survivors of the "Pilgrim," and consequently hesitated before he actually condemned him for conduct so base and heartless. What could be done? he repeatedly asked himself. On board ship the boy captain might perchance have been able to devise some plan for the safety of those so strangely committed to his charge, but here on an unknown shore, he could only suffer from the burden of this responsibility the more, because he was so utterly powerless to act.

He made up his mind on one point. He determined not to alarm the poor anxious mother a moment before he was actually compelled. It was his carrying out this determination that explained why on subsequently arriving at a considerable stream, where he saw some huge heads, swollen muzzles, long tusks, and unwieldy bodies rising from amidst the rank wet grass, he uttered no word and gave no gesture of surprise ; but only too well he knew, at a glance, that he must be looking at a herd of hippopotamuses.

It was a weary march that day ; a general feeling of depression spread involuntarily from one to another ; hardly conscious to herself of her weariness, Mrs. Weldon was exhibiting manifest symptoms of lassitude ; and it was only Dick's moral energy and sense of duty that kept him from succumbing to the prevailing dejection.

About four o'clock, Tom noticed something lying in the grass, and stooping down he picked up a kind of knife ; it was of peculiar shape, being very wide and flat in the blade, while its handle, which was of ivory, was ornamented with a good deal of clumsy carving. He carried it at once to Dick, who, when he had scrutinized it, held it up to Harris, with the remark,—

"There must be natives not far off."

"Quite right, my young friend ; the hacienda must be a very few miles away,—but yet, but yet—"

He hesitated.

"You don't mean that you are not sure of your way," said Dick sharply.

"Not exactly that," replied Harris ; "yet in taking this short cut across the forest, I am inclined to think I am a mile or so out of the way. Perhaps I had better walk on a little way, and look about me."

"No ; you do not leave us here," cried Dick firmly.

"Look here! here are hands, men's hands!"

"Not against your will ; but remember, I do not undertake to guide you in the dark."

"We must spare you the necessity for that. I can answer for it that Mrs. Weldon will raise no objection to spending another night in the open air. We can start off to-morrow morning as early as we like, and if the distance be only what you represent, a few hours will easily accomplish it."

"As you please," answered Harris, with cold civility.

Just then, Dingo again burst out into a vehement fit of barking, and it required no small amount of coaxing on Dick's part to make him cease from his noise.

It was decided that the halt should be made at once. Mrs. Weldon, as it had been anticipated, urged nothing against it, being preoccupied by her immediate attentions to Jack, who was lying in her arms, suffering from a decided attack of fever. The shelter of a large thicket had just been selected by Dick as a suitable resting-place for the night, when Tom, who was assisting in the necessary preparations, suddenly gave a cry of horror.

"What is it, Tom?" asked Dick very calmly.

"Look ! look at these trees ! they are spattered with blood ! and look here ! here are hands, men's hands, cut off and lying on the ground !"

"What ?" cried Dick, and in an instant was at his side.

His presence of mind did not fail him ; he whispered,—

"Hush ! Tom ! hush ! not a word !"

But it was with a shudder that ran through his veins that he witnessed for himself the mutilated fragments of several human bodies, and saw, lying beside them, some broken forks, and some bits of iron chain.

The sight of the gory remains made Dingo bark ferociously, and Dick, who was most anxious that Mrs. Weldon's attention should not be called to the discovery, had the greatest difficulty in driving him back ; but fortunately the lady's mind was so engrossed with her patient, that she did not observe the commotion. Harris stood aloof; there was no one to notice the change that passed over his countenance, but the expression was almost diabolical in its malignity.

Poor old Tom himself seemed perfectly spell-bound. With his hands clenched, his eyes dilated, and his breast heaving with emotion, he kept repeating without anything like coherence, the words,—

"Forks! chains! forks! . . . long ago . . . remember . . . too well . . . chains!"

"For Mrs. Weldon's sake, Tom, hold your tongue!" Dick implored him.

Tom, however, was full with some remembrance of the past; he continued to repeat,—

"Long ago . . . forks . . . chains!" until Dick led him out of hearing.

A fresh halting-place was cho en a short distance further on, and supper was prepared. But the meal was left almost untasted; not so much that hunger had been overcome by fatigue, but because the indefinable feeling of uneasiness, that had taken possession of them all, had entirely destroyed all appetite.

Gradually the night became very dark. The sky was covered with heavy storm-clouds, and on the western horizon flashes of summer lightning now and then glimmered through the trees. The air was perfectly still; not a leaf stirred, and the atmosphere seemed so charged with electricity as to be incapable of transmitting sound of any kind.

Dick himself, with Austin and Bat in attendance, remained on guard, all of them eagerly straining both eye and ear to catch any light or sound that might disturb the silence and obscurity. Old Tom, with his head sunk upon his breast, sat motionless, as in a trance; he was gloomily revolving the awakened memories of the past. Mrs. Weldon was engaged with her sick child. Scarcely one of the party was really asleep, except indeed it might be Cousin Benedict, whose reasoning faculties were not of an order to carry him forwards into any future contingencies.

Midnight was still an hour in advance, when the dull air seemed filled with a deep and prolonged roar, mingled with a peculiar kind of vibration.

Tom started to his feet. A fresh recollection of his early days had struck him.

" A lion ! a lion !" he shouted.

" In vain Dick tried to repress him ; but he repeated,—

" A lion ! a lion !"

Dick Sands seized his cutlass, and, unable any longer to control his wrath, he rushed to the spot where he had left Harris lying.

The man was gone, and his horse with him !

All the suspicions that had been so long pent up within Dick's mind now shaped themselves into actual reality. A flood of light had broken in upon him. Now he was convinced, only too certainly, that it was not the coast of America at all upon which the schooner had been cast ashore ! it was not Easter Island that had been sighted far away in the west ! the compass had completely deceived him ; he was satisfied now that the strong currents had carried them quite round Cape Horn, and that they had really entered the Atlantic. No wonder that quinquinas, caoutchouc, and other South American products, had failed to be seen. This was neither the Bolivian pampas nor the plateau of Atacama. They were giraffes, not ostriches, that had vanished down the glade ; they were elephants that had trodden down the underwood ; they were hippopotamuses that were lurking by the river ; it was indeed the dreaded tzetzy that Cousin Benedict had so triumphantly discovered; and, last of all, it was a lion's roar that had disturbed the silence of the forest. That chain, that knife, those forks, were unquestionably the instruments of slave-dealers ; and what could those mutilated hands be, except the relics of their ill-fated victims ?

Harris and Negoro must be in a conspiracy !

It was with terrible anguish that Dick gnashed his teeth and muttered,—

"Yes, it is too true ; we are in Africa ! in equatorial Africa ! in the land of slavery ! in the very haunt of slave-drivers !"

END OF FIRST PART.

PRINTED BY GILBERT AND RIVINGTON, LIMITED, ST. JOHN'S SQUARE.

BOOKS BY JULES VERNE.

Large Crown 8vo. .	Containing 350 to 600 pp. and from 50 to 100 full-page illustrations.		Containing the whole of the text with some illustrations.	
WORKS.	In very handsome cloth binding, gilt edges.	In plainer binding, plain edges.	In cloth binding, gilt edges, smaller type.	Coloured Boards.
	s. *d.*	*s.* *d.*	*s.* *d.*	
Twenty Thousand Leagues under the Sea. Part I. Ditto Part II.	10 6	5 0	3 6	2 vols., 1s. each.
Hector Servadac . . .	10 6	5 0	3 6	2 vols., 1s. each.
The Fur Country . . .	10 6	5 0	3 6	2 vols., 1s. each
From the Earth to the Moon and a Trip round it	10 6	5 0	2 vols., 2s. each.	2 vols., 1s. each.
Michael Strogoff, the Courier of the Czar . .	10 6	5 0	3 6	2 vols., 1s. each.
Dick Sands, the Boy Captain	10 6	5 0	3 6	2 vols., 1s. each.
Five Weeks in a Balloon .	7 6	3 6	2 0	1s. 0d.
Adventures of Three Englishmen and Three Russians	7 6	3 6	2 0	1 0
Around the World in Eighty Days	7 6	3 6	2 0	1 0
A Floating City	7 6	3 6	2 0	1 0
The Blockade Runners .			2 0	1 0
Dr. Ox's Experiment . .			2 0	1 0
Master Zacharius . . .	7 6	3 6		
A Drama in the Air . .				
A Winter amid the Ice .			2 0	1 0
The Survivors of the "Chancellor"	7 6	3 6	2 0	2 vols. 1s. each.
Martin Paz			2 0	1 0
The Mysterious Island, 3 vols. :—	22 6	10 6	6 0	3 0
Vol. I. Dropped from the Clouds	7 6	3 6	2 0	1 0
Vol. II. Abandoned . .	7 6	3 6	2 0	1 0
Vol. III. Secret of the Island	7 6	3 6	2 0	1 0
The Child of the Cavern .	7 6	3 6	2 0	1 0
The Begum's Fortune . .	7 6	3 6		
The Tribulations of a Chinaman	7 6			
The Steam House, 2 vols.:—				
Vol. I. Demon of Cawnpore	7 6			
Vol. II. Tigers and Traitors	7 6			
The Giant Raft, 2 vols.:—				
Vol. I. Eight Hundred Leagues on the Amazon.	7 6			
Vol. II. The Cryptogram	7 6			

Celebrated Travels and Travellers. 3 vols. Demy 8vo, 600 pp., upwards of 100 full-page illustrations, 12s. 6d. ; gilt edges, 14s. each :—

(1) The Exploration of the World.

(2) The Great Navigators of the Eighteenth Century.

(3) The Great Explorers of the Nineteenth Century.

The giant clave their skulls with the butt end of his gun.

DICK SANDS

THE BOY CAPTAIN

BY

JULES VERNE.

PART II.

AUTHOR'S ILLUSTRATED EDITION.

London:

SAMPSON LOW, MARSTON, SEARLE, & RIVINGTON,

CROWN BUILDINGS, 188, FLEET STREET.

1882.

LONDON:
GILBERT AND RIVINGTON, LIMITED,
ST. JOHN'S SQUARE.

CONTENTS.

LIST OF ILLUSTRATIONS.

DICK SANDS,

THE BOY CAPTAIN.

———◇◇———

CHAPTER I.

THE DARK CONTINENT.

THE "slave-trade" is an expression that ought never to have found its way into any human language. After being long practised at a large profit by such European nations as had possessions beyond the seas, this abominable traffic has now for many years been ostensibly forbidden; yet even in the enlightenment of this nineteenth century, it is still largely carried on, especially in Central Africa, inasmuch as there are several states, professedly Christian, whose signatures have never been affixed to the deed of abolition.

Incredible as it should seem, this barter of human beings still exists, and for the due comprehension of the second part of Dick Sands' story it must be borne in mind, that for the purpose of supplying certain colonies with slaves, there continue to be prosecuted such barbarous "man-hunts" as threaten almost to lay waste an entire continent with blood, fire, and pillage.

The nefarious traffic as far as regards negroes does not appear to have arisen until the fifteenth century. The following are said to be the circumstances under which it had its origin. After being banished from Spain, the Mussulmans crossed the straits of Gibraltar and took refuge upon the shores of Africa, but the Portuguese who then occupied that portion of the coast persecuted the fugitives with the utmost severity, and having captured them in large numbers, sent them as prisoners into Portugal. They were thus the first nucleus of any African slaves that entered Western Europe since the commencement of the Christian era. The majority, however, of these Mussulmans were members of wealthy families, who were prepared to pay almost any amount of money for their release; but no ransom was exorbitant enough to tempt the Portuguese to surrender them; more precious than gold were the strong arms that should work the resources of their young and rising colonies. Thus baulked in their purpose of effecting a direct ransom of their captured relatives, the Mussulman families next submitted a proposition for exchanging them for a larger number of African negroes, whom it would be quite easy to procure. The Portuguese, to whom the proposal was in every way advantageous, eagerly accepted the offer; and in this way the slave-trade was originated in Europe.

By the end of the sixteenth century this odious traffic had become permanently established; in principle it contained nothing repugnant to the semi-barbarous thought and customs then existing; all the great states recognized it as the most effectual means of colonizing the islands of the New World, especially as slaves of negro blood, well acclimatized to tropical heat, were able to survive where white men must have perished by thousands. The transport of slaves to the American colonies was consequently regularly effected by vessels specially built for that purpose, and large depôts for this branch of commerce were established at various points of the African coast. The "goods" cost comparatively little in production, and the profits were enormous.

Yet, after all, however indispensable it might be to complete the foundation of the trans-atlantic colonies, there was

nothing to justify this shameful barter of human flesh and
blood, and the voice of philanthropy began to be heard in
protestation, calling upon all European governments, in the
name of mercy and common humanity, to decree the abolition of the trade at once.

In 1751, the Quakers put themselves at the head of the
abolitionist movement in North America, that very land
where, a hundred years later, the war of secession burst
forth, in which the question of slavery bore the most conspicuous part. Several of the Northern States, Virginia,
Connecticut, Massachusetts, and Pennsylvania prohibited
the trade, liberating the slaves, in spite of the cost, who had
been imported into their territories.

The campaign, thus commenced, was not limited to a few
provinces of the New World ; on this side of the Atlantic,
too, the partisans of slavery were subject to a vigorous
attack. England and France led the van, and energetically
beat up recruits to serve the righteous cause. " Let us lose
our colonies rather than sacrifice our principles," was the
magnanimous watchword that resounded throughout Europe,
and notwithstanding the vast political and commercial
interests involved in the question, it did not go forth in
vain. A living impulse had been communicated to the
liberation-movement. In 1807, England formally prohibited
the slave-trade in her colonies ; France following her
example in 1814. The two great nations then entered upon
a treaty on the subject, which was confirmed by Napoleon
during the Hundred Days.

Hitherto, however, the declaration was purely theoretical.
Slave-ships continued to ply their illicit trade, discharging
their living cargo at many a colonial port. It was evident
that more resolute and practical measures must be taken to
repress the enormity. Accordingly the United States in
1820, and Great Britain in 1824, declared the slave-trade to
be an act of piracy and its perpetrators to be punishable
with death. France soon gave in her adherence to the new

treaty, but the Southern States of America, and the Spanish and Portuguese, not having signed the act of abolition, continued the importation of slaves at a great profit, and this in defiance of the recognized reciprocal right of visitation to verify the flags of suspected ships.

But although the slave-trade by these measures was in a considerable measure reduced, it continued to exist; new slaves were not allowed, but the old ones did not recover their liberty. England was now the first to set a noble example. On the 14th of May, 1833, an Act of Parliament, by a munificent vote of millions of pounds, emancipated all the negroes in the British Colonies, and in August, 1838, 670,000 slaves were declared free men. Ten years later, in 1848, the French Republic liberated the slaves in her colonies to the number of 260,000, and in 1859 the war which broke out between the Federals and Confederates in the United States finished the work of emancipation by extending it to the whole of North America.

Thus, three great powers have accomplished their task of humanity, and at the present time the slave-trade is carried on only for the advantage of the Spanish and Portuguese colonies, or to supply the requirements of the Turkish or Arab populations of the East. Brazil, although she has not emancipated her former slaves, does not receive any new, and all negro children are pronounced free-born.

In contrast, however, to all this, it is not to be concealed that, in the interior of Africa, as the result of wars between chieftains waged for the sole object of making captives, entire tribes are often reduced to slavery, and are carried off in caravans in two opposite directions, some westwards to the Portuguese colony of Angola, others eastwards to Mozambique. Of these miserable creatures, of whom a very small proportion ever reach their destination, some are despatched to Cuba or Madagascar, others to the Arab or Turkish provinces of Asia, to Mecca or Muscat. The

French and English cruisers have practically very little power to control the iniquitous proceedings, because the extent of coast to be watched is so large that a strict and adequate surveillance cannot be maintained. The extent of the odious export is very considerable; no less than 24,000 slaves annually reach the coast, a number that hardly represents a tenth part of those who are massacred or otherwise perish by a deplorable end. After the frightful butcheries, the fields lie devastated, the smouldering villages are void of inhabitants, the rivers reek with bleeding corpses, and wild beasts take undisputed possession of the soil. Livingstone, upon returning to a district, immediately after one of these ruthless raids, said that he could never have recognized it for the same that he had visited only a few months previously; and all other travellers, Grant, Speke, Burton, Cameron, Stanley, describe the wooded plateau of Central Africa as the principal theatre of the barbarous warfare between chief and chief. In the region of the great lakes, throughout the vast district which feeds the market of Zanzibar, in Bornu and Fezzan, further south on the banks of the Nyassa and Zambesi, further west in the districts of the Upper Zaire, just traversed by the intrepid Stanley, everywhere there is the recurrence of the same scenes of ruin, slaughter, and devastation. Ever and again the question seems to be forced upon the mind whether slavery is not to end in the entire annihilation of the negro race, so that, like the Australian tribes of South Holland, it will become extinct. Who can doubt that the day must dawn which will herald the closing of the markets in the Spanish and Portuguese colonies, a day when civilized nations shall no longer tolerate the perpetration of this barbarous wrong?

It is hardly too much to say that another year ought to witness the emancipation of every slave in the possession of Christian states. It seems only too likely that for years to come the Mussulman nations will continue to depopulate the continent of Africa; to them is due the chief emigration of the natives, who, torn from their provinces, are sent to the eastern coast in numbers that exceed 40,000 annually. Long before the Egyptian expedition the natives of Sennaar were sold to the natives of Darfur and *vice versâ;* and even Napoleon Buonaparte purchased a considerable number of negroes, whom he organized into regiments after the fashion of the mamelukes. Altogether it may be affirmed, that although four-fifths of the present century have passed away, slave-traffic in Africa has been increased rather than diminished.

The truth is that Islamism really nurtures the slave-trade. In Mussulman provinces, the black slave has taken the place of the white slave of former times ; dealers of the most questionable character bear their part in the execrable business, bringing a supplementary population to races which, unregenerated by their own labour, would otherwise diminish and ultimately disappear.

As in the time of Buonaparte, these slaves often become soldiers ; on the Upper Niger, for instance, they still form half the army of certain chieftains, under circumstances in which their lot is hardly, if at all, inferior to that of free men.   Elsewhere, where the slave is not a soldier, he counts merely as current coin ; and in Bornu and even in Egypt, we are told by William Lejean, an eye-witness, that officers and other functionaries have received their pay in this form.

Such, then, appears to be the present actual condition of the slave-trade ; and it is stern justice that compels the additional statement that there are representatives of certain great European powers who still favour the unholy traffic with an indulgent connivance, and whilst cruisers are watching the coasts of the Atlantic and of the Indian Ocean, kidnapping goes on regularly in the interior, caravans pass along under the very eyes of certain officials, and massacres are perpetrated in which frequently ten negroes are sacrificed in the capture of a single slave.

It was the knowledge, more or less complete, of all this, that wrung from Dick Sands his bitter and heart-rending cry :—

"We are in Africa ! in the very haunt of slave-drivers !"

Too true it was that he found himself and his companions in a land fraught with such frightful peril. He could only tremble when he wondered on what part of the fatal continent the "Pilgrim" had stranded. Evidently it was at some point of the west coast, and he had every reason to fear that it was on the shores of Angola, the rendezvous for all the caravans that journey in that portion of Africa.

His conjecture was correct ; he really was in the very country that a few years later and with gigantic effort was to be traversed by Cameron in the south and Stanley in the north. Of the vast territory, with its three provinces, Congo, Angola, and Benguela, little was then known except the coast. It extends from the Zaire on the north to the Nourse on the south, and its chief towns are the ports of Benguela and of St. Paul de Loanda, the capital of the colony, which is a dependency of the kingdom of Portugal. The interior of the country had been almost entirely unexplored. Very few were the travellers who had cared to venture far inland, for an unhealthy climate, a hot, damp soil conducive to fever, a permanent warfare between the native tribes, some of which are cannibals, and the ill-feeling of the slave-dealers against any stranger who might endeavour to discover the secrets of their infamous craft, all combine to render the region one of the most hazardous in the whole of Equatorial Africa.

It was in 1816 that Tuckey ascended the Congo as far as the Yellaba Falls, a distance not exceeding 200 miles ; but the journey was too short to give an accurate idea of the interior of the country, and moreover cost the lives of nearly all the officers and scientific men connected with the expedition.

Thirty-seven years afterwards, Dr. Livingstone had

advanced from the Cape of Good Hope to the Upper Zambesi ; thence, with a fearlessness hitherto unrivalled, he crossed the Coango, an affluent of the Congo, and after having traversed the continent from the extreme south to the east he reached St. Paul de Loanda on the 31st of May, 1854, the first explorer of the unknown portions of the great Portuguese colony.

Eighteen years elapsed, and two other bold travellers crossed the entire continent from east to west, and after encountering unparalleled difficulties, emerged, the one to the south, the other to the north of Angola.

The first of these was Verney Lovett Cameron, a lieutenant in the British navy. In 1872, when serious doubts were entertained as to the safety of the expedition sent out under Stanley to the relief of Livingstone in the great lake district, Lieutenant Cameron volunteered to go out in search of the noble missionary explorer. His offer was accepted, and accompanied by Dr. Dillon, Lieutenant Cecil Murphy, and Robert Moffat, a nephew of Livingstone, he started from Zanzibar. Having passed through Ugogo, he met Livingstone's corpse, which was being borne to the eastern coast by his faithful followers. Unshaken in his resolve to make his way right across the continent, Cameron still pushed onwards to the west. He passed through Unyanyembe and Uganda, and reached Kawele, where he secured all Livingstone's papers. After exploring Lake Tanganyika he crossed the mountains of Bambarre, and finding himself unable to descend the course of the Lualaba, he traversed the provinces devastated and depopulated by war and the slave-trade, Kilemba, Urua, the sources of the Lomani, Ulanda, and Lovalé, and having crossed the Coanza, he sighted the Atlantic and reached the port of St. Philip de Benguela, after a journey that had occupied three years and five months. Cameron's two companions, Dr. Dillon and Robert Moffat, both succumbed to the hardships of the expedition.

The intrepid Englishman was soon to be followed into the

field by an American, Mr. Henry Moorland Stanley. It is universally known how the undaunted correspondent of the *New York Herald*, having been despatched in search of Livingstone, found the veteran missionary at Ujiji, on the borders of Lake Tanganyika, on the 31st of October, 1871. But what he had undertaken in the cause of humanity Stanley longed to continue in the interests of science, his prime object being to make a thorough investigation of the Lualaba, of which, in his first expedition, he had only been able to get a partial and imperfect survey. Accordingly, whilst Cameron was still deep in the provinces of Central Africa, Stanley started from Bagamoyo in November, 1874. Twenty-one months later he quitted Ujiji, which had been decimated by small-pox, and in seventy-four days accomplished the passage of the lake and reached Nyangwe, a great slave-market previously visited both by Livingstone and Cameron. He was also present at some of the horrible razzias, perpetrated by the officers of the Sultan of Zanzibar in the districts of the Marunzu and Manyuema.

In order to be in a position to descend the Lualaba to its very mouth, Stanley engaged at Nyangwe 140 porters and nineteen boats. Difficulties arose from the very outset, and not only had he to contend with the cannibals of Ugusu, but, in order to avoid many unnavigable cataracts, he had to convey his boats many miles by land. Near the equator, just at the point where the Lualaba turns north-north-west, Stanley's little convoy was attacked by a fleet of boats, manned by several hundred natives, whom, however, he succeeded in putting to flight. Nothing daunted, the resolute American pushed on to lat. 20° N. and ascertained, beyond room for doubt, that the Lualaba was really the Upper Zaire or Congo, and that, by following its course, he should come directly to the sea.

Beset with many perils was the way. Stanley was in almost daily collision with the various tribes upon the river-banks; on the 3rd of June, 1877, he lost one of his companions, Frank Pocock, at the passage of the cataracts of Massassa, and on the 18th of July he was himself carried in his boat into the Mbelo Falls, and escaped by little short of a miracle.

On the 6th of August, the daring adventurer arrived at the village of Ni Sanda, only four days from the sea ; two days later he received a supply of provisions that had been sent by two Emboma merchants to Banza M'buko, the little coast-town where, after a journey of two years and nine months, fraught with every kind of hardship and privation, he completed his transit of the mighty continent. His toil told, at least temporarily, upon his years, but he had the grand satisfaction of knowing that he had traced the whole course of the Lualaba, and had ascertained, beyond reach of question, that as the Nile is the great artery of the north, and the Zambesi of the east, so Africa possesses in the west a third great river, which in a course of no less than 2900 miles, under the names of the Lualaba, Zaire, and Congo, unites the lake district with the Atlantic Ocean.

In 1873, however, the date at which the " Pilgrim " foundered upon the coast, very little was known of the province of Angola, except that it was the scene of the western slave-trade, of which the markets of Bihe, Cassanga, and Kazunde were the chief centres. This was the country in which Dick Sands now found himself, a hundred miles from shore, in charge of a lady exhausted with fatigue and anxiety, a half-dying child, and a band of negroes who would be a most tempting bait to the slave-driver.

His last illusion was completely dispelled. He had no longer the faintest hope that he was in America, that land where little was to be dreaded from either native, wild beast, or climate ; he could no more cherish the fond impression that he might be in the pleasant region between the Cordilleras and the coast, where villages are numerous and missions afford hospitable shelter to every traveller. Far, far away were those provinces of Bolivia and Peru, to which (unless a criminal hand had interposed) the " Pilgrim " would certainly have sped her way. No: too truly this was the terrible province of Angola ; and worse than all, not the district near the coast, under the surveillance of the Portuguese authorities, but the interior of the country, traversed only by slave caravans, driven under the lash of the havildars.

Limited, in one sense, was the knowledge that Dick Sands possessed of this land of horrors ; but he had read the accounts that had been given by the missionaries of the sixteenth and seventeenth centuries, by the Portuguese traders who frequented the route from St. Paul de Loanda, by San Salvador to the Zaire, as well as by Dr. Livingstone in his travels in 1853, and consequently he knew enough to awaken immediate and complete despair in any spirit less indomitable than his own.

Anyhow, his position was truly appalling

CHAPTER II.

ACCOMPLICES.

ON the day following that on which Dick Sands and his party had made their last halt in the forest, two men met by appointment at a spot about three miles distant.

The two men were Harris and Negoro, the one lately landed from New Zealand, the other pursuing his wonted occupation of slave-dealer in the province of Angola. They were seated at the foot of an enormous banyan-tree, on the banks of a rushing torrent that streamed between tall borders of papyrus. After the conversation had turned awhile upon the events of the last few hours, Negoro said abruptly,—

"Couldn't you manage to get that young fifteen-year-old any farther into the interior?"

"No, indeed; it was a hard matter enough to bring him thus far; for the last few days his suspicions have been wide awake."

"But just another hundred miles, you know," continued Negoro, "would have finished the business off well, and those black fellows would have been ours to a dead certainty."

"Don't I tell you, my dear fellow, that it was more than time for me to give them the slip?" replied Harris, shrugging his shoulders. "Only too well I knew that our young friend was longing to put a shot into my body, and that was a sugar-plum I might not be able to digest."

The Portuguese gave a grunt of assent, and Harris went on,—

"For several days I succeeded well enough. I managed

to palm off the country as the forest of Atacama, which you may recollect I once visited ; but when the youngster began to ask for gutta-percha and humming-birds, and his mother wanted quinquina-trees, and when that old fool of a cousin was bent on finding cocuyos, I was rather nonplussed. One day I had to swear that giraffes were ostriches, but the young captain did not seem to swallow the dose at all easily. Then we saw traces of elephants and hippopotamuses, which of course are as often seen in America as an honest man in a Benguela penitentiary ; then that old nigger Tom discovered a lot of forks and chains left by some runaway slaves at the foot of a tree ; but when, last of all, a lion roared,—and the noise, you know, is rather louder than the mewing of a cat,—I thought it was time to take my horse and decamp."

Negoro repeated his expression of regret that the whole party had not been carried another hundred miles into the province.

"It really cannot be helped," rejoined the American ; "I have done the best I could ; and I think, mate," he added confidentially, "that you have done wisely in following the caravan at a good distance ; that dog of theirs evidently owes you a grudge, and might prove an ugly customer."

"I shall put a bullet into that beast's head before long," growled Negoro.

"Take care you don't get one through your own first," laughed Harris ; "that young Sands, I warn you, is a first-rate shot, and between ourselves, is rather a fine fellow of his kind."

"Fine fellow, indeed !" sneered Negoro ; "whatever he is, he is a young upstart, and I have a long score to wipe off against him ;" and, as he spoke, an expression of the utmost malignity passed over his countenance.

Harris smiled.

"Well, mate," he said ; "your travels have not improved your temper, I see. But come now, tell me what you have been doing all this time. When I found you just after the wreck, at the mouth of the Longa, you had only time to ask me to get this party, somehow or other, up into the country. But it is just upon two years since you left Cassange with that caravan of slaves for our old master Alvez. What have you been doing since ? The last I heard of you was that you had run foul of an English cruiser, and that you were condemned to be hanged."

"So I was very nearly," muttered Negoro.

"Ah, well, that will come sooner or later," rejoined the American with philosophic indifference ; "men of our trade can't expect to die quietly in our beds, you know. But were you caught by the English ?"

"No, by the Portuguese."

"Before you had got rid of your cargo ?"

Negoro hesitated a moment before replying.

"No," he said, presently, and added, "The Portuguese have changed their game : for a long time they carried on the trade themselves, but now they have got wonderfully particular ; so I was caught, and condemned to end my days in the penitentiary at St. Paul de Loanda."

"Confound it ! " exclaimed Harris, "a hundred times better be hanged !"

"I'm not so sure of that," the Portuguese replied, "for when I had been at the galleys about a fortnight I managed to escape, and got into the hold of an English steamer bound for New Zealand. I wedged myself in between a cask of water and a case of preserved meat, and so managed to exist for a month. It was close quarters, I can tell you, but I preferred to travel incognito rather than run the risk of being handed over again to the authorities at Loanda."

"Well done ! " exclaimed the American, " and so you had a free passage to the land of the Maoris. But you didn't come back in the same fashion ? "

"No ; I always had a hankering to be here again at my old trade ; but for a year and a half . . . ."

He stopped abruptly, and grasped Harris by the arm.

"Hush," he whispered, "didn't you hear a rustling in that clump of papyrus?"

In a moment Harris had caught up his loaded gun ; and both men, starting to their feet, looked anxiously around them.

"It was nothing," said Harris presently ; "the stream is swollen by the storm, that is all ; your two years' travelling has made you forget the sounds of the forest, mate. Sit down again, and go on with your story. When I know the past, I shall be better able to talk about the future."

They reseated themselves, and Negoro went on,—

"For a whole year and a half I vegetated at Auckland. I left the hold of the steamer without a dollar in my pocket, and had to turn my hand to every trade imaginable in order to get a living."

"Poor fellow ! I daresay you even tried the trade of being an honest man," put in the American.

"Just so," said Negoro, "and in course of time the ' Pilgrim,' the vessel by which I came here, put in at Auckland. While she was waiting to take Mrs. Weldon and her party. on board, I applied to the captain for a post, for I was once mate on board a slaver, and know something of seamanship. The ' Pilgrim's ' crew was complete, but fortunately the ship's cook had just deserted ; I offered to supply his place ; in default of better my services were accepted, and in a few days we were out of sight of New Zealand."

"I have heard something about the voyage from young Sands," said Harris, "but even now I can't understand how you reached here."

"Neither does he," said Negoro, with a malicious grin. "I will tell you now, and you may repeat the story to your young friend if you like."

"Well, go on," said Harris.

"When we started," continued Negoro, "it was my intention to sail only as far as Chili : that would have brought me nearly half way to Angola ; but three weeks after leaving Auckland, Captain Hull and all his crew were lost in chasing a whale, and I and the apprentice were the only seamen left on board."

"Then why in the name of peace didn't you take command of the ship ?" exclaimed Harris.

"Because there were five strong niggers who didn't trust me ; so, on second thoughts, I determined to keep my old post as cook."

"Then do you mean to say that it was mere accident that brought you to the coast of Africa ?"

"Not a bit of it ; the only accident,—and a very lucky one it was—was meeting you on the very spot where we stranded. But it was my doing that we got so far. Young Sands understood nothing more of navigation than the use of the log and compass. Well, one fine day, you understand, the log remained at the bottom of the sea, and one night the compass was tampered with, so that the ' Pilgrim,' scudding along before a tempest, was carried altogether out of her course. You may imagine the young captain was puzzled at the length of the voyage ; it would have bewildered a more experienced head than his. Before he was aware of it, we had rounded Cape Horn ; I recognized it through the mist. Then at once I put the compass to rights again, and the ' Pilgrim ' was carried north-eastwards by a tremendous hurricane to the very place I wanted. The island Dick Sands took for Easter Island was really Tristan d'Acunha."

"Good !" said Harris ; "I think I understand now how our friends have been persuaded to take Angola for Bolivia. But they are undeceived now, you know," he added.

"I know all about that," replied the Portuguese.

"Then what do you intend to do?" said Harris.

"You will see," answered Negoro significantly ; "but first of all tell me something about our employer, old Alvez ; how is he ?"

" Oh, the old rascal is well enough, and will be delighted to see you again," replied Harris.

" Is he at the market at Bihe ? "

" No, he has been at his place at Kazoundé for a year or more."

" And how does business go on ? "

" Badly enough, on this coast," said Harris ; "plenty of slaves are waiting to be shipped to the Spanish colonies, but the difficulty is how to get them embarked. The Portuguese authorities on the one hand, and the English cruisers on the other, almost put a stop to exportation altogether ; down to the south, near Mossamedes, is the only part where it can be attempted with any chance of success. To pass a caravan through Benguela or Loande is an utter impossibility ; neither the governors nor the chefés[1] will listen to a word of reason. Old Alvez is therefore thinking of going in the other direction towards Nyangwe and Lake Tanganyika ; he can there exchange his goods for slaves and ivory, and is sure to do a good business with Upper Egypt and the coast of Mozambique, which supplies Madagascar. But I tell you, Negoro," he added gravely, " I believe the time is coming when the slave-trade will come to an end altogether. The English missionaries are advancing into the interior. That fellow Livingstone, confound him ! has finished his tour of the lakes, and is now working his way towards Angola ; then there is another man named Cameron who is talking about crossing the continent from east to west, and it is feared that Stanley the American will do the same. All this exploration, you know, is ruinous to our business, and it is to our interest that not one of these travellers should be allowed to return to tell tales of us in Europe."

Harris spoke like a merchant embarrassed by a temporary commercial crisis. The atrocious scenes to which the slave-dealers are accustomed seems to render them impervious to all sense of justice or humanity, and they learn to regard

[1] Subordinate Portuguese governors at secondary stations.

their living merchandise with as small concern as though they were dealing with chests of tea or hogsheads of sugar.

But Harris was right when he asserted that civilization must follow the wake of the intrepid pioneers of African discovery. Livingstone first, and after him, Grant, Speke, Burton, Cameron, Stanley, are the heroes whose names will ever be linked with the first dawnings of a brighter age upon the dark wilds of Equatorial Africa.

Having ascertained that his accomplice had returned unscrupulous and daring as ever, and fully prepared to pursue his former calling as an agent of old Alvez the slave-dealer, Harris inquired what he proposed doing with the survivors of the "Pilgrim" now that they were in his hands.

"Divide them into two lots," answered Negoro, without a moment's hesitation, "one for the market, the other . . . ."

He did not finish his sentence, but the expression of his countenance was an index to the malignity of his purpose.

"Which shall you sell?" asked the American.

"The niggers, of course. The old one is not worth much, but the other four ought to fetch a good price at Kazoundé."

"Yes, you are right," said Harris; 'American-born slaves, with plenty of work in them, are rare articles, and very different to the miserable wretches we get up the country. But you never told me," he added, suddenly changing the subject, "whether you found any money on board the 'Pilgrim'!"

"Oh, I rescued a few hundred dollars from the wreck, that was all," said the Portuguese carelessly; "but I am expecting . . . ." he stopped short.

"What are you expecting?" inquired Harris eagerly.

"Oh, nothing, nothing," said Negoro, apparently annoyed that he had said so much, and immediately began talking of the means of securing the living prey which he had been taking so many pains to entrap. Harris informed him that on the Coanza, about ten miles distant, there was at the present time encamped a slave caravan, under the control of

Dingo disappeared again amongst the bushes.

an Arab named Ibn Hamish ; plenty of native soldiers were there on guard, and if Dick Sands and his people could only be induced to travel in that direction, their capture would be a matter of very little difficulty.   He said that of course Dick Sands' first thought would naturally be how to get back to the coast ; it was not likely that he would venture a second time through the forest, but would in all probability try to make his way to the nearest river, and descend its course on a raft to the sea.   The nearest river was undoubtedly the Coanza, so that he and Negoro might feel quite sure of meeting " their friends " upon its banks.

" If you really think so," said Negoro, " there is not much time to be lost ; whatever young Sands determines to do, he will do at once : he never lets the grass grow under his feet."

" Let us start, then, this very moment, mate," was Harris's reply.

Both rose to their feet, when they were startled by the same rustling in the papyrus which had previously aroused Negoro's fears.   Presently a low growl was heard, and a large dog, showing his teeth, emerged from the bushes, evidently prepared for an attack.

" It's Dingo ! " exclaimed Harris.

" Confound the brute ! he shall not escape me this time," said Negoro.

He caught up Harris's gun, and raising it to his shoulder, he fired just as the dog was in the act of springing at his throat.   A long whine of pain followed the report, and Dingo disappeared again amongst the bushes that fringed the stream. Negoro was instantly upon his track, but could discover nothing beyond a few blood-stains upon the stalks of the papyrus, and a long crimson trail upon the pebbles on the bank.

" I think I have done for the beast now," was Negoro's remark as he returned from his fruitless search.

Harris, who had been a silent spectator of the whole scene, now asked coolly,—

"What makes that animal have such an inveterate dislike to you?"

"Oh, there is an old score to settle between us," replied the Portuguese.

"What about?" inquired the American.

Negoro made no reply, and finding him evidently disinclined to be communicative on the subject, Harris did not press the matter any further.

A few moments later the two men were descending the stream, and making their way through the forest towards the Coanza.

CHAPTER III.

ON THE MARCH AGAIN.

"AFRICA! Africa!" was the terrible word that echoed and re-echoed in the mind of Dick Sands. As he pondered over the events of the preceding weeks he could now understand why, notwithstanding the rapid progress of the ship, the land seemed ever to be receding, and why the voyage had been prolonged to twice its anticipated length. It remained, however, a mystery inexplicable as before, how and when they had rounded Cape Horn and passed into another ocean. Suddenly the idea flashed upon him that the compass must have been tampered with; and he remembered the fall of the first compass; he recalled the night when he had been roused by Tom's cry of alarm that Negoro had fallen against the binnacle. As he recollected these circumstances he became more and more convinced that it was Negoro who was the mainspring of all the mischief; that it was he who had contrived the loss of the "Pilgrim," and compromised the safety of all on board.

What had been the career, what could be the motives of a man who was capable of such vile machinations?

But shrouded in mystery as were the events of the past, the present offered a prospect equally obscure.

Beyond the fact that he was in Africa and a hundred miles from the coast, Dick knew absolutely nothing. He could only conjecture that he was in the fatal province of Angola, and assured as he was that Harris had acted the traitor, he was led to the conclusion that he and Negoro had been playing into each other's hands. The result of the collision, he feared, might be very disastrous to the survivors of the "Pilgrim." Yet, in what manner would the odious stratagem be accomplished? Dick could well understand that the negroes would be sold for slaves; he could only too easily imagine that upon himself Negoro would wreak the vengeance he had so obviously been contemplating; but for Mrs. Weldon and the other helpless members of the party what fate could be in store?

The situation was terrible, but yet Dick did not flinch; he had been appointed captain, and captain he would remain; Mrs. Weldon and her little son had been committed to his charge, and he was resolved to carry out his trust faithfully to the end.

For several hours he remained wrapped in thought, pondering over the present and the future, weighing the evil chances against the good, only to be convinced that the evil much preponderated. At length he rose, firm, resolute, calm. The first glimmer of dawn was breaking upon the forest. All the rest of the party, except Tom, were fast asleep. Dick Sands crept softly up to the old negro, and whispered,—

"Tom, you know now where we are!"

"Yes, yes, Mr. Dick, only too well I know it. We are in Africa!"

The old man sighed mournfully.

"Tom," said Dick, in the same low voice, "you must keep this a secret; you must not say a word to let Mrs. Weldon or any of the others know."

The old man murmured his assent, and Dick continued :—

"It will be quite enough for them to learn that we have been betrayed by Harris, and that we must consequently practise extra care and watchfulness; they will merely think we are taking precautions against being surprised by nomad Indians. I trust to your good sense, Tom, to assist me in this."

"You may depend upon me, Mr. Dick ; and I can promise you that we will all do our best to prove our courage, and to show our devotion to your service."

Thus assured of Tom's co-operation, Dick proceeded to deliberate upon his future line of action. He had every reason to believe that the treacherous American, startled by the traces of the slaves and the unexpected roaring of the lion, had taken flight before he had conducted his victims to the spot where they were to be attacked, and that consequently some hours might elapse before he would be joined by Negoro, who (to judge from Dingo's strange behaviour) had undoubtedly for the last few days been somewhere on their track.

Here was a delay that might be turned to good account, and no time was to be lost in taking advantage of it to commence their return journey to the coast. If, as Dick had every reason to suppose, he was in Angola, he hoped to find, either north or south, some Portuguese settlement whence he could obtain the means of transporting his party to their several homes.

But how was this return journey to be accomplished ? It would be difficult, not to say imprudent, to retrace their footsteps through the forest ; it would merely bring them to their starting-point, and would, moreover, afford an easy track for Negoro or his accomplices to follow. The safest and most secret means of reaching the coast would assuredly be by descending the course of some river. This would have to be effected by constructing a strong raft, from which the little party, well armed, might defend themselves alike from attacks either of the natives or of wild beasts, and which would likewise afford a comfortable means of transport for Mrs. Weldon and her little boy, who were now deprived of the use of Harris's horse. The negroes, it is true, would be only too pleased to carry the lady on a litter of branches, but this would be to occupy the services of two out of five, and under the circumstances it was manifestly advisable that all hands should be free to act on the defensive. Another great inducement towards the plan was that Dick Sands felt himself much more at home in travelling by water than by land, and was longing to be once again upon what to him was, as it were, his native element. He little dreamt that he was devising for himself the very plan that Harris, in his speculations, had laid down for him !

The most urgent matter was now to find such a stream as would suit their purpose. Dick had several reasons for feeling sure that one existed in the neighbourhood. He knew that the little river, which fell into the Atlantic near the spot where the " Filgrim " stranded, could not extend very far either to the north or east, because the horizon was bounded in both directions by the chain of mountains which he had taken for the Cordilleras. If the stream did not rise in those hills it must incline to the south, so that in either case Dick was convinced he could not be long in discovering it or one of its affluents. Another sign, which he recognized as hopeful, was that during the last few miles of the march the soil had become moist and level, whilst here and there the appearance of tiny rivulets indicated that an aqueous network existed in the subsoil. On the previous day, too, the caravan had skirted a rushing torrent, of which the waters were tinged with oxide of iron from its sloping banks.

Dick's scheme was to make his way back as far as this stream, which, though not navigable itself, would in all probability empty itself into some affluent of greater importance. The idea, which he imparted to Tom, met with the old negro's entire approval.

As the day dawned the sleepers, one by one, awoke. Mrs. Weldon laid little Jack in Nan's arms. The child was still dozing ; the fever had abated, but he looked painfully white and exhausted after the attack.

" Dick," said Mrs. Weldon, after looking round her, " where is Mr. Harris ? I cannot see him."

" Harris has left us," answered Dick very quietly.

" Do you mean that he has gone on ahead ?"

" No, madam, I mean that he has left us, and gone away entirely : he is in league with Negoro."

" In league with Negoro !" cried Mrs. Weldon. "Ah, I have had a fancy lately that there has been something wrong : but why ? what can be their motive ?"

" Indeed I am unable to tell you," replied Dick ; " I only know that we have no alternative but to return to the coast immediately if we would escape the two rascals."

" I only wish I could catch them," said Hercules, who had overheard the conversation ; " I would soon knock their heads together ;" and he shook his two fists in giving emphasis to his words.

" But what will become of my boy ?" cried Mrs. Weldon, in tones of despondency ; " I have been so sanguine in procuring him the comforts of San Felice."

" Master Jack will be all right enough, madam, when we get into a more healthy situation near the coast," said Tom.

" But is there no farm anywhere near ? no village ? no shelter ?" she pleaded.

" None whatever, madam ; I can only repeat that it is absolutely necessary that we make the best of our way back to the sea-shore."

" Are you quite sure, Dick, that Mr. Harris has deceived us ?"

Dick felt that he should be glad to avoid any discussion on the subject, but with a warning glance at Tom, he proceeded to say that on the previous night he and Tom had discovered the American's treachery, and that if he had not instantly taken to his horse and fled he would have answered for his guilt with his life. Without, however, dwelling for a moment more than he could avoid upon the past, he hurried on to detail the means by which he now proposed to reach the sea, concluding by the assertion that he hoped a very few miles' march would bring them to a stream on which they might be able to embark.

Mrs. Weldon, thoroughly ignoring her own weakness, professed her readiness not only to walk, but to carry Jack too. Bat and Austin at once volunteered to carry her in a litter; of this the lady would not hear, and bravely repeated her intention of travelling on foot, announcing her willingness to start without further delay. Dick Sands was only too glad to assent to her wish.

"Let me take Master Jack," said Hercules; "I shall be out of my element if I have nothing to carry."

The giant, without waiting for a reply, took the child from Nan's arms so gently that he did not even rouse him from his slumber.

The weapons were next carefully examined, and the provisions, having been repacked into one parcel, were consigned to the charge of Actæon, who undertook to carry them on his back.

Cousin Benedict, whose wiry limbs seemed capable of bearing any amount of fatigue, was quite ready to start. It was doubtful whether he had noticed Harris's disappearance; he was suffering from a loss which to him was of far greater importance. He had mislaid his spectacles and magnifying-glass. It had happened that Bat had picked them up in the long grass, close to the spot where the amateur naturalist had been lying, but acting on a hint from Dick Sands, he said nothing about them; in this way the entomologist, who, without his glasses could scarcely see a yard beyond his face, might be expected to be kept without trouble in the limits of the ranks, and having been placed between Actæon and Austin with strict injunctions not to leave their side, he followed them as submissively as a blind man in leading-strings.

The start was made. But scarcely had the little troop advanced fifty yards upon their way, when Tom suddenly cried out, "Where's Dingo?"

With all the force of his tremendous lungs, Hercules gave a series of reverberating shouts :—

" Dingo ! Dingo ! Dingo !"

Not a bark could be distinguished in reply.

" Dingo ! Dingo ! Dingo !" again echoed in the air.

But all was silence.

Dick was intensely annoyed at the non-appearance of the dog ; his presence would have been an additional safeguard in the event of any sudden surprise.

" Perhaps he has followed Harris," suggested Tom.

" Far more likely he is on the track of Negoro," rejoined Dick.

" Then Negoro, to a dead certainty," said Hercules, " will put a bullet into his head."

" It is to be hoped," replied Bat, " that Dingo will strangle him first."

Dick Sands, disguising his vexation, said,—

" At any rate, we have no time to wait for the animal now : if he is alive, he will not fail to find us out. Move on, my lads ! move on ! "

The weather was very hot ; ever since daybreak heavy clouds had been gathering upon the horizon, and it seemed hardly likely that the day would pass without a storm. Fortunately the woods were sufficiently light to ensure a certain amount of freshness to the surface of the soil. Here and there were large patches of tall, rank grass enclosed by clumps of forest trees. In some places, fossilized trunks, lying on the ground, betokened the existence of one of the coal districts that are common upon the continent of Africa. Along the glades the carpet of verdure was relieved by crimson stems and a variety of flowers ; ginger-blossoms, blue and yellow, pale lobelias, and red orchids fertilized by the numerous insects that incessantly hovered about them. The trees did not grow in impenetrable masses of one species, but exhibited themselves in infinite variety. There was also a species of palm producing an oil locally much valued ; there were cotton-plants growing in bushes eight or ten feet high, the cotton attached in long shreds to the ligneous stalks; and there were copals from which, pierced by the proboscis of certain insects, exudes an odorous resin that flows on to the ground and is collected by the natives. Then there were citrons and wild pomegranates, and a score of other arborescent plants, all testifying to the fertility of this plateau of Central Africa. In many places, too, the air was fragrant with the odour of vanilla, though it was not possible to discover the shrub from which the perfume emanated.

In spite of it being the dry season, so that the soil had only been moistened by occasional storms, all trees and plants were flourishing in great luxuriance. It was the time of year for fever, but according to Dr. Livingstone's observation, the disorder may generally be cured by quitting the locality where it has been contracted. Dick expressed his hope that, in little Jack's case, the words of the great traveller would be verified, and in encouragement of this sanguine view, pointed out to Mrs. Weldon that although it was past the time for the periodical return of the fever, the child was still slumbering quietly in Hercules' arms.

The march was continued with as much rapidity as was consistent with caution. Occasionally, where the bushes and brushwood had been broken down by the recent passage of men or beasts, progress was comparatively easy; but much more frequently, greatly to Dick's annoyance, obstacles of various sorts impeded their advance. Climbing plants grew in such inextricable confusion that they could only be compared to a ship's rigging involved in hopeless entanglement; there were creepers resembling curved scimitars, thickly covered with sharp thorns; there were likewise strange growths, like vegetable serpents, fifty or sixty feet long, which seemed to have a cruel faculty for torturing every passenger with their prickly spines. Axe in hand, the negroes had repeatedly to cut their road through these bewildering obstructions that clothed the trees from their summit to their base.

Animal life was no less remarkable in its way than the vegetation. Birds in great variety flitted about in the ample foliage, secure from any stray shot from the little band, whose chief object it was to preserve its incognito. Guinea-fowls were seen in considerable numbers, francolins in several varieties, and a few specimens of the bird to which the Americans, in imitation of their note, have given the name of " whip-poor-will." If Dick had not had too much evidence in other ways to the contrary, he might almost have imagined himself in a province of the New World.

Hitherto they had been unmolested by any dangerous wild beasts. During the present stage of their march a herd of giraffes, startled by their unexpected approach, rushed fleetly past ; this time, however, without being represented as ostriches. Occasionally a dense cloud of dust on the edge of the prairie, accompanied by the sound like the roll of heavily laden chariots, betokened the flight of a herd of buffaloes ; but with these exceptions no animal of any magnitude appeared in view.

For about two miles Dick followed the course of the rivulet, in the hope that it would emerge into a more important stream, which would convey them without much difficulty or danger direct to the sea.

Towards noon about three miles had been accomplished, and a halt was made for rest. Neither Negoro nor Harris had been seen, nor had Dingo reappeared. The encampment for the midday refreshment was made under the shelter of a clump of bamboos, which effectually concealed them all. Few words were spoken during the meal. Mrs. Weldon could eat nothing ; she had again taken her little boy into her arms, and seemed wholly absorbed in watching him. Again and again Dick begged her to take some nourishment, urging upon her the necessity of keeping up her strength.

"We shall not be long in finding a good current to carry us to the coast," said the lad brightly.

Mrs. Weldon raised her eyes to his animated features. With so sanguine and resolute a leader, with such devoted servants as the five negroes in attendance, she felt that she ought not utterly to despair. Was she not, after all, on friendly soil? what great harm could Harris perpetrate against her or her belongings? She would hope still, hope for the best.

Rejoiced as he was to see something of its former brightness return to her countenance, Dick nevertheless had scarcely courage steadily to return her searching gaze. Had she known the whole truth, he knew that her heart must fail her utterly.

CHAPTER IV.

ROUGH TRAVELLING.

JUST at this moment Jack woke up and put his arms round his mother's neck. His eyes were brighter, and there was manifestly no return of fever.

"You are better, darling !" said Mrs. Weldon, pressing him tenderly to her.

"Yes, mamma, I am better ; but I am very thirsty."

Some cold water was soon procured, which the child drank eagerly, and then began to look about him. His first inquiry was for his old friends, Dick and Hercules, both of whom approached at his summons and greeted him affectionately.

"Where is the horse ?" was the next question.

"Gone away, Master Jack ; I am your horse now," said Hercules.

"But you have no bridle for me to hold," said Jack, looking rather disappointed.

"You may put a bit in my mouth if you like, Master Jack," replied Hercules, extending his jaws, "and then you may pull as hard as you please."

"O, I shall not pull very hard," said Jack ; "but haven't we nearly come to Mr. Harris's farm ?"

Mrs. Weldon assured the child that they should soon be where they wanted to be, and Dick, finding that the conversation was approaching dangerous ground, proposed that the journey should be now resumed. Mrs. Weldon assented ;

the encampment was forthwith broken up, and the march continued as before.

In order not to lose sight of the watercourse, it was necessary to cut a way right through the underwood; progress was consequently very slow; and a little over a mile was all that was accomplished in about three hours. Footpaths had evidently once existed, but they had all become what the natives term "dead," that is, they had become entirely overgrown with brushwood and brambles. The negroes worked away with a will; Hercules, in particular, who temporarily resigned his charge to Nan, wielded his axe with marvellous effect, all the time giving vent to stentorian groans and grunts, and succeeded in opening the woods before him as if they were being consumed by a devouring fire.

Fortunately this heavy labour was not of very long duration.

After about a mile, an opening of moderate width, converging towards the stream and following its bank, was discovered in the underwood. It was a passage formed by elephants, which apparently by hundreds must be in the habit of traversing this part of the forest. The spongy soil, soaked by the downpour of the rainy season, was everywhere indented with the enormous impressions of their feet.

But it soon became evident that elephants were not the only living creatures that had used this track. Human bones gnawed by beasts of prey, whole human skeletons, still wearing the iron fetters of slavery, everywhere strewed the ground. It was a scene only too common in Central Africa, where like cattle driven to the slaughter, poor miserable men are dragged in caravans for hundreds of weary miles, to perish on the road in countless numbers beneath the trader's lash, to succumb to the mingled horrors of fatigue, privation, and disease, or, if provisions fail, to be butchered, without pity or remorse, by sword and gun.

That slave-caravans had passed that way was too obvious

It was a scene only too common in Central Africa.

to permit a doubt. For at least a mile, at almost every step Dick came in contact with the scattered bones ; while ever and again huge goat-suckers, disturbed by the approach of the travellers, rose with flapping wings, and circled round their heads.

The youth's heart sank with secret dismay lest Mrs. Weldon should divine the meaning of this ghastly scene, and appeal to him for explanation, but fortunately she had again insisted on carrying her little patient, and although the child was fast asleep, he absorbed her whole attention. Nan was by her side, almost equally engrossed. Old Tom alone was fully alive to the significance of his surroundings, and with downcast eyes he mournfully pursued his march. Full of amazement, the other negroes looked right and left upon what might appear to them as the upheaval of some vast cemetery, but they uttered no word of inquiry or surprise.

Meantime the bed of the stream had increased both in breadth and depth, and the rivulet had in a degree lost its character of a rushing torrent. This was a change which Dick Sands observed hopefully, interpreting it as an indication that it might itself become navigable, or would empty itself into some more important tributary of the Atlantic. His resolve was fixed : he would follow its course at all hazards. As soon, therefore, as he found that the elephant's track was quitting the water's edge, he made up his mind to abandon it, and had no hesitation in again resorting to the use of the axe. Once more, then, commenced the labour of cutting a way through the entanglement of bushes and creepers that were thick upon the soil. It was no longer forest through which they were wending their arduous path ; trees were comparatively rare ; only tall clumps of bamboos rose above the grass, so high, however, that even Hercules could not see above them, and the passage of the little troop could only have been discovered by the rustling in the stalks.

In the course of the afternoon the soil became soft and

marshy. It was evident that the travellers were crossing plains that in a long rainy season must be inundated. The ground was carpeted with luxuriant mosses and graceful ferns, and the continual appearance of brown hematite wherever there was a rise in the soil, betokened the existence of a rich vein of metal beneath.

Remembering what he had read in Dr. Livingstone's account of these treacherous swamps, Dick bade his companions take their footing warily. He himself led the way. Tom expressed his surprise that the ground should be so soaked when there had been no rain for some time.

"I think we shall have a storm soon," said Bat.

"All the more reason, then," replied Dick, "why we should get away from these marshes as quickly as possible. Carry Jack again, Hercules; and you, Bat and Austin, keep close to Mrs. Weldon, so as to be able to assist her if she wants your help. But take care, take care, Mr. Benedict!" he cried out in sudden alarm; "what are you doing, sir?"

"I'm slipping in," was poor Benedict's helpless reply. He had trodden upon a kind of quagmire and, as though a trap had been opened beneath his feet, was fast disappearing into the slough. Assistance was immediately rendered, and the unfortunate naturalist was dragged out, covered with mud almost to his waist, but thoroughly satisfied because his precious box of specimens had suffered no injury. Actæon undertook for the future to keep close to his side, and endeavour to avoid a repetition of the mishap.

The accident could not be said to be altogether free from unpleasant consequences. Air-bubbles in great numbers had risen to the surface of the mire from which Benedict had been extricated, and as they burst they disseminated an odious stench that was well-nigh intolerable. The passage of these pestilential districts is not unfrequently very dangerous, and Livingstone, who on several occasions waded through them in mud that reached to his breast, compares them to great sponges composed of black porous earth, in which every footstep causes streams of moisture to ooze out.

For well-nigh half a mile they had now to wend their cautious way across this spongy soil. Mrs. Weldon, ankle-deep in the soft mud, was at last compelled to come to a stand-still ; and Hercules, Bat, and Austin, all resolved that she should be spared further discomfort, and insisted upon weaving some bamboos into a litter, upon which, after much reluctance to become such a burden, she was induced, with Jack beside her, to take her place.

After the delay thus caused, the procession again started on its perilous route. Dick Sands continued to walk at the head, in order to test the stability of the footing ; Actæon followed, holding Cousin Benedict firmly by the arm ; Tom took charge of old Nan, who without his support would certainly have fallen into the quagmire ; and the three other negroes carried the litter in the rear. It was a matter of the greatest difficulty to find a path that was sufficiently firm ; the method they adopted was to pick their way as much as possible on the long rank grass that on the margin of the swamps was tolerably tough ; but in spite of the greatest precaution, there was not one of them who escaped occa-sionally sinking up to his knees in slush.

At about five o'clock they were relieved by finding them-selves on ground of a more clayey character ; it was still soft and porous below, but its surface was hard enough to give a secure foothold. There were watery pores that percolated the subsoil, and these gave evident witness to the proximity of a river-district.

The heat would have been intolerably oppressive if it had not been tempered by some heavy storm-clouds which obstructed the direct influence of the sun's rays. Lightning was observed to be playing faintly about the sky, and there was now and again the low growl of distant thunder. The indications of a gathering storm were too manifest to be disregarded, and Dick could not help being very uneasy. He had heard of the extreme violence of African storms, and knew that torrents of rain, hurricanes that no tree could resist, and thunderbolt after thunderbolt were the usual accompaniment of these tempests. And here in this lowland desert, which too surely would be completely inundated, there would not be a tree to which they could resort for shelter, while it would likewise be utterly vain to hope to obtain a refuge by excavation, as water would be found only two feet below the surface.

After scrutinizing the landscape, however, he noticed some low elevations on the north that seemed to form the boundary of the marshy plain. A few trees were scattered along their summits; if his party could get no other shelter here, he hoped they would be able to find themselves free from any danger caused by the rising flood.

"Push on, friends, push on!" he cried; "three miles more, and we shall be out of this treacherous lowland."

His words served to inspire a fresh confidence, and in spite of all the previous fatigue, every energy was brought into play with renewed vigour. Hercules, in particular, seemed ready to carry the whole party, if it had been in his power.

The storm was not long in beginning. The rising ground was still two miles away. Although the sun was above the horizon, the darkness was almost complete; the over-hanging volumes of vapour sank lower and lower towards the earth, but happily the full force of the deluge which must ultimately come did not descend as yet. Lightning, red and blue, flashed on every side and appeared to cover the ground with a network of flame.

Ever and again the little knot of travellers were in peril of being struck by the thunderbolts which, on that treeless plain, had no other object of attraction. Poor little Jack, who had been awakened by the perpetual crashes, buried his face in terror in Hercules' breast, anxious, however, not to distress his mother by any outward exhibition of alarm. The good-natured negro endeavoured to pacify him by promises that the lightning should not touch him, and the child, ever confident in the protection of his huge friend, lost something of his nervousness.

But it could not be long before the clouds would burst and discharge the threatened down-pour.

" What are we to do, Tom ? " asked Dick, drawing up close to the negro's side.

" We must make a rush for it; push on with all the speed we can."

" But where ? " cried Dick.

" Straight on," was the prompt reply ; " if the rain catches us here on the plain, we shall all be drowned."

" But where are we to go ? " repeated Dick, in despair ; " if only there were a hut !   But look, look there ! "

A vivid flash of lightning had lit up the country, and Dick declared that he could see a camp which could hardly be more than a quarter of a mile ahead.

The negro looked doubtful.

" I saw it too," he assented : " but if it be a camp at all, it would be a camp of natives ; and to fall into that would involve us in a worse fate than the rain."

Another brilliant flash brought the camp once again into relief ; it appeared to be made up of about a hundred conical tents, arranged very symmetrically, each of them being from twelve to fifteen feet in height.   It had the appearance, from a distance, of being deserted ; if it were really so, it would afford just the shelter that was needed ; otherwise, at all hazards, it must be most carefully avoided.

" I will go in advance," said Dick, after a moment's reflection, " and reconnoitre it."

" Let one of us, at least, go with you," replied Tom.

" No, stay where you are ; I shall be much less likely to be discovered if I go alone."

Without another word, he darted off, and was soon lost in the sombre darkness that was only broken by the frequent lightning.

Large drops of rain were now beginning to fall.

Tom and Dick had been walking some little distance in advance of the rest of the party, who consequently had not overheard their conversation. A halt being made, Mrs. Weldon inquired what was the matter. Tom explained that a camp or village had been noticed a little way in front, and that the captain had gone forward to investigate it. Mrs. Weldon asked no further questions, but quietly waited the result. It was only a few minutes before Dick returned.

"You may come on," he cried.

"Is the camp deserted?" asked Tom.

"It is not a camp at all; it is a lot of ant-hills!"

"Ant-hills!" echoed Benedict, suddenly aroused into a state of excitement.

"No doubt of it, Mr. Benedict," replied Dick; "they are ant-hills twelve feet high at least: and I hope we shall be able to get into them."

"Twelve feet!" the naturalist repeated; "they must be those of the termites, the white ants; there is no other insect that could make them. Wonderful architects are the termites."

"Termites, or whatever they are, they will have to turn out for us," said Dick.

"But they will eat us up!" objected Benedict.

"I can't help that," retorted Dick; "go we must, and go at once."

"But stop a moment," continued the provoking naturalist; "stop, and tell me: I can't be wrong: I always thought that white ants could never be found elsewhere than in Africa."

"Come along, sir, I say; come along, quick!" shouted Dick, terrified lest Mrs. Weldon should have overheard him.

They hurried on. A wind had risen; large spattering drops were now beginning to fall more heavily on the ground, and in a few minutes it would be impossible to stand against the advancing tempest. The nearest of the accumulation of ant-hills was reached in time, and however dangerous their occupants might be, it was decided either to expel them, or to share their quarters. Each cone was formed of a kind of reddish clay, and had a single opening at its base. Hercules took his hatchet, and quickly enlarged the aperture till it would admit his own huge body. Not an ant made its appearance. Cousin Benedict expressed his extreme surprise. But the structure unquestionably was empty, and one after another the whole party made their way inside.

The rain by this time was descending in terrific torrents, strong enough to extinguish, one would think, the most violent explosions of the electric fluid. But the travellers were secure in their shelter, and had nothing to fear for the present ; their tenement was of greater stability than a tent or a native hut. It was one of those marvellous structures erected by little insects, which to Cameron appeared even more wonderful than the upraising of the Egyptian pyramids by human hands. To use his own comparison, it might be likened to the construction of a Mount Everest, the loftiest of the Himalayan peaks, by the united labour of a nation.

CHAPTER V.

WHITE ANTS.

THE storm had now burst in full fury, and fortunate it was that a refuge had been found. The rain did not fall in separate drops as in temperate zones, but descended like the waters of a cataract, in one solid and compact mass, in a way that could only suggest the outpour of some vast aerial basin. containing the waters of an entire ocean. Contrary, too, to the storms of higher latitudes, of which the duration seems ordinarily to be in inverse ratio to their violence, these African tempests, whatever their magnitude, often last for whole days, furrowing the soil into deep ravines, changing plains to lakes and brooks to torrents, and causing rivers to overflow and cover vast districts with their inundations. It is hard to understand whence such volumes of vapour and electric fluid can accumulate. The earth, upon these occasions, might almost seem to be carried back to the remote period which has been called the "diluvian age."

Happily, the walls of the ant-hill were very thick; no beaver-hut formed of pounded earth could be more perfectly water-tight, and a torrent might have passed over it without a particle of moisture making its way through its substance.

As soon as the party had taken possession of the tenement, a lantern was lighted, and they proceeded to examine the interior. The cone, which was about twelve feet high inside, was eleven feet wide at the base, gradually narrowing to a sugar-loaf top. The walls and partitions between

the tiers of cells were nowhere less than a foot thick throughout.

These wonderful erections, the result of the combined
labour of innumerable insects, are by no means uncommon
in the heart of Africa. Smeathman, a Dutch traveller of
the last century, has recorded how he and four companions
all at one time occupied the summit of one of them in
Loundé. Livingstone noticed some made of red clay, of
which the height varied from fifteen to twenty feet; and
in Nyangwé, Cameron several times mistook one of these
colonies for a native camp pitched upon the plain. He
described some of these strange edifices as being flanked
with small spires, giving them the appearance of a cathedral-
dome.

The reddish clay of which the ant-hill was composed could
leave no doubt upon the mind of a naturalist that it had
been formed by the species known as " termes bellicosus ;"
had it been made of grey or black alluvial soil, it might
have been attributed to the "termes mordax" or "termes
atrox," formidable names that must awaken anything but
pleasure in the minds of all but enthusiast entomologists.

In the centre was an open space, surrounded by roomy
compartments, ranged one upon another, like the berths of
a ship's cabin, and lined with the millions of cells that had
been occupied by the ants. This central space was inadequate to hold the whole party that had now made their
hurried resort to it, but as each of the compartments was
sufficiently capacious to admit one person to occupy it in a
sitting posture, Mrs. Weldon, Jack, Nan, and Cousin Benedict were exalted to the upper tier, Austin, Bat, and Actæon
occupied the next story, whilst Tom and Hercules, and Dick
Sands himself remained below.

Dick soon found that the soil beneath his feet was beginning to get damp, and insisted upon having some of the dry
clay spread over it from the base of the cone.

"It is a long time," he said, " since we have slept with a

roof over our heads; and I am anxious to make our refuge as secure as possible. It may be that we shall have to stay here for a whole day or more; on the first opportunity I shall go and explore; it may turn out that we are near the stream we are seeking; and perhaps we shall have to build a raft before we start again."

Under his direction, therefore, Hercules took his hatchet, and proceeded to break down the lowest range of cells and to spread the dry, brittle clay of which they were composed a good foot thick over the damp floor, taking care not in any way to block up the aperture by which the fresh air penetrated into the interior.

It was indeed fortunate that the termites had abandoned their home; had it swarmed with its multitudes of voracious Neuroptera, the ant-hill would have been utterly untenable for human beings. Cousin Benedict's curiosity was awakened, and he was intensely interested in the question of the evacuation, so that he proceeded at once to investigate, if he could, whether the emigration had been recent or otherwise. He took the lantern, and as the result of his scrutiny he soon discovered in a recess what he described as the termites' "storehouse," or the place where the indefatigable insects keep their provisions. It was a large cavity, not far from the royal cell, which, together with the cells for the reception of the young larvæ, had been destroyed by Hercules in the course of his flooring operations. Out of this receptacle Benedict drew a considerable quantity of gum and vegetable juices, all in a state so liquid as to demonstrate that they had been deposited there quite recently.

"They have only just gone," he exclaimed, with an air of authority, as if he imagined that some one was about to challenge his assertion.

"We are not going to dispute your word, Mr. Benedict," said Dick; "here we are; we have taken their place, and shall be quite content for them to keep out of the way, without caring when they went, or where they have gone."

"But we must care," retorted Benedict testily ; "why they have gone concerns us a good deal ; these juices make it evident, from the liquid state in which we find them, that the ants were here this morning ; they have not only gone, but they have carried off their young larvæ with them ; they have been sagacious enough to take warning of some impending danger."

"Perhaps they heard that we were coming," said Hercules, laughing.

A look of withering scorn was the only answer that the entomologist deigned to give.

"Yes, I say," repeated Hercules, "perhaps they heard that we were coming."

"Pshaw!" said Benedict contemptuously ; "do you imagine they would be afraid of you? they would reduce your carcase to a skeleton in no time, if they found it across their path."

"No doubt, if I were dead," replied Hercules, "they could pick my bones pretty clean ; but while I had the use of my limbs I think I could crush them by thousands."

"Thousands!" ejaculated Benedict, with increasing warmth ; "you think you could demolish thousands ; but what if they were hundreds of thousands, millions, hundreds of millions? Alive as much as dead, I tell you, they wouldn't be long in consuming every morsel of you."

During this brisk little discussion Dick Sands had been pondering over what Benedict had said. There was no doubt that the amateur naturalist was well acquainted with the habits of white ants, and if, as he affirmed, the insects had instinctively quitted their abode on account of some approaching danger, Dick asked himself whether it was safe or prudent for his party to remain. But the fury of the storm was still so great that all possibility of removing from the shelter seemed precluded for the present, and, without inquiring farther into the mystery, he merely said,—

"Although the ants, Mr. Benedict, have left us their provisions, we must not forget that we have brought our own. We will have our supper now, and to-morrow, when the storm is over, we will see what is to be done."

Fatigue' had not taken away the appetite of the energetic travellers, and they gladly set about the preparation of their meal. The provisions, of which they had enough for another two days, had not been injured by the rain. For some minutes the crunching of hard biscuit was the only sound to be heard ; Hercules, in particular, seemed to pound away with his huge jaws as with a pair of mill-stones.

Mrs. Weldon was the only one of the party who ate little ; and that little was only taken at Dick's earnest solicitation ; he could not help noticing, with much concern, that although Jack seemed to be satisfactorily recovering, and, without sign of fever, was sleeping calmly enough on a bed made up of clothes spread out in one of the cells, yet his mother had lost much of her courage, and seemed pre-occupied and depressed.

Cousin Benedict did due honour to the simple evening repast ; not on account of its quantity or quality, but because it gave him an opportunity of holding forth upon the subject of termites. He was much vexed that he had been unable to discover a single specimen in the deserted ant-hill with which he might illustrate his lecture, but notwithstanding this deficiency he continued to talk, heedless whether any one was listening.

" They are wonderful insects," he said ; " they belong to the order of the Neuroptera, which have the antennæ longer than the head ; their mandibles are well-developed, and the inferior pair of wings is generally as large as the superior. There are five families of them ; the Panorpidæ, the Myrmeilonidæ, the Hemerobiidæ, the Termitinæ, and the Perlidæ. I need hardly say that what we are now occupying is a dwelling of the Termitinæ."

At this point Dick became all attention ; he was anxious

to ascertain whether this discovery of white ants had aroused any suspicion in Benedict's mind that they must be on African soil. The naturalist, now fairly mounted on a favourite hobby, went on with his discourse.

"I am sorry not to have a specimen to show you, but these Termitinæ have four joints in the tarsi, and strong horny mandibles. The family includes, as genera, the Mantispa, the Raphidia, and the Termes, the last commonly known as white ants, amongst which are 'Termes fatalis, Termes lucifugans, Termes mordax,' and several others more or less rare."

"And which of them built this ant-hill?" inquired Dick.

"The bellicosi!" replied Benedict, pronouncing the name with as much pride as if he were eulogizing the Macedonians or some warlike nation of antiquity. "Bellicosi," he continued, "are to be found of every size. There is as much difference between the largest and the smallest of them as there is between Hercules and a dwarf; the workers are about one-fifth of an inch long; the soldiers, or fighting-ants, are half an inch; whilst the males and females measure four-fifths of an inch. There is another curious species, called 'sirafoos,' which are about half an inch long, and have pincers instead of mandibles, and heads larger than their bodies, like sharks. In fact, if sharks and sirafoos were placed in competition, I should be inclined to back the sirafoos."

"And where are these sirafoos most generally to be found?" said Dick cautiously.

"In Africa, in the southern and central provinces. Africa may truly be termed the land of ants. Livingstone, in the notes brought home by Stanley, describes a battle which he was fortunate enough to witness between an army of black ants and an army of red. The black ants, or drivers, which are what the natives call sirafoos, got the best of it; and the red ants, or 'tchoongoos,' after a very resolute defence, were obliged to retire defeated, carrying their eggs and young ones with them. Livingstone avows that he never saw the warlike instinct so strongly developed as in these sirafoos; the stoutest man, the largest animal, a lion or an elephant, quails before the grip of their mandibles: no obstacle impedes their progress; no tree is too lofty for them to scale, and they contrive to cross wide streams by forming their own bodies into a kind of suspension bridge. Equally amazing are their numbers; Du Chaillu, another African traveller, relates how it took more than twelve hours for a column of ants to file past him, without a moment's pause in their march. These numbers, however, cease to be so surprising when it is explained that their fecundity is such that a single female of the termites bellicosi has been estimated to produce as many as sixty thousand eggs a day. These Neuroptera furnish the natives with a favourite food, grilled ants being considered a great delicacy."

"Have you ever tasted them?" asked Hercules, with a grin.

"Never," answered the naturalist; "but I am in hopes I shall have a chance of doing so very soon."

"Surely you don't imagine yourself in Africa!" said Tom suddenly.

"Africa! no; why should I?" replied Benedict; "but, as I have already seen a tzetsy in America, I do not despair of having the satisfaction of discovering white ants there too. You do not know the sensation I shall make in Europe when I publish my folio volume and its illustrations."

It was evident that no inkling of the truth had yet entered poor Benedict's brain, and it seemed likely that it would require demonstration far more striking than any natural phenomena to undeceive the minds of such of the party as were not already in possession of the fatal secret.

Although it was nine o'clock, Cousin Benedict went on talking incessantly, regardless of the fact that one by one his audience were falling to sleep in their separate cells. Dick Sands did not sleep, but neither did he interrupt the entomologist by farther questions; Hercules kept up his attention longer than the rest, but at length he too succumbed to weariness, and his eyes and ears were closed to all external sights and sounds.

But endurance has limits, and at last Cousin Benedict, having worn himself out, clambered up to the topmost cell of the cone, which he had chosen for his dormitory, and fell into a peaceful slumber.

The lantern had been already extinguished. All was darkness and silence within, whilst the storm without still raged with a violence that gave no sign of abatement.

Dick Sands himself was the only one of the party who was not partaking in the repose that was so indispensable to them all; but he could not sleep; his every thought was absorbed in the responsibility that rested on him to rescue those under his charge from the dangers that threatened them. Again and again he recalled every incident that had occurred since the loss of Captain Hull and his crew; he remembered the occasion when he had stood with his pistol pointed at Negoro's head; why, oh why, had his hand faltered then? why had he not at that moment hurled the miserable wretch overboard, and thus relieved himself and his partners in trouble from the catastrophe that had since befallen them? Peril was still staring them in the face, and his sole drop of consolation in the bitter cup of despondency was that Mrs. Weldon was still ignorant of their real situation.

At that moment, just in the fever of his agony, he felt a light breath upon his forehead; a hand was laid upon his shoulder, and a gentle voice murmured in his ear,—

" My poor boy, I know everything. God will help us ! His will be done ! "

CHAPTER VI.

A DIVING-BELL.

THIS sudden revelation that Mrs. Weldon was acquainted with the true state of things left Dick speechless. Even had he been capable of replying, she gave him no opportunity, but immediately retired to the side of her son. The various incidents of the march had all gradually enlightened her, and perhaps the exclamation of Cousin Benedict on the preceding evening had crowned them all ; anyhow the brave lady now knew the worst. Dick felt, however, that she did not despair; neither would he.

He lay and longed for the dawn, when he hoped to explore the situation better, and perchance to find the watercourse which he was convinced could not be far distant. Moreover, he was extremely anxious to be out of the reach of the natives whom, it was only too likely, Negoro and Harris might be putting on their track.

But as yet no glimmer of daylight penetrated the aperture of the cone, whilst the heavy rumblings, deadened as they were by the thickness of the walls, made it certain that the storm was still raging with undiminished fury. Attentively Dick listened, and he could distinctly hear the rain beating around the base of the ant-hill ; the heavy drops splashed again as they fell, in a way altogether different to what they would upon solid ground, so that he felt sure that the adjacent land was by this time completely flooded. He was getting very drowsy when it suddenly occurred to him that it was not unlikely the aperture was getting blocked up

with damp clay ; in that case he knew that the breath of
the inmates would quickly vitiate the internal atmosphere.
He crept along the ground and had the satisfaction of finding that the clay embankment was still perfectly dry ; the
orifice was quite unobstructed, allowing not only a free passage to the air, but admitting the glare of the occasional
flashes of lightning, which the descending volumes of water
did not seem to stay.

Having thus far satisfied himself that all was well, and
that there was no immediate danger, Dick thought that he
might now resign himself to sleep as well as the rest : he
took the precaution, however, of stretching himself upon
the embankment within easy reach of the opening, and with
his head supported against the wall, after a while dozed
off.

How long his light slumber had lasted he could not say,
when he was aroused by a sensation of cold. · He started
up, and to his horror discovered that the water had entered
the ant-hill and was rising rapidly ; it could not be long, he
saw, before it reached the cells which were occupied by
Hercules and Tom. He woke them at once, and told them
what he had observed. The lantern was soon lighted, and
they set to work to ascertain what progress the water was
making. It rose for about five feet, when it was found to
remain stationary.

"What is the matter, Dick ?" inquired Mrs. Weldon,
disturbed by the movements of the men.

"Nothing very alarming," answered Dick promptly ;
"only some water has found its way into the lower part of
the place ; it will not reach your upper cells ; probably some
river has overflowed its boundaries."

"The very river, perhaps," suggested Hercules assuringly,
"that is to carry us to the coast."

Mrs. Weldon made no reply.

Cousin Benedict was still sleeping as soundly as if he were
himself a white ant ; the negroes were peering down on to

the sheet of water which reflected back the rays of the lantern, ready to carry out any orders given by Dick, who was quietly gauging the inundation, and removing the provisions and fire-arms out of its reach.

"Did the water get in at the opening, Mr. Dick?" asked Tom.

"Yes, Tom, and consequently we are coming to the end of our stock of fresh air," was Dick's reply.

"But why should we not make another opening above the water level?" Tom inquired.

"A thing to be thought about," said Dick; "but we have to remember that if we have five feet of water here inside, there is probably a depth of six or seven outside. In rising here the flood has compressed the air, and made it an obstacle to further progress, but if we allow the air to escape, we may perhaps only be letting the water rise too high for our safety. We are just as if we were in a diving-bell."

"Then what is to be done?" asked the old negro.

"No doubt," replied Dick, "we must proceed very cautiously. An inconsiderate step will jeopardize our lives."

Dick Sands was quite correct in comparing the cone to an immersed diving-bell. In that mechanical contrivance, however, the air can always be renewed by means of pumps, so that it can be occupied without inconvenience beyond what is entailed by a somewhat confined atmosphere; but here the interior space had already been reduced by a third part through the encroachment of the water, and there was no method of communicating with the outer air except by opening a new aperture, an operation in which there was manifest danger.

Dick did not entertain the slightest apprehension that the ant-hill would be carried away bodily by the inundation; he knew that it would adhere to its base as firmly as a beaver-hut; what he really dreaded was that the storm would last so long that the flood would rise high above the plain, perhaps submerging the ant-hill entirely, so that ultimately all air would be expelled by the persistent pressure.

The more he pondered the more he felt himself driven to the conviction that the inundation would be wide and deep. It could not be, he felt sure, entirely owing to the downpour from the clouds that the rapid flood was rising; there must have been the sudden overflowing of some stream to cause such a deluge over the low-lying plain. It could not be proved that the ant-hill was not already under water, so that escape might be no longer possible, even from its highest point.

With all Dick's courage, it was yet evident that he was very uneasy; he did not know what to do, and asked himself again and again whether patient waiting or decisive action would be his more prudent course.

It was now about three o'clock in the morning. All within the ant-hill were silent and motionless, listening to the incessant turmoil which told that the strife of the elements had not yet ceased.

Presently, old Tom pointed out that the height of the water was gradually increasing, but only by very slow ascent. Dick could only say that if the flood continued to rise, however slowly, it must inevitably drive out the air.

As if struck by a sudden thought, Bat called out,—

"Let me try and get outside. Perhaps I might dive and get through the opening."

"I think I had better make that experiment myself," answered Dick.

"That you never shall," interposed Tom peremptorily; "you must let Bat go. It may not be possible to get back, and your presence is indispensable here. Think, sir, think of Mrs. Weldon, and Master Jack," he added in a lower tone.

"Well, well," Dick assented, "if it must be so, Bat shall go."

And turning to Bat, he continued,—

"Do not try to come back again ; we will try, if we can, to follow you the same way ; but if the top of the cone is still above water, knock hard on it with your hatchet, and we shall take it as a signal that we may break our way out. Do you understand ? "

"All right ! " he said, " all right, sir."

And after wringing his father's hand, he drew a long breath, and plunged into the water that filled the lower section of the ant-hill.

It was an exploit that required considerable agility ; the diver would have to find the orifice, make his way through it, and, without loss of a moment, let himself rise to the surface outside. Full half a minute elapsed, and Dick was making sure that the negro had been successful in his effort, when his black head emerged from the water. There was a general exclamation of surprise.

"It is blocked up," gasped Bat, as soon as he had re-covered breath enough to speak.

" Blocked up ? " cried Tom.

"Yes," Bat affirmed ; " I have felt all round the wall very carefully with my hand, and I am sure there is no hole left ; I suppose the water has dissolved the clay."

" If you cannot find a hole," exclaimed Hercules, " I can very soon make one ;" and he was just about to plunge his hatchet into the side of the ant-hill, when Dick prevented him.

"Stop, stop ! you must not be in such a hurry ! "

He reflected for a few moments, and went on,—

" We must be cautious ; an impetuous step may be de-struction ; perhaps the water is over the top ; if it is allowed to enter, then at once is an end of all."

" But whatever we do," urged Tom, " must be done at once ; there is no time to lose."

He was right ; the water had risen till it was quite six feet deep ; none but Mrs. Weldon, Jack, Nan, and Cousin

Benedict, who were lodged in the upper cells, were fairly above its surface.

Dick now came to his determination. At about a foot above the water-level, that is, about seven feet from the ground, he resolved to bore a hole through the clay. If he should find himself in communication with the open air, he would have the proof he desired that the top of the cone was still uncovered; if, on the other hand, he should ascertain that he had pierced the wall below the surface of the external water, he would be prepared to plug up the hole instantaneously, and repeat the experiment higher up. It was true that the inundation might have risen even fifteen feet above the plain ; in that case the worst had come and there was no alternative but that they must all die of asphyxia.

Carefully considering the chances of his undertaking, Dick calmly and steadily set about his task. The best instrument that suggested itself for his purpose was the ramrod of a gun, which, having a sort of corkscrew at the end for extracting the wadding, would serve as an auger. The hole would be very small, but yet large enough for the requisite test. Hercules showed him all the light he could by holding up the lantern. There were several candles left, so that they were not in fear of being altogether in darkness.

The operation hardly took a minute ; the ramrod passed through the clay without difficulty ; a muffled sound was distinguished as of air-bubbles rushing through a column of water. As the air escaped, the water in the cone rose perceptibly. The hole had been pierced too low. A handful of clay was immediately forced into the orifice, which was thus effectually plugged ; and Dick turned round quietly, and said,—

"We must try again."

The water had again become stationary, but its last rise had diminished the amount of breathing space by more than eight inches. The supply of oxygen was beginning to fail respiration was becoming difficult, and the flame of the candle burned red and dim.

About a foot higher than the first hole, Dick now set about boring a second. The experiment might again prove a failure, and the water rise yet higher in the cone; but the risk must be run.

Just as the auger was being inserted, a loud exclamation of delight was heard proceeding from Cousin Benedict's cell. Dick paused, and Hercules turned the lantern towards the excited naturalist, who seemed beaming with satisfaction.

"Yes, yes; I see it all well enough," he cried; " I know now why the termites left their home; they were wide-awake; they were more clever than we are; they knew that the storm was coming !"

Finding that this was all the worthy entomologist had to communicate, Dick, without comment, turned back again to his operation. Again the gurgling noise ! again the water's upward rush ! For the second time he had failed to effect an aperture to the outer air !

The situation was to the last degree alarming. The water had all but reached Mrs. Weldon, and she was obliged to take her boy into her arms. Every one felt nearly stifled. A loud singing was heard in the ears, and the lantern showed barely any light at all. A few minutes more and the air would be incapable of supporting life. One chance alone remained. They must bore another hole at the very summit of the cone. Not that they were unaware of the imminent danger of this measure, for if the ant-hill were really submerged the water from below would immediately expel the remaining air and death must be instantaneous. A few brief words from Dick explained the emergency of the crisis. Mrs. Weldon recognized the necessity,—

" Yes, Dick, do it ; there is nothing else to be done."

While she was speaking the light flickered out, and they were in total darkness.

All fired simultaneously at the nearest boat.

Mounted on the shoulders of Hercules, who was crouching in one of the side-cells, his head only just above water, Dick proceeded to force the ramrod into the clay, which at the vertex of the ant-hill was considerably harder and thicker than elsewhere.

A strange mingling of hope and fear thrilled through Dick Sands as he applied his hand to make the opening which was to admit life and air, or the flood of death!

The silence of the general expectation was broken by the noise of a sharp hissing; the water rose for eight inches, but all at once it ceased to rise; it had found its level. No need this time to close the orifice; the top of the ant-hill was higher than the top of the flood; and for the present, at least, they could all rejoice that their lives were spared!

A general cheer, led by the stentorian voice of Hercules, involuntarily broke from the party; cutlasses were brought into action, and the clay crumbled away beneath the vigorous assault that was made upon it. The welcome air was admitted through the new-made aperture, bringing with it the first rays of the rising sun. The summit of the ant-hill once removed, it would be quite easy to clamber to the top, whence it was hoped they would soon get away to some high ground out of reach of the flood.

Dick was the first to mount the summit; but a cry of dismay burst from his lips!

A sound only too well known to travellers in Africa broke upon his ear; that sound was the whizzing of arrows.

Hardly a hundred yards away was a large encampment; whilst, in the water, quite close to the ant-hill where he stood, he saw some long boats full of natives. From one of these had come the volley of arrows which had greeted his appearance above the opening of the cone.

To tell his people what had happened was the work of a moment. He seized his gun, and made Hercules, Bat, and Actæon take theirs, and all fired simultaneously at the nearest boat. Several of the natives were seen to fall; but shouts of defiance were raised, and shots were fired in return.

Resistance was manifestly useless. What could they do against a hundred natives? they were assailed on every hand. In accordance with what seemed a preconcerted plan, they were carried off from the ant-hill with brutal violence, in two parties, without the chance of a farewell word or sign.

Dick Sands saw that Mrs. Weldon, Jack, and Cousin Benedict were placed on board one boat, and were conveyed towards the camp, whilst he himself, with the five negroes and old Nan, was forced into another, and taken in a different direction. Twenty natives formed a body-guard around them, and five boats followed in their rear.

Useless though it were, Dick and the negroes made one desperate attempt to maintain their freedom; they wounded several of their antagonists, and would doubtless have paid their lives as a penalty for their daring, if there had not been special orders given that they should be taken alive.

The passage of the flood was soon accomplished. The boat had barely touched the shore, when Hercules with a tremendous bound sprang on to the land. Instantly two natives rushed upon him. The giant clave their skulls with the butt end of his gun, and made off. Followed though he was by a storm of bullets, he escaped in safety, and disappeared beneath the cover of the woods.

Dick Sands and the others were guarded to the shore, and fettered like slaves.

CHAPTER VII.

A SLAVE CARAVAN.

THE storm of the previous night, by swelling the tributaries of the Coanza, had caused the main river to overflow its banks. The inundation had entirely changed the aspect of the country, transforming the plain into a lake, where the peaks of a number of ant-hills were the sole objects that emerged above the watery expanse.

The Coanza, which is one of the principal rivers of Angola, falls into the Atlantic about a hundred miles from the spot at which the " Pilgrim " was stranded. The stream, which a few years later was crossed by Cameron on his way to Benguela, seems destined to become the chief highway of traffic between Angola and the interior ; steamers already ply upon its lower waters, and probably ten years will not elapse before they perform regular service along its entire course.

Dick Sands had been quite right in searching north-wards for the navigable stream he had been so anxious to find ; the rivulet he had been following fell into the Coanza scarce a mile away, and had it not been for this unexpected attack he and his friends might reasonably have hoped to descend the river upon a raft, until they reached one of the Portuguese forts where steam vessels put in. But their fate was ordered otherwise.

The camp which Dick had descried from the ant-hill was pitched upon an eminence crowned by an enormous syca-more-fig, one of those giant trees occasionally found in Central Africa, of which the spreading foliage will shelter some five hundred men. Some of the non-fruit-bearing kind of banyan-trees formed the background of the landscape.

Beneath the shelter of the sycamore, the caravan which had been referred to in the conversation between Negoro and Harris had just made a halt. Torn from their villages by the agents of the slave-dealer Alvez, the large troop of natives was on its way to the market of Kazonndé, thence to be sent as occasion required either to the west coast, or to Nyangwé, in the great lake district, to be dispersed into Upper Egypt or Zanzibar.

Immediately on reaching the camp, the four negroes and old Nan were placed under precisely the same treatment as the rest of the captives. In spite of a desperate resistance, they were deprived of their weapons, and fastened two and two, one behind another, by means of a pole about six feet long, forked at each end, and attached to their necks by an iron bolt. Their arms were left free, that they might carry any burdens, and in order to prevent an attempt to escape a heavy chain was passed round their waists. It was thus in single file, unable to turn either right or left, they would have to march hundreds of miles, goaded along their toilsome road by the havildar's whip. The lot of Hercules seemed preferable, exposed though undoubtedly he would be in his flight to hunger, and to the attacks of wild beasts, and to all the perils of that dreary country. But solitude, with its worst privations, was a thing to be envied in comparison to being in the hands of those pitiless drivers, who did not speak a word of the language of their victims, but communicated with them only by threatening gestures or by actual violence.

As a white man, Dick was not attached to any other captive. The drivers were probably afraid to subject him to the same treatment as the negroes, and he was left unfettered, but placed under the strict surveillance of a havildar. At first he felt considerable surprise at not seeing Harris or Negoro in the camp, as he could not entertain a doubt that it was at their instigation the attack had been made upon their retreat; but when he came to reflect that Mrs. Weldon, Jack, and Cousin Benedict had not been allowed to come with them, but had been carried off in some other direction, he began to think it probable that the two rascals had some scheme to carry out with regard to them elsewhere.

The caravan consisted of nearly eight hundred, including about five hundred slaves of both sexes, two hundred soldiers and freebooters, and a considerable number of havildars and drivers, over whom the agents acted as superior officers.

These agents are usually of Portuguese or Arab extraction; and the cruelties they inflict upon the miserable captives are almost beyond conception; they beat them continually, and if any unfortunate slave sinks from exhaustion, or in any way becomes unfit for the market, he is forthwith either stabbed or shot. As the result of this brutality it rarely happens that fifty per cent. of the slaves reach their destination; some few may contrive to escape, and many are left as skeletons along the line of route.

Such of the agents as are Portuguese are (as it may well be imagined) of the very lowest dregs of society, outlaws, escaped criminals, and men of the most desperate character; of this stamp were the associates of Negoro and Harris, now in the employ of José Antonio Alvez, one of the most notorious of all the slave-dealers of Central Africa, and of whom Commander Cameron has given some curious information.

Most frequently the soldiers who escort the captives are natives hired by the dealers, but they do not possess the entire monopoly of the forays made for the purpose of securing slaves; the native negro kings make war upon each other with this express design, and sell their vanquished antagonists, men, women, and children, to the traders for calico, guns, gunpowder, and red beads; or in times of famine, according to Livingstone, even for a few grains of maize.

The escort of old Alvez's caravan was an average specimen of these African soldiers. It was simply a horde of half-naked banditti, carrying old flint-locked muskets, the barrels of which were decorated with copper rings. The agents are very often put to their wits' end to know how to manage them ; their orders are called in question, halts are continually demanded, and in order to avert desertion they are frequently obliged to yield to the obstreperous will of their undisciplined force.

Although the slaves, both male and female, are compelled to carry burdens whilst on their march, a certain number of porters, called *pagazis*, is specially engaged to carry the more valuable merchandize, and principally the ivory. Tusks occasionally weigh as much as 160 lbs., and require two men to carry them to the depôts, whence they are sent to the markets of Khartoom, Natal, and Zanzibar. On their arrival the *pagazis* are paid by the dealers according to contract, which is generally either by about twenty yards of the cotton stuff known as *merikani*, or by a little powder, by a handful or two of cowries, by some beads, or if all these be scarce, they are paid by being allotted some of the slaves who are otherwise unsalable.

Among the five hundred slaves in the caravan, very few were at all advanced in years. The explanation of this circumstance was that whenever a raid is made, and a village is set on fire, every inhabitant above the age of forty is mercilessly massacred or hung upon the neighbouring trees ; only the children and young adults of both sexes are reserved for the market, and as these constitute only a small proportion of the vanquished, some idea may be formed of the frightful depopulation which these vast districts of Equinoctial Africa are undergoing.

Nothing could be more pitiable than the condition of this miserable herd. All alike were destitute of clothing, having nothing on them but a few strips of the stuff known as *mbuza*, made from the bark of trees ; many of the women were

covered with bleeding wounds from the drivers' lashes, and
had their feet lacerated by the constant friction of the road,
but in addition to other burdens were compelled to carry
their own emaciated children ; young men, too, there were
who had lost their voices from exhaustion, and who, to
use Livingstone's expression, had been reduced to "ebony
skeletons " by toiling under the yoke of the fork, which is
far more galling than the galley-chain.   It was a sight that
might have moved the most stony-hearted, but yet there was
no symptom of compassion on the part of those Arab and
Portuguese drivers whom Cameron pronounces " worse than
brutes."[1]

The guard over the prisoners was so strict that Dick
Sands felt it would be utterly useless for him to make any
attempt to seek for Mrs. Weldon.   She and her son had
doubtless been carried off by Negoro, and his heart sank
when he thought of the dangers to which too probably she
would be exposed.   Again and again he repeated his re-
proaches on himself that he had ever allowed either Negoro
or Harris to escape his hands.   Neither Mrs. Weldon nor
Jack could expect the least assistance from Cousin Benedict ;
the good man was barely able to consult for himself.   All
three of them would, he conjectured, be conveyed to some
remote district of Angola ; the poor mother, like some miser-

[1] Cameron says, "In order to obtain the fifty women of whom
Alvez is the owner, ten villages, containing altogether a population
of not less than 1500, were totally destroyed.   A few of the inhabitants contrived to escape, but the majority either perished in the
flames, were slain in defending their families, or were killed by
hunger or wild beasts in the jungle. . . . . The crimes which are
perpetrated in Africa, by men who call themselves Christians,
seem incredible to the inhabitants of civilized countries.   It is
impossible that the government at Lisbon can be aware of the
atrocities committed by those who boast of being subject to her
flag."—*Tour du Monde*.

N.B.—Against these assertions of Cameron, loud protestations
have been made in Portugal.

able slave, would insist upon carrying her own sick son until her strength failed her, and, exhausted by her endurances, she sank down helpless on the the way.

A prisoner, and powerless to help! the very thought was itself a torture to poor Dick. Even Dingo was gone! It would have been a satisfaction to have had the dog to send off upon the track of the lost ones. One only hope remained. Hercules still was free. All that human strength could attempt in Mrs. Weldon's behalf, Hercules would not fail to try. Perhaps, too, under cover of the night, it was not altogether improbable that the stalwart negro would mingle with the crowd of negroes (amongst whom his dark skin would enable him to pass unnoticed), and make his way to Dick himself; then might not the two together elude the vigilance of the watch? might they not follow after and overtake Mrs. Weldon in the forest? would they not perchance be able either by stealth or by force to liberate her, and once free they would effect an escape to the river, and finally accomplish the undertaking in which they had been so lamentably frustrated. Such were the sanguine visions in which Dick permitted himself to indulge; his temperament overcame all tendency to despair, and kept him alive to the faintest chance of deliverance.

The next thing of importance was to ascertain the destination of the caravan. It was a matter of the most serious moment whether the convoy of slaves were going to be carried to one of the depôts of Angola, or whether they were to be sent hundreds of miles into the interior to Nyangwé, in the heart of the great lake district that Livingstone was then exploring. To reach the latter spot would occupy some months, and to return thence to the coast, even if they should be fortunate enough to regain their liberty, would be a work of insuperable difficulty.

He was not long left in suspense. Although he could not understand the half-African, half-Arab dialect that was used by the leaders of the caravan, he noticed that the word

Kazonndé occurred very frequently, and knowing it as the name of an important market in the province, he naturally concluded that it was there the slaves were to be disposed of ; whether for the advantage of the king of the district, or of one of the rich traders, he had no means of telling. Unless his geographical knowledge was at fault, he was aware that Kazonndé must be about 400 miles from St. Paul de Loanda, and consequently that it could hardly be more than 250 miles from the part of the Coanza where they were now encamped. Under favourable circumstances it was a journey that could not be accomplished in less than twelve or fourteen days, but allowing for the retarded progress of a caravan already exhausted by a lengthened march, Dick was convinced that they could not reach the place for at least three weeks.

He was most anxious to communicate to his companions in adversity his impression that they were not to be carried into the heart of the country, and began to cogitate whether some plan could not be devised for exchanging a few words with them.

Forked together, as it has been said, two and two, the four negroes were at the right-hand extremity of the camp ; Bat attached to his father, Austin to Actæon. A havildar, with twelve soldiers, formed their guard. Dick, at first, was about fifty yards away from the group, but being left free to move about, contrived gradually to diminish the distance between himself and them. Tom seemed to apprehend his intention, and whispered a word to his companions that they should be on the look-out. Without moving they were all on their guard in a moment. Dick, careful to conceal his design, strolled backward with a feigned indifference, and succeeded in getting so near that he might have called out and informed Tom that they were going to Kazonndé. But he was desirous of accomplishing more than this ; he wanted to get an opportunity of having some conversation as to their future plans, and he ventured to approach still nearer.

His heart beat high as he believed he was on the point of attaining his object, when all at once the havildar, becoming aware of his design, rushed upon him like a madman, summoned some soldiers, and with considerable violence sent him back to the front. Tom and the others were quickly removed to another part of the encampment.

Exasperated by the rough attack that was made upon him, Dick had seized the havildar's gun and broken it, almost wrenching it from his hands, when several soldiers simultaneously assailed him, and would have struck him down and killed him upon the spot, had not one of the chiefs, an Arab of huge stature and ferocious countenance, interfered to stop them.

This Arab was the Ibn Hamish of whom Harris had spoken to Negoro. He said a few words which Dick could not understand, and the soldiers, with manifest reluctance, relaxed their hold and retired. It was evident that although Dick was not to be permitted to hold any communication with the rest of his party, orders had been given that his life was to be protected.

It was now nine o'clock, and the beating of drums and the blowing of coodoo [2] horns gave the signal that the morning march was to be continued. Instantly chiefs, soldiers, porters, and slaves were upon their feet, and arranged themselves in their various groups with a havildar bearing a bright-coloured banner at their head.

The order was given; the start was made. A strange song was heard rising in the air. It was a song, not of the victors, but of the vanquished. The slaves were chanting an imprecation on their oppressors ; and the burden of the chorus was that captured, tortured, slain—after death they would return and avenge their wrongs upon their murderers !

[2] Coodoo, a ruminant common in Africa.

CHAPTER VIII.

NOTES BY THE WAY.

THE storm of the preceding evening had now passed away, but the sky was still cloudy and the weather far from settled. It was the 19th of April, the time of the *masika* or second period of the rainy season, so that for the next two or three weeks the nights might be expected to be wet.

On leaving the banks of the Coanza the caravan proceeded due east. Soldiers marched at the head and in the rear, as well as upon the flanks of the troop ; any escape of the prisoners, therefore, even if they had not been loaded with their fetters, would have been utterly impossible. They were all driven along without any attempt at order, the havildars using their whips unsparingly upon them whenever they showed signs of flagging. Some poor mothers could be seen carrying two infants, one on each arm, whilst others led by the hand naked children, whose feet were sorely cut by the rough ground over which they had trod.

Ibn Hamish, the Arab who had interfered between Dick and the havildar, acted as commander to the caravan, and was here, there, and everywhere ; not moved in the least by the sufferings of the captives, but obliged to be attentive to the importunities of the soldiers and porters, who were perpetually clamouring for extra rations, or demanding an immediate halt. Loud were the discussions that arose, and the uproar became positively deafening when the quarrelsome voices rose above the shrieks of the slaves, many of whom found themselves treading upon soil already stained by the blood of the ranks in front.

No chance again opened for Dick to get any communication with his friends, who had been sent to the van of the procession. Urged on by the whip they continued to march in single file, their heads in the heavy forks. If ever the havildar strolled a few yards away, Bat took the opportunity of murmuring a few words of encouragement to his poor old father, while he tried to pick out the easiest path for him, and to relax the pace to suit his enfeebled limbs. Large tears rolled down old Tom's cheeks when he found that his son's efforts only resulted in bringing down upon his back some sharp cuts of the havildar's whip. Actæon and Austin, subject to hardly less brutality, followed a few steps behind, but all four could not help feeling envious at the luck of Hercules, who might have dangers to encounter, but at least had his liberty.

Immediately upon their capture, Tom had revealed to his companions the fact that they were in Africa, and informing them how they had been betrayed by Harris, made them understand that they had no mercy to expect.

Old Nan had been placed amongst a group of women in the central ranks. She was chained to a young mother with two children, the one at the breast, the other only three years old, and scarcely able to walk. Moved by compassion, Nan took the little one into her own arms, thus not only saving it from fatigue, but from the blows it would very likely have received for lagging behind. The mother shed tears of gratitude, but the weight was almost too much for Nan's strength, and she felt as if she must break down under her self-imposed burden. She thought fondly of little Jack, and imagining him borne along in the arms of his weary mother, could not help asking herself whether she should ever see him or her kind mistress again.

Far in the rear, Dick could not see the head of the caravan except occasionally, when the ground was rather on the rise. The voices of the agents and drivers, harsh and excited as they were, scarcely roused him from his melancholy reflections.' His thoughts were not of himself nor of his own sufferings ; his whole attention was absorbed in looking for some traces of Mrs. Weldon's progress ; if she, too, was being taken to Kazonndé, her route must also lie this way. But he could discover no trace of her having been conducted by this line of march, and could only hope that she was being spared the cruelties which he was himself witnessing.

The forest extended for about twenty miles to the east of the Coanza, but whether it was that the trees had been destroyed by the ravages of insects, or broken down before they had made their growth by being trampled on by elephants, they were growing much less thickly than in the immediate vicinity of the river. There were numbers of cotton-trees, seven or eight feet high, from which are manufactured the black-and-white striped stuffs that are worn in the interior of the province ; but, upon the whole, progress was not much impeded either by shrubs or underwood. Occasionally the caravan plunged into jungles of reeds like bamboos, their stalks an inch in diameter, so tall that only an elephant or giraffe could have reared above them, and through which none excepting such as had a very intimate knowledge of the country could possibly have made their way.

Starting every morning at daybreak they marched till noon, when an hour's halt was made. Packets of manioc were then unfastened, and doled out in sparing quantities among the slaves ; sometimes, when the soldiers had plundered some village, a little goat's flesh or some sweet potatoes were added to the meal ; but generally the fatigue, aggravated by inadequate rest, took away the appetite, and when meal-time arrived many of the slaves could hardly eat at all.

During the first eight days march from the Coanza no less than twenty unfortunate wretches had fallen upon the road, and had been left behind, a prey to the lions, panthers, and leopards that prowled in the wake. As Dick heard their roars in the stillness of the night, he trembled as he thought of Hercules. Nevertheless, had the opportunity offered itself, he would not for a moment have hesitated in making his own escape to the wilderness.

The two hundred and fifty miles between the river and Kazonndé were accomplished in what the traders call marches of ten miles each, including the halts at night and midday. The journey cannot be better described than by a few rough notes that Dick Sands made upon his way.

April 25th.—Saw a village surrounded with bamboo palisading, eight or nine feet high. Fields round planted with maize, beans, and sorghum. Two negroes captured, fifteen killed, rest took to flight.

26th.—Crossed a torrent 150 yards wide. Bridge formed of trunks of trees and creepers. Piles nearly gave way ; two women fastened to a fork ; one of them, carrying a baby, fell into the water. Water quickly tinged with blood ; crocodiles seen under bridge ; risk of stepping into their very jaws.

28th.—Crossed a forest of bauhinias ; great trees, the iron-wood of the Portuguese. Heavy rain ; ground sodden ; marching difficult. Caught sight of Nan in the middle of caravan ; she was toiling along with a black child in her arms ; the woman with her limping, and blood trickling from her shoulder.

29th.—Camp at night under a huge baobab, with white flowers and light green leaves. Lions and leopards roaring all night. A soldier fired at a panther. What has become of Hercules ?

30th.—Rainy season said to be over till November. First touch of African winter. Dew very heavy. Plains all flooded. Easterly winds : difficulty of respiration ; susceptibility to

The caravan had been attacked on the flank by a dozen or more crocodiles.

fever. No trace of Mrs. Weldon ; cannot tell whether she is ahead. Fear Jack may have a return of fever.

May 5th.—Forced to march several stages across flooded plains, water up to the waist ; many leeches sticking to the skin. Lotus and papyrus upon higher ground. Great heavy leaves, like cabbages, beneath the water, make many stumble as they walk. Saw large numbers of little fish, silurus-species ; these are caught by the natives, and sold to the caravans.

7th.—Plain still inundated. Last night, no halting-place to be found. Marched on through the darkness. Great misery. Except for Mrs. Weldon, life not worth having ; for her sake must hold out. Loud cries heard. Saw, by the lightning, soldiers breaking large boughs from the resinous trees that emerged from the water. The caravan had been attacked on the flank by a dozen or more crocodiles ; women and children seized and carried off to what Livingstone calls their "pasture-lands," the holes where they deposit their prey until it is decomposed. Myself grazed by the scales of one of them. A slave close beside me torn out of the fork, which was snapped in half. How the poor fellow's cry of agony rings in my ear ! This morning, twenty missing. Tom and the others, thank God, are still alive. They are on in front. Once Bat made a sharp turn, and Tom caught sight of me. Nothing to be seen of Nan ; was she, poor creature, one of those that the crocodiles had got?

8th.—After twenty-four hours in the water we have crossed the plain. We have halted on a hill. The sun helps to dry us. Nothing to eat except a little manioc and a few handfuls of maize. Only muddy water to drink. Impossible for Mrs. Weldon to survive these hardships ; I hope from my heart that she has been taken some other way. Small-pox has broken out in the caravan ; those that have it are to be left behind.

9th.—Started at dawn. No stragglers allowed ; sick and weary must be kept together by havildars' whip ; the losses were considerable. Living skeletons all round. Rejoiced once more to catch sight of Nan. She was not carrying the child any longer; she was alone; the chain was round her waist, but she had the loose end thrown over her shoulder. I got close to her; suppose I am altered, as she did not know me. After I had called her by name several times she stared at me, and at last said, "Ah, Mr Dick, is it you? you will not see me here much longer." Her cadaverous look pained my very soul, but I tried to speak hopefully. Poor Nan shook her head. "I shall never see my dear mistress again; no, nor master Jack; I shall soon die." Anxious to help her, I would gladly have carried the end of the chain which she had been obliged to bear because her fellow-prisoner was dead. A rough hand was soon upon my shoulder; a cruel lash had made Nan retreat to the general crowd, whilst, at the bidding of an Arab chief, I was hustled back to the very hindmost rank of the procession. I overheard the word Negoro, in a way that convinced me that it is under the direction of the Portuguese that I am subject to this hard indignity.

11*th*.—Last night encamped under some large trees on the skirts of a forest. Several escaped prisoners recaptured; their punishment barbarously cruel. Loud roaring of lions and hyenas heard at nightfall, also snorting of hippopotamuses; probably some lake or water-course not far off. Tired, but could not sleep; heard a rustling in the grass; felt sure that something was going to attack me; what could I do? I had no gun. For Mrs. Weldon's sake must, if possible, preserve my life. The night was dark; no moon; two eyes gleamed upon me; I was about to utter a cry of alarm; fortunately, I suppressed it; the creature that had sprung to my feet was Dingo! The dog licked my hands all over, persisting in rubbing his neck against them, evidently to make me feel there; found a reed fastened to the well-known collar upon which the initials S.V. had so often awakened our curiosity; breaking open the reed, I took a note from inside; it was too dark for me to see to read it

I tried, by caressing Dingo, to detain him; but the dog appeared to know that his mission with me was at an end; he licked my hands affectionately, made a sudden bound, and disappeared in the long grass as mysteriously as he had come. The howling of the wild beasts increased. How I dreaded that the faithful creature would become their prey! No more sleep this night for me. It seemed that daylight would never dawn; at length it broke with the suddenness that marks a tropical morn. I was able cautiously to read my note; the handwriting, I knew at a glance, was that of Hercules; there were but a few lines in pencil :—

"Mrs. Weldon and Jack carried away in a kitanda. Harris and Negoro both with them. Mr. Benedict too. Only a few marches ahead, but cannot be communicated with at present. Found Dingo wounded by a gun-shot. Dear Mr. Dick, do not despair; keep up your courage. I may help you yet.

"Your ever true and faithful

"HERCULES."

As far as it went, this intelligence was satisfactory. A kitanda, I know, is a kind of litter made of dry grass, protected by a curtain, and carried on the shoulders of two men by a long bamboo. What a relief to know that Mrs. Weldon and Jack have been spared the miseries of this dreadful march! May I not indulge the hope of seeing them at Kazonndé?

12*th*.—The prisoners getting more and more weary and worn out. Blood-stains on the way still more conspicuous. Many poor wretches are a mass of wounds. One poor woman for two days has carried her dead child, from which she refuses to be parted.

16*th*.—Small-pox raging; the road strewn with corpses. Still ten days before we reach Kazonndé. Just passed a tree from which slaves who had died from hunger were hanging by the neck.

18*th*.—Must not give in, but I am almost exhausted. Rains

have ceased.   We are to make what the dealers call *trikesa*, extra marches in the after-part of the day.   Road very steep ; runs through *nyassi*, tall grass of which the stalks scratch my face, and the seeds get under my tattered clothes and make my skin smart painfully.   My boots fortunately are thick, and have not worn out.   More slaves sick and abandoned to take their chance.   Provisions running very short ; soldiers and pagazis must be satisfied, otherwise they desert ; consequently the slaves are all but starved.   "They can eat each other," say the agents.   A young-slave, apparently in good health, dropped down dead.   It made me think of Livingstone's description of how free-born men, reduced to slavery, will suddenly press their hand on their side, and die of a broken heart.

24th.—Twenty captives, incapable any longer of keeping pace with the rest, put to death by the havildars, the Arab chief offering no opposition.   Poor old Nan one of the victims of this horrible butchery.   My foot struck her corpse as I passed, but I was not permitted to give her a decent burial. Poor old Nan ! the first of the survivors of the " Pilgrim " to go to her long rest !   Poor old Nan !

Every night I watch for Dingo ; but he never comes.   Has Hercules nothing more to communicate ? or has any mishap befallen him ?   If he is alive he will do what mortal strength can do to aid us.

CHAPTER IX.

KAZONNDÉ.

BY the 26th of May, when the caravan reached Kazonndé, the number of the slaves had diminished by more than half, so numerous had been the casualties along the road. But the dealers were quite prepared to make a market of their loss; the demand for slaves was very great, and the price must be raised accordingly.

Angola at that time was the scene of a large negro-traffic, and as the caravans principally wended their way towards the interior, the Portuguese authorities at Loanda and Benguela had practically no power to prevent it. The barra ckson the shore were crowded to overflowing with prisoners, the few slave-ships that managed to elude the cruisers being quite inadequate to embark the whoie number for the Spanish colonies to America.

Kazonndé, the point whence the caravans diverge to the various parts of the lake district, is situated three miles from the mouth of the Coanza, and is one of the most important *lakonis*, or markets of the province. The open market-place where the slaves are exposed for sale is called the *chiloka*.

All the larger towns of Central Africa are divided into two distinct parts; one occupied by the Arab, Portuguese, or native merchants, and containing their slave-barracks; the other being the residence of the negro king, often a fierce drunken potentate, whose rule is a reign of terror, and who lives by subsidies allowed him by the traders.

The commercial quarter of Kazonndé now belonged to José Antonio Alvez. It was his largest depôt, although he had another at Bihé, and a third at Cassangé, where Cameron subsequently met him. It consisted of one long street, on each side of which were groups of flat-roofed houses called *tembés*, built of rough earth, and provided with square yards for cattle. The end of it opened into the *chitoka*, which was surrounded by the barracks. Above the houses some fine banyan-trees waved their branches, surmounted here and there by the crests of graceful palms. There was at least a score of birds of prey that hovered about the streets, and came down to perform the office of public scavengers. At no great distance flowed the Loohi, a river not yet explored, but which is supposed to be an affluent or sub-affluent of the Congo.

Adjoining the commercial quarter was the royal residence, nothing more nor less than a collection of dirty huts, extending over an area of nearly a square mile.

Some of these huts were unenclosed; others were surrounded by a palisade of reeds, or by a hedge of bushy figs.

In an enclosure within a papyrus fence were about thirty huts appropriated to the king's slaves, another group for his wives, and in the middle, almost hidden by a plantation of manioc, a *tembé* larger and loftier than the rest, the abode of the monarch himself.

He had sorely declined from the dignity and importance of his predecessors, and his army, which by the early Portuguese traders had been estimated at 20,000, now numbered less than 4000 men ; no longer could he afford, as in the good old time, to order a sacrifice of twenty-five or thirty slaves at one offering.

His name was Moené Loonga. Little over fifty, he was prematurely aged by drink and debauchery, and scarcely better than a maniac. His subjects, officers, and ministers, were all liable to be mutilated at his pleasure, and noses and ears, feet and hands, were cut off unsparingly whenever his caprice so willed it. His death would have been a cause of regret to no one, with the exception, perhaps, of Alvez, who was on very good terms with him. Alvez, moreover, feared that in the event of the present king's death, the succession of his chief wife, Queen Moena, might be disputed, and that his dominions would he invaded by a younger and more active neighbour, one of the kings of Ukusu, who had already seized upon some villages dependent on the government of Kazonndé, and who was in alliance with a rival trader named Tipo-Tipo, a man of pure Arab extraction, from whom Cameron afterwards received a visit at Nyangwé.

To all intents and purposes Alvez was the real sovereign of the district, having fostered the vices of the brutalized king till he had him completely in his power. He was a man considerably advanced in years; he was not (as his name might imply) a white man, but had merely assumed his Portuguese title for purposes of business; his true name was Kendélé, and he was a pure negro by birth, being a native of Dondo on the Coanza. He had commenced life as a slave-dealer's agent, and was now on his way towards becoming a first-class trader; that is to say, he was a consummate rascal under the guise of an honest man. He it was whom Cameron met at the end of 1874 at Kilemba, the capital of Urua, of which Kasongo is chief, and with whose caravan he travelled to Bihé, a distance of seven hundred miles.

It was midday when the caravan entered Kazonndé. The journey from the Coanza had lasted thirty-eight days, more than five weeks of misery as great as was within human power to endure. Amidst the noise of drums and coodoo-horns the slaves were conducted to the market-place. The soldiers of the caravan discharged their guns into the air, and old Alvez's resident retinue responded with a similar salute. The bandits, than which the soldiers were nothing better, were delighted to meet again, and would celebrate their return by a season of riot and excess.

The slaves, reduced to a total of about two hundred and

fifty, were many of them almost dead from exhaustion ; the forks were removed from their necks, though the chains were still retained, and the whole of them were driven into barracks that were unfit even for cattle, to await (in company with 1200 to 1500 other captives already there) the great market which would be held two days hence.

The *pagazis*, after delivering their loads of ivory, would only stay to receive their payment of a few yards of calico or other stuff, and would then depart at once to join some other caravan.

On being relieved from the forks which they had carried for so many weary days, Tom and his companions heartily wrung each other's hands, but they could not venture to utter one word of mutual encouragement. The three younger men, more full of life and vigour, had resisted the effects of the fatigue, but poor old Tom was nearly exhausted, and had the march been protracted for a few more days he must have shared Nan's fate and been left behind, a prey to the wild beasts.

Upon their arrival all four were packed into a narrow cell, where some food was provided, and the door was immediately locked upon them.

The *chitoka* was now almost deserted, and Dick Sands was left there under the special charge of a havildar : he lost no opportunity of peering into every hut in the hope of catching a glimpse of Mrs. Weldon, who, if Hercules had not misinformed him, had come on hither just in front.

But he was very much perplexed. He could well understand that Mrs. Weldon, if still a prisoner, would be kept out of sight, but why Negoro and Harris did not appear to triumph over him in his humiliation was quite a mystery to him. It was likely enough that the presence of either one or the other of them would be the signal for himself to be · exposed to fresh indignity, or even to torture, but Dick would have welcomed the sight of them at Kazonndé, were it only as an indication that Mrs. Weldon and Jack were there also.

It disappointed him, too, that Dingo did not come back. Ever since the dog had brought him the first note, he had kept an answer written ready to send to Hercules, imploring him to look after Mrs. Weldon, and to keep him informed of every-thing. He began to fear that the faithful creature must be dead, perhaps perished in some attempt to reach himself; it was, however, quite possible that Hercules had taken the dog in some other direction, hoping to gain some depôt in the interior.

But so thoroughly had Dick persuaded himself that Mrs. Weldon had preceded him to Kazonndé that his disap-pointment became more and more keen when he failed to discover her. For a while he seemed to yield to despair, and sat down sorrowful and sick at heart.

Suddenly a chorus of voices and trumpets broke upon his ear; he was startled into taking a new interest in what was going on.

"Alvez! Alvez!" was the cry again and again repeated by the crowd.

Here, then, was the great man himself about to appear. Was it not likely that Harris or Negoro might be with him?

Dick stood erect and resolute, his eye vivid with expecta-tion; he felt all eagerness to stand face to face with his betrayers; boy as he was, he was equal to cope with them both.

The *kitanda*, which came in sight at the end of the street, was nothing more than a kind of hammock covered by a faded and ragged curtain. An old negro stepped out of it. His attendants greeted him with noisy acclamations.

This, then, was the great trader, José Antonio Alvez.

Immediately following him was his friend Coïmbra, son of the chief Coïmbra of Bihé, and, according to Cameron, the greatest blackguard in the province. This sworn ally of Alvez, this organizer of his slave-raids, this commander, worthy of his own horde of bandits, was utterly loathsome in his appearance, his flesh was filthily dirty, his eyes were bloodshot, his skin yellow, and his long hair all dishevelled. He had no other attire than a tattered shirt, a tunic made of grass, and a battered straw hat, under which his countenance appeared like that of some old hag.

Alvez himself, whose clothes were like those of an old Turk the day after a carnival, was one degree more respectable in appearance than his satellite, not that his looks spoke much for the very highest class of African slave-dealers. To Dick's great disappointment, neither Harris nor Negoro was among his retinue.

Both Alvez and Coïmbra shook hands with Ibn Hamish, the leader of the caravan, and congratulated him on the success of the expedition. Alvez made a grimace on being told that half the slaves had died on the way, but on the whole he seemed satisfied; he could meet the demand that at present existed, and would lose no time in bartering the new arrival for ivory or *hannas*, copper in the shape of a St. Andrew's cross, the form in which the metal is exported in Central Africa.

After complimenting the havildars upon the way in which they had done their work, the trader gave orders that the porters should be paid and dismissed. The conversations were carried on in a mixture of Portuguese and native idioms, in which the African element abounded so largely that a native of Lisbon would have been at a loss to understand them. Dick, of course, could not comprehend what was said, and it was only when he saw a havildar go towards the cell in which Tom and the others were confined, that he realized that the talk was about himself and his party.

When the negroes were brought out, Dick came close up, being anxious to learn as much as he could of what was in contemplation. The old trader's eyes seemed to brighten as he glanced upon the three strapping young men who, he knew, would soon be restored to their full strength by rest and proper food. They at least would get a good price; as for poor old Tom, he was manifestly so broken down by infirmity and age, that he would have no value in the market.

In a few words of broken English, which Alvez had picked up from some of his agents, he ironically gave them all a welcome.

"Glad to see you!" he said, with a diabolical grin.

Tom knew what he meant, and drew himself up proudly.

"We are free men!" he protested, "free citizens of the United States!"

"Yes, yes!" replied Alvez, grinning, "you are Americans; very glad to see you!"

"Very glad to see you!" echoed Coïmbra, and walking up to Austin he felt his chest and shoulders, and they proceeded to open his mouth in order to examine his teeth.

A blow from Austin's powerful fist sent the satellite staggering backwards.

Some soldiers made a dash and seized the young negro, evidently ready to make him pay dearly for his temerity; but Alvez was by no means willing to have any injury done to his newly-acquired property, and called them off. He hardly attempted to conceal his amusement at Coïmbra's discomfiture, although the blow had cost him one of his front teeth.

After he had recovered somewhat from the shock, Coïmbra stood scowling at Austin, as if mentally vowing vengeance on some future occasion.

Dick Sands was now himself brought forward in the custody of a havildar. It was clear that Alvez had been told all about him, for after scanning him for a moment, he stammered out in his broken English,—

"Ah! ah! the little Yankee!"

"Yes," replied Dick; "I see you know who I am. What are you going to do with me and my friends?"

"Yankee! little Yankee!" repeated the trader, who either did not or would not comprehend the meaning of Dick's question.

Dick turned to Coïmbra and made the same inquiry of him ; in spite of his degraded features, now still farther disfigured by being swollen from the blow, it was easy to recognize that he was not of native origin.   He refused to answer a word, and only stared again with the vicious glare of malevolence.

Meanwhile, Alvez had begun to talk to Ibn Hamish. Dick felt sure that they intended to separate him from the negroes, and accordingly took the opportunity of whispering a few words to them.

"My friends, I have heard from Hercules.   Dingo brought me a note from him, tied round his neck.   He says Harris and Negoro have carried off Mrs. Weldon, Jack, and Mr. Benedict.   He did not know where.   Have patience, and we will find them yet."

"And where's Nan ?" muttered Tom, in a low voice.

"Dead," replied Dick, and was about to add more, when a hand was laid upon his shoulder, and a voice that he knew too well exclaimed,—

"Well, my young friend, how are you ?   I am glad to see you again."

He turned round quickly.   Harris stood before him.

"Where is Mrs. Weldon ?" asked Dick impetuously.

"Ah, poor thing !" answered Harris, with an air of deep commiseration.

"What ! is she dead ?" Dick almost shrieked ; "where is her child ?"

"Poor little fellow !" said Harris, in the same mournful tone.

These insinuations, that those in whose welfare he was so deeply interested had succumbed to the hardships of the journey, awoke in Dick's mind a sudden and irresistible desire for vengeance.   Darting forwards he seized the cutlass that Harris wore in his belt, and plunged it into his heart.

With a yell and a curse, the American fell dead at his feet.

CHAPTER X.

MARKET-DAY.

So sudden was Dick's action that it had been impossible to parry his blow. Several of the natives rushed on him, and in all likelihood would have struck him down upon the spot had not Negoro arrived at that very moment. At a sign from him the natives drew back, and proceeded to raise and carry away Harris's corpse.

Alvez and Coïmbra were urgent in their demand that Dick should forthwith be punished by death, but Negoro whispered to them that they would assuredly be the gainers by delay, and they accordingly contented themselves with ordering the youth to be placed under strict supervision.

This was the first time that Dick had set eyes upon Negoro since he had left the coast; nevertheless, so heart-broken was he at the intelligence he had just received, that he did not deign to address a word to the man whom he knew to be the real author of all his misery. He cared not now what became of him.

Loaded with chains, he was placed in the dungeon where Alvez was accustomed to confine slaves who had been condemned to death for mutiny or violence. That he had no communication with the outer world gave him no concern; he had avenged the death of those for whose safety he had felt himself responsible, and could now calmly await the fate which he could not doubt was in store for him; he did not dare to suppose that he had been temporarily spared otherwise than that he might suffer the cruellest tortures that native ingenuity could devise. That the "Pilgrim's" cook now held in his power the boy captain he so thoroughly hated was warrant enough that the sternest possible measure of vengeance would be exacted.

Two days later, the great market, the *lakoni*, commenced. Although many of the principal traders were there from the interior, it was by no means exclusively a slave-mart ; a considerable proportion of the natives from the neighbouring provinces assembled to dispose of the various products of the country.

Quite early the great *chitoka* of Kazonndé was all alive with a bustling concourse of little under five thousand people, including the slaves of old Alvez, amongst whom were Tom and his three partners in adversity—an item by no means inconsiderable in the dealer's stock.

Accompanied by Coïmbra, Alvez himself was one of the first arrivals. He was going to sell his slaves in lots to be conveyed in caravans into the interior. The dealers for the most part consisted of half-breeds from Ujiji, the principal market on Lake Tanganyika, whilst some of a superior class were manifestly Arabs.

The natives that were assembled were of both sexes, and of every variety of age, the women in particular displaying an aptitude in making bargains that is shared by their sisters elsewhere of a lighter hue ; and it may be said that no market of the most civilized region could be characterized by greater excitement or animation, for amongst the savages of Africa the customer makes his offer in equally noisy terms as the vendor.

The *lakoni* was always considered a kind of fête-day ; consequently the natives of both sexes, though their clothing was scanty in extent, made a point of appearing in a most lavish display of ornaments. Their head-gear was most remarkable. The men had their hair arranged in every variety of eccentric device ; some had it divided into four parts, rolled over cushions and fastened into a chignon, or mounted in front into a bunch of tails adorned with red feathers; others plastered it thickly with a mixture of red mud and oil similar to that used for greasing machinery, and formed it into cones or lumps, into which they inserted a medley of iron pins and ivory skewers; whilst the greatest dandies had a glass bead threaded upon every single hair, the whole being fastened together by a tattooing-knife driven through the glittering mass.

As a general rule, the women preferred dressing their hair in little tufts about the size of a cherry, arranging it into the shape of a cap, with corkscrew ringlets on each side of the face. Some wore it simply hanging down their backs, others in French fashion, with a fringe across the forehead; but every *coiffure*, without exception, was daubed and caked either with the mixture of mud and grease, or with a bright red extract of sandal-wood called *nkola*.

But it was not only on their heads that they made this extraordinary display of ornaments; the lobes of their ears were loaded till they reached their shoulders with a profusion of wooden pegs, open-work copper rings, grains of maize, or little gourds, which served the purpose of snuff-boxes; their necks, arms, wrists, legs, and ankles were a perfect mass of brass and copper rings, or sometimes were covered with a lot of bright buttons. Rows of red beads, called *sames-sames*, or *talakas*, seemed also very popular. As they had no pockets, they attached their knives, pipes and other articles to various parts of their body; so that altogether, in their holiday attire, the rich men of the district might not inappropriately be compared to walking shrines.

With their teeth they had all played the strangest of vagaries; the upper and lower incisors had generally been extracted, and the others had been filed to points or carved into hooks, like the fangs of a rattlesnake. Their finger-nails were allowed to grow to such an immoderate length as to render the hands well-nigh useless, and their swarthy skins were tattooed with figures of trees, birds, crescents and discs, or, not unfrequently, with those zigzag lines which Livingstone thinks he recognizes as resembling those observed in ancient Egyptian drawings. The tattooing is effected by means of a blue substance inserted into incisions previously made in the skin. Every child is tattooed in precisely the same pattern as his father before him, and thus it may always be ascertained to what family he belongs. Instead of carrying his armorial bearings upon his plate or upon the panels of his carriage, the African magnate wears them emblazoned on his own bosom !

The garments that were usually worn were simply aprons of antelope-skins descending to the knees, but occasionally a short petticoat might be seen made of woven grass and dyed with bright colours. The ladies not unfrequently wore girdles of beads attached to green skirts embroidered with silk and ornamented with bits of glass or cowries, or sometimes the skirts were made of the grass cloth called *lambda*, which, in blue, yellow, or black, is so much valued by the people of Zanzibar.

Garments of these pretensions, however, always indicated that the wearers belonged to the upper classes ; the lower orders, such as the smaller dealers, as well as the slaves, had hardly any clothes at all.

The women commonly acted as porters, and arrived at the market with huge baskets on their backs, which they secured by means of straps passed across the forehead. Having deposited their loads upon the chitoka, they turned out their goods, and then seated themselves inside the empty baskets.

As the result of the extreme fertility of the country all the articles offered for sale were of a first-rate quality. There were large stores of rice, which had been grown at a profit a hundred times as great as the cost, and maize which, producing three crops in eight months, yielded a profit as large again as the rice. There were also sesame, Urua pepper stronger than Cayenne, manioc, nutmegs, salt, and palm-oil. In the market, too, were hundreds of goats, pigs and sheep, evidently of a Tartar breed, with hair instead of wool; and there was a good supply of fish and poultry. Besides all these there was an attractive display of bright-coloured pottery, the designs of which were very symmetrical.

In shrill, squeaky voices, children were crying several varieties of native drinks; banana-wine, *pombé*, which, whatever it was, seemed to be in great demand; *malofoo*, a kind of beer compounded of bananas, and mead, a mixture of honey and water, fermented with malt.

But the most prominent feature in the whole market was the traffic in stuffs and ivory. The pieces could be counted by thousands of the unbleached *merikani* from Salem in Massachusetts, of the blue cotton, *kaniki*, thirty-four inches wide, and of the checked *sohari*, blue and black with its scarlet border. More expensive than these were lots of silk *diulis*, with red, green, or yellow grounds, which are sold in lengths of three yards, at prices varying from seven dollars to eighty, when they are interwoven with gold.

The ivory had come from well-nigh every part of Central Africa, and was destined for Khartoom, Zanzibar, and Natal, many of the merchants dealing in this commodity exclusively.

How vast a number of elephants must be slaughtered to supply this ivory may be imagined when it is remembered that over 200 tons, that is, 1,125,000 lbs, are exported annually to Europe. Of this, much the larger share goes to England, where the Sheffield cutlery consumes about 382,500 lbs. From the West Coast of Africa alone the produce is nearly 140 tons.

The average weight of a pair of tusks is 28 lbs., and the ordinary value of these in 1874 would be about 60*l*.; but here in Kazonndé were some weighing no less than 165 lbs., of that soft, translucent quality which retains its whiteness far better than the ivory from other sources.

As already mentioned, slaves are not unfrequently used as current money amongst the African traders, but the natives themselves usually pay for their goods with Venetian glass beads, of which the chalk-white are called *catchokolos*, the black *bubulus*, and the red *sikunderetches*. Strung in ten rows, or *khetés*, these beads are twisted twice round the neck, forming what is called a *foondo*, which is always reckoned of considerable value. The usual measure by which they are sold is the *frasilah*, containing a weight of about 70 lbs. Livingstone, Cameron and Stanley always took care to be well provided with this kind of currency. In default of beads, the picé, a Zanzibar coin worth something more than a farthing, and *vioongooas*, shells peculiar to the East Coast, are recognized as a medium of exchange in the market. Amongst the cannibal tribes a certain value is attached to human teeth, and at the lakoni some natives might be seen wearing strings of teeth, the owners of which they had probably, at some previous time, devoured. This species of currency, however, was falling rapidly into disuse.

Towards the middle of the day the excitement of the market reached its highest pitch, and the uproar became perfectly deafening. The voices of the eager sellers mingled with those of indignant and overcharged customers ; fights were numerous, and as there was an utter absence of any kind of police, no effort was made to restore peace or order amongst the unruly crowd.

It was just noon when Alvez gave orders that the slaves he wished to dispose of should be placed on view. Thereupon nearly two thousand unfortunates were brought forward, many of whom had been confined in the dealer's barracks for several months. Most of the stock, however, had been so carefully attended to that they were in good condition, and it was only the last batch that looked as if they would be improved by another month's rest ; but as the demand upon the East Coast was now very large, Alvez hoped to get a good price for all, and determined to part with even the last arrivals for whatever sum he could obtain.

Amongst these latter, whom the havildars drove like a herd of cattle into the middle of the chitoka, were Tom and his three friends. They were closely chained, and rage and shame were depicted in their countenances.

Bat passed a quick and scrutinizing gaze around him, and said to the others,—

" I do not see Mr. Dick."

Tom answered mournfully,—

" Mr. Dick will be killed, if he is not dead already. Our only hope is that we may now all be bought in one lot ; it will be a consolation to us if we can be all together."

Tears rose to Bat's eyes as he thought of how his poor old father was likely to be sold, and carried away to wear out his days as a common slave.

The sale now commenced. The agents of Alvez proceeded to divide the slaves, men, women, and children, into lots, treating them in no respect better than beasts in a cattle-market. Tom and the others were paraded about from customer to customer, an agent accompanying them to proclaim the price demanded. Strong, intelligent-looking Americans, quite different to the miserable creatures brought from the banks of the Zambesi and Lualaba, they at once attracted the observation of the Arab and half-breed dealers. Just as though they were examining a horse, the buyers felt their limbs, turned them round and round, looked at their teeth, and finally tested their paces by throwing a stick to a distance and making them run to fetch it.

All the slaves were subjected to similar humiliations ; and all alike, except the very young children, seemed deeply sensible of their degradation. The cruelty exhibited towards them was very vile. Coïmbra, who was half drunk, treated them with the utmost brutality ; not that they had any reason to expect any gentler dealings at the hands of the new masters who might purchase them for ivory or any other commodity. Children were torn away from their parents, husbands from their wives, brothers from sisters, and without even the indulgence of a parting word, were separated never to meet again.

The scenes that occur at such markets as this at Kazonndé are too heartrending to be described in detail.

It is one of the peculiar requirements of the slave-trade that the two sexes should have an entirely different destination. In fact, the dealers who purchase men never purchase women. The women, who are required to supply the Mussulman harems, are sent principally to Arab districts to be exchanged for ivory; whilst the men, who are to be put to hard labour, are despatched to the coast, East and West, whence they are exported to the Spanish colonies, or to the markets of Muscat or Madagascar.

To Tom and his friends the prospect of being transported to a slave colony was far better than that of being retained in some Central African province, where they could have no chance of regaining their liberty; and the moment, to them, was accordingly one of great suspense.

Altogether, things turned out for them better than they dared anticipate. They had at least the satisfaction of finding that as yet they were not to be separated. Alvez, of course, had taken good care to conceal the origin of this exceptional lot, and their own ignorance of the language thoroughly prevented them from communicating it; but the anxiety to secure so valuable a property rendered the competition for it very keen ; the bidding rose higher and higher, until at length the four men were knocked down to a rich Arab dealer, who purposed in the course of a few days to take them to Lake Tanganyika, and thence to one of the depôts of Zanzibar.

This journey, it is true, would be for 1500 miles across the most unhealthy parts of Central Africa, through districts harassed by internal wars ; and it seemed improbable that

Tom could survive the hardships he must meet ; like poor
old Nan, he would succumb to fatigue ; but the brave fellows
did not suffer themselves to fear the future, they were only
too happy to be still together ; and the chain that bound
them one to another was felt to be easier and lighter to
bear.

Their new master knew that it was for his own interest
that his purchase should be well taken care of ; he looked
to make a substantial profit at Zanzibar, and sent them off
at once to his own private barracks ; consequently they saw
no more of what transpired at Kazonndé.

CHAPTER XI.

A BOWL OF PUNCH.

THE afternoon was passing away, and it was now past four o'clock, when the sound of drums, cymbals, and a variety of native instruments was heard at the end of the main thoroughfare. The market was still going on with the same animation as before ; half a day's screeching and fighting seemed neither to have wearied the voices nor broken the limbs of the demoniacal traffickers; there was a considerable number of slaves still to be disposed of, and the dealers were haggling over the remaining lots with an excitement of which a sudden panic on the London Stock Exchange could give a very inadequate conception.

But the discordant concert which suddenly broke upon the ear was the signal for business to be at once suspended. The crowd might cease its uproar, and recover its breath. The King of Kazonndé, Moené Loonga, was about to honour the *lakoni* with a visit.

Attended by a large retinue of wives, officers, soldiers, and slaves, the monarch was conveyed to the middle of the market-place in an old palanquin, from which he was obliged to have five or six people to help him to descend. Alvez and the other traders advanced to meet him with the most exaggerated gestures of reverence, all of which he received as his rightful homage.

He was a man of fifty years of age, but might easily have

The potentate beneath whose sway the country trembled for a hundred miles round.

passed for eighty. 'He looked like an old, decrepit monkey.
On his head was a kind of tiara, adorned with leopards
claws dyed red, and tufts of greyish-white hair ; this was the
usual crown of the sovereigns of Kazonndé, from his waist
hung two skirts of coodoo-hide, stiff as blacksmiths' aprons,
and embroidered with pearls. The tattooings on his breast
were so numerous that his pedigree, which they declared,
might seem to reach back to time immemorial. His wrists
and arms were encased in copper bracelets, thickly encrusted
with beads ; he wore a pair of top-boots, a present from
Alvez some twenty years ago ; in his left hand he carried a
great stick surmounted by a silver knob ; in his right a fly-
flapper with a handle studded with pearls ; over his head
was carried an old umbrella with as many patches as a
Harlequin's coat, whilst from his neck hung Cousin Benedict's
magnifying-glass, and on his nose were the spectacles which
had been stolen from Bat's pocket.

Such was the appearance of the potentate beneath whose
sway the country trembled for a hundred miles round.

By virtue of his sovereignty Moené Loonga claimed to be
of celestial origin ; and any subject who should have the
audacity to raise a question on this point would have been
despatched forthwith to another world. All his actions, his
eating and drinking, were supposed to be performed by
divine impulse. He certainly drank like no other mortal ;
his officers and ministers, confirmed tipplers as they were,
appeared sober men in comparison with himself, and he
seemed never to be doing anything but imbibing strong
pombé, and over-proof spirit with which Alvez kept him
liberally supplied.

In his harem Moené Loonga had wives of all ages from
forty to fourteen, most of whom accompanied him on his
visit to the *lakoni*. Moena, the chief wife, who was called
the queen, was the eldest of them all, and, like the rest, was
of royal blood. She was a vixenish-looking woman, very

gaily attired ; she wore a kind of bright tartan over a skirt of woven grass, embroidered with pearls ; round her throat was a profusion of necklaces, and her hair was mounted up in tiers that toppled high above her head, making her resemble some hideous monster.   The younger wives, all of them sisters or cousins of the king, were less elaborately dressed. They walked behind her, ready at the slightest sign to perform the most menial services.   Did his Majesty wish to sit down, two of them would immediately stoop to the ground and form a seat with their bodies, whilst others would have to lie down and support his feet upon their backs : a throne and footstool of living ebony.

Amidst the staggering, half-tipsy crowd of ministers, officers, and magicians that composed Moené Loonga's suite, there was hardly a man to be seen who had not lost either an eye, an ear, or hand, or nose.   Death and mutilation were the only two punishments practised in Kazonndé, and the slightest offence involved the instant amputation of some member of the body.   The loss of the ear was considered the severest penalty, as it prevented the possibility of wearing earrings !

The governors of districts, or *kilolos*, whether hereditary or appointed for four years, were distinguished by red waistcoats and zebra-skin caps; in their hands they brandished long rattans, coated at one extremity with a varnish of magic drugs.

The weapons carried by the soldiers consisted of wooden bows adorned with fringes and provided with a spare bowstring, knives filed into the shape of serpents' tongues, long, broad lances, and shields of palm wood, ornamented with arabesques.   In the matter of uniform, the royal army had no demands to make upon the royal treasury.

Amongst the attendants of the king there was a considerable number of sorcerers and musicians.   The sorcerers, or *mganga*, were practically the physicians of the court, the savages having the most implicit faith in divinations and incantations of every kind, and employing fetishes, clay of wooden figures, representing sometimes ordinary human beings, and sometimes fantastic animals. Like the rest of the retinue, these magicians were, for the most part, more or less mutilated, an indication that some of their prescriptions on behalf of the king had failed of success.

The musicians were of both sexes, some performing on shrill rattles, some on huge drums, whilst others played on instruments called *marimbas*, a kind of dulcimer made of two rows of different-sized gourds fastened in a frame, and struck by sticks with india-rubber balls at the end. To any but native ears the music was perfectly deafening.

Several flags and banners were carried in the procession, and amongst these was mixed up a number of long pikes, upon which were stuck the skulls of the various chiefs that Moené Loonga had conquered in battle.

As the king was helped out of his palanquin, the acclamations rose higher and higher from every quarter of the market-place. The soldiers attached to the caravans fired off their old guns, though the reports were almost too feeble to be heard above the noisy vociferations of the crowd ; and the havildars rubbed their black noses with cinnabar powder, which they carried in bags, and prostrated themselves. Alvez advanced and presented the king with some fresh tobacco, " the appeasing herb," as it is called in the native dialect; and certainly Moené Loonga seemed to require some appeasing, as, for some unknown reason, he was in a thoroughly bad temper.

Coïmbra, Ibn Hamish and the dealers all came forward to pay their court to the monarch, the Arabs greeting him with the cry of *marhaba*, or welcome ; others clapped their hands and bowed to the very ground; while some even smeared themselves with mud, in token of their most servile subjection.

But Moené Loonga scarcely took notice of any of them ; he went staggering along, rolling like a ship upon a stormy sea, and made his way past the crowds of slaves, each of whom, no less than their masters, trembled lest he should think fit to claim them for his own.

Negoro, who kept close at Alvez' side, did not fail to render his homage along with the rest. Alvez and the king were carrying on a conversation in the native language, if that could be called a conversation in which Moené Loonga merely jerked out a few monosyllables from his inflamed and swollen lips. He was asking Alvez to replenish his stock of brandy.

"We are proud to welcome your majesty at the market of Kazonndé," Alvez was saying.

"Get me brandy," was all the drunken king's reply.

"Will it please your majesty to take part in the business of the *lakoni ?*" Alvez tried to ask.

"Drink !" blurted out the king, impatiently.

Alvez continued,—

"My friend Negoro here is anxious to greet your majesty after his long absence."

"Drink !" roared the monarch again.

"Will the king take pombé or mead ? " asked Alvez, at last obliged to take notice of the demand.

"Brandy ! give me fire-water !" yelled the king, in a fury. "For every drop you shall have—"

"A drop of a white man's blood !" suggested Negoro glancing at Alvez.

"Yes, yes ; kill a white man," assented Moené Loonga, his ferocious instincts all aroused by the proposition.

"There is a white man here," said Alvez, "who has killed my agent. He must be punished for his act."

"Send him to King Masongo !" cried the king ; "Masongo and the Assuas will cut him up and eat him alive."

Only too true it is that cannibalism is still openly practised in certain provinces of Central Africa. Livingstone records that the Manyuemas not only eat men killed in war, but even buy slaves for that purpose ; it is said to be the avowal of these Manyuemas that " human flesh is slightly salt, and requires no seasoning." Cameron relates how in the dominions of Moené Booga dead bodies were soaked for a few days in running water as a preparation for their being devoured ; and Stanley found traces of a widely-spread cannibalism amongst the inhabitants of Ukusu.

But however horrible might be the manner of death proposed by Moené Loonga, it did not at all suit Negoro's purpose to let Dick Sands out of his clutches.

" The white man is here," he said to the king; "it is here he has committed his offence, and here he should be punished."

" If you will," replied Moené Loonga ! " only I must have fire-water ; a drop of fire-water for every drop of the white man's blood."

" Yes, you shall have the fire-water," assented Alvez, " and what is more, you shall have it all alight. We will give your majesty a bowl of blazing punch."

The thought had struck Alvez, and he was himself delighted with the idea, that he would set the spirit in flames. Moené Loonga had complained that the " fire-water " did not justify its name as it ought, and Alvez hoped that perhaps, administered in this new form, it might revivify the deadened membranes of the palate of the king.

Moené Loonga did not conceal his satisfaction. Wives and courtiers alike were full of anticipation. They had all drunk brandy, but they had not drunk brandy alight. And not only was their thirst for alcohol to be satisfied ; their thirst for blood was likewise to be indulged ; and when it is remembered how, even amongst the civilized, drunkenness reduces a man below the level of a brute, it may be imagined to what barbarous cruelties Dick Sands was likely to be exposed. The idea of torturing a white man was not altogether repugnant to the coloured blood of either Alvez or Coïmbra, while with Negoro the spirit of vengeance had completely over powered all feeling of compunction.

Night, without any intervening twilight, was soon drawing on, and the contemplated display could hardly fail to be effective. The programme for the evening consisted of two parts; first, the blazing punch-bowl; then the torture, culminating in an execution.

The destined victim was still closely confined in his dark and dreary dungeon; all the slaves, whether sold or not, had been driven back to the barracks, and the chitoka was cleared of every one except the slave-dealers, the havildars, and the soldiers, who hoped, by favour of the king, to have a share of the flaming punch.

Alvez did not long delay the proceedings. He ordered a huge caldron, capable of containing more than twenty gallons, to be placed in the centre of the market-place. Into this were emptied several casks of highly-rectified spirit, of a very inferior quality, to which was added a supply of cinnamon and other spices, no ingredient being omitted which was likely to give a pungency to suit the savage palate.

The whole royal retinue formed a circle round the king. Fascinated by the sight of the spirit, Moené Loonga came reeling up to the edge of the punch-bowl, and seemed ready to plunge himself head foremost into it. Alvez held him back, at the same time placing a lucifer in his hand.

" Set it alight ! " cried the slave-dealer, grinning slily as he spoke.

The king applied the match to the surface of the spirit. The effect was instantaneous. High above the edge of the bowl the blue flame rose and curled. To give intensity to

the process Alvez had added a sprinkling of salt to the
mixture, and this caused the fire to cast upon the faces of all
around that lurid glare which is generally associated with
apparitions of ghosts and phantoms. Half intoxicated
already, the negroes yelled and gesticulated; and joining
hands, they performed a fiendish dance around their
monarch. Alvez stood and stirred the spirit with an enormous metal ladle, attached to a pole, and as the flames rose
yet higher and higher they seemed to throw a more and more
unearthly glamour over the ape-like forms that circled in their
wild career.

Moené Loonga, in his eagerness, soon seized the ladle
from the slave-dealer's hands, plunged it deep into the bowl,
and bringing it up again full of the blazing punch, raised it
to his lips.

A horrible shriek brought the dancers to a sudden standstill. By a kind of spontaneous combustion, the king had
taken fire internally; though it was a fire that emitted little
heat, it was none the less intense and consuming. In an
instant one of the ministers in attendance ran to the king's
assistance, but he, almost as much alcoholized as his master,
caught fire as well, and soon both monarch and minister lay
writhing on the ground in unutterable agony. Not a soul
was able to lend a helping hand. Alvez and Negoro were
at a loss what to do; the courtiers dared not expose
themselves to so terrible a fate; the women had all fled
in alarm, and Coïmbra, awakened to the conviction
of the inflammability of his own condition, had rapidly
decamped.

To say the truth, it was impossible to do anything: water
would have proved unavailing to quench the pale blue flame
that hovered over the prostrate forms, every tissue of which
was so thoroughly impregnated with spirit, that combustion,
though outwardly extinguished, would continue its work
internally.

In a few minutes life was extinct, but the bodies continued long afterwards to burn ; until, upon the spot where they had fallen, a few light ashes, some fragments of the spinal column, some fingers and some toes, covered with a thin layer of stinking soot, were all that remained of the King of Kazonndé and his ill-fated minister.

CHAPTER XII.

ROYAL OBSEQUIES.

ON the following morning the town of Kazonndé presented
an aspect of unwonted desolation. Awe-struck at the event
of the previous evening, the natives had all shut themselves
up in their huts. That a monarch who was to be assumed
as of divine origin should perish with one of his ministers by
so horrible a death was a thing wholly unparalleled in their
experience. Some of the elder part of the community
remembered having taken part in certain cannibal preparations, and were aware that the cremation of a human body
is no easy matter, yet here was a case in which two men
had been all but utterly consumed without any extraneous
application. Here was a mystery that baffled all their
comprehension.

Old Alvez had also retired to the seclusion of his own
residence ; having been warned by Negoro that he would
probably be held responsible for the occurrence, he deemed
it prudent to keep in retirement. Meanwhile Negoro
industriously circulated the report that the king's death had
been brought about by supernatural means reserved by the
great Manitoo solely for his elect, and that it was sacred
fire that had proceeded from his body. The superstitious
natives readily received this version of the affair, and at once
proceeded to honour Moené Loonga with funeral rites worthy
of one thus conspicuously elevated to the rank of the gods.
The ceremony (which entailed an expenditure of human

blood incredible except that it is authenticated by Cameron and other African travellers) was just the opportunity that Negoro required for carrying out his designs against Dick, whom he intended to take a prominent part in it.

The natural successor to the king was the queen Moena. By inaugurating the funeral without delay and thus assuming the semblance of authority, she forestalled the King of Ukusu or any other rival who might venture to dispute her sovereignty; and moreover, by taking the reins of government into her hands she avoided the fate reserved for the other wives who, had they been allowed to live, might prove somewhat troublesome to the shrew. Accordingly, with the sound of coodoo horns and marimbas, she caused a proclamation to be made in the various quarters of the town, that the obsequies of the deceased monarch would be celebrated on the next evening with all due solemnity.

The announcement met with no opposition either from the officials about the court or from the public at large. Alvez and the traders generally were quite satisfied with Moena's assumption of the supremacy, knowing that by a few presents and a little flattery they could make her sufficiently considerate for their own interests.

Preparations began at once. At the end of the chief thoroughfare flowed a deep and rapid brook, an affluent of the Coango, in the dry bed of which the royal grave was to be formed. Natives were immediately set to work to construct a dam by means of which the water should be diverted, until the burial was over, into a temporary channel across the plain; the last act in the ceremonial being to undam the stream and allow it to resume its proper course.

Negoro had formed the resolution that Dick Sands should be one of the victims to be sacrificed upon the king's tomb. Thoroughly aware as he was that the indignation which had caused the death of Harris extended in at least an equal degree to himself, the cowardly rascal would not have ventured to approach Dick under similar circumstances at the risk of meeting a similar fate ; but knowing him to be a prisoner bound hand and foot, from whom there could be nothing to fear, he resolved to go to him in his dungeon. Not only did he delight in torturing his victims, but he derived an especial gratification from witnessing the torture.

About the middle of the day, accordingly, he made his way to the cell where Dick was detained under the strict watch of a havildar. There, bound with fetters that penetrated his very flesh, lay the poor boy ; for the last four and twenty hours he had not been allowed a morsel of food, and would gladly have faced the most painful death as a welcome relief to his miseries.

But at the sight of Negoro all his energy revived ; instinctively he made an effort to burst his bonds, and to get a hold upon his persecutor ; but the strength of a giant would have been utterly unavailing for such a design. Dick felt that the struggle he had to make was of another kind, and forcing himself to an apparent composure, he determined to look Negoro straight in the face, but to vouchsafe no reply to anything he might say.

"I felt bound," Negoro began, "to come and pay my respects to my young captain, and to tell him how sorry I am that he has not the same authority here that he had on board the ' Pilgrim.' "

Finding that Dick returned no answer, he continued,—

" You remember your old cook, captain : I have come to know what you would like to order for your breakfast."

Here he paused to give a brutal kick at Dick's foot, and went on,—

" I have also another question to ask you, captain ; can you tell me how it was that you landed here in Angola instead of upon the coast of America ? "

The way in which the question was put more than ever confirmed Dick's impression that the " Pilgrim's " course had been altered by Negoro, but he persevered in maintaining a contemptuous silence.

"It was a lucky thing for you, captain," resumed the vindictive Portuguese, "that you had a good seaman on board, otherwise the ship would have run aground on some reef in the tempest, instead of coming ashore here in a friendly port."

Whilst he was speaking, Negoro had gradually drawn nearer to the prisoner, until their faces were almost in contact. Exasperated by Dick's calmness, his countenance assumed an expression of the utmost ferocity, and at last he burst forth in a paroxysm of rage.

"It is my turn now! I am master now.! I am captain here! You are in my power now! Your life is in my hands!"

"Take it, then," said Dick quietly ; " death has no terrors for me, and your wickedness will soon be avenged."

"Avenged!" roared Negoro; "do you suppose there is a single soul to care about you? Avenged! who will concern himself with what befalls you? except Alvez and me, there is no one with a shadow of authority here ; if you think you are going to get any help from old Tom or any of those niggers, let me tell you that they are every one of them sold and have been sent off to Zanzibar."

"Hercules is free," said Dick.

"Hercules!" sneered Negoro ; "he has been food for lions and panthers long ago. I am only sorry that I did not get the chance of disposing of him myself."

"And there is Dingo," calmly persisted Dick ; "sure as fate, he will find you out some day."

"Dingo is dead!" retorted Negoro with malicious glee : "I shot the brute myself, and I should be glad if every survivor of the 'Pilgrim' had shared his fate."

"But remember," said Dick, "you have to follow them all yourself;" and he fixed a sharp gaze upon his persecutor's eye.

The Portuguese villain was stung to the quick ; he made a dash towards the youth, and would have strangled him upon the spot, but remembering that any such sudden action would be to liberate him from the torture he was determined he should undergo, he controlled his rage, and after giving strict orders to the havildar, who had been a passive spectator of the scene, to keep a careful watch upon his charge, he left the dungeon.

So far from depressing Dick's spirits, the interview had altogether a contrary effect; his feelings had undergone a reaction, so that all his energies were restored. Possibly Negoro in his sudden assault had unintentionally loosened his fetters, for he certainly seemed to have greater play for his limbs, and fancied that by a slight effort he might succeed in disengaging his arms. Even that amount of freedom, however, he knew could be of no real avail to him; he was a closely-guarded prisoner, without hope of succour from without; and now he had no other wish than cheerfully to meet the death that should unite him to the friends who had gone before.

The hours passed on. The gleams of daylight that penetrated the thatched roof of the prison gradually faded into darkness; the few sounds on the chitoka, a great contrast to the hubbub of the day, became hushed into silence, and night fell upon the town of Kazonndé.

Dick Sands slept soundly for about a couple of hours, and woke up considerably refreshed. One of his arms, which was somewhat less swollen than the other, he was able to withdraw from its bonds; it was at any rate a relief to stretch it at his pleasure.

The havildar, grasping the neck of a brandy-bottle which he had just drained, had sunk into a heavy slumber, and Dick Sands was contemplating the possibility of getting possession of his gaoler's weapons when his attention was arrested by a scratching at the bottom of the door. By the help of his liberated arm he contrived to crawl noiselessly to the threshold, where the scratching increased in violence. For a moment he was in doubt whether the noise proceeded from the movements of a man or an animal. He gave a glance at the havildar, who was sound asleep, and placing his lips against the door murmured "Hercules!"

A low whining was the sole reply.

"It must be Dingo," muttered Dick to himself; "Negoro may have told me a lie; perhaps, after all, the dog is not dead."

As though in answer to his thoughts, a dog's paw was pushed below the door. Dick seized it eagerly; he had no doubt it was Dingo's; but if the dog brought a message, it was sure to be tied to his neck, and there seemed to be no means of getting at it, except the hole underneath could be made large enough to admit the animal's head. Dick determined to try and scrape away the soil at the threshold, and commenced digging with his nails. But he had scarcely set himself to his task when loud barkings, other than Dingo's, were heard in the distance. The faithful creature had been scented out by the native dogs, and instinct dictated an immediate flight. Alarm had evidently been taken, as several gun-shots were fired; the havildar half roused himself from his slumber, and Dick was fain to roll himself once more into his corner, there to await the dawn of the day which was intended to be his last.

Throughout that day, the grave-digging was carried on with unremitted activity. A large number of the natives, under the superintendence of the queen's prime minister, were set to work, and according to the decree of Moena, who seemed resolved to continue the rigorous sway of her departed husband, were bound, under penalty of mutilation, to accomplish their task within the prescribed time.

As soon as the stream had been diverted into its temporary channel, there was hollowed out in the dry river bed a pit, fifty feet long, ten feet wide, and ten feet deep. This, towards the close of the day, was lined throughout with living women, selected from Moené Loonga's slaves; in ordinary cases it would have been their fate to be buried alive beside their master ; but in recognition of his miraculous death it was ordained that they should be drowned beside his remains.[1]

Generally, the royal corpse is arrayed in its richest vestments before being consigned to the tomb, but in this case, when the remains consisted only of a few charred bones, another plan was adopted. An image of the king, perhaps rather flattering to the original, was made of wicker-work ; inside this were placed the fragments of bones and skin, and the effigy itself was then arrayed in the robes of state, which, as already mentioned, were not of a very costly description. Cousin Benedict's spectacles were not forgotten, but were firmly affixed to the countenance of the image. The masquerade had its ludicrous as well as its terrible side.

When the evening arrived, a long procession was seen wending its way to the place of interment ; the uproar was perfectly deafening ; shouts, yells, the boisterous incantations of the musicians, the clang of musical instruments, and the reports of many old muskets, mingled in wild confusion.

The ceremony was to take place by torch-light, and the whole population of Kazonndé, native and otherwise, was bound to be present. Alvez, Coïmbra, Negoro, the Arab dealers and their havildars all helped to swell the numbers, the queen having given express orders that no one who had been at the lakoni should leave the town, and it was not deemed prudent to disobey her commands.

The remains of the king were carried in a palanquin in the rear of the cortége, surrounded by the wives of the second class, some of whom were doomed to follow their master beyond the tomb. Queen Moena, in state array, marched behind the catafalque.

[1] The horrible hecatombs that commemorate the death of any powerful chief in Central Africa defy all description. Cameron relates that more than a hundred victims were sacrificed at the obsequies of the father of the King of Kassongo.

Night was well advanced when the entire procession reached the banks of the brook, but the resin-torches, waved on high by their bearers, shed a ruddy glare upon the teeming crowd. The grave, with its lining of living women, bound to its side by chains, was plainly visible; fifty slaves, some resigned and mute, others uttering loud and piteous cries, were there awaiting the moment when the rushing torrent should be opened upon them.

The wives who were destined to perish had been selected by the queen herself and were all in holiday attire. One of the victims, who bore the title of second wife, was forced down upon her hands and knees in the grave, in order to form a resting-place for the effigy, as she had been accustomed to do for the living sovereign ; the third wife had to sustain the image in an upright position, and the fourth lay down at its feet to make a footstool.

In front of the effigy, at the end of the grave, a huge stake, painted red, was planted firmly in the earth. Bound to this stake, his body half naked, exhibiting marks of the tortures which by Negoro's orders he had already undergone, friendless and hopeless, was Dick Sands !

The time, however, for opening the flood-gate had not yet arrived. First of all, at a sign from the queen, the fourth wife, forming the royal footstool, had her throat cut by an executioner, her blood streaming into the grave. This barbarous deed was the commencement of a most frightful butchery. One after another, fifty slaves fell beneath the slaughterous knife, until the river-bed was a very cataract of blood. For half an hour the shrieks of the victims mingled with the imprecations of their murderers, without evoking one single expression of horror or sympathy from the gazing crowd around.

At a second signal from the queen, the barrier, which retained the water above, was opened. By a refinement of cruelty the torrent was not admitted suddenly to the grave, but allowed to trickle gradually in.

The first to be drowned were the slaves that carpeted the bottom of the trench, their frightful struggles bearing witness to the slow death that was overpowering them. Dick was immersed to his knees, but he could be seen making what might seem one last frantic effort to burst his bonds.

Steadily rose the water; the stream resumed its proper course ; the last head disappeared beneath its surface, and soon there remained nothing to indicate that in the depth below there was a tomb where a hundred victims had been sacrificed to the memory of the King of Kazonndé.

Painful as they are **to** describe, it is impossible to ignore the reality of such scenes.

CHAPTER XIII.

IN CAPTIVITY.

So far from Mrs. Weldon and Jack having succumbed to
the hardships to which they had been exposed, they were
both alive, and together with Cousin Benedict were now in
Kazonndé. After the assault upon the ant-hill they had all
three been conveyed beyond the encampment to a spot
where a rude palanquin was in readiness for Mrs. Weldon
and her son. The journey hence to Kazonndé was consequently accomplished without much difficulty ; Cousin Benedict, who performed it on foot, was allowed to entomologize
as much as he pleased upon the road, so that to him the
distance was a matter of no concern. The party reached
their destination a week sooner than Ibn Hamish's caravan,
and the prisoners were lodged in Alvez' quarters.

Jack was much better. After leaving the marshy districts
he had no return of fever, and as a certain amount of indulgence had been allowed them on their journey, both he and
his mother, as far as their health was concerned, might be
said to be in a satisfactory condition.

Of the rest of her former companions Mrs. Weldon could
hear nothing. She had herself been a witness of the escape
of Hercules, but of course knew nothing further of his fate ;
as for Dick Sands, she entertained a sanguine hope that his
white skin would protect him from any severe treatment ;
but for Nan and the other poor negroes, here upon African
soil, she feared the very worst.

Being entirely shut off from communication with the outer world, she was quite unaware of the arrival of the caravan ; even if she had heard the noisy commotion of the market she would not have known what it meant, and she was in ignorance alike of the death of Harris, of the sale of Tom and his companions, of the dreadful end of the king, and of the royal obsequies in which poor Dick had been assigned so melancholy a share. During the journey from the Coanza to Kazonndé, Harris and Negoro had held no conversation with her, and since her arrival she had not been allowed to pass the enclosure of the establishment, so that, as far as she knew, she was quite alone, and being in Negoro's power, was in a position from which it seemed only too likely nothing but death could release her.

From Cousin Benedict, it is needless to repeat, she could expect no assistance ; his own personal pursuits engrossed him, and he had no care nor leisure to bestow upon external circumstances. His first feeling, on being made to understand that he was not in America, was one of deep disappointment that the wonderful things he had seen were no discoveries at all ; they were simply African insects common on African soil. This vexation, however, soon passed away, and he began to believe that "the land of the Pharaohs" might possess as much entomological wealth as "the land of the Incas."

"Ah," he would exclaim to Mrs. Weldon, heedless that she gave him little or no attention, "this is the country of the manticoræ, and wonderful coleoptera they are, with their long hairy legs, their sharp elytra and their big mandibles ; the most remarkable of them all is the tuberous manticora. And isn't this, too, the land of the golden-tipped calosomi ? and of the prickly-legged goliaths of Guinea and Gabon ? Here, too, we ought to find the spotted anthidia, which lay their eggs in empty snail-shells ; and the sacred atenchus, which the old Egyptians used to venerate as divine."

"Yes, yes ;" he would say at another time, "this is the

proper habitat of those death's head sphinxes which are now so common everywhere; and this is the place for those 'Idias Bigoti,' so formidable to the natives of Senegal. There must be wonderful discoveries to be made here if only those good people will let me."

The "good people" referred to were Negoro and Harris, who had restored him much of the liberty of which Dick Sands had found it necessary to deprive him. With freedom to roam and in possession of his tin box, Benedict would have been amongst the most contented of men, had it not been for the loss of his spectacles and magnifying-glass, now buried with the King of Kazonndé. Reduced to the necessity of poking every insect almost into his eyes before he could discover its characteristics, he would have sacrificed much to recover or replace his glasses, but as such articles were not to be procured at any price, he contented himself with the permission to go where he pleased within the limits of the palisade. His keepers knew him well enough to be satisfied that he would make no attempt to escape, and as the enclosure was nearly a mile in circumference, containing many shrubs and trees and huts with thatched roofs, besides being intersected by a running stream, it afforded him a very fair scope for his researches, and who should say that he would not discover some novel specimen to which, in the records of entomological science, his own name might be assigned?

If thus the domain of Antonio Alvez was sufficient to satisfy Benedict, to little Jack it might well seem immense. But though allowed to ramble over the whole place as he liked, the child rarely cared to leave his mother; he would be continually inquiring about his father, whom he had now so long been expecting to see: he would ask why Nan and Hercules and Dingo had gone away and left him; and perpetually he would be expressing his wonder where Dick could be, and wishing he would come back again. Mrs. Weldon could only hide her tears and answer him by caresses.

Nothing, however, transpired to give the least intimation that any of the prisoners were to be treated otherwise than they had been upon the journey from the Coanza. Excepting such as were retained for old Alvez' personal service, all the slaves had been sold, and the storehouses were now full of stuffs and ivory, the stuffs destined to be sent into the central provinces and the ivory to be exported. The establishment was thus no longer crowded as it had been, and Mrs. Weldon and Jack were lodged in a different hut to Cousin Benedict. All three, however, took their meals together, and were allowed a sufficient diet of mutton or goat's-flesh, vegetables, manioc, sorghum and native fruits. With the traders' servants they held no communication, but Halima, a young slave who had been told off to attend to Mrs. Weldon, evinced for her new mistress an attachment which, though rough, was evidently sincere.

Old Alvez, who occupied the principal house in the depôt, was rarely seen ; whilst the non-appearance of either Harris or Negoro caused Mrs. Weldon much surprise and perplexity. In the midst of all her troubles, too, she was haunted by the thought of the anxiety her husband must be suffering on her account. Unaware of her having embarked on board the " Pilgrim," at first he would have wondered at steamer after steamer arriving at San Francisco without her. After a while the " Pilgrim " would have been registered amongst the number of missing ships ; and it was certain the intelligence would be forwarded to him by his correspondents, that the vessel had sailed from Auckland with his wife and child on board. What was he to imagine ? he might refuse to believe that they had perished at sea, but he would never dream of their having been carried to Africa, and would certainly institute a search in no other direction than on the coast of America, or amongst the isles of the Pacific. She had not the faintest hope of her whereabouts being discovered, and involuntarily her thoughts turned to the possibility of making an escape. She might well feel her heart sink within her at the bare idea ; even if she should succeed in eluding the vigilance of the watch, there were two hundred miles of dense forest to be traversed before the coast could be reached ; nevertheless, it revealed itself to her as her last chance, and, failing all else, she resolved to hazard it.

But, first of all, she determined, if it were possible, to discover the ultimate design of Negoro. She was not kept long in suspense. On the 6th of June, just a week after the royal funeral, the Portuguese entered the depôt, in which he had not set foot since his return, and made his way straight to the hut in which he knew he should find the prisoner. Benedict was out insect-hunting ; Jack, under Halima's charge, was being taken for a walk. Mrs. Weldon was alone.

Negoro pushed open the door, and said abruptly,—

" Mrs. Weldon, I have come to tell you, that Tom and his lot have been sold for the Ujiji market ; Nan died on her way here ; and Dick Sands is dead too."

Mrs. Weldon uttered a cry of horror.

" Yes, Mrs. Weldon," he continued ; " he has got what he deserved ; he shot Harris, and has been executed for the murder. And here you are alone ! mark this ! alone and in my power ! "

What Negoro said was true ; Tom, Bat, Actæon, and Austin had all been sent off that morning on their way to Ujiji.

Mrs. Weldon groaned bitterly.

Negoro went on.

" If I chose, I could still further avenge upon you the ill-treatment I got on board that ship ; but it does not suit my purpose to kill you. You and that boy of yours, and that idiot of a fly-catcher, all have a certain value in the market. I mean to sell you."

" You dare not ! " said Mrs. Weldon firmly ; " you know you are making an idle threat ; who do you suppose would purchase people of white blood ? "

" I know a customer who will give me the price I mean to ask," replied Negoro with a brutal grin.

She bent down her head; only too well she knew that such things were possible in this horrid land.

"Tell me who he is!" she said; "tell me the name of the man who . . . ."

"James Weldon," he answered slowly.

"My husband!" she cried; "what do you mean?

"I mean what I say. I mean to make your husband buy you back at my price; and if he likes to pay for them, he shall have his son and his cousin too."

"And when, and how, may I ask, do you propose to manage this?" replied Mrs. Weldon, forcing herself to be calm.

"Here, and soon too. I suppose Weldon will not mind coming to fetch you."

"He would not hesitate to come; but how could he know we are here?"

"I will go to him. I have money that will take me to San Francisco."

"What you stole from the 'Pilgrim'?" said Mrs. Weldon.

"Just so," replied Negoro; "and I have plenty more. I suppose when Weldon hears that you are a prisoner in Central Africa, he will not think much of a hundred thousand dollars."

"But how is he to know the truth of your statement?"

"I shall take him a letter from you. You shall represent me as your faithful servant, just escaped from the hands of savages."

"A letter such as that I will never write; never," said Mrs. Weldon decisively.

"What? what? you refuse?"

"I refuse."

She had all the natural cravings of a woman and a wife, but so thoroughly was she aware of the treachery of the man she had to deal with, that she dreaded lest, as soon as he had touched the ransom, he would dispose of her husband altogether.

PART II. X

There was a short silence.

" You will write that letter," said Negoro.

" Never ! " repeated Mrs. Weldon.

" Remember your child ! "

Mrs. Weldon's heart beat violently, but she did not answer a word.

" I will give you a week to think over this," hissed out Negoro.

Mrs. Weldon was still silent.

" A week ! I will come again in a week ; you will do as I wish, or it will be the worse for you."

He gnashed his teeth, turned on his heel, and left the hut.

CHAPTER XIV.

A RAY OF HOPE.

MRS. WELDON'S first feeling on being left alone was a sense of relief at having a week's respite. She had no trust in Negoro's honesty, but she knew well enough that their "marketable value" would secure them from any personal danger, and she had time to consider whether some compromise might be effected by which her husband might be spared the necessity of coming to Kazonndé. Upon the receipt of a letter from herself, he would not hesitate for a moment in undertaking the journey, but she entertained no little fear that after all perhaps her own departure might not be permitted ; the slightest caprice on the part of Queen Moena would detain her as a captive, whilst as to Negoro, if once he should get the ransom he wanted, he would take no further pains in the matter.

Accordingly, she resolved to make the proposition that she should be conveyed to some point upon the coast, where the bargain could be concluded without Mr. Weldon's coming up the country.

She had to weigh all the consequences that would follow any refusal on her part to fall in with Negoro's demands. Of course, he would spend the interval in preparing for his start to America, and when he should come back and find her still hesitating, was it not likely that he would find scope for his revenge in suggesting that she must be separated from her child.

The very thought sent a pang through her heart, and she clasped her little boy tenderly to her side.

"What makes you so sad, mamma?" asked Jack.

"I was thinking of your father, my child," she answered; "would you not like to see him?"

"Yes, yes; is he coming here?"

"No, my boy, he must not come here."

"Then let us take Dick, and Tom, and Hercules, and go to him."

Mrs. Weldon tried to conceal her tears.

"Have you heard from papa?"

"No."

"Then why do you not write to him?"

"Write to him?" repeated his mother, "that is the very thing I was thinking about."

The child little knew the agitation that was troubling her mind.

Meanwhile Mrs. Weldon had another inducement which she hardly ventured to own to herself for postponing her final decision. Was it absolutely impossible that her liberation should be effected by some different means altogether?

A few days previously she had overheard a conversation outside her hut, and over this she had found herself continually pondering.

Alvez and one of the Ujiji dealers, discussing the future prospects of their business, mutually agreed in denouncing the efforts that were being made for the suppression of the slave-traffic, not only by the cruisers on the coast, but by the intrusion of travellers and missionaries into the interior.

Alvez averred that all these troublesome visitors ought to be exterminated forthwith.

"But kill one, and another crops up," replied the dealer.

"Yes, their exaggerated reports bring up a swarm of them," said Alvez.

Dr. Livingstone.

It seemed a subject of bitter complaint that the markets of Nyangwé, Zanzibar, and the lake-district had been invaded by Speke and Grant and others, and although they congratulated each other that the western provinces had not yet been much persecuted, they confessed that now that the travelling epidemic had begun to rage, there was no telling how soon a lot of European and American busy-bodies might be among them. The depôts at Cassange and Bihé had both been visited, and although Kazonndé had hitherto been left quiet, there were rumours enough that the continent was to be tramped over from east to west.[1]

"And it may be," continued Alvez, "that that missionary fellow, Livingstone, is already on his way to us ; if he comes there can be but one result ; there must be freedom for all the slaves in Kazonndé."

" Freedom for the slaves in Kazonndé !"   These were the words which in connexion with Dr. Livingstone's name had arrested Mrs. Weldon's attention, and who can wonder that she pondered them over and over again, and ventured to associate them with her own prospects ?

Here was a ray of hope !

The mere mention of Livingstone's name in association with this story seems to demand a brief survey of his career.

Born on the 19th of March, 1813, David Livingstone was the second of six children of a tradesman in the village of Blantyre, in Lanarkshire. After two years' training in medicine and theology, he was sent out by the London Missionary Society, and landed at the Cape of Good Hope in 1840, with the intention of joining Moffat in South Africa. After exploring the country of the Bechuanas, he returned to Kuruman, and, having married Moffat's daughter, proceeded in 1843 to found a mission in the Mabotsa valley.

---

[1] This extraordinary feat was, it is universally known, subsequently accomplished by Cameron.

After four years he removed to Kolobeng in the Bechuana district, 225 miles north of Kuruman, whence, in 1849, starting off with his wife, three children, and two friends, Mr. Oswell and Mr. Murray, he discovered Lake Ngami, and returned by descending the course of the Zouga.

The opposition of the natives had prevented his proceeding beyond Lake Ngami at his first visit, and he made a second with no better success. In a third attempt, however, he wended his way northwards with his family and Mr. Oswell along the Chobé, an affluent of the Zambesi, and after a difficult journey at length reached the district of the Makalolos, of whom the chief, named Sebituané, joined him at Linyanté. The Zambesi itself was discovered at the end of June, 1851, and the doctor returned to the Cape for the purpose of sending his family to England.

His next project was to cross the continent obliquely from south to west, but in this expedition he had resolved that he would risk no life but his own. Accompanied, therefore, by only a few natives, he started in the following June, and skirting the Kalahari desert entered Litoubarouba on the last day of the year; here he found the Bechuana district much ravaged by the Boers, the original Dutch colonists, who had formed the population of the Cape before it came into the possession of the English. After a fortnight's stay, he proceeded into the heart of the district of the Bamangonatos, and travelled continuously until the 23rd of May, when he arrived at Linyanté, and was received with much honour by Sekeletoo, who had recently become sovereign of the Makalolos. A severe attack of fever detained the traveller here for a period, but he made good use of the enforced rest by studying the manners of the country, and became for the first time sensible of its terrible sufferings in consequence of the slave-trade.

Descending the course of the Chobé to the Zambesi, he next entered Naniele, and after visiting Katonga and

Libonta, advanced to the point of confluence of the Leeba with the Zambesi, where he determined upon ascending the former as far as the Portuguese possessions in the west; it was an undertaking, however, that required considerable preparation, so that it was necessary for him to return to Linyanté.

On the 11th of November he again started. He was accompanied by twenty-seven Makalolos, and ascended the Leeba till, in the territory of the Balonda, he reached a spot where it received the waters of its tributary the Makondo. It was the first time a white man had ever penetrated so far.

Proceeding on their way, they arrived at the residence of Shinté, the most powerful of the chieftains of the Balonda, by whom they were well received, and having met with equal kindness from Kateema, a ruler on the other side of the Leeba, they encamped, on the 20th of February, 1853, on the banks of Lake Dilolo.

Here it was that the real difficulty commenced; the arduous travelling, the attacks of the natives, and their exorbitant demands, the conspiracies of his own attendants, and their desertions, would soon have caused any one of less energy to abandon his enterprise; but David Livingstone was not a man to be daunted; resolutely he persevered, and on the 4th of April reached the banks of the Coango, the stream that forms the frontier of the Portuguese possessions, and joins the Zaire on the north.

Six days later he passed through Cassangé. Here it was that Alvez had seen him. On the 31st of May he arrived at St. Paul de Loanda, having traversed the continent in about two years.

It was not long, however, before he was off again. Following the banks of the Coanza, the river which was to bring such trying experiences to Dick Sands and his party, he reached the Lombé, and having met numbers of slave-caravans on his way, again passed through Cassangé, crossed the Coango, and reached the Zambesi at Kewawa. By the 8th of the following June he was again at Lake Dilolo, and descending the river, he re-entered Linyanté. Here he stayed till the 3rd of November, when he commenced his second great journey, which was to carry him completely across Africa from west to east.

After visiting the famed Victoria Falls, the intrepid explorer quitted the Zambesi, and took a north-easterly route. The transit of the territory of the Batokas, a people brutalized by the inhalation of hemp ; a visit to Semalemboni the powerful chief of the district ; the passage of the Kafoni; a visit to king Mbourouma ; an inspection of the ruins of Zumbo, an old Portuguese town ; a meeting with the chief Mpendé, at that time at war with the Portuguese ; these were the principal events of this journey, and on the 22nd of April, Livingstone left Teté, and having descended the river as far as its delta, reached Quilimané, just four years after his last departure from the Cape. On the 12th of July he embarked for the Mauritius, and on the 22nd of December, 1856, he landed in England after an absence of sixteen years.

Loaded with honours by the Geographical Societies of London and Paris, brilliantly entertained by all ranks, it would have been no matter of surprise if he had surrendered himself to a well-earned repose ; but no thought of permanent rest occurred to him, and on the 1st of March, 1858, accompanied by his brother Charles, Captain Bedingfield, Dr. Kirk, Dr. Miller, Mr. Thornton, and Mr. Baines, he started again, with the intention of exploring the basin of the Zambesi, and arrived in due time at the coast of Mozambique.

The party ascended the great river by the Kongone mouth ; they were on board a small steamer named the "Ma-Robert," and reached Teté on the 8th of September.

During the following year they investigated the lower

course of the Zambesi, and its left affluent the Shiré, and having visited Lake Shirwa, they explored the territory of the Manganjas, and discovered Lake Nyassa. In August, 1860, they returned to the Victoria Falls.

Early in the following year, Bishop Mackenzie and his missionary staff arrived at the mouth of the Zambesi.

In March an exploration of the Rovouma was made on board the "Pioneer," the exploring party returning afterwards to Lake Nyassa, where they remained a considerable time. The 30th of January, 1862, was signalized by the arrival of Mrs. Livingstone, and by the addition of another steamer, the "Lady Nyassa;" but the happiness of reunion was very transient; it was but a short time before the enthusiastic Bishop Mackenzie succumbed to the unhealthiness of the climate, and on the 27th of April Mrs. Livingstone expired in her husband's arms.

A second investigation of the Rovouma soon followed, and at the end of November the doctor returned to the Zambesi, and reascended the Shiré. In the spring of 1863 he lost his companion Mr. Thornton, and as his brother and Dr. Kirk were both much debilitated, he insisted upon their return to Europe, while he himself returned for the third time to Lake Nyassa, and completed the hydrographical survey which already he had begun.

A few months later found him once more at the mouth of the Zambesi; thence he crossed over to Zanzibar, and after five years' absence arrived in London, where he published his work, "The exploration of the Zambesi and its affluents."

Still unwearied and insatiable in his longings, he was back again in Zanzibar at the commencement of 1866, ready to begin his fourth journey, this time attended only by a few sepoys and negroes. Witnessing on his way some horrible scenes which were perpetrated as the result of the prosecution of the slave-trade, he proceeded to Mokalaosé on the shores of Lake Nyassa, where nearly all his attendants deserted him, and returned to Zanzibar with the report that he was dead.

Dr. Livingstone meanwhile was not only alive, but undaunted in his determination to visit the country between the two lakes Nyassa and Tanganyika. With none to guide him except a few natives, he crossed the Loangona, and in the following April discovered Lake Liemmba. Here he lay for a whole month hovering between life and death, but rallying a little he pushed on to the north shore of Lake Moero. Taking up his quarters at Cazembé for six weeks, he made two separate explorations of the lake, and then started farther northwards, intending to reach Ujiji, an important town upon Lake Tanganyika ; overtaken, however, by floods, and again abandoned by his servants, he was obliged to retrace his steps. Six weeks afterwards he had made his way southwards to the great lake Bangweolo, whence once more he started towards Tanganyika.

This last effort was most trying, and the doctor had grown so weak that he was obliged to be carried, but he reached Ujiji, where he was gratified by finding some supplies that had been thoughtfully forwarded to him by the Oriental Society at Calcutta.

His great aim now was to ascend the lake, and reach the sources of the Nile. On the 21st of September he was at Bambarré, in the country of the cannibal Manyuema, upon the Lualaba, the river afterwards ascertained by Stanley to be the Upper Zaire or Congo. At Mamobela the doctor. was ill for twenty-four days, tended only by three followers who continued faithful ; but in July he made a vigorous effort, and although he was reduced to a skeleton, made his way back to Ujiji.

During this long time no tidings of Livingstone reached Europe, and many were the misgivings lest the rumours of his death were only too true. He was himself, too, almost despairing as to receiving any help. But help was closer at hand than he thought. On the 3rd of November, only eleven days after his return to Ujiji, some gun-shots were heard within half a mile of the lake. The doctor went out to ascertain whence they proceeded, and had not gone far before a white man stood before him.

"You are Dr. Livingstone, I presume," said the stranger, raising his cap.

"Yes, sir, I am Dr. Livingstone, and am happy to see you," answered the doctor, smiling kindly.

The two shook each other warmly by the hand.

The new arrival was Henry Stanley, the correspondent of the *New York Herald*, who had been sent out by Mr. Bennett, the editor, in search of the great African explorer. On receiving his orders in October, 1870, without a day's unnecessary delay he had embarked at Bombay for Zanzibar, and, after a journey involving considerable peril, had arrived safely at Ujiji.

Very soon the two travellers found themselves on the best of terms, and set out together on an excursion to the north of Tanganyika. They proceeded as far as Cape Magala, and decided that the chief outlet of the lake must be an affluent of the Lualaba, a conclusion that was subsequently confirmed by Cameron.

Towards the end of the year Stanley began to prepare to return. Livingstone accompanied him as far as Kwihara and on the 3rd of the following March they parted.

"You have done for me what few men would venture to do; I am truly grateful," said Livingstone.

Stanley could scarcely repress his tears as he expressed his hope that the doctor might be spared to return to his friends safe and well.

"Good-bye!" said Stanley, choked with emotion.

"Good-bye!" answered the veteran feebly.

Thus they parted, and in July, 1872, Stanley landed at Marseilles.

Again David Livingstone resumed his researches in the interior. After remaining five months at Kwihara he gathered together a retinue consisting of his faithful followers Suzi, Chumah, Amoda, and Jacob Wainwright, and fifty-six men sent to him by Stanley, and lost no time in proceeding towards the south of Tanganyika. In the course of the ensuing month the caravan encountered some frightful storms, but succeeded in reaching Moura. There had previously been an extreme drought, which was now followed by the rainy season, which entailed the loss of many of the beasts of burden, in consequence of the bites of the tzetsy.

On the 24th of January they were at Chitounkwé, and in April, after rounding the east of Lake Bangweolo, they made their way towards the village of Chitambo. At this point it was that Livingstone had parted company with certain slave-dealers, who had carried the information to old Alvez that the missionary traveller would very likely proceed by way of Loanda to Kazonndé.

But on the 13th of June, the very day before Negoro reckoned on obtaining from Mrs. Weldon the letter which should be the means of securing him a hundred thousand dollars, tidings were circulated in the district that on the 1st of May Dr. Livingstone had breathed his last.

The report proved perfectly true. On the 29th of April the caravan had reached the village of Chitambo, the doctor so unwell that he was carried on a litter. The following night he was in great pain, and after repeatedly murmuring in a low voice, "Oh dear, oh dear!" he fell into a kind of stupor. A short time afterwards he called up Suzi, and having asked for some medicine, told his attendant that he should not require anything more.

"You can go now."

About four o'clock next morning, when an anxious visit was made to his room, the doctor was found kneeling by the bed-side, his head in his hands, in the attitude of prayer. Suzi touched him, but his forehead was icy with the coldness of death. He had died in the night.

His body was carried by those who loved him, and in spite of many obstacles was brought to Zanzibar, whence, nine months after his death, it was conveyed to England. On the 12th of April, 1874, it was interred in Westminster Abbey, counted worthy to be deposited amongst those whom the country most delights to honour.

CHAPTER XV.

AN EXCITING CHASE.

To say the truth, it was the very vaguest of hopes to which Mrs. Weldon had been clinging, yet it was not without some thrill of disappointment that she heard from the lips of old Alvez himself that Dr. Livingstone had died at a little village on Lake Bangweolo. There had appeared to be a sort of a link binding her to the civilized world, but it was now abruptly snapped, and nothing remained for her but to make what terms she could with the base and heartless Negoro.

On the 14th, the day appointed for the interview, he made his appearance at the hut, firmly resolved to make no abatement in the terms that he had proposed, Mrs. Weldon, on her part, being equally determined not to yield to the demand.

" There is only one condition," she avowed, " upon which I will acquiesce. My husband shall not be required to come up the country here."

Negoro hesitated ; at length he said that he would agree to her husband being taken by ship to Mossamedes, a small port in the south of Angola, much frequented by slavers, whither also, at a date hereafter to be fixed, Alvez should send herself with Jack and Benedict ; the stipulation was confirmed that the ransom should be 100,000. dollars, and it was further made part of the contract that Negoro should be allowed to depart as an honest man.

Mrs. Weldon felt she had gained an important point in

thus sparing her husband the necessity of a journey to Kazonndé, and had no apprehensions about herself on her way to Mossamedes, knowing that it was to the interest of Alvez and Negoro alike to attend carefully to her wants.

Upon the terms of the covenant being thus arranged, Mrs. Weldon wrote such a letter to her husband as she knew would bring him with all speed to Mossamedes, but she left it entirely to Negoro to represent himself in whatever light he chose. Once in possession of the document, Negoro lost no time in starting on his errand. The very next morning, taking with him about twenty negroes, he set off towards the north, alleging to Alvez as his motive for taking that direction, that he was not only going to embark somewhere at the mouth of the Congo, but that he was anxious to keep as far as possible from the prison-houses of the Portuguese, with which already he had been involuntarily only too familiar.

After his departure, Mrs. Weldon resolved to make the best of her period of imprisonment, aware that it could hardly be less than four months before he would return. She had no desire to go beyond the precincts assigned her, even had the privilege been allowed her ; but warned by Negoro that Hercules was still free, and might at any time attempt a rescue, Alvez had no thought of permitting her any unnecessary liberty. Her life therefore soon resumed its previous monotony.

The daily routine went on within the enclosure pretty much as in other parts of the town, the women all being employed in various labours for the benefit of their husbands and masters. The rice was pounded with wooden pestles ; the maize was peeled and winnowed, previously to extracting the granulous substance for the drink which they call *mtyellé;* the sorghum had to be gathered in, the season of its ripening being marked by festive observances ; there was a fragrant oil to be expressed from a kind of olive named the *mpafoo;* the cotton had to be spun on spindles, which were hardly less than a foot and a half in length ; there was the bark of trees to be woven into textures for wearing ; the manioc had to be dug up, and the cassava procured from its roots ; and besides all this, there was the preparation of the soil for its future plantings, the usual productions of the country being the *moritsané* beans, growing in pods fifteen inches long upon stems twenty feet high, the *arachides*, from which they procure a serviceable oil, the *chilobé* pea, the blossoms of which are used to give a flavour to the insipid sorghum, cucumbers, of which the seeds are roasted as chestnuts, as well as the common crops of coffee, sugar, onions, guavas, and sesame.

To the women's lot, too, falls the manipulation of all the fermented drinks, the *malafoo*, made from bananas, the *pombé*, and various other liquors. Nor should the care of all the domestic animals be forgotten ; the cows that will not allow themselves to be milked unless they can see their calf, or a stuffed representative of it ; the short-horned heifers that not unfrequently have a hump ; the goats that, like slaves, form part of the currency of the country; the pigs, the sheep, and the poultry.

The men, meanwhile, smoke their hemp or tobacco, hunt buffaloes or elephants, or are hired by the dealers to join in the slave-raids ; the harvest of slaves, in fact, being a thing of as regular and periodic recurrence as the ingathering of the maize.

In her daily strolls, Mrs. Weldon would occasionally pause to watch the women, but they only responded to her notice by a long stare or by a hideous grimace ; a kind of natural instinct made them hate a white skin, and they had no spark of commiseration for the stranger who had been brought among them ; Halima, however, was a marked exception, she grew more and more devoted to her mistress, and by degrees, the two became able to exchange many sentences in the native dialect.

Jack generally accompanied his mother. Naturally enough he longed to get outside the enclosure, but still he found considerable amusement in watching the birds that built in a huge baobab that grew within; there were maraboos making their nests with twigs; there were scarlet-throated *souimangas* with nests like weaver-birds; widow birds that helped themselves liberally to the thatch of the huts; *calaos* with their tuneful song; grey parrots, with bright red tails, called *roufs* by the Manyema, who apply the same name to their reigning chiefs; and insect-eating *drongos*, like grey linnets with large red beaks. Hundreds of butterflies flitted about, especially in the neighbourhood of the brooks; but these were more to the taste of Cousin Benedict than of little Jack; over and over again the child expressed his regret that he could not see over the walls, and more than ever he seemed to miss his friend Dick, who had taught him to climb a mast, and who he was sure would have fine fun with him in the branches of the trees, which were growing sometimes to the height of a hundred feet.

So long as the supply of insects did not fail, Benedict would have been contented to stay on without a murmur in his present quarters. True, without his glasses he worked at a disadvantage; but he had had the good fortune to discover a minute bee that forms its cells in the holes of worm-eaten wood, and a "sphex" that practises the craft of the cuckoo, and deposits its eggs in an abode not prepared by itself. Mosquitoes abounded in swarms, and the worthy naturalist was so covered by their stings as to be hardly recognizable; but when Mrs. Weldon remonstrated with him for exposing himself so unnecessarily, he merely scratched the irritated places on his skin, and said,—

" It is their instinct, you know ; it is their instinct."

On the 17th of June an adventure happened to him which was attended with unexpected consequences. It was about eleven o'clock in the morning. The insufferable heat had driven all the residents within the depôt indoors, and not a native was to be seen in the streets of Kazonndé. Mrs. Weldon was dozing; Jack was fast asleep. Benedict himself, sorely against his will, for he heard the hum of many an insect in the sunshine, had been driven to the seclusion of his cabin, and was falling into an involuntary siesta.

Suddenly a buzz was heard, an insect's wing vibrating some fifteen thousand beats a second !

"A hexapod!" cried Benedict, sitting up.

Short-sighted though he was, his hearing was acute, and his perception made him thoroughly convinced that he was in proximity to some giant specimen of its kind. Without moving from his seat he did his utmost to ascertain what it was ; he was determined not to flinch from the sharpest of stings if only he could get the chance of capturing it. Presently he made out a large black speck flitting about in the few rays of daylight that were allowed to penetrate the hut. With bated breath he waited in eager expectation. The insect, after long hovering above him, finally settled on his head. A smile of satisfaction played about his lips as he felt it crawling lightly through his hair. Equally fearful of missing or injuring it, he restrained his first impulse to grasp it in his hand.

" I will wait a minute," he thought ; " perhaps it may creep down my nose ; by squinting a little perhaps I shall be able to see it."

For some moments hope alternated with fear. There sat Benedict with what he persuaded himself was some new African hexapod perched upon his head, and agitated by doubts as to the direction in which it would move. Instead of travelling in the way he reckoned along his nose, might it not crawl behind his ears or down his neck, or, worse than all, resume its flight in the air ?

Fortune seemed inclined to favour him. After threading the entanglement of the naturalist's hair the insect was felt

to be descending his forehead. With a fortitude not
unworthy of the Spartan who suffered his breast to be gnawed
by a fox, nor of the Roman hero who plunged his hand into
the red-hot coals, Benedict endured the tickling of the six
small feet, and made not a motion that might frighten the
creature into taking wing.   After making repeated circuits of
his forehead, it passed just between his eyebrows ; there was
a moment of deep suspense lest it should once more go
upwards ; but it soon began to move again ; neither to the
right nor to the left did it turn, but kept straight on over the
furrows made by the constant rubbing of the spectacles, right
along the arch of the cartilage till it reached the extreme tip
of the nose.   Like a couple of movable lenses, Benedict's two
eyes steadily turned themselves inwards till they were
directed to the proper point.

" Good ! " he whispered to himself.

He was exulting at the discovery that what he had been
waiting for so patiently was a rare specimen of the tribe
of the Cicindelidæ, peculiar to the districts of Southern
Africa.

" A tuberous manticora ! " he exclaimed.

The insect began to move again, and as it crawled down
to the entrance of the nostrils the tickling sensation became
too much for endurance, and Benedict sneezed. He made
a sudden clutch, but of course he only caught his own nose.
His vexation was very great, but he did not lose his composure ; he knew that the manticora rarely flies very high,
and that more frequently than not it simply crawls.
Accordingly he groped about a long time on his hands and
knees, and at last he found it basking in a ray of sunshine
within a foot of him. His resolution was soon taken. He
would not run the risk of crushing it by trying to catch it,
but would make his observations on it as it crawled ; and so
with his nose close to the ground, like a dog upon the scent,
he followed it on all fours, admiring it and examining it as it
moved. Regardless of the heat he not only left the doorway

of his hut, but continued creeping along till he reached the enclosing palisade.

At the foot of the fence the manticora, according to the habits of its kind, began to seek a subterranean retreat, and coming to the opening of a mole-track entered it at once. Benedict quite thought he had now lost sight of his prize altogether, but his surprise was very great when he found that the aperture was at least two feet wide, and that it led into a gallery which would admit his whole body. His momentary feeling of astonishment, however, gave way to his eagerness to follow up the hexapod, and he continued burrowing like a ferret.

Without knowing it, he actually passed under the palisading, and was now beyond it;—the mole-track, in fact, was a communication that had been made between the interior and exterior of the enclosure. Benedict had obtained his freedom, but so far from caring in the least for his liberty he continued totally absorbed in the pursuit upon which he had started.

He watched with unflagging vigilance, and it was only when the hexapod expanded its wings as if for flight that he prepared to imprison it in the hollow of his hand.

All at once, however, he was taken by surprise ; a whizz and a whirr and the prize was gone !

Disappointed rather than despairing, Benedict raised himself up, and looked about him. Before long the old black speck was again flitting just above his head. There was every reason to hope that it would ultimately settle once more upon the ground, but on this side of the palisade there was a large forest a little way to the north, and if the manticora were to get into its mass of foliage all hope of keeping it in view would be lost, and there would be an end of the proud expectation of storing it in the tin box, to be preserved among the rest of the entomological wonders.

After a while the insect descended to the earth ; it did not rest at all, nor crawl as it had done previously, but made its advance by a series of rapid hops. This made the chase for the near-sighted naturalist a matter of great difficulty ; he put his face as close to the ground as possible, and kept starting off and stopping and starting off again with his arms extended like a swimming frog, continually making frantic clutches to find as continually that his grasp had been cluded.

After running till he was out of breath, and scratching his hands against the brushwood and the foliage till they bled, he had the mortification of feeling the insect dash past his ear with what might be a defiant buzz, and finding that it was out of sight for ever.

" Ungrateful hexapod !" he cried in dismay, " I intended to honour you with the best place in my collection."

He knew not what to do, and could not reconcile himself to the loss ; he reproached himself for not having secured the manticora at the first ; he gazed at the forest till he persuaded himself he could see the coveted insect in the distance, and, seized with a frantic impulse, exclaimed,—

" I will have you yet ! "

He did not even yet realize the fact that he had gained his liberty, but heedless of everything except his own burning disappointment, and at the risk of being attacked by natives or beset by wild beasts, he was just on the very point of dashing into the heart of the wood when suddenly a giant form confronted him, as suddenly a giant hand seized him by the nape of his neck, and, lifting him up, carried him off with apparently as little exertion as he could himself have carried off his hexapod !

For that day at least Cousin Benedict had lost his chance of being the happiest of entomologists.

CHAPTER XVI.

A MAGICIAN.

On finding that Cousin Benedict did not return to his quarters at the proper hour, Mrs. Weldon began to feel uneasy. She could not imagine what had become of him; his tin box with its contents were safe in his hut, and even if a chance of escape had been offered him, she knew that nothing would have induced him voluntarily to abandon his treasures. She enlisted the services of Halima, and spent the remainder of the day in searching for him, until at last she felt herself driven to the conviction that he must have been confined by the orders of Alvez himself; for what reason she could not divine, as Benedict had undoubtedly been included in the number of prisoners to be delivered to Mr. Weldon for the stipulated ransom.

But the rage of the trader when he heard of the escape of the captive was an ample proof that he had had no hand in his disappearance. A rigorous search was instituted in every direction, which resulted in the discovery of the mole-track. Here beyond a question was the passage through which the fly-catcher had found his way.

"Idiot! fool! rascal!" muttered Alvez, full of rage at the prospect of losing a portion of the redemption-money; "if ever I get hold of him, he shall pay dearly for this freak."

The opening was at once blocked up, the woods were scoured all round for a considerable distance, but no trace of Benedict was to be found. Mrs. Weldon was bitterly grieved and much overcome, but she had no alternative except to resign herself as best she could to the loss of her unfortunate relation ; there was a tinge of bitterness in her anxiety, for she could not help being irritated at the recklessness with which he had withdrawn himself from the reach of her protection.

Meanwhile the weather for the time of year underwent a very unusual change. Although the rainy reason is ordinarily reckoned to terminate about the end of April, the sky had suddenly become overcast in the middle of June, rain had recommenced falling, and the downpour had been so heavy and continuous that all the ground was thoroughly sodden. To Mrs. Weldon personally this incessant rainfall brought no other inconvenience beyond depriving her of her daily exercise, but to the natives in general it was a very serious calamity.

The ripening crops in the low-lying districts were completely flooded, and the inhabitants feared that they would be reduced to the greatest extremities ; all agricultural pursuits had come to a standstill, and neither the queen nor her ministers could devise any expedient to avert or mitigate the misfortune. They resolved at last to have recourse to the magicians, not those who are called in request to heal diseases or to procure good luck, but to the *mganga*, sorcerers of a superior order, who are credited with the faculty of invoking or dispelling rain.

But it was all to no purpose. It was in vain that the *mganga* monotoned their incantations, flourished their rattles, jingled their bells, and exhibited their amulets ; it was equally without avail that they rolled up their balls of dirt and spat in the faces of all the courtiers : the pitiless rain continued to descend, and the malign influences that were ruling the clouds refused to be propitiated.

The prospect seemed to become more and more hopeless, when the report was brought to Moena that there was a most wonderful *mganga* resident in the north of Angola. He had never been seen in this part of the country, but fame declared him to be a magician of the very highest order. Application, without delay, should be made to him; he surely would be able to stay the rain.

Early in the morning of the 25th a great tinkling of bells announced the magician's arrival at Kazonndé. The natives poured out to meet him on his way to the *chitoka*, their minds being already predisposed in his favour by a moderation of the downpour, and by sundry indications of a coming change of wind.

The ordinary practice of the professors of the magical art is to perambulate the villages in parties of three or four, accompanied by a considerable number of acolytes and assistants. In this case the *mganga* came entirely alone. He was a pure negro of most imposing stature, more than six feet high, and broad in proportion. All over his chest was a fantastic pattern traced in pipe-clay, the lower portion of his body being covered with a flowing skirt of woven grass, so long that it made a train. Round his neck hung a string of birds' skulls, upon his head he wore a leathern helmet ornamented with pearls and plumes, and about his waist was a copper girdle, to which was attached bells that tinkled like the harness of a Spanish mule. The only instrument indicating his art was a basket he carried made of a calabash containing shells, amulets, little wooden idols and other fetishes, together with what was more important than all, a large number of those balls of dung, without which no African ceremony of divination could ever be complete.

One peculiarity was soon discovered by the crowd; the *mganga* was dumb, and could utter only one low, guttural sound, which was quite unintelligible; this was a circumstance, however, that seemed only to augment their faith in his powers.

With a stately strut that brought all his tinkling paraphernalia into full play, the magician proceeded to make the circuit of the market-place. The natives followed in a troop behind, endeavouring, like monkeys, to imitate his every movement. He turned into the main thoroughfare, and began to make his way direct to the royal residence, whence, as soon as the queen heard of his approach, she advanced to meet him. On seeing her, the *mganga* bowed to the very dust ; then, rearing himself to his full height, he pointed aloft, and by the significance of his animated gestures indicated that, although the fleeting clouds were now going to the west, they would soon return eastwards with a rotatory motion irresistibly strong.

All at once, to the surprise of the beholders, he stooped and took the hand of the mighty sovereign of Kazonndé.

The courtiers hurried forward to check the unprecedented breach of etiquette, but the foremost was driven back with so staggering a blow that the others deemed it prudent to retire.

The queen herself appeared not to take the least offence at the familiarity; she bestowed a hideous grimace, which was meant for a smile, upon her illustrious visitor, who, still keeping his hold upon her hand, started off walking at a rapid pace, the crowd following in the rear. He directed his steps towards the residence of Alvez, and finding the door closed, applied his strong shoulder to it with such effect, that it feel bodily to the ground, and the passive sovereign stood within the limits of the enclosure. The trader was about to summon his slaves and soldiers to repel the unceremonious invasion of his premises, but on beholding the queen all stepped back with respectful reverence.

Before Alvez had time to ask the sovereign to what cause he was indebted for the honour of her visit, the magician had cleared a wide space around him, and had once again commenced his performances. Brandishing his arms wildly he pointed to the clouds as though he were arresting them in their course ; he inflated his huge cheeks and blew with all his strength, as if resolved to disperse the heavy masses, and then stretching himself to his full height, he appeared to clutch them in his giant grasp.

Deeply impressed, the superstitious Moena was half beside herself with excitement; she uttered loud cries and involuntarily began herself to imitate every one of the *mganga's* gestures. The entire crowd joined in, and very soon the low guttural note of the sorcerer was lost, totally drowned in the turmoil of howls, shrieks, and discordant songs.

To the chagrin, however, both of the queen and her subjects, there was not the slightest intimation that the clouds above were going to permit a rift by which the rays of the tropical sun could find a passage. On the contrary, the tokens of improvement in the weather, which had been observed in the early morning, had all disappeared, the atmosphere was darker than ever, and heavy storm-drops began to patter down.

A reaction was beginning to take place in the enthusiasm of the crowd. After all, then, it would seem that this famous *mganga* from whom so much had been expected, had no power above the rest. Disappointment every moment grew more keen, and soon there was a positive display of irritation. The natives pressed around him with closed fists and threatening gestures. A frown gathered on Moena's face, and her lips opened with muttered words clear enough to make the magician understand that his ears were in jeopardy. His position was evidently becoming critical.

An unexpected incident suddenly altered the aspect of affairs.

The *mganga* was quite tall enough to see over the heads of the crowd, and all at once pausing in the midst of his incantations, he pointed to a distant corner of the enclosure. All eyes were instantly turned in that direction. Mrs. Weldon and Jack had just come out of their hut, and catching sight of them, the *mganga* stood with his left hand pointing towards them and his right upstretched towards the heavens.

Intuitively the multitude comprehended his meaning. Here was the explanation of the mystery. It was this white

The entire crowd joined in.

woman with her child that had been the cause of all their misery, it was owing to them that the clouds had poured down this desolating rain. With yells of execration the whole mob made a dash towards the unfortunate lady who, pale with fright and rigid as a statue, stood clasping her boy to her side. The *mganga*, however, anticipated them. Having pushed his way through the infuriated throng, he seized the child and held him high in the air, as though about to hurl him to the ground, a peace-offering to the offended gods.

Mrs. Weldon gave a piercing shriek, and fell senseless to the earth.

Lifting her up, and making a sign to the queen that all would now be right, the *mganga* retreated carrying both mother and child through the crowd, who retreated before him and made an open passage.

Alvez now felt that it was time to interfere. Already one of his prisoners had eluded his vigilance, and was he now to see two more carried off before his eyes? was he to lose the whole of the expected ransom? no, rather would he see Kazonndé destroyed by a deluge, than resign his chance of securing so good a prize. Darting forwards he attempted to obstruct the magician's progress; but public opinion was against him; at a sign from the queen, he was seized by the guards, and he was aware well enough of what would be the immediate consequence of resistance. He deemed it prudent to desist from his obstruction, but in his heart he bitterly cursed the stupid credulity of the natives for supposing that the blood of the white woman or the child could avail to put an end to the disasters they were suffering.

Making the natives understand that they were not to follow him, the magician carried off his burden as easily as a lion would carry a couple of kids. The lady was still unconscious, and Jack was all but paralyzed with fright. Once free of the enclosure the *mganga* crossed the town, entered the forest, and after a march of three miles, during which he did not slacken his pace for a moment, reached the bank of a river which was flowing towards the north.

Here in the cavity of a rock, concealed by drooping foliage, a canoe was moored, covered with a kind of thatched roof; on this the magician deposited his burden, and sending the light craft into mid-stream with a vigorous kick, exclaimed in a cheery voice,—

"Here they are, captain! both of them! Mrs. Weldon and Master Jack, both! We will be off now! I hope those idiots of Kazonndé will have plenty more rain yet! Off we go!"

CHAPTER XVII.

DRIFTING DOWN THE STREAM.

"OFF we go!" It was the voice of Hercules addressing Dick Sands, who, frightfully debilitated by recent sufferings, was leaning against Cousin Benedict for support. Dingo was lying at his feet.

Mrs. Weldon gradually recovered her consciousness. Looking around her in amazement she caught sight of Dick.

"Dick, is it you?" she muttered feebly.

The lad with some difficulty arose, and took her hand in his, while Jack overwhelmed him with kisses.

"And who would have thought it was you, Hercules, that carried us away?" said the child; "I did not know you a bit; you were so dreadfully ugly."

"I was a sort of a devil, you know, Master Jack," Hercules answered; "and the devil is not particularly handsome;" and he began rubbing his chest vigorously to get rid of the white pattern with which he had adorned it.

Mrs. Weldon held out her hand to him with a grateful smile.

"Yes, Mrs. Weldon, he has saved you, and although he does not own it, he has saved me too," said Dick.

"Saved!" repeated Hercules, "you must not talk about safety, for you are not saved yet."

And pointing to Benedict, he continued,—

"That's where your thanks are due; unless he had come

and informed me all about you and where you were, I should have known nothing, and should have been powerless to aid you."

It was now five days since he had fallen in with the entomologist as he was chasing the manticora, and unceremoniously had carried him off.

As the canoe drifted rapidly along the stream, Hercules briefly related his adventures since his escape from the encampment on the Coanza. He described how he had followed the kitanda which was conveying Mrs. Weldon ; how in the course of his march he had found Dingo badly wounded ; how he and the dog together had reached the neighbourhood of Kazonndé, and how he had contrived to send a note to Dick, intending to inform him of Mrs. Weldon's destination. Then he went on to say that since his unexpected *rencontre* with Cousin Benedict he had watched very closely for a chance to get into the guarded depôt, but until now had entirely failed. A celebrated *mganga* had been passing on his way through the forest, and he had resolved upon impersonating him as a means of gaining the admittance he wanted. His strength made the undertaking sufficiently easy ; and having stripped the magician of his paraphernalia, and bound him securely to a tree, he painted his own body with a pattern like that which he observed on his victim's chest, and having attired himself with the magical garments was quite equipped to impose upon the credulous natives. The result of his stratagem they had all that day witnessed.

He had hardly finished his account of himself when Mrs. Weldon, smiling at his success, turned to Dick.

"And how, all this time, my dear boy, has it fared with you ? " she asked.

Dick said,—

"I remember very little to tell you. I recollect being fastened to a stake in the river-bed and the water rising and rising till it was above my head. My last thoughts were about yourself and Jack. Then everything became a blank, and I knew nothing more until I found myself amongst the papyrus on the river-bank, with Hercules tending me like a nurse."

"You see I am the right sort of *mganga*," interposed Hercules; "I am a doctor as well as a conjuror."

"But tell me, Hercules, how did you save him?"

"Oh, it was not a difficult matter by any means,' answered Hercules modestly; "it was dark, you know, so that at the proper moment it was quite possible to wade in amongst the poor wretches at the bottom of the trench, and to wrench the stake from its socket. Anybody could have done it. Cousin Benedict could have done it. Dingo, too, might have done it. Perhaps, after all, it was Dingo that did it."

" No, no, Hercules, that won't do," cried Jack ; "besides, look, Dingo is shaking his head; he is telling you he didn't do it."

"Dingo must not tell tales, Master Jack," said Hercules, laughing.

But, nevertheless, although the brave fellow's modesty prompted him to conceal it, it was clear that he had accomplished a daring feat, of which few would have ventured to incur the risk.

Inquiry was next made after Tom, Bat, Actæon, and Austin. His countenance fell, and large tears gathered in his eyes as Hercules told how he had seen them pass through the forest in a slave-caravan. They were gone ; he feared they were gone for ever.

Mrs. Weldon tried to console him with the hope that they might still be spared to meet again some day ; but he shook his head mournfully. She then communicated to Dick the terms of the compact that had been entered into for her own release, and observed that under the circumstances it might really have been more prudent for her to remain in Kazonndé.

"Then I have made a mistake; I have been an idiot, in bringing you away," said Hercules, ever ready to depreciate his own actions.

"No," said Dick; "you have made no mistake; you could not have done better; those rascals, ten chances to one, will only get Mr. Weldon into some trap. We must get to Mossamedes before Negoro arrives; once there, we shall find that the Portuguese authorities will lend us their protection, and when old Alvez arrives to claim his 100,000 dollars—"

"He shall receive a good thrashing for his pains," said Hercules, finishing Dick's sentence, and chuckling heartily at the prospect.

It was agreed on all hands that it was most important that Negoro's arrival at Mossamedes should be forestalled. The plan which Dick had so long contemplated of reaching the coast by descending some river seemed now in a fair way of being accomplished, and from the northerly direction in which they were proceeding it was quite probable that they would ultimately reach the Zaire, and in that case not actually arrive at St. Paul de Loanda; but that would be immaterial, as they would be sure of finding help anywhere in the colonies of Lower Guinea.

On finding himself on the river-bank, Dick's first thought had been to embark upon one of the floating islands that are continually to be seen upon the surface of the African streams, but it happened that Hercules during one of his rambles found a native boat that had run adrift. It was just the discovery that suited their need. It was one of the long, narrow canoes, thirty feet in length by three or four in breadth, that with a large number of paddles can be driven with immense velocity, but by the aid of a single skull can be safely guided down the current of a stream.

Dick was somewhat afraid that, to elude observation, it would be necessary to proceed only by night, but as the loss of twelve hours out of the twenty-four would double the length of the voyage, he devised the plan of covering the canoe with a roof of long grass, supported by a horizontal pole from stem to stern, and this not only afforded a shelter from the sun, but so effectually concealed the craft, rudder-scull and all, that the very birds mistook it for one of the natural islets, and red-beaked gulls, black *arringhas* and grey and white kingfishers would frequently alight upon it in search of food.

Though comparatively free from fatigue, the voyage must necessarily be long, and by no means free from danger, and the daily supply of provisions was not easy to procure. If fishing failed, Dick had the one gun which Hercules had carried away with him from the ant-hill, and as he was by no means a bad shot, he hoped to find plenty of game, either along the banks or by firing through a loop-hole in the thatch.

The rate of the current, as far as he could tell, was about two miles an hour, enough to carry them about fifty miles a day; it was a speed, however, that made it necessary for them to keep a sharp look-out for any rocks or submerged trunks of trees, as well as to be on their guard against rapids and cataracts.

Dick's strength and spirits all revived at the delight of having Mrs. Weldon and Jack restored to him, and he assumed his post at the bow of the canoe, directing Hercules how to use the scull at the stern. A litter of soft grass was made for Mrs. Weldon, who spent most of her time lying thoughtfully in the shade. Cousin Benedict was very taci-turn; he had not recovered the loss of the manticora, and frowned ever and again at Hercules, as if he had not yet forgiven him for stopping him in the chase. Jack, who had been told that he must not be noisy, amused himself by playing with Dingo.

The first two days passed without any special incident. The stock of provisions was quite enough for that time, so that there was no need to disembark, and Dick merely lay to for a few hours in the night to take a little necessary repose.

The stream nowhere exceeded 150 feet in breadth. The floating islands moved at the same pace as the canoe, and except from some unforeseen circumstance, there could be no apprehension of a collision. The banks were destitute of human inhabitants, but were richly clothed with wild plants, of which the blossoms were of the most gorgeous colours ; the asclepiæ, the gladiolus, the clematis, lilies, aloes, umbelliferæ, arborescent ferns and fragrant shrubs, combining on either hand to make a border of surpassing beauty. Here and there the forest extended to the very shore, and copal-trees, acacias with their stiff foliage, bauhinias clothed with lichen, fig-trees with their masses of pendant roots, and other trees of splendid growth rose to the height of a hundred feet, forming a shade which the rays of the sun utterly failed to penetrate.

Occasionally a wreath of creepers would form an arch from shore to shore, and on the 27th, to Jack's great delight a group of monkeys was seen crossing one of these natural bridges, holding on most carefully by their tails, lest the aërial pathway should snap beneath their weight. These monkeys, belonging to a smaller kind of chimpanzee, which are known in Central Africa by the name of *sokos*, were hideous creatures with low foreheads, bright yellow faces, and long, upright ears ; they herd in troops of about ten, bark like dogs, and are much dreaded by the natives on account of their alleged propensity to carry off young children ; there is no telling what predatory designs they might have formed against Master Jack if they had spied him out, but Dick's artifice effectually screened him from their observation.

Twenty miles further on the canoe came to a sudden standstill.

"What's the matter now, captain ?" cried Hercules from the stern.

"We have drifted on to a grass barrier, and there is no hope for it, we shall have to cut our way through," answered Dick.

"All right, I dare say we shall manage it," promptly replied Hercules, leaving his rudder to come in front.

The obstruction was formed by the interlacing of masses of the tough, glossy grass known by the name of *tikatika*, which, when compressed, affords a surface so compact and resisting that travellers have been known by means of it to cross rivers dry-footed. Splendid specimens of lotus plants had taken root amongst the vegetation.

As it was nearly dark, Hercules could leave the boat without much fear of detection, and so effectually did he wield his hatchet that, in two hours after the stoppage, the barrier was hewn asunder, and the light craft resumed the channel.

It must be owned that it was with a sense of reluctance that Benedict felt the boat was again beginning to move forward; the whole voyage appeared to him to be perfectly uninteresting and unnecessary; not a single insect had he observed since he left Kazonndé, and his most ardent wish was that he could return there and regain possession of his invaluable tin box. But an unlooked-for gratification was in store for him.

Hercules, who had been his pupil long enough to have an eye for the kind of creature Benedict was ever trying to secure, on coming back from his exertions on the grass-barrier, brought a horrible-looking animal, and submitted it to the sullen entomologist.

"Is this of any use to you?"

The amateur lifted it up carefully, and having almost poked it into his near-sighted eyes, uttered a cry of delight,—

"Bravo, Hercules! you are making amends for your past mischief; it is splendid! it is unique!"

"Is it really very curious?" said Mrs. Weldon.

"Yes, indeed," answered the enraptured naturalist ; " it is really unique ; it belongs to neither of the ten orders ; it can be classed neither with the coleoptera, neuroptera, nor to the hymenoptera : if it had eight legs I should know how to classify it ; I should place it amongst the second section of the arachnida ; but it is a hexapod, a genuine hexapod ; a spider with six legs ; a grand discovery ; it must be entered on the catalogue as ' Hexapodes Benedictus.'" Once again mounted on his hobby, the worthy enthusiast continued to discourse with an unwonted vivacity to his indulgent if not over attentive audience.

Meanwhile the canoe was steadily threading its way over the dark waters, the silence of the night broken only by the rattle of the scales of some crocodiles, or by the snorting of hippopotamuses in the neighbourhood. Once the travellers were startled by a loud noise, such as might proceed from some ponderous machinery in motion : it was caused by a troop of a hundred or more elephants that, after feasting through the day on the roots of the forest, had come to quench their thirst at the river-side.

But no danger was to be apprehended ; lighted by the pale moon that rose over the tall trees, the canoe throughout the night pursued in safety its solitary voyage.

CHAPTER XVIII.

AN ANXIOUS VOYAGE.

THUS the canoe drifted on for a week, the forests that for many miles had skirted the river ultimately giving place to extensive jungles that stretched far away to the horizon. Destitute, fortunately for the travellers, of human inhabitants, the district abounded in a large variety of animal life; zebras, elands, caamas, sported on the bank, disappearing at night-fall before howling leopards and roaring lions.

It was Dick's general custom, as he lay to for a while in the afternoon, to go ashore in search of food, and as the manioc, maize, and sorghum that were to be found were of a wild growth and consequently not fit for consumption, he was obliged to run the risk of using his gun. On the 4th of July he succeeded by a single shot in killing a *pokoo*, a kind of antelope about five feet long, with annulated horns, a tawny skin dappled with bright spots, and a white belly. The venison proved excellent, and was roasted over a fire procured by the primitive method, practised, it is said, even by gorillas, of rubbing two sticks together.

In spite of these halts, and the time taken for the night's rest, the distance accomplished by the 8th could not be estimated at less than a hundred miles. The river, augmented by only a few insignificant tributaries, had not materially increased in volume; its direction, however, had slightly changed more to the north-west. It afforded a very fair supply of fish, which were caught by lines made of the long stems of creepers furnished with thorns instead of fish-hooks, a considerable proportion being the delicate *sandjikas*, which when dried may be transported to any climate; besides these there were the black *usakas*, the wide-headed *mounds*, and occasionally the little *dagalas*, resembling Thames whitebait.

Next day, Dick met with an adventure that put all his courage and composure to the test. He had noticed the horns of a caama projecting above the brushwood, and went ashore alone with the intention of securing it. He succeeded in getting tolerably close to it and fired, but he was terribly startled when a formidable creature bounded along some thirty paces ahead, and took possession of the prey he had just wounded.

It was a majestic lion, at least five feet in height, of the kind called *káramoo*, in distinction to the maneless species known as the *Nyassi-lion*. Before Dick had time to reload, the huge brute had caught sight of him, and without relaxing its hold upon the writhing antelope beneath its claws, glared upon him fiercely. Dick's presence of mind did not forsake him; flight he knew was not to be thought of; his only chance he felt intuitively would be by keeping perfectly still; and aware that the beast would be unlikely to give up a struggling prey for another that was motionless, he stood face to face with his foe, not venturing to move an eyelid. In a few minutes the lion's patience seemed to be exhausted; with a grand stateliness, it picked up the caama as easily as a dog would lift a hare, turned round, and lashing the bushes with its tail, disappeared in the jungle.

It took Dick some little time to recover himself sufficiently to return to the canoe. On arriving, he said nothing of the peril to which he had been exposed, but heartily congratulated himself that they had means of transport without making their way through jungles and forests.

As they advanced, they repeatedly came across evidences

He stood face to face with his foe.

that the country had not been always, as now it was, utterly
devoid of population ; more than once, they observed traces
which betokened the former existence of villages ; either
some ruined palisades or the *débris* of some thatched huts,
or some solitary sacred tree within an enclosure would
indicate that the death of a chief had, according to custom,
made a native tribe migrate to new quarters.

If natives were still dwelling in the district, as was just
probable, they must have been living underground, only
emerging at night like beasts of prey, from which they were
only a grade removed.

Dick Sands had every reason to feel convinced that
cannibalism had been practised in the neighbourhood.
Three times, as he was wandering in the forest, he had come
upon piles of ashes and half-charred human bones, the
remnants, no doubt, of a ghastly meal, and although he
mentioned nothing of what he had seen to Mrs. Weldon, he
made up his mind to go ashore as seldom as possible, and
as often as he found it absolutely necessary to go, he gave
Hercules strict directions to push off into mid-stream at the
very first intimation of danger.

A new cause of anxiety arose on the following evening,
and made it necessary for them to take the most guarded
measures of precaution. The river-bed had widened out
into a kind of lagoon, and on the right side of this, built
upon piles in the water, not only was there a collection of
about thirty huts, but the fires gleaming under the thatch,
made it evident that they were all inhabited. Unfortunately
the only channel of the stream flowed close under the huts,
the river elsewhere being so obstructed with rocks that
navigation of any kind was impossible. Nothing was
more probable than that the natives would have set their
nets all across the piles, and if so, the canoe would be sure
to be obstructed, and an alarm must inevitably be raised.
Every caution seemed to be unavailing, because the canoe
must follow the stream ; however, in the lowest of whispers

Dick order Hercules to keep clear as much as he could of the worm-eaten timber. The night was not very dark, which was equally an advantage and a disadvantage, as while it permitted those on board to steer as they wanted, it did not prevent them from being seen.

The situation became more and more critical. About a hundred feet ahead, the channel was very contracted; two natives, gesticulating violently, were seen squatting on the pilework; a few moments more and their voices could be heard; it was obvious that they had seen the floating mass; apprehending that it was going to destroy their nets, they yelled aloud and shouted for assistance; instantly five or six negroes scrambled down the piles, and perched themselves upon the cross-beams.

On board the canoe the profoundest silence was maintained. Dick only signalled his directions to Hercules, without uttering a word, while Jack performed his part by holding Dingo's mouth tightly closed, to stop the low growlings which the faithful watch-dog seemed resolved to make; but fortunately every sound was overpowered by the rushing of the stream and the clamour of the negroes, as they hurriedly drew in their nets. If they should raise them in time, all might be well, but if, on the other hand, the canoe should get entangled, the consequences could hardly fail to be disastrous. The current in its narrow channel was so strong that Dick was powerless either to modify his course or to slacken it.

Half a minute more, and the canoe was right under the woodwork, but the efforts of the natives had already elevated the nets so that the anticipated danger was happily escaped; but it chanced that in making its way through the obstacle, a large piece of the grass-thatch got detached. One of the negroes raised a sudden shout of alarm, and it seemed only too probable that he had caught a sight of the travellers below and was informing his companions. This apprehension, too, was only momentary; the current had changed almost to a rapid, and carried the canoe along with such velocity that the lacustrine village was quickly out of sight.

"Steer to the left!" cried Dick, finding that the river-bed had again become clear.

A stiff pull at the tiller made the craft fly in that direction.

Dick went to the stern, and scanned the moonlit waters. All was perfectly still, no canoe was in pursuit; perhaps the natives had not one to use; but certain it was that when daylight dawned no vestige of an inhabitant was to be seen. Nevertheless Dick thought it prudent for a while to steer close under the shelter of the left-hand shore.

By the end of the next four days the aspect of the country had undergone a remarkable change, the jungle having given place to a desert as dreary as the Kalahari itself. The river appeared interminable, and it became a matter of serious consideration how to get a sufficiency of food. Fish was scarce, or at least hard to catch, and the arid soil provided no means of sustenance for antelopes, so that nothing was to be gained from the chase. Carnivorous animals also had quite disappeared, and the silence of the night was broken, not by the roar of wild beasts, but by the croaking of frogs in a discordant chorus, which Cameron has compared to the clanking of hammers and the grating of files in a ship-builder's yard.

Far away both to the east and west the outlines of hills could be faintly discerned, but the shores on either hand were perfectly flat and devoid of trees. Euphorbias, it is true, grew in considerable numbers, but as they were only of the oil-producing species, and not the kind from which cassava or manioc is procured, they were useless in an alimentary point of view.

Dick was becoming more and more perplexed, when Hercules happened to mention that the natives often eat young fern-fronds and the pith of the papyrus, and that before now he had himself been reduced to the necessity of subsisting on nothing better.

"We must try them," said Dick.

Both ferns and papyrus abounded on the banks, and a meal was prepared, the sweet soft pith of the papyrus being found very palatable. Jack in particular appeared to enjoy it extremely, but it was not in any way a satisfying diet.

Thanks to Cousin Benedict, a fresh variety in the matter of food was found on the following day. Since the discovery of the "Hexapodes Benedictus" he had recovered his spirits, and, having fastened his prize safely inside his hat, he wandered about, as often as he had a chance, in his favourite pursuit of insect-hunting. As he was rummaging in the long grass, he put up a bird which flew but a very short distance. Benedict recognized it by its peculiar note, and, seeing Dick take his gun to aim at it, exclaimed,—

"Don't fire! don't fire! that bird will be worth nothing for food among five of us."

"It will be dinner enough for Jack," said Dick, who, finding that the bird did not seem in a hurry to make its escape, delayed his shot for a moment, without intending to be diverted from his purpose of securing it.

"You mustn't fire," insisted Benedict, "it is an indicator; it will show you where there are lots of honey."

Aware that a few pounds of honey would really be of more value than a little bird, Dick lowered his gun, and in company with the entomologist set off to follow the indicator, which seemed, by alternately flying and stopping, to be inviting them to come on, and they had but a little way to go before they observed several swarms of bees buzzing around some old stems hidden amongst the euphorbias. Notwithstanding Benedict's remonstrances against depriving the bees of the fruits of their industry, Dick instantly set to work, and without remorse suffocated them by burning dry grass underneath. Having secured a good amount of honey, he left the comb to the indicator as its share of the booty, and went back with his companion to the canoe.

The honey was acceptable, but it did not do much to alleviate the cravings of hunger.

Next day it happened that they had just stopped for their accustomed rest, when they observed that an enormous swarm of grasshoppers had settled at the mouth of a creek close by. Two or three deep they covered the soil, myriads and myriads of them adhering to every shrub.

"The natives eat those grasshoppers," said Benedict, "and like them too."

The remark produced an instant effect ; all hands were busied in collecting them, and a large supply was quickly gathered : the canoe might have been filled ten times over. Grilled over a slow fire, they were found to be very palatable eating, and, spite of his qualms of conscience, Benedict himself made a hearty meal.

But although the gnawings of absolute hunger were thus assuaged, all the travellers began to long most anxiously for the voyage to come to an end. The mode of transit indeed might be less exhausting to the bodily powers than a land march would have been, but the excessive heat by day, the damp mists at night, and the incessant attacks of mosquitoes, all combined to render the passage extremely trying. There was no telling how long it would last, and Dick was equally uncertain whether it might end in a few days, or be protracted for a month. The direction which the stream was taking was itself a subject of perplexity.

A fresh surprise was now in store.

As Jack, a few mornings afterwards, was standing at the bow peering through an aperture in the grass canopy above him, he suddenly turned round and cried,—

"The sea ! the sea !"

Dick started forwards, and looked eagerly in the same direction. A large expanse of water was visible in the horizon, but after having surveyed it for a moment or two, he said,—

" No, Jack, it is not the sea, it is a great river ; it is running west, and I suppose this river runs into it.   Perhaps it is the Zaire."

" Let us hope it is," said Mrs. Weldon earnestly.

Most cordially did Dick Sands re-echo her words, being well aware that at the mouth of that river were Portuguese villages, where a refuge might assuredly be found.

For several succeeding days the canoe, still concealed by its covering, floated on the silvery surface of this new-found stream.   On either side the banks became less arid, and there seemed everything to encourage the few survivors of the " Pilgrim " to believe that they would soon see the last of the perils and toils of their journey.

They were too sanguine.   Towards three o'clock on the morning of the 18th, Dick, who was at his usual post at the bow, fancied he heard a dull rumbling towards the west. Mrs. Weldon, Jack, and Benedict, were all asleep.   Calling Hercules to him, he asked him whether he could not hear a strange noise.   The night was perfectly calm, and not a breath of air was stirring.   The negro listened attentively, and suddenly,'his eyes sparkling with delight, exclaimed,—

" Yes, captain, I hear the sea !"

Dick shook his head and answered,—

" It is not the sea, Hercules."

" Not the sea !" cried the negro, " then what can it be ?"

" We must wait till daybreak," replied Dick, " and meanwhile we shall have to keep a sharp look-out."

Hercules returned to his place, but only to continue listening with ever-increasing curiosity.   The rumbling perceptibly increased till it became a continued roar.

With scarcely any intervening twilight night passed into day.   Just in front, scarcely more than half a mile ahead, a great mist was hanging over the river ; it was not an ordinary fog, and when the sun rose, the light of the dawn caused a brilliant rainbow to arch itself from shore to shore.

In a voice so loud that it awoke Mrs. Weldon, Dick gave his order to Hercules to steer for the bank :—

"Quick, quick, Hercules ! ashore ! ashore ! there are cataracts close ahead !"

And so it was. Within little more than a quarter of a mile the bed of the river sank abruptly some hundred feet, and the foaming waters rushed down in a magnificent fall with irresistible velocity. A few minutes more and the canoe must have been swallowed in the deep abyss.

CHAPTER XIX.

AN ATTACK.

THE canoe inclined to the west readily enough; the fall in the river-bed was so sudden that the current remained quite unaffected by the cataract at a distance of three hundred yards.

On the bank were woods so dense that sunlight could not penetrate the shade. Dick was conscious of a sad misgiving when he looked at the character of the territory through which they must necessarily pass. It did not seem practicable by any means to convey the canoe below the falls.

As they neared the shore, Dingo became intensely agitated. At first Dick suspected that a wild beast or a native might be lurking in the papyrus, but it soon became obvious that the dog was excited by grief rather than by rage.

"Dingo is crying," said Jack; "poor Dingo!" and the child laid his arms over the creature's neck.

The dog, however, was too impatient to be caressed; bounding away, he sprang into the water, swam across the twenty feet that intervened between the shore, and disappeared in the grass.

In a few moments the boat had glided on to a carpet of confervæ and other aquatic plants, starting a few kingfishers and some snow-white herons. Hercules moored it to the stump of a tree, and the travellers went ashore.

There was no pathway through the forest, only the trampled moss showed that the place had been recently visited either by animals or men.

Dick took his gun and Hercules his hatchet, and they set out to search for Dingo. They had not far to go before they saw him with his nose close to the ground, manifestly following a scent; the animal raised his head for a moment, as if beckoning them to follow, and kept on till he reached an old sycamore-stump. Having called out to the rest of the party to join them, Dick made his way farther into the wood till he got up to Dingo, who was whining piteously at the entrance of a dilapidated hut.

The rest were not long in following, and they all entered the hut together. The floor was strewn with bones whitened by exposure.

"Some one has died here," said Mrs. Weldon.

"Perhaps," added Dick, as if struck by a sudden thought, "it was Dingo's old master. Look at him! he is pointing with his paw."

The portion of the sycamore-trunk which formed the farther side of the hut had been stripped of its bark, and upon the smooth wood were two great letters in dingy red almost effaced by time, but yet plain enough to be distinguished.

"S. V.," cried Dick, as he looked where the dog's paw rested; "the same initials that Dingo has upon his collar. There can be no mistake. S. V."

A small copper box, green with verdigris, caught his eye, and he picked it up. It was open, but contained a scrap of discoloured paper. The writing upon this consisted of a few sentences, of which only detached words could be made out, but they revealed the sad truth only too plainly.

"Robbed by Negoro—murdered—Dingo—Help—Negoro guide—120 miles from coast—December 3rd, 1871—write no more.

"S. VERNON."

Here was the clue to a melancholy story. Samuel Vernon, under the guidance of Negoro, and taking with him his dog Dingo, had set out on an exploration of a district of Central Africa; he had taken a considerable quantity of money to procure the necessary supplies on the way, and this had excited the cupidity of his guide, who seized the opportunity, whilst they were encamping on the banks of the Congo, to assassinate his employer, and get possession of his property. Negoro, however, had not escaped; he had fallen into the hands of the Portuguese, by whom he was recognized as an agent of the slave-dealer Alvez, and condemned to spend the rest of his days in prison. He contrived after a while to make his escape, and, as has been already mentioned, found his way to New Zealand, whence he had returned by securing an engagement on board the " Pilgrim." Between the time when he was attacked by Negoro and the moment of his death, Vernon had managed to write the few brief lines of which the fragments still survived, and to deposit the document in the box from which the money had been stolen, and by a last effort had traced out his initials in blood upon the naked wood which formed the wall of the hut. For many days Dingo watched beside his master, and throughout that time his eyes were resting so perpetually upon the two crimson letters in front of him, that mere instinct seemed to fasten them indelibly on his memory. Quitting his watch one day, perhaps to pacify his hunger, the dog wandered to the coast, where he was picked up by the captain of the " Waldeck," afterwards to be transferred to the very ship on which his owner's murderer had been engaged as cook.

All throughout this time poor Vernon's bones had been bleaching in the African forest, and the first resolution of Dick and Mrs. Weldon was to give the residue of his remains some semblance of a decent burial. They were just proceeding to their task when Dingo gave a furious growl, and dashed out of the hut; another moment, and a terrible shriek made it evident that he was in conflict with some dread antagonist.

Hercules was quickly in pursuit, and the whole party followed in time to witness the giant hurl himself upon a man with whom already Dingo was in mortal combat. The dog was gripping the man by the throat, the man was lifting his cutlass high above the head of the dog.

That man was Negoro. The rascal, on getting his letter at Kazonndé, instead of embarking at once for America, had left his native escort for a while, and returned to the scene of his crime to secure the treasure which he had left buried at a little distance in a spot that he had marked. At this very moment he was in the act of digging up the gold he had concealed; some glistening coins scattered here and there betrayed his purpose; but in the midst of his labours he had been startled by the dashing forward of a dog; another instant, and the dog had fixed itself upon his throat, whilst he, in an agony of desperation, had drawn his cutlass and plunged it deep into the creature's side.

Hercules came up at the very climax of the death-struggle.

"You villain! you accursed villain! I have you now!" he cried, about to seize hold of his victim.

But vengeance was already accomplished. Negoro gave no sign of life; death had overtaken him on the very scene of his guilt. Dingo, too, had received a mortal wound; he dragged himself back to the hut, lay down beside the remains of his master, and expired.

The sad task of burying Vernon's bones and laying his faithful dog beside them having been accomplished, the whole party was obliged to turn their thoughts to their own safety. Although Negoro was dead, it was very likely that the natives that he had taken with him were at no great distance, and would come to search for him.

A hurried conference was held as to what steps had best be taken. The few words traceable on the paper made them aware that they were on the banks of the Congo, and that they were still 120 miles from the coast. The fall just ahead was probably the cataract of Ntemo, but whatever it was, no doubt it effectually barred their farther progress by water. There seemed no alternative but that they should make their way by one bank or the other a mile or two below the waterfall, and there construct a raft on which once again they could drift down the stream. The question that pressed for immediate settlement was which bank it should be. Here, on the left bank, would be the greater risk of encountering the negro escort of Negoro, while as to the farther shore they could not tell what obstacles it might present.

Altogether Mrs. Weldon advocated trying the other side, but Dick insisted upon crossing first by himself to ascertain whether an advance by that route were really practicable.

"The river is only about 100 yards wide," he urged; "I can soon get across. I shall leave Hercules to look after you all."

Mrs. Weldon demurred for a while, but Dick seemed resolute, and as he promised to take his gun and not to attempt to land if he saw the least symptom of danger, she at last consented, but with so much reluctance that even after he had entered the canoe she said,—

"I think, Dick, it would be really better for us all to go together."

"No, Mrs. Weldon, indeed, no; I am sure it is best for me to go alone; I shall be back in an hour."

"If it must be so, it must," said the lady.

"Keep a sharp look-out, Hercules!" cried the youth cheerily, as he pushed off from the land.

The strength of the current was by no means violent, but quite enough to make the direction of Dick's course somewhat oblique. The roar of the cataract reverberated in his ears, and the spray, wafted by the westerly wind, brushed lightly past his face, and he shuddered as he felt how near they must have been to destruction if he had relaxed his watch throughout the night.

It took him hardly a quarter of an hour to reach the opposite bank, and he was just preparing to land when there arose a tremendous shout from about a dozen natives, who, rushing forward, began to tear away the canopy of grass with which the canoe was covered.

Dick's horror was great. It would have been greater still if he had known that they were cannibals. They were the natives settled at the lacustrine village higher up the river. When the piece of thatch had been knocked off in passing the piles, a glimpse had been caught of the passengers below, and aware that the cataract ahead must ultimately bring them to a standstill, the eager barbarians had followed them persistently day by day for the last eight days.

Now they thought they had secured their prize, but loud was their yell of disappointment when on stripping off the thatch they found only one person, and that a mere boy, standing beneath it.

Dick stood as calmly as he could at the bow, and pointed his gun towards the savages, who were sufficiently acquainted with the nature of fire-arms to make them afraid to attack him.

Mrs. Weldon with the others, in their eagerness to watch Dick's movements, had remained standing upon the shore of the river, and at this instant were caught sight of by one of the natives, who pointed them out to his companions. A sudden impulse seized the whole of them, and they sprang into the canoe; there seemed to be a practised hand amongst them, which caught hold of the rudder-oar, and the little craft was quickly on its way back.

Although he gave up all as now well-nigh lost, Dick neither moved nor spoke. He had one lingering hope yet left. Was it not possible even now that by sacrificing his own life he could save the lives of those that were entrusted to him?

When the canoe had come near enough to the shore for his voice to be heard, he shouted with all his might,—

"Fly, Mrs. Weldon; fly, all of you; fly for your lives!"

But neither Mrs. Weldon nor Hercules stirred; they seemed rooted to the ground.

"Fly, fly, fly!" he continued shouting.

But though he knew they must hear him, yet he saw them make no effort to escape. He understood their meaning; of what avail was flight when the savages would be upon their track in a few minutes after?

A sudden thought crossed his mind. He raised his gun and fired at the man who was steering; the bullet shattered the rudder-scull into fragments.

The cannibals uttered a yell of terror. Deprived of guidance, the canoe was at the mercy of the current, and, borne along with increasing speed, was soon within a hundred feet of the cataract.

The anxious watchers on the bank instantly discerned Dick's purpose, and understood that in order to save them he had formed the resolution of precipitating himself with the savages into the seething waters.

Nothing could avail to arrest the swift descent. Mrs. Weldon in an agony of despair waved her hands in a last sad farewell, Jack and Benedict seemed paralyzed, whilst Hercules involuntarily extended his great strong arm that was powerless to aid.

Suddenly the natives, impelled by a last frantic effort to reach the shore, plunged into the water, but their movement capsized the boat.

Face to face with death, Dick lost nothing of his indomitable presence of mind. Might not that light canoe, floating bottom upwards, be made the means for yet another grasp at life? The danger that threatened him was twofold; there was the risk of suffocation as well as the peril of being drowned; could not the inverted canoe be used for a kind of float at once to keep his head above water and to serve as a screen from the rushing air? He had some faint recollection of how it had been proved possible under some such conditions to descend in safety the falls of Niagara.

Quick as lightning he seized hold of the cross-bench of the canoe, and with his head out of water beneath the up-turned keel, he was dashed down the furious and well-nigh perpendicular fall.

The craft sank deep into the abyss, but rose quickly again to the surface. Here was Dick's chance; he was a good swimmer, and his life depended now upon his strength of arm.

It was a hard struggle, but he succeeded. In a quarter of an hour he had landed on the left-hand bank, where he was greeted with the joyful congratulations of his friends, who had hurried to the foot of the fall to assure themselves of his fate.

The cannibals had all disappeared in the surging waters. Unprotected in their fall, they had doubtless ceased to breathe before reaching the lowest depths of the cataract, where their lifeless bodies would soon be dashed to pieces against the sharp rocks that were scattered along the lower course of the stream.

CHAPTER XX.

A HAPPY RE-UNION.

TWO days after Dick's marvellous deliverance the party had the good fortune to fall in with a caravan of honest Portuguese ivory-traders on their way to Emboma, at the mouth of the Congo. They rendered the fugitives every assistance, and thus enabled them to reach the coast without further discomfort.

This meeting with the caravan was a most fortunate occurrence, as any project of launching a raft upon the Zaire would have been quite impracticable, the river between the Ntemo and Yellala Falls being a continuous series of cataracts. Stanley counted as many as sixty-two, and it was hereabouts that that brave traveller sustained the last of thirty-one conflicts with the natives, escaping almost by a miracle from the Mbelo cataract.

Before the middle of August the party arrived at Emboma, where they were hospitably received by M. Motta Viega and Mr. Harrison. A steamer was just on the point of starting for the Isthmus of Panama; in this they took their passage, and in due time set foot once more upon American soil.

Forthwith a message was despatched to Mr. Weldon, apprising him of the return of the wife and child over whose loss he had mourned so long. On the 25th the railroad deposited the travellers at San Francisco, the only thing to mar their happiness being the recollection that Tom and his partners were not with them to share their joy.

Mr. Weldon had every reason to congratulate himself that Negoro had failed to reach him. No doubt he would have been ready to sacrifice the bulk of his fortune, and without a moment's hesitation would have set out for the coast of Africa, but who could question that he would there have been exposed to the vilest treachery? He felt that to Dick Sands and to Hercules he owed a debt of gratitude that it would be impossible to repay; Dick assumed more than ever the place of an adopted son, whilst the brave negro was regarded as a true and faithful friend.

Cousin Benedict, it must be owned, failed to share for long the general joy. After giving Mr. Weldon a hasty shake of the hand, he hurried off to his private room, and resumed his studies almost as if they had never been interrupted. He set himself vigorously to work with the design of producing an elaborate treatise upon the " Hexapodes Benedictus " hitherto unknown to entomological research. Here in his private chamber spectacles and magnifying-glass were ready for his use, and he was now able for the first time with the aid of proper appliances to examine the unique production of Central Africa.

A shriek of horror and disappointment escaped his lips. The Hexapodes Benedictus was not a hexapod at all. It was a common spider. Hercules, in catching it, had unfortunately broken off its two front legs, and Benedict, almost blind as he was, had failed to detect the accident. His chagrin was most pitiable, the wonderful discovery that was to have exalted his name high in the annals of science belonged simply to the common order of the arachnidæ. The blow to his aspirations was very heavy; it brought on a fit of illness from which it took him some time to recover.

For the next three years Dick was entrusted with the education of little Jack during the intervals he could spare from the prosecution of his own studies, into which he threw himself with an energy quickened by a kind of re-morse.

"If only I had known what a seaman ought to know when I was left to myself on board the 'Pilgrim,'" he would continually say, "what misery and suffering we might have been spared!"

So diligently did he apply himself to the technical branches of his profession that at the age of eighteen he received a special certificate of honour, and was at once raised to the rank of a captain in Mr. Weldon's firm.

Thus by his industry and good conduct did the poor foundling of Sandy Hook rise to a post of distinction. In spite of his youth, he commanded universal respect; his native modesty and straightforwardness never failed him, and for his own part, he seemed to be unconscious of those fine traits in his character which had impelled him to deeds that made him little short of a hero.

His leisure moments, however, were often troubled by one source of sadness; he could never forget the four negroes for whose misfortunes he held himself by his own inexperience to be in a way responsible. Mrs. Weldon thoroughly shared his regret, and would have made many sacrifices to discover what had become of them. This anxiety was at length relieved.

Owing to the large correspondence of Mr. Weldon in almost every quarter of the world, it was discovered that the whole of them had been sold in one lot, and that they were now in Madagascar. Without listening for a moment to Dick's proposal to apply all his savings to effect their liberation, Mr. Weldon set his own agents to negotiate for their freedom, and on the 15th of November, 1877, Tom, Bat, Actæon, and Austin awaited their welcome at the merchant's door. It is needless to say how warm were the greetings they received.

Out of all the survivors of the "Pilgrim" that had been cast upon the fatal coast of Africa, old Nan alone was wanting to complete the number. Considering what they had all undergone, and the perils to which they had been exposed, it seemed little short of a miracle that she and poor Dingo should be the only victims.

High was the festivity that night in the house of the Californian merchant, and the toast, proposed at Mrs. Weldon's request, that was received with the loudest acclamation was

"DICK SANDS, THE BOY CAPTAIN!"

THE END.